LOST

(Book Two of the Displacement Cycle)

BARRIE DURRANT

ISBN: 9781658630757

Independently published

For my dad.

The greatest role model anyone could ever wish for.

May the sun be forever over the yardarm.

Acknowledgements

To my wife, Michelle. Thank you for your love, help and support.
May the sacred pink pen never run dry.

To all of my family and friends, for their continued encouragement.

To Clint and Stephen Martin. Thank you both for battling through the initial drafts and giving me the benefit of your sage wisdom.
Really appreciate it.

Prologue

The boy ran as fast he could, stumbling as he tried to keep his fatigued legs from giving way. He did not know for how long he had been running, but his lungs burned terribly and his aching muscles began to spasm painfully as he fled. He pelted out of the narrow street that he had been following and entered a deserted avenue. Ahead of him he spotted the familiar buildings of the city council and so, drawing heavily upon his dwindling energy reserves, he forced his legs to keep moving, desperate to find help.

The creature was still back there. No matter how hard he ran, he simply could not escape it. The boy could hear its ragged breathing as the monster pursued him. But what did it want? Why did it chase him? He did not know the answer to these questions, so out of desperation he kept running, hoping that somehow he could evade whatever it was that dogged his every step.

The boy stopped to draw breath. He was on the verge of collapse, but the council building seemed just as far away. It was as though the building itself retreated from him, just as the creature behind slowly gained ground. The monster was still there, shambling towards him along the deserted street, wreathed in a shadowy haze, its face no more than a featureless grey mask. It never tired, or had to stop to rest its aching lungs. Its form was familiar somehow, although the boy could not quite remember where he had seen it before.

It spotted him. As if recognising that he had briefly halted his frantic flight, the creature raised one ghostly arm in the air, as if waving in greeting. The boy squinted, hoping to discern some new detail about the figure that followed him, something to help him recognise who or what it was. He needed to know, to understand why it followed, but he was too terrified to confront his pursuer.

'What do you want?' he screamed, suddenly angry with the creature. The shadowy figure stopped and looked up at him. Although the features of its face could not be seen, the boy felt something pass between them, almost as if the creature had somehow recognised his voice. It raised its arm once more, and shambled forward.

The boy ran again, as the shadowed creature lumbered in his direction. He turned onto another street, one he recognised and which was usually filled with people going about their daily business. This time however, it was deserted, devoid of all life. He looked around, calling out for help, desperate to find someone to make the nightmare go away. But there was no answer, and the nightmare refused to end. The creature was close now and he could hear its ragged breathing growing louder with every passing moment. He was gripped by an intense feeling of panic. What should he do? He could not run forever, of that he was certain. He was exhausted, nearly spent, and must find a place of safety soon, somewhere that he could hide until the creature was gone and he was rested once more. But where?

He spotted the council chamber again, directly ahead of him. He pushed his aching body beyond its limits, desperate to reach the safety offered by its walls and the protection of those who would surely be inside. He was nearly there, just a few more steps. His legs were burning ferociously and his lungs felt as though they were about to burst from his heaving chest. He frantically pushed open the huge doors, almost falling through, desperate to evade his pursuer.

The boy cried out with panic. Where was everybody? It was completely dark inside the council chambers. The air was cold and uninviting and not a single torch burned in the wall sconces. It was as though nobody had been there for a very long time. A thick carpet of dust lay undisturbed on the stone floor and huge spiders skittered through their webs, suddenly alerted to his intrusion.

Where was the creature? It had not yet caught up with him. The boy tried frantically to close the huge wooden doors, desperate to bar the way, to prevent his pursuer from following him. At the very last moment, a pale, almost ghostly hand grabbed the side of the large wooden door. He struggled against the creature, but it pushed back against him in a desperate attempt to get inside. The boy heaved back with all his might, using his fear to push his muscles to their very limits. But it was not enough. The creature was far stronger and the door slowly creaked open.

The boy fell backwards, landing heavily on his rump, kicking up a small dust storm as he tried to regain his footing. The shadowy figure stood in the doorway, illuminated by the dull light from outside. It wore a long white cloak that appeared to have been torn in many places, as if shredded by the claws of a wild beast, and which was somehow familiar. The creature entered the building, shambling forward and hunched over as if pain. Its face was obscured by its hood but as it approached the boy, who was still lying on the dusty floor, too terrified to move, its hands reached out towards him, as if seeking comfort.

The boy was struck by a sudden feeling of familiarity. The creature reminded him of someone he once knew, but had not seen for some time now. He recognised this creature, this man, who had plagued his dreams for what seemed like an eternity. If only he could remember from where he knew him, perhaps he might be able to make contact and end the terrifying chase that he had endured for so very long.

The creature stood above him, looking down, its face still obscured by the cloak that it wore. It reached up and slowly peeled back the edge of the hood, revealing the shadowed face beneath.

The boy screamed. . . .

One

Professor Marcus Klein stood on the bridge of his small ship, looking out over the tranquil waters of the harbour below the city of Nesteris. The sun was shining down fiercely from high in the blue skies above and only a thin layer of cloud was visible, way up in the upper atmosphere. It was nearly always hot and sunny here and Marcus watched with amusement as groups of adolescent Aellindi jumped from the rocks at the harbour entrance, splashing into the clear blue waters. They were revelling in its refreshing coolness, just as the children would do during the hot summer months back on his own world. The harbour below the city was busy and ships of all sizes were going to and fro, bringing in delicious spices from the east or sending luxury cloth to the Kingdom of the Isles in the north. There was always something going on, something new and exciting to watch.

Marcus's own ship, the *Drake*, was moored behind a small breakwater, away from the busy piers. She was unlike any of the other ships that were currently coursing through the waters within the harbour. The *Drake* belonged to a different world, a futuristic world, where ships were constructed entirely from metal and utilised advanced electronic systems to navigate the busy shipping lanes. Here though, on the world of the Aellindi, the ships that plied the oceans were constructed from timber and relied on wind power to get to their destinations. They bore vast canvas sheets, to catch the wind and propel them forwards, much like the early wooden craft used by the namesake of his own vessel, *Sir Francis Drake*.

When he had first arrived here, a little over two years ago, the *Drake* had been running at peak efficiency, having just received multiple upgrades to her systems. So advanced had she been that he could control almost every system directly from the bridge, aided by the artificial intelligence that he had installed. However, the ravages of time were now clearly visible on her red and white painted hull. Prior to his failed time travel experiment, her livery had been splendid, as if she had just emerged from the shipwright's yard, with champagne still running down her bow. Now the flaking paint was losing the inexorable battle against the ever growing patches of rust that were the inevitable consequence of extended exposure to salty water. Several of the integrated systems, some of which he had installed himself, had failed, or had been cannibalised for his current projects. This meant that it was no longer possible for him to take the ship to sea without help. Worse still, without the resources of his own world, he was unable to repair the failed systems. This meant that slowly, system by system, his ship was dying.

Marcus looked across the harbour towards the great tower, which sat like some watchful sentinel at the far entrance. It was known throughout the world as the great lighthouse of Nesteris, although its true name was the *Beacon of Rhasad*. It was a huge, towering construction, erupting from the rocky plateaux on which it was built. It was not a conical structure, like most of the lighthouses on his own world, but consisted of three steeply sloped sides, like some triangular plant stem. On top of the sturdy structure sat a large domed chamber, constructed almost entirely of a see-through material that afforded fantastic views all around. The beacon had been built by the ancient inhabitants of this world, known to the Aellindi as the Ancestors, who they believed to have created and nurtured them. It was one of many such structures left behind when the Ancestors had departed, and Marcus had spent the last two years exploring them, trying to reactivate as many of the beacons' technological wonders as he could. The Aellindi had even allowed him to make his home within the *Beacon of Rhasad*, a testament to the high esteem in which he was now held, ever since he had aided them in defeating the evil demon lord. He firmly believed that, in the times when the Ancestors still walked the lands, there had been many more of these beacons. He was certain that the Ancestors had used them for communication and transport, but so far he had only managed to discern a few of the abilities which he believed they were capable of.

'I've finished, Marcus,' said a voice from beside him, startling him slightly and making him jump.

The voice had a slightly gurgled sound to it, as if the owner had been trying to talk to him from under water. Marcus looked down on the individual who had spoken, and who was holding out one of his webbed hands in which he clutched a selection of shiny metal discs.

'Excellent, Klestin. Can I see?'

The small man, who was from the water-logged lands known as Vilnarr, handed Marcus the shiny objects, which clattered together as they came into close proximity, sticking firmly to one another. Klestin smiled up at Marcus, clearly pleased with the objects that his tutor was now inspecting. He was a little less than four foot tall, which was slightly smaller than the average for a Vilnarri adult, and he made Marcus look quite tall as the pair stood together on the bridge of the *Drake*. Marcus himself was only a little over five feet, with a lean wiry build and thinning white-blonde hair. Since coming to the world of the Aellindi his usually pale skin had taken on the olive complexion that was associated with the people of the Mediterranean nations back home, making him look healthier than he had in years.

'I kept them in the magnetic field for several minutes, just as you instructed,' said Klestin, clearly eager to win Marcus's approval. The strange gill slits on his neck opening and closing involuntarily as he waited for his tutor to inspect the objects.

'Yes, the magnets look good to me, Klestin. Nice and powerful. I think they should work out nicely, don't you?'

'I sure hope so!'

'So, shall we go and find the others? I think it's about time that we put these to good use.'

The Vilnarri man nodded enthusiastically and followed Marcus as he left the bridge. The pair ambled down the gangplank and onto the pier. From there they headed towards the nearby stable where their two tharen, which always reminded Marcus of the horses from his own world, were currently enjoying the contents of a grain-filled nosebag. The animals whinnied softly as the two men entered the stable and began to lead them out onto the busy streets of the harbour.

Marcus and Klestin rode across the harbour and up into the city of Nesteris, which was nestled on the cliffs above. It was a beautiful city, sprawled out on a grassy plateau. The magnificent buildings were constructed mostly from blocks of bright white marble, with windows covered by ornate wooden shutters and topped with blue-grey roof tiles. Many of the buildings, especially those in the more affluent areas, had decorative pieces of lapis lazuli set into their walls. The fantastic blue colour added a wonderful contrast to the stark white of the marble blocks.

They continued across to the other side of the city, dismounting next to a small building which had been constructed near a rapid flowing stream, not far from where the torrent of water disappeared over the edge of the huge cliffs, spilling down into the sea below. Three other individuals were already there, waiting patiently for them to arrive. There were two Aellindi females and a stout man from the Kingdom of the Isles.

Even now it was sometimes hard for Marcus to accept what had happened to him, especially when he was in the company of the Aellindi people, who were the most alien of the inhabitants of this world. Outwardly they appeared to be a race of sentient lizards, larger than the average human. However, having lived with them for some time now, he had grown to recognise the distinct differences between them. There were many different types of Aellindi on this world, ranging from the stocky, fearsome warriors, to those individuals who were gifted with large, powerful wings, and the seemingly peaceful members of their race who always appeared calm and reserved. Marcus firmly believed that they were more akin to the equivalent of evolved dinosaurs, or at least what he imagined the dinosaurs might have become had they not been wiped out. Many Aellindi were highly skilled in the arcane arts, due to their deep connection with the mystical energy of the aether. Marcus had seen some of what could be done when wielding this powerful force, although he was unable to comprehend the scientific mechanisms that drove it. It was as if the aether did not follow the laws of physics that he was so familiar with, and he desperately wished to uncover these new secrets.

'Hello, Lethis,' said Klestin, in that warbling accent for which his people were so well known, 'are you ready for the magnets to be installed?'

'Yes,' replied one of the Aellindi females, hissing slightly in the sibilant way that Marcus had initially found so hard to understand, 'all is ready.'

'Shall we go inside then?' said Marcus, indicating for Lethis to lead the way.

The inside of the building was illuminated by several spherical crystals that sat in ornate cradles and which emitted a bright white light from their highly faceted surfaces. The nearby stream had been diverted slightly and part of it now flowed directly through the centre of the building. It was very noisy inside, as the fast flowing water dropped down over a series of artificial water falls that had been built into the stone floor. The stream entered at the highest end of the building and disappeared through an outlet in the lowest section of the floor, where it re-joined the main water course before plunging over the cliffs.

Marcus moved over to a large work table on the far side of the building and placed the recently magnetised metal discs beside another set of similar looking objects.

'So, who wants to install the magnets in the generator?' he asked.

The three students who had been waiting for them at the stream all indicated that the honour should go to Klestin, who had spent the morning magnetising them in the electrical current produced by the generators aboard the *Drake*.

Klestin eagerly stepped forward and picked up the stack of magnets from the table, struggling slightly to prise them apart, his webbed fingers making it difficult for him to grip the metal discs. Finally all twelve had been separated and placed on the table, sufficiently far apart so as to prevent them from clattering together again. He picked up a large oval object from the table and turned it on its side, exposing the circular holes in which the magnets were to be housed. Slowly, carefully, the young Vilnarri placed each magnetic disc into position. He then covered the side of the object with a thin piece of wood, sealing in the internal components of the device.

'Good,' said Marcus, smiling enthusiastically. 'Brune, can you take the generator and connect it up to the system, please?'

'Sure,' replied the stout man from the city of Karnith.

Brune hefted the object that Klestin had just finished constructing and carried it over towards the fast flowing water. He briefly struggled to open a panel on the side of the huge water wheel, which was currently in a locked position, and then placed Klestin's generator inside, attaching it to some cabling which had been installed previously. He looked back at Marcus, who nodded almost imperceptibly at him, before closing the panel and unlocking the water wheel. Before long, the wheel was turning swiftly, pushed into motion by the constant gushing water as it flowed through the building.

'Excellent,' said Marcus joyfully, 'now we just need to test it out. Samir, can you place the light spheres in the charger, please?'

'Of course,' replied the Aellindi woman, as she gathered up a small pile of translucent spherical crystals and walked over to a large object with multiple holes in the top surface, which was sitting beside the water wheel. She placed the crystals into the circular recesses on top of the device and moved back to stand beside her colleagues.

The crystals began to emit a faint glow, which increased in intensity with every passing minute, soon becoming indistinguishable from the objects which illuminated the interior of the building.

'Fantastic!' exclaimed Marcus. 'That went really well, don't you think?'

The four students all nodded in agreement, pleased with their achievement and with the praise being lavished on them by their tutor.

Marcus was currently teaching these four individuals about technology. They had been selected, from the numerous applicants, to study with him and to learn about the amazing objects that he had brought from his own world. They would also help him to learn about the workings of the beacons. His friends had dubbed him "The Technomancer", although he still thought of himself as just an ordinary teacher, especially given his lack of affinity with the aether, something which all magi apparently possessed. Klestin and Brune were similarly devoid of connection to the magical energy, whereas Lethis and Samir, as members of the Aellindi race, were already powerful magi in their own right. What these four young individuals all had in common though, was a deep desire to learn about science and technology, to improve their way of life and to expand their understanding of the world around them.

The light crystals had been an accidental discovery, just like so many of the scientific breakthroughs on his own world. Marcus had been travelling across K'vith with his wife, Indrani, when they had been caught in a sudden thunderstorm. They had taken shelter in a nearby cave and huddled close to the entrance, watching as giant spears of lightning arced down from the heavens above. One of the lightning bolts had hit a nearby rock face, causing it to explode and shower the area with small fragments of stone and several strange, ball-shaped crystals.

When the storm had passed, Marcus went out to investigate the area where the lightning had struck and was amazed to find that the crystals were glowing brightly. Indrani explained that the crystals were fairly common in the mountains, but to find ones which had been energised by a lightning strike was unusual, as the light would fade over the course of several hours. Electromancers had been known to use the crystals in their rituals, but a more practical use for them had yet to be found.

Marcus brought several back to Nesteris with him and began to experiment on them. It was not long before he discovered that a modest electrical current was all that was required to bring the crystals to life, and that once energised, they emitted a bright light for many hours before needing to be recharged. This simple discovery had set Marcus on a course that had revolutionised the lives of the Aellindi. No longer did they need to burn pitch coated wooden torches in order to light their homes at night, or maintain a constant link to the powers of the aether, which was a tiring process, even for the most gifted magi. These crystals would provide all the light they required and did not represent a fire hazard. Furthermore, the crystals were easily recharged using the hydroelectric generators that he and his students had recently constructed.

So profound was the discovery that merchants from the lands of K'vith, Vilnarr and the Kingdom of the Isles were almost fighting one another to obtain the technology that he had created.

'Well,' said Marcus, 'I think we've done enough for today. How about we get something to eat?'

They all agreed and so teacher and students exited the noisy building, emerging once more into the bright, warm sunlight.

'Where should we go?' asked Samir.

'I know a great place,' replied Brune, 'down at the waterfront, just outside of the harbour.'

'Let's go then, shall we?' added Marcus, as he clambered onto his tharen.

As the group made their way back down the steep road towards the harbour of Nesteris, they discussed the new projects that Marcus had planned for them, and ideas that they themselves had been pondering. Marcus had always loved teaching and was overjoyed to be doing so once more, even though he was on a completely different world.

Samir had asked Marcus a question about the different people who inhabited his world, and Marcus was doing his best to explain that where he came from, humans were the only sentient species. He was giving a brief history, to the best of his ability, about the rise of mankind and how it had evolved from earlier species of intelligent apes and then spread across the entire planet. His tale was suddenly interrupted by a thunderous bellow, reminding him of the powerful air horns which the old-fashioned steamships used to carry. It was extremely loud and made them jump, startling their tharen.

'What was that?' asked Klestin, as he struggled to keep his skittish mount under control.

'I dunno!' replied Brune. 'Never heard anything like it before.'

'Sounds like a ship's horn to me,' added Marcus. 'Let's go and have a look.'

The group jumped down from their mounts and headed over to a small viewpoint, nestled in the cliff, about halfway down the steep road to the harbour. The sight which greeted Marcus was enough to take his breath away.

Steaming slowly into the harbour was the biggest ship he had seen since departing his own world. It was like one of the old ironclad warships that plied the oceans during the American civil war. She was totally covered in iron plating, coursing low through the water, which gave her a predatory visage. There were several huge ballistae mounted on the decks, which made her look like some chimeric amalgamation of the ancient and the modern. The ship clearly bore a striking similarity to those old dreadnoughts, and Marcus had a feeling he knew exactly who would be at the helm. She was definitely a steamer, although Marcus could detect no hint of the foul black smoke which should have accompanied such a vessel. The horn blew once more, announcing the ship's entry to the harbour and warning any vessels in her way that they ought to make haste to avoid a collision.

'Is that Admiral Mochus's latest flagship?' asked Brune, his keen eyes drinking in the sleek lines of the new arrival.

'Yes, I believe it is,' replied Marcus.

'It's huge,' said Lethis.

'Bigger even than your ship, Marcus,' added Klestin.

'Hmm, you might well be correct,' replied Marcus. 'I think I'll head down and greet him, so you'll have to go and eat without me.'

The four students jumped back onto their tharen and, wishing Marcus a pleasant evening, headed off in search of some well-earned refreshment. Marcus watched the huge ship for a while longer, as it ponderously approached the empty pier that was reserved for visiting dignitaries. Finally, he too clambered back onto his tharen and headed down to the harbour to await the arrival of his old friend.

Two

Panx stood at the top of the *Beacon of Andin*, close to the edge of the glass-domed structure at the apex of the tower, looking down at the dense forest below. The trees, which had once reached all the way up to the base of the beacon, had been felled in great numbers and the perimeter of the forest was now some distance away. The clearing that had been created by the rapid deforestation had revealed a vast number of ruins, which the young magus believed to be the ancient dwellings of the Ancestors. He felt certain that the original inhabitants of this world had lived here; perhaps many thousands of years ago, before the ancient cataclysm had killed them, or forced them to abandon their homeworld.

As he stood looking down at the ruined city, he watched several of his team scurrying through the trees. They picked their way meticulously through the ancient buildings, looking for some clue as to who had occupied them, and when. He had recently decided that he needed some time away from the Mages College, to unwind and relax, and to do that he knew that he had to get away from the study of magic.

His gaze shifted out into the dense forest, beyond the current line of deforestation. Although the trees no longer surrounded the beacon, they still harboured dangerous creatures, which meant that regular armed patrols needed to head into the forest to flush out and destroy the most threatening inhabitants of the small island. Panx could still clearly remember, and would probably never forget, that night when he and his friends had been attacked in this very forest. They had been searching for the *Beacon of Olon*, believing it to be at the centre of the island, and were making their way through the trees when they had been set upon. The creatures, a mixture of different types of giant insect, working in unison to ambush their prey, had attacked without warning, taking two of the group back to their lair to be used as incubation chambers for their unborn young. He would never forget the feeling of revulsion at seeing the insect's larvae spill forth from one of its previous victims, or the feeling of helpless despair as he burnt the area to ash, releasing his friends from their unending torment.

Fortunately, the beacon at the centre of the island, although not the ancient structure that they had been seeking, had provided them with answers. The deaths of their companions had therefore not been in vain. The *Beacon of Andin*, which they had discovered surrounded by the almost impenetrable forest, had been restored to life by the off-worlder, Marcus Klein. It had told them how to find the *Beacon of Olon* and given them the secret to defeating Valken, the malevolent demon lord who had attempted to conquer their world and feast upon the magical power of the aether that perfused it.

Panx was certain that the ancient city they were uncovering below stretched out across the entire island and out into the shallow sea beyond. As the ships had brought in men and supplies for the archaeological expedition, they had noticed numerous ruins and even some statues lying on the seabed just a few metres below them. They had excitedly reported their discovery to Panx, who had immediately led a small group of aquamancers on an exploratory dive to see exactly what lay beneath the surface of the water. His team were now meticulously cataloguing the waters around the entire island, and so far had discovered a fantastic range of buildings, monuments and artefacts.

The young man's mind returned to their previous quest for the *Beacon of Olon*. They had been successful in sending Valken and his army of darkness back to their own world, although Marcus had been captured and brutally tortured by the dark lord. Their little group had managed to rescue the professor, but they had lost several friends to the demons during their foray into the dark citadel. Panx especially wished that Navesh was here now to witness the grand discovery of the lost city of the Ancestors. His brown eyes glistened in the light of the beacon's control room, and a tear ran down the young man's cheek as he remembered his friend's noble sacrifice, his valiant last stand against the brutal monsters that pursued them, allowing the others to return safely to their own world.

'This is for you, Navesh,' he whispered.

Panx had kept himself busy since the defeat of Valken. He had divided his time as evenly as possible between helping to rebuild the Mages College in Brind, which had been decimated during the demon invasion, and completing his own studies in the use of water magic. The number of student magi that were now attending the college was finally reaching a level equivalent to that of before the war, although it would still take many years to fully recover. He himself had recently graduated as a master aquamancer, much to the annoyance of his colleagues, several years before most of the new magi would even complete their basic studies. He was much younger than the other masters, seeming to possess a natural affinity for tapping into the power of the aether. In fact, since returning from Valken's dark world, where the aether had been scarce and difficult to control, he had felt the arcane power coursing through him at all times. On occasions he had even found it difficult to sleep, as the aether pulsed almost rhythmically through his body, as if it were looking for some means of release.

He had not restricted his studies to that of aquamancy either, but had expanded his skills by learning the secrets of several other schools of magic. During the search for the *Beacon of Olon*, he had managed to cast some very powerful spells from the school of pyromancy, all but mastering this form of magic. He had since turned his attention to understanding the secrets of wind, lightning and illusion. Many of his colleagues were clearly jealous of his mastery of the arcane energies, passing it off as a fluke of nature, but Panx knew differently. He had spent much of his spare time, the little that he had managed to find, delving into the secrets held within the ancient tomes that had belonged to his grandfather, Jorinde, who was known to have been a very powerful magus. Before he had died, Jorinde had mastered all of the known schools of magic and, to the best of Panx's knowledge, was even able to combine them into new and powerful forms; something which was thought to be impossible. In fact, after reading some of the ancient texts for himself, Panx too had achieved minor success with combining some of the magical disciplines, although he had kept this to himself for the time being.

During his periods of study he had received some instruction from Fireen, the leader of the Aellindi people. She had revealed to him new ways to reach even deeper into the aether, seeking out every last drop of power with which to cast his spells. He had always returned from these visits with renewed vigour and a sense of determination to master the arcane secrets.

One thing which he had always struggled to comprehend was why the casting of certain spells took so long to achieve. In fact, some of the most powerful incantations took so long to cast that they were all but useless if required at some sudden moment of desperate need. So he had begun to think about ways to overcome this handicap, to reduce the casting time required for the most potent of spells. He was certain that there was a way to access the power of the aether without the need for extensive incantations and flamboyant gesticulation. His current idea involved simple words of power, which could be uttered at a moment's notice, unleashing the aether and greatly improving the efficiency of the casting. So far, however, his initial attempts had not been successful.

The portal in the *Beacon of Andin* flared to life, distracting Panx from his musings. He watched as it coalesced into a shimmering oval of blue light, with energy crackling and fizzing at the edges, reaching out into the air around it. The portals fascinated him, even though he still could not understand how they worked. Marcus had managed to reactivate many of the systems within the *Beacon of Andin*, including the energy portal, which was now used regularly to travel to and from Nesteris. The professor had postulated that the beacons utilised some sort of energy that was capable of warping space and creating something which he called a wormhole. But Panx could not even begin to understand what the professor was describing. He understood the aether and how to manipulate it, but Marcus's technology was mostly beyond his ability to comprehend.

As he watched the newly formed portal, two of the Aellindi emerged from the shimmering energy field. Panx recognised them as the pair that had recently travelled back to Nesteris to retrieve some ancient texts, and he wandered over to greet them. They smiled at the young magus as he approached them, their sharp white teeth flashing in the blue light of the active portal and their heads swaying gently from side to side on elongated necks.

'Greetings, Panx,' said one of the Aellindi scholars, 'it's good to be back here again.'

'Hello, Matixis,' replied Panx. 'Did you find what you were looking for?'

'Yes, we did,' hissed Matixis, excitedly indicating for his colleague to show Panx one of the massive tomes that they had brought with them.

The second Aellindi scholar placed a huge book down onto one of the workstations within the beacon, which was glowing with some form of rapidly scrolling text that had yet to be deciphered. She opened the book at some previously marked chapter and pointed with undisguised glee at the illustrations contained in its pages.

'You see,' she said, 'those statues that we discovered were made in the likeness of the Ancestors themselves! Isn't it amazing?'

'Yes, it certainly is,' replied Panx, excited by the latest discovery. 'I think we should try and get them up from the seabed. What say you?'

'Yes, agreed,' hissed the Aellindi scholars in perfect unison.

Panx was about to continue the discussion about how to best raise several heavy stone statues from the shallow waters around the island, when the door to the lift in the beacon's central shaft whooshed open, revealing another member of his team. The man was similar in appearance to Panx, being just a few years older and also coming from Brind, the capital city of the Kingdom of the Isles. He too had a deep olive complexion, although, in contrast to Panx's thick curly brown hair, his scalp was smoothly shaven.

'Panx!' he shouted. 'You must come and see this!'

'See what?' replied the young magus, turning to face the newcomer. 'What's got you so fired up?'

'We've found a new ruin, just inside the trees. It's much bigger than most of the others that we've come across so far and is still filled with ancient artefacts. Some of them look almost new!'

'Excellent,' replied Panx. 'I'll be down shortly. I've just got to finish what I'm doing here.'

'I'm sorry, Panx,' he replied, 'but that's not really the interesting bit.'

'Oh?' replied Panx. 'Now you've really got me intrigued.'

'We found a set of steps, remarkably preserved, leading down to a doorway at the bottom. And it's open, Panx. The door is unlocked.'

The four scholars stood there for a few moments, taking in all that had just been said.

'What's inside?' asked Panx, suddenly released from his momentary paralysis.

'A room. A very large room. Much like this one really, although underground, obviously, and not currently active,' continued the young archaeologist, babbling almost incoherently.

'Well that's that then!' said Panx. 'Sorry Matixis, but I don't think this can wait. Would you care to join us?'

The two Aellindi indicated that they would indeed like to view this latest discovery for themselves and the four scholars headed over to the waiting lift, eager to find out what lay beneath the ground, undisturbed for so many years.

*   *   *

Indrani meandered through the busy marketplace, which was filled with many wondrous things. There was fine clothing, made from exotic materials, and ripe fruits, some of which she had never seen before. The traders were selling almost anything you could think of, and small children darted out from beside them, calling at the shoppers as they passed by, desperate to entice them to make a purchase from their parents' stalls.

She stopped to examine a stunning silver necklace, which was adorned with a beautiful pendant in the shape of an intricately detailed sea shell. The vendor was clearly desperate to sell his wares and instantly started to pester the Visnach magus, showing her numerous other items, in the hope that she might decide to buy one. However, unbeknown to the man, Indrani had travelled extensively across the known world and was quite experienced at haggling with desperate salesmen.

She started by feigning an interest in the necklace, but let her disappointment show when he suggested a price, deliberately placing the jewellery back on his table and turning away. He instantly lowered his asking price, grabbing at her shoulder, in the hope of attracting her back to his stall. Indrani smiled at the man, turning back towards him and pretending to give consideration to his new offer.

I have you now! she thought, as she countered his new price with an offer of her own.

'Ah, there you are, Indrani. I think I've found exactly what we're looking for.'

'Excellent, Leandra,' replied Indrani, turning to face her Visnach guide as she pushed her way through the bustling market.

The two women moved to one side of the busy street on which the marketplace was located. They looked rather out of place here in the land of the Reznari, far to the south of K'vith, the Visnach homeland. Although Indrani and Leandra were of average height for their people, they were dwarfed by the natives of Reznar, who were very tall and slender. Their height was not the only factor setting them apart from the local people here, as their pale skin, violet-coloured irises, long red hair and pointed ears contrasted totally with the Reznari, who had light brown skin, brown eyes and short black hair. Their ears were ordinarily shaped, although most Reznari wore multiple coloured hoops through their lobes, with the number and size of the rings indicating an individual's rank in society.

Reznar itself was a vast land mass, almost entirely covered in dense, humid rainforest, with a long range of mountains rising up to tower over the south-eastern edge. Both Visnach women had long since shed their travel cloaks in favour of simple light tunics, which helped them to withstand the heavy, oppressive heat that blanketed the entire continent. There were several large cities and many smaller settlements scattered across Reznar, although most were built within the trees themselves, as the people here lived in close harmony with their natural surroundings, choosing to reside high up in the dense canopies.

Indrani had travelled here in search of a special kind of silk, produced exclusively in the lands of the Reznari using the string-like threads excreted by the ixoden, a twelve legged insect that lived deep within the forest. The journey from Nesteris had been fairly pleasant, travelling as a guest of Tordin's friend, Ellis Bellithar, who owned several ships that plied the trade routes between Nesteris and Reznar.

At one point during their journey the wind had died down, leaving them becalmed and drifting slowly with the current back towards K'vith. Luckily, Indrani was a master aeromancer and had called upon the power of the aether to create a wind which countered the currents and drove them on towards Reznar. By the time the natural wind returned, Indrani had been channelling the magical energy for nearly three days, leaving her extremely fatigued. But she had saved them from floating aimlessly in the sea, and had gained the gratitude of the captain and his crew.

She needed the silk for her latest project, the creation of a flying machine, which Marcus had called an *airship*. Over the last two years Indrani had watched a number of films, which Marcus had brought with him, showing the amazing machines that soared through the skies of his world. She was amazed at the speed at which some of the aircraft could travel, and she had decided that this was something worth pursuing. Marcus told her that the technology to build such machines was simply not available here on the world of the Aellindi, and they would need to focus on a far simpler solution.

They had researched several designs of the early flying machines and had decided that the construction of an airship might just be possible. The fusion generator aboard the *Drake* could be used to create the lighter-than-air gas, which would lift the airship into the skies, but they would need some sort of material to contain it. Indrani had suggested the ixoden silk, known for its strong, tight weave, and their plan had developed rapidly from there.

After petitioning the council of Nesteris for help with the construction, they had set about building a prototype airship, which they hoped would demonstrate that their design had merit. Their hard work had paid dividends, and the prototype had greatly impressed both the council of Nesteris and King Elridan, of the Kingdom of the Isles. Indrani had proposed that she train a group of aeromancers to fly the airships and to create a fledgling air force to defend the skies above them.

King Elridan, impressed by the display, immediately promised to fund the creation of these wondrous machines, stating that such an institution would be invaluable in the defence of the realm. Marcus had, rather excitedly, wanted to call their new defence force, "*The RAF*", although she had not really liked his idea, and he had sulked for quite some time about it.

'So the merchant can supply all of the silk we need?' asked Indrani.

'Yes,' replied Leandra. 'It's slightly more expensive than we'd anticipated, but he can supply all the bolts of fabric that you require, and has them ready for us to take away immediately.'

'Wonderful,' replied Indrani, the sun glinting off her newly purchased necklace. 'Leave the final haggling over price to me. Perhaps I might be able to get him to drop it slightly.'

'Oh, I'm sure you'll be able to persuade him,' replied Leandra, grinning wickedly as the two Visnach women headed off to speak with the silk merchant.

Indrani led the procession through the forest, heading back to the busy port where Ellis's ship waited for them to return. The forest road had been quiet, and they had passed only a few other merchants heading in the opposite direction. To either side of the road lay the dense rain forest, and Indrani could only see a few metres into the thick tangle of bushes. Unlike the untamed forest on the island in the shallow sea, where they had discovered the *Beacon of Andin*, these forests seemed to be devoid of dangerous creatures, and were generally considered safe to travel through. Perhaps, if she left the safety of the road and headed deep into the trees, there would be dangers lurking in the shadows, waiting to pounce. But here, on the path, all appeared safe.

As the company rode along the track, mounted on their tharen, with several heavily laden carts trailing along behind, Indrani's mind wandered to Marcus. She found herself thinking about all that had happened since he had come to their world and changed her life forever. She had initially been suspicious of him, but had soon discovered that he was a gentle and honourable person, who genuinely wanted to help them defeat Valken and his army of darkness. There was something about his quiet, unassuming personality that had drawn her towards the stranger from another world, and she had soon found herself deeply in love with him.

She had known from the start that Marcus had been married before, and that his wife, Lydia, had died several years before he had come to the world of the Aellindi. At first he had been reluctant to commit himself to the new relationship, but Indrani had sensed that his deep sadness at the loss of Lydia was lessening with each passing day and that she was helping him to recover, to be the man that he used to be.

They had settled down together on Nesteris, where they had continued to get to know one another and finally had a child, Navesh, who was now just over six months old. Marcus was still amazed that Visnach children were born after just six months, claiming that, on his world, this sort of thing took nine. Navesh had grown quickly, as all Visnach children do, and he was already running around, causing Marcus to tear out his remaining hair as he tried to catch him.

Their son had been named in honour of their Aellindi friend, who had nobly sacrificed himself in Valken's dark world, so that the others could make it home. He was currently staying with her parents, with whom she had, at Marcus's insistence, repaired the rift between them before it had grown too deep.

The group continued on through the forest, following the meandering path back towards the coast. Indrani considered the paths, which bore a striking resemblance to those that they had found on the island in the shallow sea. Could it be that the Ancestors had been here too? Had they constructed these paths? She made a mental note to mention it to Panx when they next got together. He was fascinated by these things and she expected that he would be excited by the prospect of travelling across the continent of Reznar, which, as far as she knew, had yet to be fully explored. Indrani continued her musings as the procession headed along the trail, the shadows lengthening as evening approached.

Three

The sun was high in the sky, beating down mercilessly onto the small procession that trundled through the golden sand beneath its fierce, baking rays. The scorching sands of the great desert swirled in the afternoon winds, blowing into the faces of the men and women of the caravan as they struggled to cover their exposed skin, before the abrasive dust caused it to blister and bleed. Several of those in the procession were rubbing at their eyes, desperately trying to dislodge the grainy particles. However, without the long, specialised eyelashes with which their beasts of burden were gifted, they stood very little chance of succeeding.

The caravan had been crossing the great desert for many days now, slowly making its way from the eastern cities towards their counterparts on the western coast. It was not the best time of the year to make the journey, as the sun was at its highest position in the skies above. It glared down on all those caught out in the open, threatening to dry them out, like the desiccated remains that lay in the tombs on the edge of the ancient settlements. The caravan master had insisted on making the crossing straight away, rather than wait for the cooler season, and had made his way from oasis to oasis as he crisscrossed the well-used trade routes. Without these ancient water sources, travel across the desert would be all but impossible.

Although they could not see them through the swirling sandstorm that had suddenly picked up, they were close to the ancient ruins at the centre of the desert. They had already passed through the huge, monolithic pylon, which marked the entry to the great city, and were currently making their way towards the central area of the deserted settlement. They were headed towards the great tower, which marked the very core of the abandoned city, but at present they could not tell how far away it was, or if they were even headed in the right direction.

'I hope this wretched sandstorm doesn't last much longer,' muttered one of the caravan teamsters, as his beasts of burden trudged through the sand, hauling one of the wagons behind them.

'Damn right,' cursed his companion, who was standing up on his seat, looking for the tower. 'I've got so much sand in my eyes that I don't think I'll ever be able to shut 'em again.'

'I sure hope Denir knows what he's doin'. I don't wanna be caught out in the open tonight.'

'Don't worry kid. I've travelled with him before. If he says that we're close, then we're close. Shut yer whining and keep an eye on the wagon in front. If we lose sight of 'em, spending the night out in the open will be the least of yer worries.'

The caravan trundled on, slowly making its way towards its destination. The wind was finally dying down, and the harsh, choking dust was slowly settling on the ground once more, allowing the caravan drivers to finally catch a glimpse of the tower that was to be their home for the evening.

'What did I tell ya!' said the man standing up on the wagon. 'Didn't I say that Denir would get us to the tower before sunset?'

'Yeah, you did,' replied the driver, gazing in wonder at the monstrous tower which rose up out of the desert sands. 'Have ya been here before, Geran? I hear that the tower was once the home of an evil wizard, and that it's haunted!'

'Don't be stupid!' replied Geran, sitting back down in the seat beside the young caravan teamster. 'I've been through here several times now. There're wild animals running through the ruins hereabouts, but I ain't seen no spirits, ghosts or ghouls, and I ain't ever seen any evil wizard either.'

'I hope you're right,' replied the young man. 'There's just something about this place that frightens me. The hairs on the back of my neck are tingling.'

The caravan continued on towards the high tower, passing through the ancient streets of the long deserted city in the desert. The six wagons, each pulled by a team of four strong animals, seemed to pick up the pace as their destination grew ever nearer, the thought of a well-earned break spurring them on. The tower rose up in front of them, casting its long shadow over the desert sands, as the glowing orange sun finally began its slow descent towards the horizon. Most of the other ancient buildings and ruins were low and humble looking, open to the elements, with their once-tiled roofs stripped bare by the ravages of time. Not that rain would ever have posed much of a threat here. There were a few larger ruins that looked as though they might have once been temples, dedicated to whichever gods the inhabitants of the city worshipped.

Only the tower looked as though it had withstood the endless assault from the sun, wind and sand. For some unknown reason, unlike the city ruins nearby, which were half buried by the drifting dunes, the tower seemed to be immune to the desert's eternal onslaught, standing fast, as if forcing the sand to retreat before it. The slender structure gleamed brightly in the setting sun, its stark white surface reflecting the light down onto the approaching caravan teamsters, who were forced to shield their eyes from the glare. Small blue stones, set within the marble-like surface and polished to crystal clarity, glistened in the fading evening light. There was a small doorway in the base of the tower, dark and uninviting. Geran had informed his young companion that inside the tower was a long staircase that wound up to the summit. As the young man looked up at the apex of the tower, which now rose ominously before the approaching caravan, he could clearly make out the huge glass-domed structure which perched on top.

Denir, the master of the caravan, called a halt at the base of the great tower, indicating that the wagons should be formed into a large semicircle in front of the small doorway. The animals were to be fed, watered and tethered for the night. The slaves, who were crammed into the wagons, were allowed a brief moment to exercise their aching bodies before being put to work assembling the tents that would provide them with shelter. The caravan had brought with it all the supplies required for the passage across the great desert, and soon a small fire was crackling inside the protective wagon enclosure, with the evening meal bubbling gently above it.

*   *   *

Nadarru approached the well, which was located several streets away from the mighty tower, built around the ancient oasis site beside which the city had initially sprung. She was tall and slender, with black fur covering most of her lean body and a long tail trailing behind her as she walked. Unusually for a Ligarian, she had a mane of long fur on the back of her head which was braided into tightly plaited strings and decorated with colourful beads. She sang softly to herself as she meandered along the ancient dust covered street; a song which her mother had sung when she was a child. Away from the campsite it was peaceful, and she could clearly see stars twinkling in the dark sky. The temperature was dropping rapidly, as it always did out here in the middle of the desert, the residual heat from the recently departed sun leaching away into the glittering heavens above. She shivered and pulled her cloak tightly about her shoulders, warding off the chilly air.

As she lowered the bucket into the cool water of the oasis, turning the cogged mechanism slowly, she marvelled at how long this ancient water source had existed. Many oases had simply vanished as the waters had ceased flowing. Others had suddenly appeared, as if by magic, as the cool liquid found its way to the surface, bubbling up through the layers of rock that were buried beneath the hot sand. But here, in the shadow of the great tower, this source of water never failed to provide much needed hydration to weary travellers or desperate animals as they passed through the ruins. Here, the water had created a vibrant patch of green, allowing trees and small shrubs to flourish, sprouting from the dusty sand. Not far away from the life-giving water the plant life ended abruptly, as the unforgiving desert took control once more.

As the bucket, now filled with water, emerged from the darkness of the deep well, she began her short walk back to the campsite where the other members of the caravan were waiting for her. Although she was technically still a slave, Denir had long since released her from the physical bonds in which she had initially been held. He had taken to her almost immediately, attracted by her quiet, brooding intelligence and athletic body. She had, at first, resisted his advances, but after seeing exactly what lay in store for the other slaves that he routinely transported across the desert, she had accepted her fate. She was well treated, well fed, and as the property of the caravan master, protected from the advances of the other teamsters. However, for all the comforts offered by Denir, she was still a slave.

Nadarru emerged into the circle of the caravan, the firelight reflecting majestically from deep within her eyes. Her route took her directly past the group of slaves that were huddled beneath one of the wagons, trying to preserve what little warmth their meagre clothes and precious blankets could provide. She deliberately did not look at them, or engage in conversation, her guilt at their plight leaving a gnawing pit in her stomach. There were about thirty slaves on this trip across the desert, mainly scrawny men, destined to work in the mines or fight in the gladiatorial pits that were favoured on the west coast. Nestled protectively between the men were several women and small children, who would be sold to the wealthy citizens of the affluent city districts, where they would be run ragged, cooking, cleaning and looking after their master's household. They were hungry, dirty, and clearly frightened. All of them fearfully watched the teamsters as they ate, drank and made merry.

Standing beside the small fire she placed the water bucket down on the dusty ground, motioning for one of the teamsters to come and take some to the slaves. She stirred the thick stew, which was simmering gently above the fire, before scooping out a large, steaming portion into wooden bowl and filling a pitcher with water from the bucket. Grabbing a small loaf of bread from the table beside the fire, she walked gracefully towards the door leading into the dark interior of the tower.

As she moved across the firelit campsite she could feel the eyes of the newest teamster upon her, a young man who had been recruited by Denir just a few days before their departure. The other teamsters jeered at her as she passed them by, calling out lurid remarks, and asking her to come and warm them up. The youngster did not join in with their fun, but watched her silently as she went about her business. He had watched her intently as she toiled at the fire, and now his gaze followed her as she headed towards the tower, where Denir waited for her to return. He was a good looking young man and, if circumstances had been different for her, she might have crept under his blanket for the night. As it was though, she belonged to Denir, and he would not tolerate her going with any other man but himself.

The young teamster stood up, his knees wobbling slightly from drinking a little too much of the potent brew that the caravan team had brought with them. He shook his head slightly, as if trying to steady his spinning vision, and took several steps towards the beautiful Ligarian woman.

'I wouldn't do that, kid,' said Geran softly, looking up from the dice game he was currently engaged in. 'Denir doesn't take too kindly to people who touch his property.'

The young man looked down at the older, wiser teamster, as if trying to decide whether he was telling the truth. Several of the other teamsters were now looking up at the young man, clearly enjoying his confusion.

'Come back over here,' continued Geran, 'sit down, have another drink and join us for a couple of rounds of Sirok.'

'Uhh . . . okay, Geran,' muttered the young man, looking over once more at the slender form of Nadarru, as she disappeared through the doorway of the tower.

Nadarru sat to one side of the little fire that burned at the top of the ancient tower, watching Denir as he ate and drank. By the time she had returned with the food, he had already consumed several large mugs of the amber-coloured brew which he favoured. He had allowed her to try it once, and she remembered how strong it was, how it seemed to scorch her throat as she swallowed, leaving her retching and gasping for breath.

When she was satisfied that he was close to passing out, she stood up and quietly made her way over to the stairs leading down to the bottom of the tower.

'Where're ya goin'?' slurred Denir, looking up, trying to focus his bloodshot eyes on her.

'Outside, Denir,' she replied quietly. 'Call of nature.'

The caravan master tried unsuccessfully to stand up. He rolled heavily to one side as he lost his balance, spilling his drink over his already stained cloak.

Nadarru smiled and headed down the stairs, away from the drunken stink of her master, towards the cool outside air. *At least I'll have some peace tonight, without him climbing under my blanket for comfort*, she thought, as she passed through the circle of wagons and into the darkness of the ancient city.

She liked to get away from Denir whenever the opportunity presented itself, to sit alone and think about what her life might be like if she ever managed to escape from him. She had once considered sneaking into the campsite, when all the teamsters were blind drunk, and releasing the slaves. She would make a run for it along with the other captives, and hopefully they could make it to safety. But she never followed her dream through. Where would they go? There was nothing around here for them, except capture by bandits or falling prey to one of the great desert predators. No, her escape would have to wait. But escape she would, one day.

A noise in the distance caught her attention. It was back towards the tower, and sounded like the humming sound made by a great swarm of desert insects. There was an odd light too, a shimmering blue-coloured hue, which grew brighter with each passing moment. It illuminated the ancient tower, giving it an eerie, almost ethereal appearance. When she heard the screams she froze, rooted to the spot. Her heart was thumping rapidly in her chest and she was uncertain what to do, a feeling of vulnerability washing over her.

'Did ya hear that?' said Geran loudly, nudging the sleeping form of the young teamster with his boot. 'Wake up you lazy git,' he added, more urgently this time, standing up to look around.

Several of the other teamsters had come over to find out what the fuss was about, although the young man was still asleep, having consumed far too much of the potent ale.

'There's something, or someone, out there,' said Geran, pointing out beyond the protective ring of wagons.

'Let's have a look then, shall we?' said another of the teamsters, picking up his heavy blade, unsheathing it and heading off into the darkness.

Geran looked down at the sleeping youth, deciding that he would be of no use in a fight anyway. He made a mental note to teach him a lesson tomorrow, before picking up his own weapon and following after his companions.

The teamsters headed out beyond the wagon perimeter, swords in hand, squinting into the darkness as they waited for their night vision to recover. Geran indicated that they should fan out slightly and creep through the ruined buildings. Whoever was out here had gone quiet, and the veteran teamster was worried about being ambushed by bandits. He headed into a collapsed dwelling and peered up the ancient street.

The buzzing sound started suddenly, although Geran could not determine from which direction it was coming. It was as if it were all around him. The darkness was suddenly lit up by a bright blue light. A pulse of energy shot through air, flying noisily along the street, where it struck one of the teamsters. Geran was not sure who had been hit, but whoever it had been was now screaming in agony, as the blue light consumed his flesh. Geran squinted as he watched the spectacle, transfixed by the bright light as it illuminated the dying man. For a moment he was treated to the most gruesome sight that he had ever witnessed, as the light provided a clear image of the dead man's skeletal remains, before the bones collapsed in a pile on the dusty floor. Then it all went dark, leaving him momentarily blinded.

He hunkered down inside the ruined building, waiting for his vision to clear. *What the heck just happened?* he thought, as he rubbed at his watering eyes. Looking out through the doorway onto the ancient street, he thought he could see figures creeping through the shadows, although he was uncertain whether they were friend or foe. He gripped his sword tightly and moved through another collapsed wall, hoping to circle around and take the attackers by surprise.

The silence was shattered by another noisy energy discharge and the bright blue glow lit up the area once more. The sound of another man's agony told Geran that the target had been one of his fellows and he gritted his teeth, determined to hunt down whomever, or whatever was responsible.

He moved as stealthily as he could back towards the base of the tower, hoping that he might find some safety there. As he crept under one of the wagons, peering into the firelit circle, his blood froze and his heart seemed to stop beating. There were six unknown creatures standing at the base of the tower, beside the entrance doorway. He was a tall man himself, but Geran reckoned that these creatures would tower over him. In the flickering firelight he could see that they had blue-coloured skin and long dark hair, which fell upon their shoulders. Each of them carried a long spear, made from some sort of shiny metal, topped by a glowing blue crystal shard.

The floor within the circle of wagons was littered with the skeletal remains of the teamsters and their slaves. Geran looked around, but was unable to see any of his fellow teamsters. Even the young boy was gone. Somewhere in the ruins of the ancient city he heard another scream, evidence that the hunt was still continuing.

He decided to make a run for it, to creep back into the ruins and hide until the raiding party had left. Just as he was about to slide out from under the wagon, Denir emerged from inside the tower. He was wobbling noticeably, no doubt from excess drink, and looked around at the decimation that had been wrought upon his caravan. As he was about to make some angry exclamation, to chastise those responsible for the wanton destruction of his possessions, one of the creatures levelled their spear in his direction and fired. Within moments the caravan master had been enveloped in a burning blue glow and his flesh had been stripped from his bones. Geran watched in horror as the skin and muscle melted from his employer's body, leaving behind a skeletal after image, before the bones clattered to the ground.

Geran cursed loudly and scrabbled to escape the carnage, desperate to reach the safety of the ancient city and the welcoming darkness in which he hoped to hide. However, he had never been a lucky man, and his fortunes were not about to improve. The creatures spotted him and in unison they levelled their blue-tipped spears at him and fired. The wagon erupted in a ball of flame and Geran screamed in agony as his flesh began to burn.

*   *   *

Nadarru watched from the top of her favourite hiding place, a building which she had discovered on a previous visit to the ancient city. From here she could see the tower, the flickering firelight and the wagons of the caravan. She watched in terror as the wagons were ripped apart by some terrific energy discharge, as the wood and fabric caught fire and burnt to dust in mere moments. She heard the screams as the teamsters were killed, and she spotted the blue flashes in the deserted streets as the attackers hunted down those who sought to escape. She dared not move, for fear of being noticed. And so she sat there, concealed beside the partially ruined stone wall, waiting for the daylight to arrive.

Four

Marcus arrived at the pier just as the huge warship was being securely tied to the mooring stanchions. He clambered down from atop his tharen, tying it to a nearby post, and wandered along the pier towards the waiting crowd that had gathered there.

He spotted his old friend, Admiral Tordin Mochus, high up in the bridge, looking down on the spectators as the vessel came to rest. The professor was surprised to see that he had shaved off his stubbly beard and moustache, giving his deeply tanned complexion a much younger visage. However, the Admiral had yet to be persuaded to part with his long dark hair, which was sitting untidily upon his broad shoulders. He waved down at Marcus, his ever present smile even wider than usual, clearly a very happy man.

Through the crowd, standing close to the gangplank that was being hauled over to the ship, Marcus spotted a pair of familiar faces and he moved over to stand beside them.

'Greetings,' he said as he approached them. 'What a fantastic ship!'

'Hello, Marcus,' replied Fireen, the Aellindi leader. 'It is a wondrous construction.'

'Hi, Saven,' said Marcus, extending his hand to greet his friend and one time bodyguard.

'It's good to see you, Marcus,' she replied, clasping his hand firmly in hers. 'Have you been practising your sword strokes?' she added, with a mischievous glint in her eye.

'Now and then,' he replied, smiling sheepishly, 'you know me.'

'Have you come to see the new ship too?' asked Fireen.

'Well, I hadn't intended to come down to the pier today,' replied Marcus. 'I didn't know Tordin was coming to Nesteris. I happened to be passing by and heard the ship's horn as she entered the harbour.'

'He wanted to surprise you,' added Saven, chuckling sibilantly to herself. 'But his arrival was loud enough to wake the dead!'

'How are your new students progressing, Marcus?' asked Fireen.

'Very well, thanks. The latest hydropower plant is up and running and the new lighting crystals are in very high demand. I've had to send out an expedition to K'vith to bring back some more. I plan to build several more generators around the island, so that the light crystals can be enjoyed by more citizens.'

'Excellent!' replied Fireen, clearly delighted by his news.

'How is Indrani?' asked Saven.

'Oh she's fine,' replied Marcus. 'She's in Reznar at the moment, purchasing ixoden silk for our airships.'

'And little Navesh, how is he?' she added.

'Growing away, much quicker than I expected! He's staying with Indrani's parents, on K'vith.'

The three friends continued talking amongst themselves as they waited for Tordin to complete the docking of the ship.

'Well, what d'ya think?' asked Tordin, beaming at his friends as he swept his arm out to encompass the entire length of his ship. 'This is the *Hammer*, isn't she wonderful?'

'It is very impressive, Admiral,' replied Fireen, her long neck swaying gently from side to side, as it so often did when she was excited.

'It's a ship!' added Saven, grinning with undisguised mirth at the beaming Tordin.

'Just a ship!' he replied, clutching theatrically at his chest, apparently gravely wounded by her casual dismissal of his vessel. 'Come aboard and take a look around. She's the first all-metal ship to sail these waters. Well, native all-metal ship I should add, Marcus. Obviously the *Drake* was *the* first!'

'She does look very strong and powerful, Tordin,' added Marcus.

'Yeah, I designed her using the schematics found in those video documentaries that you brought with you from your world. I based her on the very early ironclads that once ruled your oceans.'

Tordin had spent much of his spare time rooting through the computer files that were loaded onto the *Drake's* on-board systems. He was constantly on the lookout for something new and exciting, some fresh idea that he could use to give his precious navy the upper hand. There was nothing else even remotely like this new ship sailing through the waters on the Aellindi homeworld, and with her thick armour plating, not even the most powerful arrow or bolt would be capable of penetrating the hull.

'How does the ship manage to cut so swiftly through the water, without sails?' asked Fireen, keen to allow the Admiral to exhaust his detailed explanations as quickly as possible.

'Steam power!' replied Tordin. 'She's got a huge boiler deep within her hull. It's filled with water, and when that's heated up it produces steam which is used to turn the propeller that pushes her through the water.'

'But you don't use coal to heat the water, do you?' asked Marcus, enjoying Tordin's explanation.

'No. We tried that, as you know, but it was really messy, and the coal was quite difficult to obtain. No, instead of coal, we use magic!'

'Magic?' said Fireen, taken aback. 'How?'

'Well, the water is heated by magically charged crystals, which we found to be much longer lasting, and cleaner, than burning wood or coal. The only downside is that we've got to have a dedicated group of magi on-board to help keep the *Hammer* running smoothly. This is something which is new to us, although we're slowly getting used to relying on the power of the aether, rather than the wind.'

'Wow!' said Marcus. 'That's impressive. What about weapons?'

'She's heavily armed, Marcus, by our standards anyway. Those huge missiles that you have on your world are a little out of our league at the moment, so we settled for these,' replied Tordin, pointing to several huge ballistae which were mounted on the deck. 'They're rapid loading, but still use conventional steel-tipped bolts. Perhaps I'll get to work on some cannons next,' he added, beaming proudly at Marcus.

'That would be something!' replied Marcus. 'With a fleet of these ships, nothing will be able to stand against you.'

'True,' replied Tordin, his jovial face suddenly serious, 'although the *Hammer* was terribly expensive to construct, so I'm not sure how quickly we can expect to have an entire fleet.'

'Progress of this sort takes time, Admiral,' added Fireen. 'She is already the most powerful vessel afloat.'

'So what are you doing here?' asked Marcus.

'I wanted to see if you fancied a little trip? A shakedown cruise to see how the *Hammer* responds.'

'I'd be delighted. Do you mind if my students come along for the ride? They'll enjoy the opportunity to look at the technology.'

'No problem at all,' replied Tordin. 'Shall we say first thing tomorrow morning?'

'Great, I'll go and speak to them now.'

'Before you leave, Marcus,' said Fireen, interrupting the two friends' excited chattering, 'I need to see you about a matter of some urgency. I had planned on stopping by the beacon this evening, but Tordin's arrival has changed things. Would you both accompany us back to the council chambers? I think you will be very interested in what I have to tell you.'

Marcus and Tordin exchanged a worried glance and then indicated for Fireen to lead the way, eager to find out what it was that she so urgently had to tell them. The four friends headed back along the pier and up towards the city of Nesteris.

In a small antechamber, just along the corridor from the main audience chamber, the council of Nesteris huddled around an old wooden table. In addition to the councillors, Marcus and Tordin were also present, as well as two other individuals, a young boy and his mother, who Marcus recognised as Navesh's mate and eldest child. Navesh, a powerful Aellindi hero, who had once been a member of the council, had been lost during the invasion that had very nearly seen Valken destroy their world. He had nobly sacrificed himself for his friends and his people, and would be remembered forever more as the man who cast the demons back to their own domain.

The young boy looked scared, so Marcus smiled at him, trying to transmit some small comfort to reassure him that he was not in danger here and that he was amongst friends. Although still a child, the young Aellindi bore an uncanny resemblance to his father. His skin had the same golden markings and his long neck was covered with small plates protruding from his spine, which ran all the way up to his bony head. It was as if he were cast in his father's image. Navesh's mate, Tethine, gently squeezed his hand and whispered encouraging words, attempting to instil some measure of resolve.

Sitting on Marcus's left was Tordin, and to his right was Rikoth, the powerful Aellindi warrior who had nearly been slain in a brutal clash with Valken. He had been left severely weakened by the encounter, and it was only when Panx had recovered the demon lord's evil blade that the noble champion's life force had been restored. He talked quietly with Fireen, his restored body muscly and powerful, and he exuded a smouldering, violent energy, which threatened to erupt at any moment. Marcus had gotten to know him well enough since taking up residence in the city, and smiled inwardly as he watched one of Rikoth's clawed hands scratch idly at the wooden table, as if imbued with a life of its own.

Apart from Fireen, Saven and Rikoth, Marcus did not know the other councillors well. He knew that they were enlightened Aellindi citizens from across the island of Nesteris, and had been chosen to serve on the council for their great wisdom, strength and their knowledge of the ancient texts and histories.

'If I may begin,' said Fireen, suddenly standing up to formally address those in the room. 'I would like to introduce Tethine, life-mate of our beloved friend, Navesh, and their child, Idris.'

The individuals seated around the wooden table mumbled their warmest greetings to Tethine and Idris, waiting for Fireen to continue her briefing.

'For some time now, young Idris has been suffering from terrible nightmares. Horrifying visions that have left him traumatised, with flashbacks that appear randomly throughout the day.'

Idris was visibly shaken at Fireen's mention of his nightmares. His eyes were wide with fear and his mother squeezed his hand once more, trying desperately to calm him down.

'Would you be able to tell us exactly what you have seen, young Idris?' hissed Fireen softly. 'It is perfectly safe to tell us, for we will be able to help you. But first, you must tell the council exactly what you have already told me. Can you do this for us?'

'Yes,' replied Idris quietly.

'Good. Please continue, when you are ready.'

The young man stood up, shaking ever so slightly in apprehension at what he was being asked to do. After gathering his thoughts, he informed the council that for many cycles of the moons he had been plagued by a recurring nightmare in which he was stalked by a ghostly, robed figure. The frightening dreams were always the same. A shadowy creature hunted him through the deserted streets of Nesteris. It did not matter where he went, or how fast he ran, he could not shake off his dogged pursuer. And the nightmare always had the same ending. He had managed to find the council chambers and had pushed open the great doors, hoping to find some help from within. But the chambers were always deserted, cold and uninviting.

Somehow he manages to push the huge doors to a close, but just as he is about to seal the entrance the creature forces its way inside, causing him to stumble backwards and fall to the ground.

'What happens next?' prompted Fireen, as the boy momentarily faltered in his recounting of the nightmares.

After a moment, to steel himself once more, Idris informed them that he had sensed something familiar about the creature that had chased him. It was as if it were reaching out towards him, beckoning him to come closer. But he could do nothing but lay there on the dusty floor, too scared to flee.

'The creature lowers its hood, revealing its face to me,' said Idris quietly, almost whispering. 'That's when I wake up screaming.'

'Do you recognise the face of the creature?' asked one of the councillors, after a moment of quiet thought.

'Yes,' replied Idris. 'It's my father's.'

Several of the council members gasped at the revelation and began to chatter noisily to one another, until Fireen hushed them back into silence, indicating that the boy's mother wished to add something.

'At first we thought that it was just a bad dream,' said Tethine. 'A very vivid, bad dream, brought on by the loss of his father and the memories that were rising to the surface of his young mind as he came of age. But the dreams didn't go away. In fact they seem to be coming ever more frequently, and they're always the same, in every little detail. We just don't know what to do. It's as if Idris is haunted somehow by his father's ghost.'

'It is troubling, yes,' hissed Fireen, 'but there is more to add to this story that I have not yet told anybody.'

Her declaration was sufficient to draw the attention of everyone in the room. Their eyes were fixed upon her as they waited for her to clarify and expand upon the statement.

'I too have been having visions, in my sleep,' she continued, once she was certain that everyone in the room was listening. 'They are neither frightening nor recurrent, as yours are, Idris,' she added, looking at the young man with warm affection. 'I have spent many hours in quiet meditation, contemplating the meaning of these visions, and I have always come to the same conclusion. Navesh is not dead. He lives.'

'But how can that be?' asked Saven, standing up and pacing about the room, interrupting Fireen's account of her visions. 'He was mortally wounded and chose to stay behind in the dark world, giving up his life so that we might escape!'

'Please, Saven. I understand that this is difficult to hear, but allow me to finish relating the details of my visions. Then, perhaps, you will understand how I came to this conclusion.'

Saven nodded to Fireen, silently apologising for her outburst, and sat down once more to hear the rest of the account.

Fireen told them all that she believed that Navesh survived somehow. She did not know how he had achieved this, but she was certain that he had not perished in the dark citadel, and was desperately trying to communicate with them. He was reaching out, connecting with the power of the aether, touching the minds of those close to him. Somehow, his desperate callings had found their way to her and Idris. She told the young man that his father would never willing scare him, so the nightmares from which he was suffering must be being twisted as they traversed the aetherium. She explained that in some of her visions she had seen Navesh within a dark citadel, which she assumed to belong to Valken, being chased by groups of vile demons, harried at every turn. In other visions she had seen him leading a large group of tired, emaciated people through a high mountain range. They are clearly still on the dark world, with its blood-red sky, but are no longer trapped within the walls of the citadel. They are fleeing for their lives, forever looking fearfully behind them, terrified of the creatures which they know are hunting them. Somehow, Navesh keeps them safe. She has seen him wielding the power of the aether, swinging his golden spear, cutting down scores of demons with its keen edge, defying the very creatures that seem intent on his destruction.

'Perhaps my father's fear of the hunters has twisted my vision into the nightmare that plagues my sleep,' said Idris thoughtfully. 'He is being forced to live out my very nightmare, running every day from those dreadful creatures and in constant fear of capture.'

'Yes,' hissed Fireen, 'you may well be correct, Idris. I had not considered that. Well done, young man. Clearly you have your father's gift for logical thought.'

Idris smiled back at Fireen, and his mother put her arm around his shoulders, proud of her son's mature reasoning.

Fireen continued to describe her visions to the council. She told of a group of blue-skinned warriors, with shoulder length dark hair, each wielding a glowing spear of deadly power, attacking their foes with brutal force, killing all who stood in their way. She recounted a vision in which a blue-skinned woman, a queen, wearing a heavy carved stone crown, sat on a throne, ornately chiselled from the wall of the chamber in which she sat.

'The visions I have had are jumbled together,' said Fireen, coming to the end of her narration, trying to make some sense of what she had just described. 'They are garbled, with no clear timeline with which to order and make sense of them. But I remain convinced that Navesh and many others from our world are trapped in the dark realm, in desperate peril.

'I must confess that I have never seen these blue-skinned creatures before. Their kind did not appear to have been part of Valken's army of darkness, and I do not know how they fit into these visions.

'There is but one final thing that I have to tell you, which is of greater importance than anything we have discussed so far. I have had a vision of the lost stone of power! It is, somehow, in the possession of the blue-skinned queen. I do not know how she acquired it, or where she is located, but she is clearly using it for her own dark purposes.'

Everyone was quiet for several minutes, looking blankly at one another as the enormity of what Fireen had just related to them began to sink in. Fireen waited patiently, observing each of them in turn, waiting for them to process the information. She had already thought about what they should do next, but wanted to hear her companions' views and ideas before she made the final decision.

'How can it be true?' asked Saven, finally breaking the oppressive silence that had engulfed the room. 'I saw Navesh's wound for myself. It would almost certainly have been fatal, even if we'd been able to access the aether and the healing magic. But at that moment in time, the aether was proving difficult to control, even for young Panx. I hope you're right, Fireen, I truly do, but he's been gone for two years now, how could he have possibly survived for so long in that foul place?'

'So where exactly is he?' asked Endina, an aged Aellindi female who had only recently been appointed to the council. 'If, as you've indicated, he's no longer in the dark citadel, he could be anywhere on Valken's world. We have no conception of the size of that realm, and to find Navesh would be like looking for a small fish in the depths of the great sea.'

'Thank you both for your comments,' said Fireen. 'I truly value your opinions on these matters. In answer to your question, Saven, yes I do believe that the visions are real and that they are showing us the true fate that poor Navesh has had to endure. I do not know exactly how he survived, but survive he did, I am certain. And Endina, your question is equally important, but one which I have already considered. If Navesh did escape the confines of the dark citadel then you are correct, he could be anywhere. But you forget one thing, my friend. If he is truly calling out to me through the aether, sending a desperate plea for help, then we will be able to locate him by following the aether trail back to its source. It will lead us directly to him.'

Saven and Endina both nodded respectfully, acknowledging Fireen's logical approach to the unusual predicament that they faced.

'So these others,' said Marcus, speaking up for the first time since joining the council assembly, 'the ones that Navesh is shepherding, do you recognise any of them?'

'No, Marcus, not specifically,' she replied, 'but there are men and women of the Kingdom amongst their number, and also several of the Aellindi people.'

'Thinking back to the moment that I killed Valken,' continued Marcus, 'as soon as he was dead, the chains which had previously bound my ankles and hands were released. It was as if he were somehow animating them, controlling them, and that when he died, the connection was severed. Perhaps these refugees also escaped when their bonds were similarly removed?'

'That is a good explanation, Marcus,' said Fireen, her acknowledgement accompanied by the vigorous nodding heads of the others in the room. 'It would certainly explain the number of people that appear to be in Navesh's company. We already know that many prisoners were dragged back to Valken's realm before the tear in the void was repaired, and we had assumed that those poor unfortunate souls had perished.'

'So what can we possibly do?' asked Tordin pragmatically. 'Obviously we don't want to leave Navesh and the others on that world. Surely their luck will run out sooner or later and the demons will catch up with them. We need to mount a rescue, of course we do, but how do we get back to that horrible place? It was Navesh who opened the portal to the dark world in the first place, with the help of the Ancestors. We didn't even know how to close it properly. All we did was yank that shard out of the socket! It seems to me that we're a bit out of our depth here.'

There was a lengthy discussion about portals and the manipulation of the aether to open passageways between different realms. The general consensus between the Aellindi scholars was that it was possible to travel between worlds using the aether as a conduit, but very few individuals were familiar with the necessary incantations. Finally, when the ideas began to fizzle out, Fireen asked Marcus and Tordin to go and summon Panx and Indrani. Perhaps they will have ideas of their own on how to handle the problem.

'When you return, Marcus, we will discuss matters further,' she said, calling the council meeting to an end.

Marcus and Tordin raced back to the *Beacon of Rhasad*, pushing their tharen a little harder than normal, dodging through the crowded streets of the port, desperate to contact Panx and Indrani. They were both still in shock at finding out that Navesh might still be alive, and they knew that any delay now might prove fatal for their long lost friend. Marcus knew exactly where Panx would be, having seen him recently. The young magus had travelled between the *Beacon of Rhasad* and the *Beacon of Andin*, to the island in the shallow sea, where he intended to spend some time exploring the ancient ruins. As far as Marcus was aware, Panx had not yet returned to Nesteris, so the two friends decided to go and seek him out. Once they had retrieved Panx they would return to Nesteris and head south to Reznar, where Indrani was currently searching for ixoden silk. Marcus quickly activated the portal at the top of the beacon, its energy field coalescing into a shimmering oval doorway and the two men prepared to step through.

Five

The sun peaked over the horizon, slowly lifting the veil of darkness which had blanketed the desert. Its golden light glinted off the glass-domed structure at the heart of the ancient, long abandoned city. It promised to be a fine day, and already the deep black of the night was fading, to be replaced by the faint orange colour which usually perfused the morning sky. Later, as the sun rose higher into the heavens above, the sky would change to the beautiful blue colour and the burning desert heat would force all but the most determined traveller to seek shelter.

Nadarru sat within an ancient dwelling. Its roof and one of its walls had long since collapsed, but she had managed to crawl underneath a fallen stone block that had come to rest against the steps that had once led to the floor above. The night had been long and cold, but she had dared not leave her stony shelter for fear of being discovered. She had lain there, as silent as a desert rodent, shaking with terror and curled into a foetal ball, trying to preserve what little warmth her shivering body could generate. She knew that the night would pass, to be replaced by the light of the new day and the welcome warmth of the sun, but lying there on the cold and dusty ground she felt vulnerable and alone.

Who, or what, were those creatures? Nadarru wondered. Previously, from the vantage point in the ruined top story of her hideout, she had watched as the tall creatures had stalked through the caravan site, dispensing an agonising death to those they had found there. Her keen eyes had managed to see, by the light of the small fire and the blinding flashes of their weapons, that the creatures carried some sort of magical spear, which they used to engulf their victims in searing flames. She had watched in horror, covering her mouth with her hands to prevent her from screaming, as Denir had stumbled from the tower and had been struck down by the invaders.

The sudden, brutal assault, had not lasted long and soon only small pockets of resistance remained, given away by the occasional flash from the attackers' spears. A few of the caravan teamsters had made it out into the ruins of the city, and she had heard them calling softly to one another. Perhaps they had hoped to regain the initiative and take back the caravan, or perhaps they were simply preparing to flee deeper into the city. She watched as the blue-skinned warriors left the firelit camp site and headed out into the deserted streets, to hunt down the escaping teamsters.

She had crept down to the ground level and crawled under the stone block, lying there in the darkness, listening to the occasional scream as her comrades were dispatched. After a while, it occurred to her that the desert was quiet once more. The hunt must be complete.

As the early morning sun filtered through the ruins of the ancient city, Nadarru slowly emerged from her secret hiding place, careful not to make any noise that might alert the intruders to her whereabouts. She had not heard any sounds of violence for many hours now, but she was concerned that they might still be here, perhaps searching the caravan for items of value.

She was hungry and very thirsty, and decided that if she were to carefully climb up to the top of the dwelling in which she had hidden, she might be able to see if the caravan site was still occupied. She clambered up the remains of the stone staircase, her long tail flicking out to aid her balance, and then stepped with feline grace onto the lintel of the old doorway. From there she scrambled up to the stone blocks which would have once supported the timber floor.

Gingerly she peered over the old window ledge, which afforded her a view along the ancient street, towards the tower where the caravan had been. There was rubble strewn about the caravan site, but no sign of movement. The wagons were gone, destroyed in the attack, but there were still many items lying on the ground at the base of the tower. She watched for a long time, waiting to see if there was any sign of the attackers, but as the sun began to creep ever higher into the blue skies above she decided that they must have left by now.

Slowly, still fearful of discovery, she crept down and emerged onto the street, staying within the shadows cast by the tumbled ruins. She moved along the ancient thoroughfare, dodging in and out of the ruined buildings, creeping ever closer to the huge tower that loomed over her. She heard no voices and saw no movement, and her fear began to lift as she edged closer to ruined caravan.

Reaching the final dwelling before the open area in front of the tower, Nadarru stopped and peered stealthily around the corner of a stone wall that had partially tumbled onto the dusty street. The caravan site was abandoned. She waited for a while longer, and when nobody moved, ran as fast as she could over to the entrance to the tower, ducking inside the doorway and into its shadowed safety. She peered around the doorway, glimpsing for the first time the carnage that had been wrought on the caravan and its inhabitants. There were no bodies to be seen. Instead, there were piles of white bones lying around the area, the flesh completely stripped away, leaving behind only the skeletal structure which had once supported it. A wave of nausea passed over her, forcing her to lean on the doorway for support. She wretched onto the ground, spilling what little remained in her stomach. *Who could have done this?* She wondered, *and why?*

Nadarru slumped to the ground, sitting on the sand beside the steaming pool of her own vomit. What was she going to do now? She had no idea how far it was to the next oasis, or even in which direction she would need to travel. Denir kept these little secrets all to himself. She knew, from previous trips, that it was still many days to the western coast and the cities that occupied the lush green land beyond the edge of the great desert. But she did not know the way. Perhaps Denir kept a map? Surely he must have had some record of the route through the barren wasteland in the centre of the continent.

She stood up with renewed determination, intent on finding a way out of her desperate plight. Moving slowly around the ruined campsite, she carefully picked through the debris which lay strewn across a wide area in front of the great tower. Surprisingly, she found many useful things, including food, water bottles, clothing and even a substantial quantity of golden coins. *Why hadn't the raiders taken these?* She wondered. *What were they after if not food and money?*

She meticulously piled all the useful items up beside the tower, loading up a tattered backpack with food, water and clothing. She took some money too, although it was heavy and she could only carry so much. The remaining coins were bundled up in an old blanket and buried behind the tower, for retrieval at some later time. The single most valuable item she found amongst the remains of the caravan was Denir's map of the desert. She had felt certain that he must have kept such a document, and silently thanked the gods that it had survived the carnage of the previous night's raid. The map showed the route that they had taken from the eastern cities, across the desert. It showed the location of the many oases that were spread out across the vast sandy wastes. Some were crossed through, which she assumed to mean they had dried up, and others appeared to have been added more recently. The map showed the tower where she was currently standing, in the very centre of the desert, and it showed her the way to the western cities and the route that Denir would have taken. She briefly considered the journey back to the east, but decided that there would be nothing for her there, except perhaps servitude to a new master.

Without the cover provided by the wagons to shelter her from the scorching rays of the afternoon sun, Nadarru decided that she ought to travel only at night, early evening and early morning, while the heat was bearable. She swung the heavy pack onto her back, preparing to head back into the ancient ruined city to seek out shelter from the heat, when she heard a noise coming from the entrance to the great tower. Someone was calling her name. It sounded like Denir, but she had seen him die at the hands of the raiders. *It couldn't be him, could it?* She waited, rooted to the spot, listening for any further sounds. Then she heard Denir's voice again, calling out to her with an urgency that she had never heard from him before. He must be still alive, up in the tower, and he must be injured.

'Nadarru, is that you? Help me, please help me!'

She took a step towards the tower entrance, and then halted. *What if it was a trap?* She thought. *He's dead, you saw it happen.* Her mind raced as she tried to decide what to do. *What if he's still alive up there?* She argued silently with herself, maybe he could help her to escape this barren desert. Denir called again, more insistent this time, and Nadarru took several steps towards the tower. Before she could stop herself she had started climbing the stairs, almost running now, eager to get to the top of the tower. But when she reached the summit, emerging into the glass-domed room, there was nobody there. She stopped, looking around in confusion. Where was he?

As she moved across the room looking for Denir, she was startled as four blue-skinned warriors suddenly appeared. She found that she was frozen to the spot, her fear preventing her from moving.

'Ahhh, there you are,' said a voice, a woman's voice this time. 'I've been waiting for you to arrive. What took you so long?'

Nadarru bolted towards the stairs, suddenly freed from her momentary paralysis, desperate to reach the freedom of the outside world. However, her captors had clearly anticipated her every move and two more warriors appeared on the stairwell, blocking her escape route. A pair of strong blue arms grabbed her from behind and, no matter how hard she struggled, she could not free herself.

'They won't harm you, Nadarru,' said the woman's voice calmly, 'but you must promise not to try and escape. Do you promise?'

'Yes, I promise,' replied the terrified Ligarian, still unable to move. She had no alternative but to acquiesce to her captors' demands, for now.

'Good,' replied the voice.

She was immediately released from the warrior's strong embrace, although she noted that the two on the stairs did not move. Clearly they did not yet trust her to keep her word.

Before she could consider her next move, the air was filled with an intense buzzing sound and the pressure inside the glass-domed room began to increase, causing her to clutch at her ears in pain. A bright light filled the centre of the room and a shimmering disc of energy began to materialise right in front of her. As the disc grew larger, almost touching the dome itself, the buzzing sound ceased and the disc coalesced into a shimmering wall of energy, shrinking back in size so that it was just larger than the blue-skinned warriors.

'It's time, my loyal followers, bring her through.'

Nadarru panicked as the warriors gently ushered her towards the shimmering wall of light. She struggled again, although there was no escape as her captors had moved in to surround her. As she was pushed closer and closer to the glowing energy disc, she became aware of a tingling sensation across her skin. She felt as though the fur on the back of her neck was standing on end, and was terrified as small sparks began jumping from the surface of the disc, flying through the air to strike her body. For a moment she panicked, fearing that she was about to be reduced to a pile of sun-bleached bones. But then one of the blue-skinned warriors grabbed her firmly from behind and pushed her closer to the glowing energy field.

'Have no fear,' he said in a cold, calm voice. 'It doesn't hurt.'

The warrior shoved her through the wall of energy and Nadarru tumbled into the disc, feeling as if she were falling from a great height, her body spinning out of control as she plummeted.

The feeling of weightlessness was overwhelming, forcing her stomach up into her throat and leaving her with an odd sensation in her gut. She fell in total silence. Even her desperate screams failed to reach her ears. There was a pulsating blue light all around her, and

46

flashes of lightning struck her as she fell, passing through her body as if it were nothing more than an ethereal phantom. In front of her she could see nothing but a long black tunnel, snaking through the flashing blue light which surrounded it.

The buzzing sound returned, growing in volume to near deafening proportions. Then, unexpectedly, the sensation of falling was gone. She was standing in a large cavern, her body shaking violently from the experience. The fur on the back of her neck was no longer standing up, although her skin felt hot and flushed and her fingers and toes tingled with an unpleasant burning feeling.

'There, that wasn't so bad, was it?' said the feminine voice that she had heard at the top of the ancient tower.

Looking around she finally saw who the commanding voice belonged to. Another of the blue-skinned people, a beautiful woman, was standing beside her. She was tall, equally as tall as Nadarru herself, although not as imposing as her lieutenants, who were taller still and had heavily muscled bodies. The woman was smiling cruelly, as if secretly enjoying the look of fear and discomfort that Nadarru was no doubt displaying. Behind her the six warriors emerged from the glowing energy disc, fanning out to surround their captive. They showed no signs of discomfort, or any after effects from the journey through the strange portal. Perhaps they were used to such means of travel, or perhaps their bodies simply withstood the physical effects of the transition better than hers.

As the disorientating effects of the journey through the portal began to dissipate, Nadarru looked around, taking in the sights of the room in which she was now standing. The voluminous cavern was stark, with the walls bare and undecorated. The air was very cold and her breath turned instantly to a steaming mist with each exhalation. However, considering that she was used to the warm desert, she did not feel cold inside. Perhaps it was some form of magic that kept her warm, she did not know, but with each passing moment since her emergence from the portal, she felt an increasing sense of calm.

'How do you like my palace?' asked the woman.

'It's colder than the desert,' replied Nadarru, unsure of what to say. 'Where is this place?'

'Far away from your homeland, child,' replied the woman.

Nadarru looked around again, noticing for the first time that the woman wore an ornately carved circlet of stone that rested on top of her head, supported by the sharply pointed ears that poked through her dark, shoulder length hair. The cavern, or palace as the woman had said, did not look much like the opulent homes of the kings and queens of her imagination. The only features to be seen were a large dais, which rose up in the centre of the room, and a stone throne which sat atop it. There were many more blue-skinned people in the throne room than she had at first noticed. There were warriors, tall and powerfully built, each carrying one of the strange energy spears, with curved swords strapped across their backs. There were others, females mostly, who wore the garb of priests, and appeared to be engaged in some form of ritual. Many were kneeling down, as if in prayer, and others were chanting in a strange language, waving their arms in the air in odd circular motions.

'Who are you?' asked Nadarru, looking at the woman who she assumed to be the leader of these people.

'I am Queen Karmina, known to my followers as the Stone Queen. You belong at my side now, Nadarru.'

Nadarru felt strangely sanguine as she watched the priests continue their incantations, bringing whatever ritual they had been performing to a close. She did not appear concerned with Queen Karmina's declaration that she now belonged at her side. She was, apparently, still a slave. She just hoped that Queen Karmina would be less cruel than Denir had been. Although she did not yet know the purpose of her transportation here, she appeared, outwardly at least, quite calm. Inside however, she was screaming. Something was not right here and she had to escape. But the inner voice was weak and not strong enough to be heard. It soon began to fade until it was but a faint whisper in the back of her mind, as the will of the Stone Queen asserted its control.

Nadarru noticed that a small group of people were being brought into the throne room. They were chained together and were being ushered past the stone dais by the armed guards, their spears lowered with undisguised malice. However, the prisoners were not of the same race as Queen Karmina and her followers. There were people of a similar kind amongst them, although they had pale skin and long red hair. There were also some of Denir's people, although these too had pale skin, like those from the western lands. She watched intently as the prisoners were gently shepherded to where the priests had just been standing. Her interest turned to horror as she saw the blue-skinned warriors lower their spears and fire at the prisoners. Their bodies began to sizzle and burn as the fire consumed their flesh. Nadarru closed her eyes, trying to shield them from the bright light. But the energy was too powerful and she was left with a ghostly after image of the gruesome spectacle, as if the brutal murder of these people had been forever etched into her mind.

'Watch, my child,' said Queen Karmina softly.

Nadarru opened her eyes once more, unable to resist the Queen's commands. The prisoners were all dead, the flesh stripped from their bodies as if eaten by some ravenous plague. Where, just moments before, the frightened captives had stood, piles of bleached white bones now lay. It was exactly the same as the scene she had discovered outside of the ancient tower in the desert, where Denir's caravan team had been massacred.

The Stone Queen walked forward, coming to stand in front of the bones which now littered the floor. She began to chant in a language which Nadarru did not comprehend, and soon a glowing light emanated from her fingertips, reaching out to touch each and every one of the lifeless bones. At first, Nadarru thought her eyes were deceiving her, for the bones appeared to be moving, scraping across the cold floor, moving with an odd jerking motion as they danced to Queen Karmina's rhythmic tune. Within moments the bones had somehow joined together, reforming the skeletons which had once been covered in flesh, skin and hair. They stood there, silently waiting for their Queen's command, their jaws slightly open as if locked in a permanent smile, and their dark eye sockets burning with some inner light.

'Behold, Nadarru, my gift to you. These will be your soldiers, the first of many that you will raise from the dust to fight for you. This power I give to you, the power to command the dead. You are to be my instrument of destruction.'

'But why?' asked Nadarru. 'Why me? I don't understand.'

'Come with me, my child, and I will reveal all to you,' replied the Queen, turning away from the reanimated bones and heading out of the throne room.

Nadarru trailed behind Queen Karmina as she led her deeper into the palace, descending into its vast icy depths. As she walked through a series of narrow corridors with ice-encrusted walls, she was surprised at how warm she felt inside. It was as if some inner warmth had infused her body, to ward away the chilly air that whistled eerily through the palace. The Queen had not spoken to her since leaving the ritual chamber and so Nadarru followed in silence, fearful of what awaited her, within the walls of the ice palace.

They finally emerged from a narrow stairwell and stepped out onto a wide platform that overlooked a vast cavernous chamber. Queen Karmina beckoned Nadarru towards a large dais that stood further along the platform. It was, like everything else in the palace, completely encrusted with a thick layer of ice.

'Don't be afraid, my child,' whispered the Queen, gently taking Nadarru by the hand and guiding her along the platform, towards the dais. 'Our lord will keep you safe. He means you no harm.'

Nadarru felt uneasy. It was as if there were numerous eyes staring at her, although she could clearly see that, except for the Queen and her, the platform was deserted. As she approached the dais, her unease grew in intensity and she began to feel an odd presence within the cavernous chamber. For a moment she was certain that there had been a strange dark mist, coalescing just above the icy dais, but when she tried to focus on what she had seen, it was no longer there. The unseen presence remained, though, filling the chamber with an oppressive tension, causing Nadarru to shiver slightly.

'Behold, my child,' whispered the Queen, sweeping her arm out before her. 'Our great lord has come.'

Nadarru looked upon the icy dais, still unable to see what the Queen was indicating, when suddenly she was pushed backwards forcefully, by some unseen power, and lifted up above the platform. Her head was tilted backwards and her face set into a grimace, as if she were in terrible pain.

'Yes, my child,' said Queen Karmina, 'the lord has accepted you. Do not resist him, for he has a wonderful gift for you!'

Nadarru tried to relax and attempted to calm herself. She tried to do as Queen Karmina instructed and forced herself to stop resisting the power that was, even now, pushing its way into her mind. Gradually the pain lessened and she felt her body descending towards the icy platform, until she was once again standing on her own two feet, with her tail swishing gently though the chilly air behind her.

'You will have power, my child,' whispered the Queen. 'More power than you've ever witnessed before. You will be our instrument of conquest on your own world. You will be our champion, and none will dare stand in your way.

Nadarru listened as Queen Karmina promised her power and an army to lead against the corrupt races that inhabited her own world. The strange force that had previously held her body rigid was now infusing her with warming energy, and she felt her muscles strengthening beyond all recognition. She felt intoxicated as the power infused her mind, opening up her senses to the arcane energies of the aether. She had never been a strong wielder of magic, and this sudden exposure to its power left her a little giddy. She tried to focus on the power and was suddenly gifted with her god's grand vision of conquest. She would lead an army of undead creatures against her enemies, in her god's mighty name, and she would be greatly feared throughout the known world.

'Never again will you be a slave, my child,' said Queen Karmina, coming to stand beside the Ligarian, as the vision slowly faded and the oppressive presence retreated from the cavernous chamber. 'You are reborn, Priestess Nadarru, and all will fear your wrath!'

*   *   *

Nadarru stood on her own world once more, in the shadow of the ancient tower. As promised, she had been gifted with the necessary power to begin Queen Karmina's conquest of her own world, and she now stood under the glaring sunshine with a small army massed before her. However, this was no ordinary army, but one that she had raised herself, from the bones of the Stone Queen's enemies. Beside her stood her six blue-skinned lieutenants, who were to accompany her throughout the conquest. They stood silently, looking out into the desert, each clutching their energy spear firmly, as if leaning on them for support. They rarely spoke, but when they did their words were uttered with an almost musical note that commanded the attention of those around them. The journey back to the tower through the shimmering energy portal had been easier the second time, although she had still been disorientated upon emerging from the glowing wall of blue light.

Before her, strewn chaotically on the dusty ground, lay the bones of the men, women and children of Denir's caravan. That other life, where she had been his servant, seemed so very far way now. It was as if it had not been real, but some bad dream that she could not quite shake off. She walked amongst the pile of bones and began to chant. Her magical song started as a soft, quiet incantation that slowly gathered urgency and her arms weaved hypnotically through the air as she channelled the aether. A golden light appeared, settling over the entire area, imbuing the dead with new life.

Slowly the bones moved across the sand, eerily reforming with their counterparts. Hands and arms joined together once more, connecting with bony shoulders that rested on hollow rib cages. As the reanimation continued, the reconstructed skeletal torsos crawled across the ground, desperate to be reunited with their legs. As the process neared completion, her headless warriors stood up and retrieved their missing skulls, placing them delicately on top of the waiting spinal column. The rebuilding of her new recruits took only moments, and before long her undead army had swelled in number. The skeletal figures stood there, patiently waiting for her to command them, with only the occasional creak of their bones and joints to break the silence which suffused the ancient city.

Nadarru moved through their ranks, carefully inspecting each and every one of them, as if looking for poorly maintained weapons or dirty clothing. She came to a halt in front of one of the silent skeletal figures, its depthless eye sockets staring into infinity.

'There you are,' she whispered, resting her hand on her soldier's hollow ribcage. 'I always knew I'd get you in the end.'

A violent burst of energy shot from her open palm, smashing into Denir's skeletal form. His reanimated bones were torn apart once more, sending them clattering to the ground where they rapidly turned into powder and mingled with the sand as it shifted gently in the desert wind.

Nadarru turned away from the tower and, without looking back, headed west into the baking sand dunes, followed by her lieutenants and her skeletal army.

Six

Panx was in heaven. When Leonar, his fellow historian from Brind, had told him about the recent discovery of an ancient dwelling filled with wondrous items, he had not been prepared for what he now found himself looking at. The building above ground had been almost too much to bear, and he had left Matixis and Rustara, his two Aellindi friends, cataloguing its contents. As Leonar had already told him, there was a long flight of stairs leading down under the building that ended in a sturdy metal doorway which, surprisingly, had been unlocked. The doorway had reminded him of the entrance to the lift in the central core of the beacon. It showed no obvious sign of corrosion, which was unusual given its underground location, and had swung effortlessly open on unseen hinges.

The space beyond the doorway had been as black as pitch, and the weak illumination from the stairwell had done little to dispel the stygian darkness. There had been a noticeable draft coming from somewhere ahead, from within the chamber itself, and a damp musty smell had assaulted his nostrils as soon as the door had been opened. The young magus had called upon the power of the aether, conjuring up a ball of light which he sent forwards, probing carefully into the gloom. The light had floated off into the darkness, illuminating the immediate area around it, although Panx was forced to recall it when it became clear that the room was too large to explore in this way. Instead, he had created multiple balls of light that he placed at intervals around the entrance to the room, which had permitted him to explore the immediate area in relative comfort. He was still unable to tell how far back the room reached, so he had sent Leonar to the surface to arrange for some torch pillars to be brought down, where they would hopefully push back the oppressive darkness. While he waited for his friend's return, he cautiously moved out into the room, illuminated by the glowing radiance of aetheric light which floated noiselessly above him as he went.

He estimated that the room was easily the size of the glass-domed construct which sat atop the *Beacon of Andin,* and as Leonar had discovered when he briefly explored the room before rushing to fetch

Panx, it was filled with the familiar workstations that seemed to be a feature of all of the Ancestors' beacons. The difference here was that this room was underground, and none of the workstations showed even the slightest sign of life.

Panx soon discovered the far end of the room and the source of the damp musty smell which filled it. There was another doorway, similar in appearance to the one at the entrance, although this one was firmly sealed. A large patch of wet ground lay before the door, and upon closer inspection he could see a fine trickle of water seeping from underneath, running away to disappear down a small metal vent in the floor.

The walls of the room were similar to those which lined the staircase inside the tower, and even featured the same strange writing that nobody had yet been able to translate. Unlike the walls of the tower, these were icy cold, although this was to be expected given their subterranean location. Panx had followed the wall in one direction from the back door and had soon discovered that the room was circular. As he had made his way around the entire circumference of the room, passing by the original entrance door on his way back to the locked rear door, he found two more locked doors which he estimated to be at equidistance from the front and rear doors. He resolved to get the three locked doors open as soon as possible.

Leonar had returned with a large team of scholars, bringing with them numerous torch pillars which immediately began to push back the oppressive darkness with their flickering orange flames, and soon the entire room had been revealed.

The Ancestors had left many wondrous things in this room, and Panx considered that very odd, as even in Nesteris, their home island, they had left very few clues about their history. Leonar was busily removing objects for further study, many of which looked as though they might be of interest to Marcus, perhaps some wondrous technology left behind by the Aellindi forebears. There were also items which Panx thought might be of an artistic nature, depicting the Ancestors themselves. However, the most amazing thing that the young man had discovered was a large stone table that sat near to one of the side doors. On top of the table was a finely detailed map, cast from some strange, hard material. The map was huge and difficult to read without standing up on a nearby workstation. They had always known that the Ancestors had been tall, far taller than their Aellindi children, but this map was proof of just how large they must have been.

As he studied the ancient map, creating several balls of aetheric light to chase away the shadows created by its highly detailed, embossed surface, it suddenly dawned on him exactly what he was looking at. Here, in this vast underground chamber, hidden for countless years, was a detailed map of the ancient world. This was how the land of the Ancestors would have appeared before the horrific cataclysm shattered it into small fragments. He nearly fell off the workstation on which he was currently standing as he leaned out a little too far, trying to examine every last detail.

'This is amazing,' he muttered to himself. 'I must get someone down here straight away to make a copy of this.'

The young magus hopped down off the workstation and, leaving his aetheric light globes behind, rushed off towards the door to the surface, intent on finding someone who could paint.

Marcus stepped through the fizzing blue portal and out into the glass-domed chamber on top of the *Beacon of Andin*, followed closely by Tordin. The room was lively, with glowing workstations flickering with rapidly scrolling text and numerous scholars going about their business. Marcus looked around for Panx, although he could not spot his young friend anywhere.

'Maybe he's in the control pit,' said Tordin, walking over to the central control station which was recessed into the floor of the chamber. He called out to the young magus, but several of the scholars, looking up from their appointed tasks, informed him that Panx was not here, that he was out in the abandoned settlement at the edge of the forest.

Marcus remembered when they had first come here, when they had discovered the beacon and the technology hidden behind the panels of the workstations. It had been a revelation, something which he could understand and which did not rely on magic or swordplay. It was something that only he could offer to the quest. He had quickly managed to get the inert beacon up and running again, partially at least, and they had managed to determine the location of the *Beacon of Olon*, which had always been their ultimate destination.

He smiled as he remembered how the others in their little group had viewed him with suspicion when he had bundled them all into the lift car, insisting that they use it to descend through the central core of the beacon rather than trudge down the stairs. He also remembered how, on a return visit to the beacon, he had discovered that the lift shaft actually went down to another level, deep underground. He had been amazed to find, when the lift doors had opened, a huge chamber below the beacon that contained what appeared to be a partially deactivated power core, which looked as if it had been deliberately turned off or sabotaged. He had managed to get the generator up and running again, although many of the beacon's functions still eluded him. This amazing discovery had led him to further explore the other known beacons. He soon found that they all shared a similar layout, although the one beyond the veil was far bigger, with more of its functions still active. There were also several doors leading away from the power core chambers, although these had all been locked and as yet he had been unable to determine what lay beyond.

'We'd better head down and find our young friend, Marcus,' said Tordin, as he came over to stand beside the professor. 'Would you care to take the stairs?' he then added, a wide grin appearing on his tanned face.

As the two friends emerged from the doorway at the base of the beacon and headed out across the ruined settlement towards the edge of the forest, they passed two Aellindi scholars who were heading back to the tower. They were heavily encumbered, carrying large boxes filled with numerous objects of wonder from the recently discovered building. Marcus could not help himself, and peered down at the objects as the scholars passed them by. He spotted what looked like a small hand gun, reminiscent of the futuristic ray guns that were depicted in the old B movies on his own world. He was just about to warn the Aellindi to be very careful with it, when Panx emerged from a large building at the edge of the forest. The young man called out to them, waving frantically in their direction as he ran across the open ground. He was puffing heavily as he skidded to a halt beside them, obviously very excited about something, and had to take a moment to catch his breath.

'Hello,' he said, his lungs still not fully recovered, 'you have to come and see this. It's wonderful!'

Without waiting for them to reply, Panx bolted back towards the building from which he had just emerged, leaving Marcus, Tordin and the two Aellindi scholars looking at each other in bewilderment.

'Is he always like this?' said Tordin, looking at the pair of Aellindi.

'Yes, quite often,' hissed Matixis, smiling back at them. 'New discoveries do seem to trigger his excitement!'

'Well then,' added Marcus, 'best not keep him waiting. Let's go.'

Marcus and Tordin headed after Panx, leaving the two Aellindi scholars to continue their journey to the beacon to offload their latest discoveries.

'Oh, Matixis, be really careful with those objects,' shouted Marcus, before heading into the building.

When they finally caught up with Panx, who had descended the steps and awaited them in the shadowy room below, they were awestruck by what they saw. Marcus and Tordin both recognised the huge map for what it was and, following Panx's lead, clambered up onto the surrounding workstations to get a better view.

'I don't recognise most of those land masses,' said Tordin, pointing to the huge map table with a broad sweep of his arm, 'so I'm not entirely sure what we're dealing with here.'

'I think it's a map of the world,' replied Panx excitedly, 'from before it was nearly destroyed by the ancient cataclysm.'

'Yes,' added Marcus, the realisation of what lay before him finally registering. 'Look, there's Nesteris, right in the middle. It looks a little different, a little larger in fact, but the basic shape is correct. If I had to make a guess, I'd say that, in addition to your world being broken into many fragments, parts of its surface have been changed too. But look, there, that has to be K'vith.'

'And that must be what we now know as the Kingdom of the Isles,' added Tordin, pointing to a land mass above Nesteris. 'The world, before it was damaged in the cataclysm, must have been huge! If this is the fragment on which we are now located,' he added, pointing to a wide area around what they believed to be Nesteris, 'then all this other land must be lost, beyond the veil somewhere, or on another fragment altogether.'

'This is amazing, Panx, truly astounding,' said Marcus. 'We must study this further.'

'I couldn't agree more,' replied Panx, watching as Marcus retrieved his small pocket camera and began to take several pictures of the huge map table, the bright flash illuminating the highly detailed model. 'So what are you both doing here, anyway?' he added. 'Not that I'm not pleased to see you of course.'

'Well, prepare to be amazed, for the second time today,' said Tordin, 'but we've just come from a meeting with Fireen and the council of Nesteris, and have just learned that Navesh is still alive. He's trapped somewhere on Valken's dark world and is calling out for our help!'

'What? How?' replied Panx, looking up from the map with undisguised shock, his jaw dropping open, disbelief registering on his face.

'His son has been having disturbing dreams,' continued Tordin, 'in which a cowled figure, who turns out to be Navesh, is chasing him through the streets of Nesteris, apparently reaching out for help. It turns out that Fireen has also seen Navesh in her dreams, although hers are little more complicated. She thinks that there are others from our world stuck in Valken's realm, and that Navesh is helping to protect them. She believes that their time is running out and that we must mount a rescue soon, before the demons catch them.'

'Well the map and this room can wait,' said Panx without hesitation. 'It's been here for a very long time already, and it'll still be here when we return. Let's go and get Navesh, before it's too late.'

Marcus took a few more pictures of the huge map and then the three companions headed back towards the *Beacon of Andin*. As they walked across the reclaimed settlement towards the ancient construct, they expanded on the descriptions of the visions which Fireen and Idris had been having. Panx was interested to hear about the lost stone of power, although he admitted that he too had never heard of these mysterious blue-skinned people.

Panx left Matixis and Rustara in charge of cataloguing the new dwelling and the underground map room, indicating that they should leave the underwater recovery for a later time. Marcus activated the portal and the three companions stepped through, back to the island of Nesteris.

Klestin looked up as the transportation portal flared to life in the control room of the *Beacon of Rhasad*. Marcus, Panx and Tordin stepped through and the fizzing energy disc faded away behind them. Lethis wandered over to greet them, clutching a new batch of recently magnetised discs for their hydroelectric generators.

'Greetings, Marcus,' she hissed softly. 'I'm glad you've come back, could you remind me how to–'

'I'm sorry, Lethis,' said Marcus, interrupting his student before she could finish asking for his help, 'but we've something of an emergency on our hands and we need to prepare the *Drake* for departure as soon as possible. Can you and Klestin go and power her up please? We'll go and find Brune and Samir, and then I'll explain everything once we're all together.'

Marcus's ship could no longer be fully controlled by Lydia, the artificial intelligence system that had been integrated throughout the entire vessel. The *Drake* was now suffering from multiple malfunctions, as several small computers had been stripped out to help with his work on the Aellindi beacons. Consequently, she required a small crew in order to safely operate at sea.

Lethis looked over at Klestin, sharing a worried look with the small Vilnarri man before turning back to Marcus. 'I'm sorry, Marcus,' she said, 'but the main generator is currently offline and the engine has been partially dismantled. We're carrying out the maintenance that you asked us to perform, and therefore the *Drake* will not be ready to go to sea for quite some time.'

'Damn it!' muttered Marcus, with a little more vehemence than he had intended, causing his students to look down at the floor, abashed by his uncharacteristic outburst. 'I'm sorry,' he quickly added, clearly ashamed of himself. 'I didn't mean to direct my frustration at you, I'd forgotten about the maintenance work.'

Lethis and Klestin indicated that they had not been offended. It was just unexpected to see such a passionate explosion from the usually calm professor.

'It's not a problem,' said Tordin, coming to Marcus's assistance. 'We can take the *Hammer* down to Reznar. I'd wanted to take her on a long voyage anyway, so this is the perfect opportunity. Panx and I'll go down and get her ready.'

Marcus nodded in approval at Tordin's quick thinking, his mind already resigned to the fact that the *Drake* was currently out of action. He tasked his students with finishing the maintenance as a top priority, and getting the ship ready for action should they require her when he returned. Klestin and Lethis departed from the tower, to locate their two companions, while Marcus picked up a few items that he thought might come in useful and followed after Panx and Tordin.

The *Hammer* ploughed through the water, heading south towards the jungles of Reznar, as Nesteris faded into the distance behind them. The rhythmic hum of the huge propeller vibrated through the deck plates as Marcus stood up on the bridge with Panx and Tordin.

They had just returned from the engine room, as Tordin had pretended that he had wanted to see how the crew were performing, although Marcus knew his friend a little better. The Admiral was simply delighted at having his two friends aboard his new ship, and had taken great pleasure in showing off her powerful steam boiler and huge rotating shaft which was currently driving the ship through the rough waters. He had known about the magical crystals that were used to generate the steam that ultimately propelled the huge ship, but had yet to see them in action. They were large oblong crystals, slightly red in colour, with a translucent, shiny surface. The *Hammer's* two resident magi had been busy recharging the crystals as their aetheric energy had been used up, replacing them in the boiler housing as and when demand from the bridge dictated. It was an efficient system, which Marcus was fascinated to see in action and was pleased to have played a small part in its design.

Tordin had tried to mimic the coal powered steam boilers, which had been popular in the early industrial era of Marcus's own world, but had found it to be a rather dirty and unpleasant business. At Marcus's insistence, the Admiral had looked for an alternative, turning to a magical solution when Panx had mentioned the heat crystals. There were still a few of the prototype coal powered steamers operating out of Brind, although they had mostly been converted to pleasure craft, taking the wealthier citizens of the Kingdom's capital city on short coastal excursions.

One of the magi, Jeban, had eagerly told them that they had also been working alongside the army's engineers to create a rudimentary rail network. This would allow the latest steam powered locomotives to move men and victuals around the city with far greater efficiency than tharen and cart. Jeban had told them that there was only a small network in operation at the present time, although it was constantly being expanded. Marcus had commented, chuckling to himself, that it was like the *Victorian Age* all over again, only much cleaner. Obviously the others had not understood the joke, and the professor had been forced to explain about the famous British monarch and the explosion of wondrous inventions that had been one of the trademarks of her reign. *If only we'd had magic on our world*, he had mused, *we could've avoided a lot of problems with pollution.*

'So what's Indrani doing in Reznar?' asked Panx.

'She's trading for ixoden silk,' replied Marcus. 'Lots of it.'

'What are you planning to do with all that silk?'

'It's for her latest project. She wants to take aeromancy to the next level and build an air defence force!'

'Oh?' added Tordin, who had been listening in to the conversation while keeping an eye on the ship's controls. 'What exactly is she planning to do?'

'Well, back on my world we had machines called airships, which were basically big balloons filled with a light gas. They were capable of carrying people and cargo from one place to another. You've probably seen them on your voyage through the documentaries stored in the *Drake's* computers.'

'You mean like the *Hindenburg*?' asked Tordin. 'If I recall, that didn't end so well!'

'No, it didn't. Quite right, Tordin, quite right. However, we learned a lot from those early disasters, especially regarding which gas to use. So there's no chance of a repeat of that awful catastrophe. Indrani's going to use the ixoden silk to create the huge balloons that will store the helium, and these will allow the airships to float. We've made a prototype already, just a small one, which seems to work quite well. It's capable of carrying three or four people. I'm trying to get her to call her new defence force "*The RAF*", but she's not having any of it!'

'I couldn't agree with her more, Marcus,' said Panx, winking mischievously at Tordin, who grinned back at him.

'Oh she'll come around in the end,' replied Marcus, smiling back at the young magus.

'Talking of Indrani,' added Tordin, 'shouldn't we try to make contact with her? To let her know that we're coming.'

'Yes, that's a good idea,' replied Marcus, fishing out the mobile comms unit which he always carried, and activating the dial-up sequence which would connect it with the paired device that Indrani had taken with her to Reznar.

Marcus tried several times to contact Indrani, but it was no use. He guessed that she was still out of range, as Reznar was quite some distance to the south, well beyond the shallow sea and the southern tips of K'vith. They would have to keep trying, and just hope that the failure to make contact was due to distance and not a sign that one, or both of the units had failed, as they had recently started to become a little temperamental.

The three friends stood on the bridge, looking out at the vast expanse of ocean as the *Hammer* pushed on through the deep blue waters, heading south as fast as its steam boilers could push it.

*   *   *

The old man wandered slowly along the track, deep within the thick, ancient forests that carpeted the land here. The narrow trail he had been following was thickly covered with fallen pine needles, allowing him to pass quietly through the trees. Huge trunks sprouted from the soft soil, reaching up towards the violet-coloured skies above. They waved their red and orange foliage in the gentle wind blowing through the dense canopy and cast a faint dappled light all around him. He noted the sound of small, ground dwelling animals that skittered nervously up the trees as he grew too close for comfort. He also spotted several large arboreal creatures swinging through the thick branches, keeping a close eye on the stranger as he passed through their territory.

He was a short man, dressed in a light brown tunic and had a shiny bald pate and a long white beard, which he absent-mindedly tugged at as he ambled through the ancient forest. He carried a long wooden staff, adorned with a glowing green gemstone, which he leaned heavily upon, as if relying on it to help keep his old legs moving.

Suddenly, the trees off to his left rustled noisily and several small animals darted across the path in front of him. Moments later, the cause of the disturbance also appeared, causing him to stop and view the newcomer with a gentle smile.

'Ah, there you are,' said the old man. 'I was wondering when you'd show yourself!'

The newcomer, a majestic white unicorn with a beautiful shiny coat and adorned with a powerful horn protruding from its mighty forehead, trotted casually up to the old man, falling in beside him as he resumed his casual stroll through the forest. The magical creature, which appeared to be glowing with an aura of smouldering power, whinnied softly in reply to the old man's gentle rebuke, which caused him to laugh out loud and shake his bald head.

'Always sticking your nose in where it doesn't belong, huh?' he said, clearly enjoying the banter.

The unicorn nudged him slightly, threatening to topple the frail looking old man onto the soft carpet of pine needles which coated the floor.

'All right, all right, you win,' he chuckled, scratching the unicorn's thick grey mane with great affection. 'So you've felt it too, I assume?' he added, looking across at his new companion, a serious expression appearing on his aged and weathered face.

The unicorn nodded its head, communicating in some ancient, long forgotten language that only they remembered.

'So it's finally begun,' continued the old man. 'Come then, my old friend, let's go. It's nearly time for us to leave this beautiful place, and we still have much work to do.'

Seven

Indrani slouched uncomfortably in the saddle as her tharen trotted along the main thoroughfare of the forest city of Jespira. The heat was oppressive here, and the vast clouds of biting insects followed wherever she went, causing her to swipe constantly at her face in an attempt to dissuade them from landing on her pale skin. She had tried using her magic to repel the swarms of creatures, but their assaults seemed to be unstoppable, so she had given up.

Leandra's tharen trotted beside her own, and the Visnach guide was looking eagerly around at the forest dwellings as they slowly passed by. They had been successful in persuading the Reznari merchant to lower his asking price for the ixoden silk, but had still ended up paying slightly more than they had initially planned. However, Indrani was impressed with the quality of the silk, and had been more than willing to purchase the merchant's entire stock, which meant that they had needed to find an extra wagon to accommodate their load.

The caravan, heavily laden with huge bolts of the dense material, rolled slowly behind them, expertly driven by the native Reznari teamsters that she had hired for the journey back to the port. She felt certain that King Elridan, who was funding the entire expedition to Reznar, would be pleased with the high quality silk that she had found. She also believed that the airships they planned to build would make a fine addition to the defence forces of the Kingdom of the Isles and Nesteris.

King Elridan, like so many others, had been initially wary of Marcus, as his sudden appearance on their world had coincided suspiciously with the brutal invasion of the demons from another realm. But Marcus had proved his worth, helping to repel the invaders and personally killing their leader. And so the King had accepted him into his innermost circle of trusted advisors. He had listened patiently, although not quite understanding every concept, as Marcus had explained the theory of flight, outlining the benefits of moving swiftly through the air rather than relying on travel by land and sea. He had been clearly fascinated by the images that Marcus had shown him of aircraft from his own world, and had eagerly agreed to allow them to create their own flying machine.

Indrani had tried to use the power of the aether to lift herself off the ground, but so far the results had been far from impressive. Only very short flights had been possible, and these required a great expenditure of magical energy. She felt that, with their present understanding of the technique, magically induced free flight was only possible over extremely short distances. In fact, the only real uses for this ability as far as she was concerned, would be to enhance a person's jumping prowess, or to prevent a gruesome death should they find themselves falling from a great height. To achieve the ability of free flight, they would need to turn to Marcus and his technology.

Panx had also expressed an interest in the subject, although he did believe that the power of the aether would allow a magus to soar through the skies, unaided by any technological device. He was reviewing the knowledge that his grandfather, a very powerful magus, had accumulated before he had died. According to Panx, free flight would require terrific power coupled with the ability to combine certain schools of magic, such as earth and air. The magus would need to make themselves lighter if they were to successfully leave the ground.

However, they had all agreed that technology offered them a much more achievable means of taking to the skies. So she had focused her efforts away from the aether, although she would still need her magic to propel the airship once they were off the ground. Marcus had assured her that the *Drake* would be capable of generating the helium gas that they would need to allow their airships to float through the skies, and that ixoden silk would be capable of containing it. She was excited to have acquired the dense material, and could not wait to return to Nesteris and put it to use.

Her quiet musing was interrupted when, from deep within an inner pocket of her tunic, her small comms device started vibrating wildly, making the particular sound that she had assigned to Marcus. He was trying to contact her. She retrieved the device and touched the sensitive screen, establishing the connection between them. The screen, which had been showing a still image of their son, flared into life, and young Navesh was replaced by a live image of his father.

'Hello, Marcus,' said Indrani, surprise showing on her face.

'Ah, Indrani, there you are. We've been trying to get through to you for ages, but the signal is really poor. I think my comms unit is playing up again.'

'Oh,' replied Indrani, screwing up her face slightly in a puzzled look. 'Who is we?'

'Panx and Tordin are here with me,' he replied, moving the comms device slightly so that she could see all three of them on the little screen.

'What's wrong?' she asked, concerned at their sudden appearance. 'Where are you?'

'We're on our way down to Reznar, almost there in fact. We've got some good, although rather disturbing news, and we're all needed back at Nesteris. We've come to pick you up.'

'What news?'

'Well, to put it succinctly, Fireen thinks that Navesh, her Navesh, the Aellindi Navesh, is still alive, and trapped in Valken's realm. We need to rescue him before he's captured.'

The screen flickered slightly as the signal was briefly disrupted. Indrani tapped it again, impatient to re-establish contact and after a few moments of fuzzy, unintelligible flashes, the screen came back to life and Marcus's face reappeared.

'How does Fireen know this?' asked Indrani, desperate to find out more, before they were cut off for good.

'Navesh's son, Idris, has been having terrible nightmares about his father, and Fireen herself has seen him in her own visions. Listen, I'm not sure what's wrong with our connection, but we're on our way to the port and we'll be there soon. I'll tell you everything once we meet up with you.'

'Okay. I'm on my way back to the port myself, so I'll wait for you there.'

'See you soon, my love,' replied Marcus, cutting the connection on the mobile devices.

The caravan trundled along through the streets of Jespira as fast as possible. Indrani was eager to get back now, and had to resist the temptation to go hurtling off on her own. *How could Navesh still be alive?* She thought. It sounded like wonderful news, although she found it a little hard to accept. *What if it's a trap?* Valken may be dead, but were they rushing headlong into a dangerous mission that would see them captured by the new ruler of that vile place. What if, in their attempt to rescue Navesh, they allowed the demons to return to their world? She shuddered at the thought as she trotted along beside the cargo-laden caravan, the hairs on the back of her neck itching more than the swarms of flies that dogged their every step.

Several hours later as the caravan rolled along the trail through the forest, having left Jespira far behind, Indrani heard a shrill whistle somewhere off in the dense treeline. No sooner had she begun to peer into the thick foliage than several tall Reznari stepped out onto the path in front of the approaching wagons.

'Halt!' said one of the lightly tanned men, who was clearly the leader of these newcomers. 'There's no need for anyone to get hurt. We just want your wagons.'

Indrani looked around, trying to determine if there was enough room to turn around and flee back towards Jespira, but she spotted a second group of tall men and women blocking the path behind. They had weapons drawn and clearly were not going to permit the escape of their quarry.

'Who are you?' she asked, as Leandra brought her own tharen to a halt beside her.

'That's not important,' replied the bandit leader, his voice making the distinctive clicking sound of the jungle dwelling Reznari. 'Just hand over the wagons and you can go free.'

Leandra looked at Indrani, her eyebrows rising ever so slightly. A silent message passed between them, and they both began to invoke the mystical power of the aether. The caravan teamsters had not been idle either, and the six Reznari men had stepped down from their wagons, weapons drawn, ready to defend themselves.

'Oh come now. You're greatly outnumbered,' said the bandit leader. 'There's no need for violence and bloodshed. But if you insist.' He smiled at them and drew a wicked looking long dagger from his belt, its blade flashing menacingly in the dappled forest light.

'Stay back,' shouted Indrani. 'I'm warning you!' She continued to invoke the power of the aether, her hands swirling rhythmically through the air, generating colourful eddies of light as they moved.

Leandra, while not as powerful as Indrani, was trained in the basic arts of pyromancy, and let loose a small ball of flames towards the nearest of the bandits. It caught the man in the chest, hurling him backwards and leaving a blackened, smouldering crater in his lightly armoured body. He lay there, unmoving, while his comrades ducked behind cover, approaching the caravan defenders with renewed caution.

The bandit leader called out something to his fellows, using a coded language that neither Indrani nor Leandra could understand. Realising that they had attacked two powerful magi, the bandits rushed forwards, letting out a shrill battle cry as they tried to overwhelm their quarry before they could unleash any further magical attacks. Indrani let fly at the lead bandit, sending a savage gust of wind towards him, knocking him backwards, where he smashed into a fallen tree trunk on the side of the path. He did not get up, although Indrani could see that he still lived, as he was moaning in pain and rubbing his head which had a deep gash running down the left side.

In the end however, the fight was over quickly. More bandits had appeared from both sides of the forest and rapidly overpowered Indrani and her little group. Leandra had managed to knock down another bandit, and Indrani had utilised her wind magic to push the attackers backwards. But even with her caravan team entering the fight, there were just too few of them and they were soon captured. Leandra had taken an arrow in the shoulder, which had interrupted her spell casting, causing her to fall to her knees. She clutched at the protruding shaft, blood already seeping through her tunic.

They were quickly rounded up at sword point. Leandra's wound was swiftly attended to, although the bandits were not particularly gentle in their ministrations. They tugged savagely at the wooden arrow until it could be withdrawn from the wound, causing her to scream out in agony. Her shoulder was bound, although it still bled profusely, and the two magi were shackled and gagged to prevent them from invoking their powers. The bandit leader, who was battered and bruised, had ordered the caravan teamsters to be tied up and bundled into the back of the wagons. The two Visnach women were forced to march alongside the wagons, accompanied by the watchful bandits.

They were led off the forest trail and into the dense tangle of trees and soon found themselves a smaller path, where the going was much easier. Indrani tried to remove her gag and wrist bindings, but found them too tightly tied. She switched her focus to her surroundings, trying to memorise the direction in which they were being taken. But the forest soon defeated her and she lost her bearings completely. *Perhaps Leandra will have more luck*, she thought, *she is a tracker after all.*

After a couple of hours travelling along the smaller, lesser known paths, they re-entered the forest and once again pushed through the trees towards some as yet unknown destination. Soon they found themselves standing in the centre of a small settlement, where other Reznari were going about their business. There were also children running around, playing games of tag, or throwing soft, ball-shaped objects to one another. The leader of the bandits called out in the strange coded language and an aged man emerged from one of the huts. He motioned for the bandit leader to take his captives to a dwelling on the edge of the village, and then went back inside the hut from which he had first appeared.

Indrani's group were roughly bundled inside the building, which was made from thick tree trunks and covered with a crude grass thatch, where they were forced to sit down on the dusty floor. A thin woman entered the hut, carrying food and water, which she passed around to the captives who had been unbound and ungagged in order to refresh themselves. The bandits remained on guard, with weapons drawn, while Indrani and her comrades consumed the food and water, after which they were swiftly secured once more.

Another Reznari individual, some sort of shaman, entered the hut and proceeded to care for the wounded Leandra. He gave her a dark liquid to drink, presumably to ease the pain. Although the Visnach were pale of skin, Indrani could see that her friend's colour had returned slightly and she looked to be more comfortable. The shaman also cleaned and dressed her wound, applying an oily salve that stopped the bleeding.

'What do you want?' Indrani managed to ask before they slipped the gag back between her teeth.

'We'll get a good ransom for you and your silk, yes?' replied the bandit leader. 'Feed our people for a long time, yes?'

All this for some food? she thought, dismayed at the lengths that people were forced to go to in order to feed themselves and their families. She felt suddenly tired and struggled to keep her eyes open. There must have been something in the water, a sedative, but it was too late now. Her comrades were also struggling to remain alert, trying desperately to fight off the effects of the drug. But it was no use. She listened to her captors as they discussed the ransom and how much the authorities might pay for the return of the foreigners. But all too soon, sleep took her.

When she awoke it was dark outside. Leandra still slept, although Indrani could see that her friend's breathing was strong, and that the bleeding on her shoulder had ceased. Several of her caravan team were already awake and they looked towards her with fear in their eyes, as if asking her what to do. She shook her head slowly as if to say, "*do nothing for now*". What could they actually do anyway? They were bound, she was gagged, and they were in the middle of a Reznar village deep in the forest. They had no other option but to let the situation play out for now, although she kept trying to loosen the bindings which held her hands together. If she could just remove her gag then perhaps she could unleash some aetheric hell upon her captors.

Indrani looked around, watching the two guards as they played a card game. One of them had a large pile of coins on the table beside him and he was grinning widely as the other bandit threw down his remaining cards, tossing another couple of small metallic discs at him.

She was suddenly aware of soft music coming from somewhere out in the village, and she looked around, trying to get a glimpse of who might be playing. Strangely, the two bandits did not look up from their game, clearly too engrossed in the moment to notice the angelic sound that was filtering in through the log framed hut. A strange light had also begun to shine outside and Indrani watched in amazement as a gently glowing figure, an old man in a brown cloak, walked straight into the hut.

The two guards suddenly noticed the old man and stood up quickly, reaching for their weapons. However, the frail looking man simply raised his left hand and, with a casual gesture, caused the guards to slump heavily back into their wooden chairs. The man walked over and nudged them gently, without any sign of fear for his own well-being. When they failed to respond he nodded to himself and turned to Indrani.

'Ah, there you are,' he said, a mischievous glint in his eye. 'Are you having fun?'

He looked familiar to her, but she could not remember where she had seen him before. He came over and knelt down beside her, gesturing with his right hand. Suddenly her bonds and gag had completely disappeared, as if they had never been there at all.

'Who are you?' she asked, looking around, noticing for the first time that Leandra and the other members of her caravan were sleeping peacefully. Apparently they had also been rendered unconscious by the old man's spell.

'Never mind that, for now,' he muttered, his voice soft and musical. 'You've lots to do, Indrani, and there's no time to delay. It's unlikely that the Reznar government would have paid for your release anyway, and by the time Marcus discovered where you were, it would have been too late.'

'Too late for what?' she asked, looking intently at the glowing figure. 'And how do you know Marcus?'

'So many questions,' he replied gently. 'Time for that later. Come on, up you get,' he added, helping her to her feet while she gently massaged the life back into her cramped limbs. 'It's time for you to go now. You must head directly to the port where Marcus will be waiting. No doubt he's very worried about you.'

'But how do we get there?' she asked. 'Our tharen and wagons have been taken from us, and we have no idea where we are, let alone how to get back to the port.'

'Trust in your friends,' he said, pointing towards Leandra, who was beginning to stir from the magically induced slumber. 'It's perfectly safe for you to leave now. There are two tharen waiting outside. You must go straight away, do not delay. Time depends on it!'

'My cargo, and the Reznari teamsters?' she asked, still struggling to comprehend what was happening.

'Don't worry about them, my dear Indrani,' he said. 'I'll ensure that they're safe and that your silk finds its way back to you on Nesteris.'

'What's going on,' whispered Leandra, who was sitting up and rubbing at her shoulder gingerly. Her bonds and gag had also disappeared. 'Why does everyone, except for us, appear to be unconscious? And how did you manage to remove our bonds?'

'I didn't,' replied Indrani. 'It was the old man.'

'What old man?' replied Leandra, looking around. 'I didn't see an old man.'

'Never mind,' replied Indrani, deciding that, for some bizarre reason, she would simply put her trust in the frail looking old man. 'We must get out of here now, before the enchantment wears off. There are tharen waiting just outside. Let's go.'

Indrani furtively peered around the doorway and looked out into the village. There was no sign of the old man, he had simply vanished. In fact, there were no signs of the villagers either, not even the groups of playful children who were having so much fun earlier that day.

'Let's go,' she whispered, scurrying across the dusty earth towards the edge of the forest.

Leandra followed closely behind, and soon the two Visnach women were climbing onto the backs of the tharen that awaited them, as if they had been placed there especially for this very occasion.

'This is all a bit strange,' said Leandra, as the two women headed into the forest. 'How did we get free? And who is this old man that you speak of?'

'I'll tell you about it later,' replied Indrani, 'but for now, can you get us back to the port?'

'Yes, I think so,' replied the Visnach guide. 'I managed to keep track of our direction when we were brought here, so I'm pretty sure I know the way back. Let's just hope we don't bump into more of those bandits!'

'Yes,' replied Indrani. *I just hope that that old man was for real*, she thought, as they moved away from the Reznari village.

*　　*　　*

Marcus paced nervously up and down the deck of the *Hammer*, his face full of worry and despair. Indrani should have been here days ago. He had tried over and over to re-establish contact with her on the comms device, but for some reason it was no longer working. Like much of the equipment that he had brought with him from his own world, a little over two years ago, the comms devices seemed to be failing with increasing regularity. He was extremely worried about Indrani, and could not help but relive the moment when he had found out that his first wife, Lydia, had been killed. He feared that he was going to lose Indrani too, and it was tearing him apart. He shook his head, trying desperately to expel the distressing thoughts from his mind. Indrani was a powerful magus, she could handle herself. *She'll be here soon!* He thought, not taking his eyes off the road leading into the port.

Panx came over and stood beside him, peering out into the harbour and resting his hand gently on his friend's shoulder.

'Tordin has acquired the tharen. Shall we head out and see if we can find Indrani and her companions?'

'Yes,' replied Marcus, his voice barely a whisper, 'lead the way, Panx.'

The two men hopped down onto the wooden pier and headed over to where Tordin was walking back towards the ship, with three tharen trailing along behind him. Marcus knew that time was running out for them, that it was extremely limited. If they did not find Indrani and her party soon, they would have no choice but to leave Reznar and head back to Nesteris. Navesh and the other captives in the dark realm were depending on them. But how could he just abandon Indrani? What if she was injured and needed his help? He felt a cold chill run down his spine at the thought of leaving without her, his beautiful wife and mother of his child. He knew then that he would never leave here without her, even if it meant parting from Tordin and Panx. He could never forgive himself.

'I'd say we can spare a day or so,' said Tordin, his face filled with worry, 'but if we haven't found them by then, we really ought to get back to Nesteris.'

Marcus did not reply to his friend's pragmatic comment, not trusting his voice at this particular moment. Tordin was a military man after all and he was used to making the hard decisions, so Marcus could not feel angry towards him. But there was no way that he was going to leave without Indrani.

'I'm sure she's alright,' added Panx, trying hard to lift his friend's spirit.

The three men had just hopped onto their tharen and were trotting slowly towards the edge of the forest when two women, also riding tharen, appeared directly ahead of them. They had burst through the treeline at a swift canter, their long red hair flowing freely as they approached, clearly in a hurry.

73

'Is that Indrani?' asked Tordin, pointing towards the approaching women.

'Yes,' replied Marcus.

'And that's Leandra with her,' added Panx, smiling brightly as the two women trotted towards them.

Marcus jumped down from his tharen, nearly twisting his ankle as he ran over to greet his wife. He hugged her fiercely as she hopped down from her own mount and they held each other as if they had been parted for years, causing the others to look away, somewhat embarrassed at the display of affection.

'What happened to you?' asked Marcus, finally disentangling himself from his lover's embrace.

'We were attacked on our way back to the port.'

'How did you get away?' asked Panx.

'I'll tell you everything once we're underway. Shall we go?'

Marcus nodded and, putting his arm around her, guided Indrani back towards the *Hammer*, closely followed by the others.

Soon, the five companions were standing on the bridge of the ship, which was slowly moving away from the port on a heading back to Nesteris.

'So, do you want to go first?' asked Marcus.

'You go first,' she replied. 'I want to know about poor Navesh. How has he managed to survive for all this time?'

As Tordin's ship picked up speed and headed back to the home of the Aellindi, the companions discussed their missing friend, how he might have managed to survive, and how they might rescue him. Indrani and Leandra explained their unexpected capture by the bandits, and the strange encounter with the old man. Finally, their conversation turned to the strange blue-skinned people and their queen, who Fireen suspected to be in possession of the lost stone of power. Who were these people, and where were they located? Hopefully, when they next saw Fireen, she would have some answers for them.

The sun was setting now and a strong wind blew across the sea, causing a large swell to rock the *Hammer* gently from side to side. The companions settled in for what promised to be a rough night, discussing the events of the last few days until, one by one, they drifted off to sleep.

Eight

Fireen sat in the chamber at the top of an ancient tower, located deep in the heart of the forest at the centre of the island of Nesteris, where the stones of power were now carefully guarded. She sat cross legged, with the two remaining stones laid out on the floor before her, their green surface glowing gently in the darkened chamber. Her eyes were closed and she breathed slowly, rhythmically, feeling the power of the aether flow through her, pulsing with the beating of her heart. Her arms rested comfortably in her lap, and her head swayed gently from side to side.

She had come here nearly every day since the defeat of Valken and the loss of the stone of power, channelling the force of the ancient magic into her meditative routines, attempting to determine its location. Her visions had given her tantalising glimpses of the artefact, and even shown her who was currently in possession of it, but as yet her attempts to define its exact location had been in vain.

The power of the aether pulsed erratically and the two remaining stones flared to life in a spectacular display of colour and sound. The light rose up from within the stones and out into the room, swirling around the motionless form of Fireen. For a moment the light was akin to a small tornado of magical energy, circling about the Aellindi leader's head. But before it could cause any physical damage it drifted down to enshroud her, giving her body a deep glowing outline before being absorbed completely by the entranced magus.

She took a sharp, sudden intake of breath and her eyes opened wide. Her pupils were abnormally dilated, reflecting the light from within the room on their black surface. She sat rigidly now, her body completely under the influence of the aether as its power coursed through her veins and visions swept through her mind. They were wild and random at first, but as the power calmed, the visions became clearer and less distorted. Finally she relaxed, her tense body easing slightly as she was shown what the aether needed her to see.

She saw the blue-skinned people again, labouring hard in their cold, stony underground chamber. Fireen studied these people closely. *Who were they?* They appeared similar in physical form to the Visnach, but had different skin colour and were more powerfully built. *Could they be related?*

Her vision shifted once more, the image blurring slightly and the colours blending together. Suddenly the image sharpened its focus and she found herself watching some sort of gruesome execution. There were humans amongst those being slaughtered, and Visnach too. *What was she watching? Where was this occurring?* Surely it could not be happening here on this world. Perhaps these blue-skinned people did originate from the dark world of Valken after all, she simply could not tell.

The blue-skinned queen was standing there, with her stone crown sitting atop her head. Beside her stood a Ligarian female, her body covered with black fur, like those from the eastern continent of Thalmira, although there was something strange about her. She had a peculiar radiance emanating from her body, as if it emitted a magical aura. The Ligarian looked shocked by the execution, as if she were forced to view it against her will. The queen was whispering something to her, but Fireen could not make out the words.

The blue-skinned warriors, who had shepherded the prisoners into the chamber, levelled their spears at them and a blue light shot forth from their pointed tips. Deadly fire engulfed the hapless victims, reducing them to piles of bleached bones in a matter of moments.

Fireen gasped, somehow just managing to hold on to the strand of aetheric energy which connected her to the vision. Slowly she calmed herself, and the vision, which had been momentarily blurred, resolved itself once more. When she finally regained control she could see that the bones of the executed prisoners had somehow been reanimated and now, standing before the Queen and her Ligarian companion, stood a row of skeletal figures.

The Queen turned around and smiled, somehow looking directly at Fireen. The Aellindi magus was startled once more, but this time she was unable to hold onto the vision. Her mind was sent reeling from the connection, flying through the aether, her consciousness returning to the tower on Nesteris with a sudden jerk. She was left feeling nauseous and weak, as she often did after such a journey, riding on the streams of magical energy that infused her world.

She sat for a moment, regaining her composure, settling her rapidly beating heart and calming her breathing. Her eyes remained closed, not trying to reconnect with the aether, but simply replaying the vision in her own mind. She tried to make sense of what she had been shown; looking for small details that she may have missed during the initial journey. A knock at the door brought her out of her meditative trance, her vision refocusing once more on the real world.

'Enter,' she said.

Endina opened the door and walked into the room, her aged body hunched over as she shuffled along. She wore a plain white tunic, and her wrinkled yellow-green skin shimmered slightly in the dappled light coming through the window. She had several bony plates protruding from the top of her head, and these were standing up straight, a sign that something troubled her deeply. She seated herself beside Fireen, although she opted for the comfort of a chair rather than the hard floor on which the council leader still sat.

'What is wrong, my friend,' asked Fireen, seeking to determine the source of Endina's discomfort.

'A messenger has arrived from the scrying chamber in Nesteris city,' hissed Endina softly.

'From King Elridan?'

Since the defeat of Valken, the allied forces from Nesteris, K'vith and the Kingdom of the Isles had agreed that they would maintain close contact with one another, allowing them to react swiftly to any possible future threat. To that end, a system of scrying chambers had been set up, manned by the magi of each nation. Most were located on the small islands in the seas that separated their nations and allowed them to swiftly pass messages between themselves, often negating the need to travel in person.

'No,' replied Endina. 'It's not from the Kingdom, but from our outpost on Thalmira.'

Fireen was momentarily shocked, thoughts flooding rapidly through her mind. *The eastern continent? But all had been quiet there for a very long time. What could have happened?* Her recent vision came to mind, in particular the Ligarian she had seen in the court of the blue queen. She had looked very much like one of those people from the east. Surely this was not a coincidence. *Perhaps the lost stone of power has been here on our world all along, hidden somewhere in Thalmira?* she wondered. Deep down she knew this could not be the case, for if it were, she would have still been able to detect its power. But still, the possibility gave her new hope. *Perhaps this queen has found a way to use the stone herself, whilst shielding its power from the other inhabitants of this world?* The thought was tantalising, although she felt as if she were grasping at the impossible.

'Something is happening over there. Word has reached Nesteris that an army of skeletal warriors, reanimated by some foul magic, has appeared suddenly from out of the deep desert. They're being led by warriors wielding powerful weapons and a strange, Ligarian female.'

Fireen's eyes opened wide at the revelation. 'I have just seen this woman and her skeletal army, in my vision,' she said, her voice an excited sibilant hiss, causing her friend to adopt a surprised expression of her own.

'Well,' continued Endina, 'from what the messenger reported, nothing seems to be able to stop these undead abominations. Even if they're cut down, they simply rise back up again and continue fighting. Even the ones which have been brutally hacked apart still keep coming, long after they should have been put down for good. What's more, this army is growing in size, fuelled by the bodies of those left behind after each conquest.'

'When did this start?'

'We're not entirely certain, but they appeared as if from thin air from the desert, and proceeded to sack the two nearest cities, swelling their ranks enormously. They're now reported to be on their way towards the coastal provinces. Do you think they might be planning to come here?'

'It is possible,' hissed Fireen. 'In my vision I saw this individual in the company of the blue-skinned queen, the same queen who appears to be in possession of the lost stone of power. Perhaps she senses the power of the other stones and covets it for herself.'

'What should we do?' asked Endina, a look of worry settling on her aged face.

'Send word to King Elridan, and also to Duchess Sybille in K'vith. We should warn them of the potential threat, and give them chance to mobilise their forces.'

'I'll send word immediately,' replied Endina, rising from her seat and moving stiffly towards the door.

'Let us also dispatch a scouting party to Thalmira,' added Fireen thoughtfully. 'We have a few Aellindi over there at the outpost, so we should send Saven and Givas to coordinate them. We need to see this army of the dead for ourselves.'

'Of course. I'll make the arrangements straight away. We've got several fast ships currently in the harbour. They can use one of those to head straight to Thalmira.'

'Good. It will take them a little while to cross the Grey Expanse, but please let me know as soon as they have arrived at the scrying outpost. We will need to assess the threat as swiftly as possible.'

Endina nodded respectfully and exited the room, leaving Fireen to her thoughts once more. *Necromancy? Could it be true? After all these years? I must consult the ancient scriptures.*

*   *   *

General Arthen Bochung, commanding officer of the northern army of the Kingdom of the Isles, sat in his chamber reading through yet another report on the skirmishes with the hill tribes. They were a breakaway faction that had decided, after the defeat of Valken, that they would be better off fending for themselves in the hills to the north of Rothford, rather than returning to their former lives as citizens of the Kingdom. And they were becoming a real thorn in his side. He had wanted to avoid bloodshed when dealing with these people. After all, they were still subjects of King Elridan and should be treated with respect. But they were a stubborn lot.

He had sent emissary after emissary up into those hills, and they had all been sent straight back. None had been harmed, which was fortunate for the people of the hill tribes, but his attempts to persuade them to rejoin the Kingdom had not gone terribly well.

Lately, there had been a few small scale skirmishes between army patrols and the hill tribes, who were clearly getting bolder in their desire for places to live. They had been steadily encroaching upon the small northern town of Nadren, where Valken's forces had first appeared, and which had been totally rebuilt in the two years since his defeat. Arthen was not certain if the hill tribes were simply looking for food, or whether they were making a move to actually conquer the town. He truly hoped it was the former, as it would indicate that they were struggling to survive on their own and might be close to accepting terms. If, however, it was conquest they desired, then he would have no choice but to bring the full force of his army to bear upon those hills.

He gently massaged his shoulders and the back of his neck. His dark unruly hair was tangled and his brown eyes were watery and a little bloodshot. He was dead tired and about to head off to bed when a knock at the door brought him back to full wakefulness.

'What is it?' he shouted, a little more grumpily than he had intended.

A young officer opened the door and peered around the wooden frame, unsure whether to enter the room or deliver his message from the safety of the corridor.

'Sorry, lieutenant. Please excuse my bad manners, I'm rather tired that's all. What can I do for you?'

'I've got a message for you, sir,' said the young man, coming to stand in front of his commanding officer, his back rigid in typical parade ground fashion.

'What's the message?' asked Arthen, raising his eyebrows in expectation of another request for an update on the hill tribe situation.

'You've been asked to return to Brind, sir, to meet with the King. It's a matter of some urgency, and you're to leave at first light tomorrow.'

Arthen was shocked and a little shaken, although he tried his hardest to keep this from showing on his face. This sort of request was unusual, and must indicate some crisis or disaster.

'Was there anything else, lieutenant?'

'Yes, sir,' replied the junior officer. 'You're ordered to bring the musketeers with you.'

'I see. Well thank you young man, you may go now.'

The young officer nodded to Arthen, snapping out a quick salute and then departed the General's quarters, closing the door softly behind him.

What's going on? thought Arthen, his bed completely forgotten. He was going to have a busy night, and so were many of those in his army, not least his new musketeers.

Since he had learned that Marcus had used a flare gun to kill Valken, Arthen had, like several of Marcus's close friends, taken to studying the professor's technology. Where Tordin was interested in all things to do with his Navy, Arthen was focused on improving the effectiveness of his soldiers.

In addition to command of the northern army, King Elridan had tasked him with the creation and training of special forces, who were to be equipped with new and powerful weapons. Arthen had actively pursued the explosive technology known to Marcus as gunpowder, after seeing several images and video clips of powerful weapons, or guns, as the professor had called them. The weapons fired deadly projectiles at great speed and accuracy, powered by the chemical reaction from the black-coloured powder following exposure to a source of ignition.

Arthen now had several regiments equipped with rudimentary gunpowder weapons that Marcus had called muskets, which were rapidly replacing his archers. What made these troops so remarkable, even more so than those on Marcus's own world, was the fact that, like bows and arrows, muskets could be magically enhanced. The magi could imbue the weapons and ammunition with a vast array of enchantments to improve such things as accuracy and range, making them the single most devastating weapon he currently had in his arsenal. It was true that these weapons were not particularly accurate in their unenchanted form, but they still represented a massive leap forward in the capabilities of his troops.

He was currently looking into the possibility of introducing rifled weapons, along with an enhanced optical eyepiece, which would increase the accuracy of his troops even when magi were absent. But this new and improved weapon was still in the testing phase. He had a limited numbers of rifles available and a small supply of ammunition for each, but he would take these with him to the capital. Perhaps it would give his new sharpshooter regiment a chance to test their metal.

Arthen left his quarters and went in search of his immediate subordinate, Commander Mawnan, who was to be left in charge of the army at Rothford. The Commander was a capable man who had fought in the demon war. He was greatly respected by the men, and Arthen knew that it would do him good to be given a taste of command.

As the General descended the stairs, leading down from his quarters at the top of the keep's northern tower, his mind was racing. While he made mental notes about this or that, his mind wandered to those who he would hopefully be able to visit while he was in Brind. He missed Kat desperately, and longed to see her again. He had grown close to the King's eldest daughter, having spent a fair bit of time in the palace after the fall of the demon lord, and the two of them had gotten to know each quite well. Kat had taken on lots of new responsibility after the war, since the demons had killed her elder brother, Oberon, and she had needed to grow up rather quickly in order to cope with the pressure.

The King had never fully recovered from the wounds inflicted on him during the war, and the toxic poison had left him weakened. Although his mind was still as sharp as ever, he now spent much of his time within the confines of the palace, only showing himself at special occasions. Much of the other routine work had fallen to his wife and their two remaining children. Kat, as the eldest daughter, had received the hardest tasks of all. He hoped that she would be pleased to see him too, assuming that he was permitted to stay in Brind for a while.

Early the next morning, before the sun had even begun to brighten the sky, Arthen marched out of Rothford accompanied by several regiments of troops, including his musketeers and new sharpshooter riflemen. Beside him marched Major Tassik, who was in command of the sharpshooters, and who was Arthen's best rifleman. The Major had excelled in the use of the musket and had been chosen to head up the new regiment, rising to the challenge and the new rank that went with it with honour and steadfast commitment.

'Did we forget anything?' asked Arthen.

'Oh yeah,' replied Tassik dryly, shrugging his shoulders with a casual nonchalance, 'I'm sure we have.'

The two men laughed as the small force of soldiers headed out of the city towards the wagons that waited to carry them south, back to Brind.

Nine

The *Hammer* steamed gracefully into the port below the ancient city of Nesteris. It turned sharply into the calm waters of the harbour, passing close to the towering beacon that guarded its entrance. Tordin paced across the cramped bridge, calling out orders to his sailors and slowing their final approach towards the busy piers.

Even though the ship had performed well during the voyage back from the forested continent of Reznar, the Admiral was already making plans to improve the designs and correct the minor flaws that had developed during the trip. He had exhaustively outlined his ideas to build many more of these vessels, improving on their capabilities with each successive design.

Panx had been especially pleased with the performance of the ship's magi, whom he had personally chosen for the task. They had honed their skills with the magically charged engines, and the heat crystals had worked perfectly. The *Hammer* had glided effortlessly through the sea for many hours each day, with only short interruptions while the crystals were changed or the water in the boiler was refilled. In fact, when compared to the old fashioned mode of sea travel that relied heavily upon the unreliable power of the wind, the actual time that the *Hammer* was able to travel under its own power was a tremendous improvement. So much so in fact, that Tordin had declared that sailing ships were now a thing of the past and that the age of steam power had arrived. Even those sailing ships that employed their own magi, channelling the power of the aether to invoke the wind, were simply no match for the mechanical power of a steam boiler coupled to a propeller.

I don't know how we ever managed before you arrived, Marcus! Tordin was fond of saying, which always managed to elicit a chuckle from the professor and a frustrated tutting noise from the others.

The journey back to Nesteris had been uneventful. The companions had used the time to discuss the revelation that Navesh was still alive, and that Fireen had made progress towards tracking down the missing stone of power. Marcus had explained to the two Visnach magi how Navesh's son, Idris, had been suffering from a recurring nightmare in which his own father stalked him through the deserted streets of Nesteris. Panx had told them that Fireen had also seen their old friend in her visions, and that he was lost somewhere in the dark realm, fighting for his life, hunted by the foul creatures that dwell there. He also told them that Fireen had decided to mount a rescue, although they were unsure as to exactly how they were going to achieve it. Indrani had asked about the lost stone of power, but all they could tell her was that Fireen had seen it in one of her visions, in the possession of a blue-skinned woman. She appeared to be using it for her own purposes, although Fireen did not know where the woman was located. They hoped that the Aellindi leader would have more information for them when they finally returned to Nesteris.

After the news of Navesh's apparent survival and the rediscovery of the lost stone had finally sunk in, Indrani and Leandra had recounted their own adventure, detailing their capture by Reznari bandits. Panx and Marcus had been especially interested to hear about the strange rescue by the frail old man. He had apparently walked straight into the bandit village and put everyone except for Indrani into some sort of magically induced slumber. Even Leandra had been affected, and she could not recall any detail from that particular encounter. Indrani still had no idea who the old man was, but she remained convinced that there something very special about him. She said that he had exuded a feeling of calm as he had spoken with her, and that she felt she could trust him completely, like she had known him for many years. He had seemed very old, and she had sensed much wisdom in his gentle voice.

As the *Hammer* made its final approach into the inner part of the harbour, slowing to a crawl as it slipped through the turquoise water, Tordin pointed out that there were far more warships than usual tied up to the piers. He had also spotted several more ships out to sea, slowly heading along the coast.

'What's happening here?' he said aloud. 'There seems to be a large scale military build-up going on.'

The companions headed down from the bridge as the ship was being tied to the mooring stanchions, coming to stand at the deck rails, looking out over the busy harbour. The sun was shining brightly and Marcus had to squint to avoid being blinded by the light as it glinted off the white stone buildings. He noted that it was not just the Aellindi navy that appeared to have been put on alert, but that their army also appeared to have been mustered for action. There were numerous squads of heavily armed warriors patrolling the streets of the busy port, ever alert for potential threats.

'Something's happened here, since we departed,' said Panx, voicing the thought that was on all of their minds.

'Let's go and find out what it is, shall we?' replied Marcus, as he thudded down the gangplank.

As they hopped down off the ship onto the wooden pier, a squad of Aellindi warriors appeared in front of them, as if from nowhere, and offered to escort them up to the city. Their presence had been requested at a meeting with the council, and their Aellindi friends were eager to begin. They followed the warriors towards a waiting transport and clambered inside. No sooner had they seated themselves than the wagon lurched forwards, picking up speed as it headed up the steep hill towards the city on the cliffs above.

Marcus and the others were ushered into the council chamber where Fireen waited for them, along with the remaining Aellindi council. A sudden feeling of déjà vu washed over him as he remembered his first visit to this place. As it had on that occasion, when they had been attacked by the demonic satyr, the room was guarded by Rikoth's elite warriors, who seemed to blend into the stone walls as if they were not there at all. There were more of them than there had been on that dreadful occasion, for which Marcus was extremely grateful. Clearly the council had decided not to take any chances this time.

As the five companions moved into the room, Fireen stood up from her seat and came over to greet them warmly, taking each of their hands in turn. She was clearly pleased to see them and relieved that they had returned safely from Reznar. The Aellindi leader returned to her seat and indicated that the newcomers should also make themselves comfortable.

As they pulled their padded chairs in under the huge table, Fireen began to explain what had occurred in their absence, and why the Aellindi defence forces had been mustered. She told them of her most recent visions, detailing the disgusting necromancy that she had witnessed in the court of the blue-skinned queen. She also told of the sudden appearance of the undead army from the deep desert on the western edge of the continent of Thalmira. She informed them of the destruction that this unnatural army seemed to leave in its wake, and that several towns and cities on the fringes of the desert had already been sacked. Fireen also told them how those who had been slaughtered by the skeletal army had themselves been reanimated to join the forces of the invaders, swelling their numbers greatly.

The occupants of the council chamber listened with rising horror as she explained that the individual who was apparently leading the undead crusade, a black-furred Ligarian female, was somehow connected to the blue-skinned queen. She reasoned that there was some connection to the appearance of this abominable army of marching dead and the lost stone of power.

'To the best of my ability,' she hissed, 'I have determined that this queen and the lost stone are not located anywhere on our world fragment.'

'But yet the Ligarian and her army of marching bones is here, on our world?' replied Rikoth, smashing his clawed fist down on the table, clearly frustrated with this latest revelation.

'Yes, my old friend,' replied Fireen calmly, 'that is correct.'

'So what's the link between them?' asked Panx, intrigued to know how the two individuals could be connected whilst existing on different world fragments.

'I am not yet certain,' replied Fireen, 'but I think we should assume that it is the blue-skinned queen who is in command of the undead army, and that the Ligarian is merely her lieutenant. Remember what I told you about my most recent vision, that it was the queen who reanimated the murdered prisoners. She may have been instructing her latest disciple, ready for an invasion of our world, but I am convinced that it is the queen who wields the true power here. For some unknown reason, she has chosen not to reveal herself yet, but to send another in her stead. I do not know for certain what it is that this queen desires, but my fear is that she has detected the remaining stones of power and covets them for herself.'

'So what should our next move be?' asked Rikoth, his anger once again under control.

'I have dispatched Saven and Givas to Thalmira,' replied Fireen, 'and from there they are in a good position to spy upon the approaching army. They have orders to report back to us when they have any further news. The army and navy are on full alert, as you well know, and we have sent messages to both King Elridan in Brind and Duchess Sybille on K'vith, informing them of the situation and recommending that they also put their armed forces on high alert.'

'What about the two remaining stones?' asked Marcus. 'Surely they must be protected?'

'They have already been moved to a new location and are now heavily guarded,' replied Fireen.

'Indeed,' added Mizarius, the newest and youngest member of the council. 'I've assigned an entire brigade to keep them safe.'

The young Aellindi councillor reminded Marcus of Navesh, not just in his physical appearance, with his long neck, bony head and golden skin colouration, but also in his steadfast devotion to his people. On the few occasions that he had seen the young man, he had always been involved with some duty or another and never seemed to relax, even for a brief moment.

'Well this is all rather badly timed!' replied Marcus, a look of concern settling on his face.

'Badly timed? How so?' asked Fireen.

'Just as we're about to descend back into Valken's cruel world, this new situation arises and complicates things even more for us. Clearly we cannot ignore the events that are unfolding out in the desert, but neither can we forget about Navesh, trapped in that dark place. Like I said, badly timed.'

Since he had arrived on this world, Marcus had come to regard Nesteris as his new home. Even though he was from a different world altogether, he had been accepted here with friendship and respect. He had become very fond, and extremely protective of this beautiful island and its normally peaceful inhabitants. He hated the thought of anyone trying to cause them harm.

'At least I'm not to blame this time!' he added, attempting to lighten the mood.

'Are you certain?' hissed Fireen, with a mischievous glint in her eye. 'Do not fear, my friends,' she continued, returning to the discussion, 'we can, and will, attend to both crises. We shall ignore nothing. No detail will be overlooked, no matter how insignificant it may appear. However, in order for us to achieve this we must divide our forces. As I said before, Saven and Givas are on their way to the eastern continent. In fact they should be there very soon, if not already. They will coordinate via the scrying network with Endina and Mizarius, who will remain here on Nesteris with the bulk of our defence force. I will travel to the dark realm, accompanied by Rikoth, Panx and a select few of our most elite warriors.'

'Is that wise?' said Mizarius, interrupting Fireen as she outlined the plan. 'Taking so few warriors with you? Surely you'd be better protected with a larger force?'

'I thank you for your concern,' replied Fireen, ignoring the young councillor's lack of decorum, 'but I believe that stealth will be our greatest ally, and therefore the fewer of us who make the crossing the better. Additionally, and I feel certain that Navesh would agree with me, I do not want to deprive our homeland of any more warriors than necessary, especially with a possible invasion looming before us.'

The others in the room nodded their heads, accepting Fireen's logical argument regarding the composition of the team she would lead through the portal.

'Marcus, I will need you and Indrani to accompany me as far as the *Beacon of Olon*,' continued Fireen. 'This is where we will attempt to open the portal and make our crossing. I am certain that I will require both of you in order to operate the wonders of the Ancestors' technology, and to keep the portal open once we have made the transition.'

Marcus and Indrani nodded in unison, pleased to have been included in the rescue team.

'Admiral Tordin,' continued Fireen, 'I would ask that you remain here in Nesteris, to take command of our naval forces.'

Tordin smiled back at the Aellindi leader, happy to accept the responsibility. 'I'll send word to King Elridan, to see if he'll put a few more ships at my disposal,' he said, knowing full well that the Kingdom fleet far outnumbered the smaller force that patrolled the seas around Nesteris.

'Excellent,' hissed Fireen, 'I will leave that in your capable hands, my friend. I have already made contact with the King myself, warning him of the potential threat, so I suspect that he will be glad to hear from you.'

The group continued their discussion for a while longer before Marcus and Indrani announced that they should head back to the *Beacon of Rhasad*. Certain things needed to be activated in order access to the *Beacon of Olon*, beyond the protective energy veil which encircled their world fragment. He had only been back to the master beacon a handful of times since Valken's demise, but Marcus had managed to activate many of its dormant systems and he wanted to gather up a few items which experience told him he might need.

'We have a few more things to discuss, regarding the protection of Nesteris and the remaining stones of power,' said Fireen, as Marcus and Indrani headed for the door, 'but we will meet you at the top of the *Beacon of Rhasad*.'

Klestin looked up as Marcus entered the glass-domed chamber at the top of the beacon. He waved his webbed hand towards his tutor and wandered over to greet him.

'Hello, Marcus,' he said, his gurgling voice full of pleasure at seeing his friend.

'It's good to see you, Klestin,' replied Marcus. 'However, I need you to go and find the others. We're about to open a portal to the *Beacon of Olon* and travel beyond the veil with Fireen.'

'Of course,' said the young student, his voice catching in the back of his throat, betraying the apprehension that had suddenly washed over him at the unexpected request, 'is anything wrong?'

'No, nothing's wrong,' replied Marcus, 'but I have a few things that I need you and the other students to do in my absence.'

'What would you have us do?'

'Is the *Drake* ready to put to sea?'

'Yes. She's all ready to go. In fact, the others are on board now, finishing up a few last checks.'

'Good, because I need the four of you to take her out and join up with Admiral Mochus, who will be on his new flagship.'

'You mean the steamship we saw the other day?'

'Yes, that's the one. Look, Klestin, I'm not going to lie to you. There may be trouble heading this way, although we don't know for sure if, or when it will actually appear. But I want the *Drake* to be available to Tordin should he have need of her.'

'I understand, Marcus. I'll head straight down to the pier now.'

'Just one more thing before you go, Klestin,' said Indrani as she entered the room. 'I'd also like you to prepare the airship for flight. Don't go anywhere with it, just leave it tied to the clamps at the base of the beacon. We might need it when we return from beyond the veil, and I'd like to know that she's ready and waiting to go. Leandra has agreed to help you, and then she'll join you on the *Drake*.'

'Sure, Indrani, we'll do that before heading out to join the Admiral. The airship is partially inflated, so it shouldn't take long to get it topped up and ready for your return.'

'Thanks, Klestin,' said Marcus and Indrani as the little man scurried inside the waiting lift car, 'and good luck.'

'And to you,' he replied, as the door whooshed closed.

*　　*　　*

Nadarru marched at the head of her shambling, undead army. The fierce desert sun beat down relentlessly onto her black fur, which seemed to radiate with some inner power. She sat astride a long dead steed, its skeletal remains bearing her weight with ease, carrying her across the hot desert sand as if it were still a living, breathing animal. It too was enveloped in Nadarru's powerful aurora, and its shadowed eye sockets blazed with blue glowing fire as they gazed across the seemingly endless dunes with malevolent intent.

In the far distance she could see the city that was her ultimate destination, with the blue shimmering sea just beyond, like some endless oasis calling to them from afar.

'We're close now,' she said, as her army marched behind her.

Her undead warriors did not reply, and nor did she expect them to. There was just the noise of the endless desert wind and the occasional creak or rattle as the reanimated bones kept pace with her.

She looked down upon her lieutenants, the blue-skinned warriors that had been sent by Queen Karmina to aid her in her quest. They strode beside her, easily keeping pace with her undead steed, using their energy spears to balance themselves in the ever shifting sands. Nadarru had been sent by the Queen to guide the army towards its ultimate destination, and to unleash it upon her enemies. The six warriors, who were all high-ranking priests of Queen Karmina's necromantic order, had apparently been sent to act as her personal bodyguards. But she knew, deep down, that they would not hesitate to betray her if the Queen demanded it.

'We'll raze this city to the ground as we have done many times before,' she said, 'and our army will grow ever more powerful.'

'The stones are near,' replied one of the warrior-priests, his voice barely a whisper. 'I can feel their power in the very air around us.'

'Yes,' replied Nadarru, 'the aether is strong on this world. We'll use its power to destroy all those who would oppose us. Once we've taken the cities on the edge of this accursed desert, we'll take their ships and seek out the stones. The Queen will be all powerful. She will be unstoppable, and she will reward us for our loyalty.'

Saven and her reconnaissance team peered out from behind a gigantic stone statue, which had long since crashed to the ground and shattered into several huge pieces. The army of the dead, led by the Ligarian female, passed slowly below them at the bottom of a rocky valley on the very edge of the desert. It was heading towards the city on the coast, not far from their current position.

The Aellindi scouts had detected their approach and sought out a suitable hiding place within a group of ancient dwellings. The long abandoned homes had been carved straight into the rock face using some colossal, ancient force to hollow out the inside of the valley wall. From their place of refuge, Saven and her warriors had watched in horror, unable to help as the enemy army had laid waste to the small group of desert folk that made this desolate valley their home. These peaceful people, who eked out a meagre living by selling their wares to the nomadic tribes that passed this way, had been no match for the hordes of reanimated creatures. They had been chased down and slaughtered. Nobody had been spared, not even the children.

Saven had watched the scene unfold, her horror turning to sickening fascination as she observed the full scale of the Ligarian's necromantic powers, unable to turn away from the gruesome spectacle. She had watched the sickening horror show as the dark magic had been invoked, from the very aether that Saven herself employed to heal her wounds following the strenuous training sessions with Rikoth. *How could the same energy be used in such a sickening way?* She had thought.

The Ligarian had been chanting in some unknown language, her arms waving above her head, as the aether was directed towards the bodies that lay there on the dusty valley floor. The Aellindi could scarcely believe what was happening, as the flesh was simply stripped away from the bones to which it had so recently been attached. They had watched as it had been turned to dust and carried away on the eddies of magical energy that flowed through the canyon. The scattered bones of the villagers had rolled across the ground, rattling back together and reforming into the same skeletal monstrosities that had so recently assaulted them in their own homes. The reanimated villagers then simply joined the ranks of the dead as they continued their inexorable march towards the coast.

'I never imagined, not even in my wildest dreams, that necromancy on this scale was even possible,' hissed Givas quietly, as he came to stand beside Saven. 'To give life to so many at the same time must take tremendous power!'

'It's not life!' replied Saven, disgusted at what she had witnessed. 'It's a powerful magic, that I grant you, but it's not true life.'

'Well, whatever it is, it's very frightening. We must find a way to reverse this terrible power. Or, at the very least, disrupt the Ligarian's hold over the dead.'

'Agreed! We must return to the outpost with all haste and send word to Fireen. She must be warned that this army of the dead is nearing the western coast of Thalmira and may soon be within striking distance of other nations. The Ligarian was clearly from these lands, most likely from the eastern cities, although she appears to have been granted the use of a powerful magic. But the blue-skinned warriors? I've never seen their like before.'

'I think they're the Visnaer. I cannot be certain, but they fit the description that I found in the ancient texts.'

'Visnaer?' replied Saven, the name rolling off her tongue with an angry, sibilant rasp. 'Are they related in some way to the Visnach?'

'Yes, very good, my friend. They're an ancient offshoot of the Visnach people, although they're said to have favoured living underground rather than in the forested regions which their red-haired cousins prefer. However, they've not been seen on our world since the cataclysm, and they were believed to have perished in the disaster. Some of our ancient scholars doubt that they existed at all, claiming they're nothing but a myth.'

'Well, clearly they're real and were not wiped out by the cataclysm,' replied Saven, her voice betraying her steely resolve to prevent these abhorrent creatures from causing any further harm. 'Wherever they've come from, wherever they've been hiding for all these years, they now pose a great threat to our world! We must send word immediately to our outpost and have them relay the message back to Nesteris with utmost haste. Fireen must be warned.'

Ten

The control room at the top of the *Beacon of Olon* was eerily quiet. Its systems appeared to be resting, in a state of dormancy with no visible light emanating from the panels and screens to disturb the darkness which enshrouded them.

Suddenly, without any prior warning, the entire glass-roofed chamber was filled with a blinding light and the beacon emerged from its slumber, its ancient systems powering up. A large oval shaped energy field began to coalesce in the central area of the room, its edges crackling with potent forces and its inner surface shimmering like shallow, sunlit water. The portal stabilised and Marcus stepped through, followed closely by Indrani. As they emerged, they were momentarily transparent in appearance, like ethereal beings from some higher plane, although they rapidly solidified as their forms were reconstructed by the advanced technology of the Ancestors. As they moved away from the still glowing portal, Fireen appeared, emerging from the event horizon with fluid grace and stepping aside so that Panx, Rikoth and his elite warriors could follow. Fireen waited beside the glowing portal for the final members of her party to emerge, and after a short delay Idris stepped through with Tethine barely two steps behind him.

The shimmering oval remained active for several moments after the last person had emerged. But when no further traffic was detected, the fizzing edge of the portal began to shrink in size until just a pinpoint of blue light was visible, which gradually faded from view altogether. The beacon's systems were now reactivated, as if it had sensed the arrival of its masters.

Marcus walked over to the edge of the chamber, as he always did when he came here, and gazed out at the panoramic vista. Through the translucent dome he could see the pier below the beacon, leading back to the water that lapped at the edge of the world. Even now, having made multiple journeys to this wondrous tower, he still found it difficult to comprehend what he was seeing. The *Beacon of Olon* stood at the very end of a long pier, like a sentinel watching over its land. However, this particular pier did not extend out over some stretch of shallow water, but out into the depths of the cosmos itself. It was surrounded by the vastness of space, with the faint light of the distant stars twinkling down from all around.

The pier reached back towards the world fragment of the Aellindi, as it floated endlessly through the black void, protected by the ancient energy veil that the Ancestors had created to keep its inhabitants safe. The veil itself was also visible from the beacon, like some enormous hazy green wall that stretched off in all directions as far as the eye could see. It was a dense green cloud, obscuring the world within. Only at the very fringe of the veil could anything from the inside be glimpsed, and Marcus could just make out the churned up waters of the ocean as they passed through the protective barrier. It appeared as though the ocean were about to pour over the very edge of the world, to boil off into the depths of space. But somehow the Ancestors' technology, or magic, prevented this from happening, and the water simply stopped at the edge, where it lapped against the strange pier that led out into space.

Looking down into what should have been the vast depths of the ocean, Marcus was unable to comprehend the power that must have been employed to hold back the water, containing it as if it were no more than a small fish tank. *Whoever these Ancestors were*, he thought, *they were truly powerful!*

'Are you okay, Marcus?' asked Indrani, coming over to stand behind him, gently placing her small hand on his shoulder.

'Yes, I'm fine. I just cannot get over this view!'

'Hmm, it's kind of unbelievable, isn't it?' she replied, although Marcus did not answer.

It had been decided at the last minute to bring young Idris along with them. His mother had not wanted to allow her son to put himself in danger. But with Fireen's assurance of his safety, she had relented, on the condition that she too would make the journey. Fireen had finally agreed when it became clear that Tethine would not take no for an answer, stubbornly refusing to leave her son's side.

The Aellindi leader believed that by employing Idris to act as a focal point when creating the portal into the dark realm, they might be able to tap into his subconscious thoughts and into the nightmarish visions that he had been having. She had informed them that a person's dreams and nightmares were stored away, locked deep within their minds. If they were able to access this information then they could feasibly use it to help them direct the portal's end location to a point near to where Navesh and his flock were hiding out. She had reasoned that if they were successful in tapping into the boy's nightmares, it would greatly advance their quest, reducing the amount of time that they would need to spend searching the dark realm for their lost friends. It would also reduce the chances of their discovery by the evil denizens of that world.

Idris had initially been reluctant to relive his nightmares, but Panx had spoken a few words of encouragement, pointing out that by adding his own power to the ritual he would learn valuable lessons and strengthen his connection with the aether.

'We must not delay,' said Fireen, invoking the power that would conjure up the portal into the dark world.

Panx had placed the *Shard of T'nath* into its receptacle, something which had been necessary the last time they had created such a portal. It had instantly begun to glow softly, as the power of the aether intensified inside the beacon's upper chamber. When they had previously connected with the dark realm, Navesh had used the *Shard of T'nath*, an ancient artefact, to channel the aether and to link with Valken's home world. They assumed that it would be necessary to use the shard on this occasion and had therefore brought it with them, hoping that its power could be reactivated.

Rikoth stood at the ready, surrounded by his retinue of elite warriors, watching intently as Fireen channelled the mystic powers of the aether through the crystal shard. Her magic was augmented by that of Panx and Indrani, who had prior experience of this particular ritual, having once lent their powers to Navesh when he made a connection to Valken's realm.

'Are you prepared, Idris?' asked Fireen, looking over at the young boy, whose eyes were open wide with a mixture of excitement and dread.

'Yes, Fireen, I'm ready,' he replied, his voice unsteady.

The young Aellindi began to chant, his arms swirling through the air, creating whirls of bright photonic light that leapt erratically from his outstretched fingers as they moved.

'Good,' whispered Fireen, 'very good.'

She increased the tempo of her chanting and reached out towards Idris. Suddenly, a stream of golden light shot forth from her clawed hands, enveloping the young boy in its aurora. Marcus watched in fascination, as he so often did when magic was employed, as the four magi continued to open the portal into another world.

'I can feel his presence,' shouted Idris, his sibilant voice struggling to be heard over the noise of Fireen's rhythmic chanting. 'Father, we're coming. Hold on!'

'Easy, Idris. Do not let your focus waver,' hissed Fireen, trying to calm the excitable youngster. 'We are nearly ready to make the connection.'

No sooner had she spoken the words than a glowing disc of light appeared in the centre of the chamber, forming the familiar oval shape of a transportation portal. Marcus watched intently as the shimmering disc stabilised. He moved back slightly, putting a little more distance between himself and the doorway into the dark world, remembering all too well how he had previously been dragged through and brutally tortured by the demon lord. The portal was surrounded by a gently strobing ribbon of energy that seemed to help prevent the gateway from losing coherence.

From a safe distance, Marcus peered into the portal, seeing for the second time in his life the frightening landscape of the dark realm. He shuddered, grateful that he was not going back there on this occasion. The view through the portal was not quite the same as it had been the first time, and the citadel could not be seen at all. There appeared to be a hilly landscape stretching off for many miles with high mountains visible in the far distance, illuminated by the eerie red sky. With any luck, he had thought, Fireen's ritual had succeeded in homing in on Navesh and maybe, just maybe, rescuing him would be a little bit easier.

Fireen relaxed slightly, the exertion of opening the portal showing on her scaled face. The *Shard of T'nath* glowed brightly as it held the doorway open, syphoning the aether through its crystal structure, redirecting it towards the linkway into the dark realm.

'We did it!' exclaimed Idris. 'We can rescue my father now?'

'Yes,' replied Fireen. 'We will go through now and attempt to locate him. Hopefully we are not too late!'

'Can I come too?' he asked hopefully.

'No way!' said Tethine, placing a firm hand on her son's shoulder, restraining the enthusiastic youth.

'I fear that we are about to head into great danger, my young friend,' replied Fireen gently. 'But know this, you have played an important part in the rescue, and I will be sure to inform your father of your great bravery.'

Idris beamed at Fireen's compliment, standing up as tall as he could, his chest thrust out with pride. His mother looked gratefully towards Fireen and bowed her head, thanking her for gently diffusing her son's eagerness without damaging his confidence. Indrani moved closer to Marcus, gently grasping his hand and squeezing. She missed their own child, who was with her parents on K'vith. He was safe for the moment, but they both hoped that the current crises would not become further inflamed and threaten the safety of everyone on their world.

'I can't see any signs of movement,' said Panx, peering intently through the portal. 'I think it's safe to go through.'

'I'll go first,' hissed Rikoth, dressed in his ancient suit of armour and wielding his mighty two handed warhammer. His armour and weapon had both been badly damaged during the demon war, but his people had possessed sufficient skill to completely restore them to their full glory. The Aellindi hero was now eager to test them out against the vile demons who had previously tried to take their world from them.

Rikoth stepped forward bravely, his armoured form momentarily shimmering in the light as he crossed the threshold. He disappeared altogether for a brief moment, causing the others to hold their breath as he made the transition through the cosmos. He reappeared moments later, having safely crossed between worlds and now waited in a watchful stance, beckoning the others to follow him through. The elite guards were next to make the transition, stepping through and reappearing beside their heroic leader. They spread out, watching for any sign that their appearance had been detected, their mighty curved swords held ready to defend themselves.

'Good luck,' said Marcus. 'I hope you find them quickly.'

'Thank you,' replied Fireen, turning to speak with Marcus and Indrani before she entered the gateway. 'Please watch the portal closely in case the denizens of the dark world should chance across it whilst we are in their realm. If there is any chance that we have been discovered and that our own world might once again be under threat, please shut down the portal immediately by removing the *Shard of T'nath.*'

'But you'll be trapped there,' gasped Idris, his young face displaying fear once more.

'It is far better that we few should perish, my young friend, than the demons gain a foothold on our world once more,' explained Fireen calmly. 'For if that were to happen, thousands would no doubt perish before we could repel them.'

'If we could repel them at all,' added Tethine gravely.

'Take care of yourself, Panx,' said Indrani, coming over to embrace her friend.

'We'll take care of one another,' he replied, hugging her back.

Fireen motioned for Panx to go first and then, with one final glance back at those who were staying behind, followed him through. Marcus watched as she calmly walked into the fizzing energy field and reappeared shortly afterwards on the other side.

'Please find my father,' said Idris, coming to stand before portal. 'Please bring him home.'

'They will return soon, my son,' whispered Tethine, placing her arm protectively around his shoulders. 'We must be patient and keep a vigilant watch here at the portal.'

As they had no idea how long Fireen and the others would be gone, they each spent a portion of their time peering through the fizzing energy gate, hoping to catch a fleeting glimpse of their friends. However, the area on the other side of the portal remained quiet, and their friends were nowhere to be seen. Thankfully, the sudden appearance of the portal had escaped the unwanted attention of the demonic abominations that resided in that place and for now all was calm.

Marcus had noticed that, in addition to the lack of demon activity, there were no animals, large or small, wandering through the wilderness. He sat quietly, pondering just what sort of life might exist on that strange world, when Indrani came over and sat down beside him.

'I forgot to tell you,' she said, her head resting gently on his shoulder, 'I found something quite interesting whilst I was travelling through Reznar.'

'Oh,' replied Marcus, 'what did you find?'

'Some sort of temple, dedicated to Nurarian!'

'The unicorn god?' said Marcus, looking away from the portal, his pondering of the lack of animal life on the dark world suddenly forgotten. 'The Traveller?'

'Yes. It was just off the main forest track, inside the thick tangle of trees. Leandra spotted it on our way into Jespira.'

'What did it look like?'

'It was quite basic really. A large circle of stones, huge monolithic blocks that had somehow been placed there. They were buried deep in the ground for stability, although they still towered above the Reznari.'

'Wow,' said Marcus, images of the various stone circles from his own world rushing through his mind. 'Anything else?'

'Yes. In the centre of the stone circle was a shrine, beside which sat a large statue of a unicorn. I guess it was meant to represent Nurarian himself, rearing up on his hind legs, with his forelegs reaching up towards the heavens. It was quite something. We spent a little time looking around, but didn't find anything else.'

'And there was nobody there? No priests?'

'No. The site appeared to have been deserted, although the forest had not encroached beyond the ring of stones. It was quite strange really. I asked about it when we finally arrived in Jespira, but most people claimed to know nothing about the shrine. There was just one old man, claiming to be an historian, who had said that there was supposed to be a mysterious cult that worshipped The Traveller and could be found living deep within the forest. He said that they came to the shrine on special occasions to offer prayers to Nurarian.'

Since his sudden arrival on the world of the Aellindi, Marcus had been intrigued by the Ancestors and by the other gods that the people who lived here had chosen to worship. He had never been a believer in such entities himself, back on his own world. Instead, he had spent most of his life worshipping science, something he could understand and believe in, if not always see and feel. But here, especially after finding out that his arrival had somehow been foretold by some ancient prophecy, he had begun to question his beliefs. He still clung to his scientific reasoning, where proof was facilitated by results and hard evidence. But his eyes had also been opened to the possibility that there were such things as divine beings.

He already accepted that the Ancestors actually existed. Or at least they had existed here at some point in history. But there were other deities that were worshipped here, by the other races who inhabited this world. One such divine being, worshipped by the Visnach people, was Nurarian. This particular god was also known as The Traveller and often took the form of a beautiful white unicorn. The professor had spent much of his spare time visiting the temples and conversing with the priests, but so far had found no concrete proof that these deities truly existed beyond the religions and beliefs of the people. But something about Indrani's chance discovery had rekindled his interest. For some reason that he did not understand, he felt that the temple in Reznar offered the key, that there he might find more than just scriptures and priests going about their worship as they had for generations.

'I think it might be worth a visit, when this is all over,' said Indrani, her voice startling Marcus from his deep thoughts, bringing him back to reality. 'Are you alright?'

'Yes, I'm fine. Sorry, I was deep in thought for a moment. Yes, definitely worth a visit.'

'You're not thinking of leaving though, are you?' she asked, worried that Marcus still harboured a desire to return to his own world.

'No, Indrani, I have no desire to leave you. But imagine if we were able to travel to my world by stepping through a portal, just like we did here with the dark world. Think of the technology we could obtain. It might even help us to unlock more of the secrets of the Ancestors!'

Indrani nodded, thinking about Marcus's homeworld. He had spoken about it often, but to actually go there would truly be an adventure. She sat with Marcus for several hours talking about his home and the things that he had left behind, until Tethine came over and informed her that it was her turn to watch the portal.

Idris walked over and tapped Marcus gently on the shoulder, waking him from the light slumber into which he had fallen.

'What is it?' he asked. 'Have you seen something through the portal?'

'No, Marcus, there's still no activity through the portal, everything is quiet. Indrani's keeping watch. But a light has started flashing over there, on that shiny surface,' said Idris, pointing to the main control panel in the centre of the room.

'Oh? That's new. Let's have a look shall we?'

He stood up and walked over to the control panel, looking down at the touch sensitive surface, trying to understand why it had suddenly come to life. A set of brightly glowing symbols was being displayed on the screen, including some familiar icons that represented the beacons that were spread out across the world. These were linked by a yellow-coloured pulsing line, and showed clearly the network of beacons to which they were currently connected. Marcus had grown used to this particular display, having seen it often in the *Beacon of Rhasad* when he wanted to open a portal to one of the other beacons.

'It's just the portal network screen. It's still active from our transition from Nesteris,' he muttered. 'Hang on a minute,' he added, 'what's this here?' His finger pointed towards another icon, one which he did not recognise and which had never appeared on the screen before. 'This symbol doesn't match any that I've seen before. Do you recognise it, Idris?'

The boy studied the symbol but could not tell Marcus anything about it. They called Tethine over and asked her if she had seen the strange symbol before. She said that although it looked familiar, she could not recall where or when she had seen it, nor did she know what, or whom it represented.

Marcus remembered that Navesh had once told him that the icons, or glyphs as he had called them, were used by the Ancestors and often represented certain individuals. He could clearly see the glyph that represented Andin as it glowed steadily on the screen, and he wondered if this new icon was dedicated to an as yet unknown Ancestor. If that truly was the case, then this flashing icon might indicate that they had discovered a new beacon.

'Look at this,' he said excitedly, beckoning Indrani over and pointing at the flashing icon. 'I think this is a new beacon. The others we're already familiar with. There's Andin, Olon, Rhasad and this one's Kolam, in Vilnarr. But this new icon is unknown to me.'

'I know that look,' said Indrani, staring at Marcus, a frown on her pale face and her hands placed firmly against her hips, 'you're going through aren't you? That's so reckless! What if you're wrong or can't get back? What then?'

'Listen, Indrani, I know that you're only concerned about me. I'd probably be saying the same thing if it were the other way round, but I need to do this. You three are more than capable of watching the portal to the dark world and removing the *Shard of T'nath* if anything goes wrong. What would I be able to do if some hairy beast were to suddenly jump through and attack us? That's something that you're better at dealing with, not me. I know that I've got a sword, and Saven says that my skills have improved greatly, but we all know that I'm not a true warrior.'

Indrani watched Marcus with a look of resigned acceptance on her face. There was no way that she was going to be able to talk him out of this.

'You know I've always felt completely out of my depth around magic and the power of the aether,' he continued. 'I've never been able to even tap into it, let alone control it. Even though you've tried to show me what to do, I just don't think I'll ever be able to control that sort of power. It still makes my skin tingle when somebody draws upon aether near me, but that's about as close as I'll ever get to making contact with your magic.

'But, with these beacons and the technology of the Ancestors, it's different. This is something that I have an affinity for. I don't really know how, or why, but I do! It's something that I understand, and therefore something that I can offer to your world and the people that live on it.'

'Fine, Marcus,' said Indrani reluctantly, 'but promise me that you'll come straight back. Don't go off exploring beyond the new beacon, no matter what you find there. We can go back later. Mount a proper expedition. But at the moment we've a duty to Fireen. We don't know how long she'll be gone, or if she'll have need of us upon her return.'

'Okay, Indrani, I promise. I'll just take a peek then I'll come straight back. Besides, Panx wouldn't speak to me again if I didn't give him the chance to visit a new beacon.'

Indrani smiled at Marcus's attempt to lighten the atmosphere between them. 'Ever the explorer,' she said, kissing him gently on the forehead.

'Can I go too?' asked Idris, who was still standing beside them.

'Certainly not,' replied Indrani, pushing the young man away from the screen, 'go and stand watch with your mother!'

Marcus touched the icon which he hoped represented an undiscovered beacon, the touch sensitive display flaring to life as his fingers made contact. Within moments a portal had coalesced beside the one into which Fireen had so recently departed, its fizzing edges holding the transportation window's oval shape. The energy arcing out from the crackling edges seemed a little more erratic than normal, but he assumed that it was a consequence of having two portals open in such close proximity. He waited for a brief moment to ensure that the portal was stable, whilst he prepared himself to step through.

'See you soon,' he said, giving Indrani a quick kiss on the cheek. He then picked up his backpack and walked confidently through the glowing energy field.

Within moments he had appeared in the control room of another of the Ancestors' beacons, the forward motion through the portal pushing him clear of the oval energy field, which spluttered and shut down almost as soon as he had fully emerged. Above him he could see the clear blue sky, shining through the glass-domed structure that was a feature of all the beacons. It was quite warm inside the room and he assumed that the automated temperature regulators must be offline.

He walked over to the edge of the chamber and peered out through the glass. Beneath the beacon he could see the remains of an ancient, long abandoned city. Beyond that he was greeted by the site of a vast golden desert that extended in all directions for as far as he could see. He let out a soft whistling sound, knowing that somehow he had found his way over to the eastern continent of Thalmira.

He spent a short while looking around the chamber, mindful that he had promised Indrani that he would come straight back. He was tempted to have a very quick look outside, but found that the lift was also inactive. There were also signs of a recent struggle in the chamber, including a large wooden table lying on its side, with one leg snapped clean off, and several sticky patches of blood. He therefore decided that he would not risk leaving the beacon after all, just in case there were any unsavoury characters in the vicinity. He would return later when he could bring a few warriors for protection.

Returning to the central console, Marcus touched the screen and waited for the image of the beacon network to appear. But the screen remained dormant. Trying desperately to ignore the rising sense of panic, he knelt down and pried off the panel underneath the screen, revealing handfuls of colourful wires which were connected to odd looking switches. He focused on the wires, recalling the systems that he had previously been required to repair inside the other beacons. Trusting to his experience he pulled several wires free from the main bundle and connected them together, attempting to reactivate the control panel.

His work was rewarded and the screen came back to life, displaying the beacon network that he so desired. It appeared to be suffering from some loss of power, and the screen was flickering randomly. He touched the icon that designated the *Beacon of Olon*, hoping that the portal would open before the power failed completely. To his relief, it flared to life and settled into the familiar oval shaped window. He wasted no time stepping back through the portal, eager to return to his companions.

He emerged in a darkened room with the stars twinkling in the black abyss outside, their distant light filtering through the glass-domed roof. The portal immediately shut down, leaving a momentary after image as the energy dissipated. He looked around, not expecting the control room to be in complete darkness and feeling a little disoriented. It certainly appeared to be the control chamber at the top of the *Beacon of Olon*, but something was not quite right. It felt cold here, much colder than it had been when he left the others just minutes ago.

He called out to Indrani, but there was no reply. He looked for the portal into the dark world, which should still be active, but found nothing. Desperate now he called out to Idris and Tethine, his voice wavering slightly as the reality washed over him like a tsunami. There was nobody here. The control panels appeared to be offline and there was no sound coming from the beacon at all.

Trying hard to fight down the rising sense of panic, Marcus walked over to the edge of the chamber. He had to scrape a layer of cold ice from the inside of the glass before he was rewarded with a view of the outside world. What he saw there chilled him to the core.

Eleven

The city of Xhaan was burning. Flames licked hungrily across the buildings and homes of the once powerful metropolis. The savage heat made no distinction between the wealthy and the poor, spreading through the narrow, crowded streets with wanton abandon. The city's citizens were screaming in fear, their lives turned upside down with frenzied panic. They hurried in all directions, trying desperately to avoid the burning flames which crackled wildly all around.

But for these hapless people, escape was all but impossible. Those that did manage to flee from the burning ruins of their homes or places of work, were set upon by the savage invaders who had appeared as if from nowhere from the hazy sands of the great desert. Hordes of skeletal warriors, reanimated by some foul magic, had smashed their way inside the walls of Xhaan. They were led by a fearless Ligarian female riding atop a nightmarish steed, accompanied by six blue-skinned devils that slowly made their way through the streets, wielding spears of deadly fire.

Nadarru watched as her army of the dead marched along a once beautiful avenue, its wide cobbled street lined with tall evergreen trees that were even now beginning to smoulder as the fire consumed the city. Roving bands of her undead warriors hurried into side streets, flushing out the city's denizens as they tried to hide or escape. Most of the victims died at the hands of her skeletal followers. Those who managed to escape the clutches of her nightmarish infantry were swiftly cut down by the Visnaer priests, struck from behind by the powerful energy weapons as they fled. She did not join the slaughter, but slowly followed the progress of her troops, drawing upon the rich energy of the aether to invoke her necromantic powers.

As she rode through the streets of the doomed city, its recently slain inhabitants rose up in her wake to bolster the ranks of her army. Their fleshless bodies scurrying away, bones grating together noisily as they hunted down the city's remaining populace.

There had been a pitched battle with the city's standing army, which had been composed of hundreds of highly trained soldiers wielding mighty swords and protected behind heavy wooden shields.

They had initially resisted the attacking army, closing the city's two huge gates and manning the walls, raining down death from above onto their unknown assailants. But to their dismay, as soon as the skeletons were felled, they were either replaced or simply stood back up, their bones clattering together once more, allowing them to continue the assault.

The defenders had quickly recognised that the only way to truly stop this abominable army was to sally forth and attempt to cut down its leaders, those who were undoubtedly responsible for reanimating the bones. They had opened one of the titanic wooden gates, lifting the huge brace from its mount and rushing out into the sands beyond the city. But the attempt had been doomed before it had even begun. Those defenders who were not immediately hacked down by the brutal skeletal attackers, pulled screaming from atop their tharen, were struck down by the energy weapons carried by the blue-skinned warriors who stood implacably beside the Ligarian.

Soon, the brave defenders who had ridden out to face the enemy had been assimilated into its ranks, and they now sat atop their skeletal tharen, waiting for the city's defences to finally falter. And falter it did, in the end, allowing Nadarru's warriors to flood into the city through the ruined gates. Then the screams had begun.

As Nadarru rounded the corner of a long avenue, which led down towards the harbour upon which the ancient city had been founded, she spotted her warrior priests engaged in hand-to-hand combat, something which she had not witnessed thus far. Usually content to cut down the fleeing populace with their energy spears, she was unaccustomed to them wading into the melee. She watched with undisguised admiration as they swung their spears towards their assailants, ducking and weaving as their attackers tried to strike back. She had not seen them tested in this way before and nudged her mount forwards to determine who it was that was putting up such fierce resistance. So far the enemy garrison, although brave and large in number, had lacked the skills to really challenge her army, but something about this small engagement intrigued her. Perhaps the city's elite warriors had been held in reserve, and had finally been unleashed upon her warriors in one final attempt to turn the tide of the battle.

She guided her skeletal mount closer and her keen eyes easily picked out the towering figures of the new combatants. Aellindi! But where had they come from? Her priests were outnumbered, although apparently not outmatched. There were already several Aellindi warriors lying on the ground, swiftly dispatched by the sharp spears as her priests swung them rapidly in a glorious display of martial prowess. She extended her powers towards the bodies of the fallen Aellindi, weaving the aether into the correct form to return those mighty warriors to life. She would help turn the tide in favour of her Visnaer guards.

I want a prisoner, she thought, sending her wishes through the aether and into the minds of her lieutenants. Soon the balance had shifted, and no longer were her priests outnumbered. Only a few of the Aellindi remained, standing close together, desperately trying to parry the deadly Visnaer spears. But as one by one they fell, the number of attackers grew, as their fallen brethren were raised from the dead.

Nadarru smiled cruelly as the final Aellindi warrior threw herself forward, desperate to avenge her fallen friends. But she was spent, and the Visnaer easily evaded her sword strokes, catching her arm as it whirled around for another thrust. The six priests moved forward in unison, and the struggling Aellindi warrior was knocked unconscious, her body dropping heavily onto the cobbled floor. The other Aellindi, who were no more than hulking skeletal bone golems, trudged off in search of new victims to slake their murderous thirst.

'Bring that one with us,' said Nadarru. 'We'll question her later.'

'As you wish,' replied one of the warrior priests, who Nadarru recognised as G'Valk, the apparent leader of her blue-skinned guards.

The Visnaer deftly bound their prisoner and hauled her into the back of a large wagon that slowly trundled along, drawn by a team of skeletal tharen. Nadarru continued to trail behind her army as it spread out through the city streets, pushing the remaining inhabitants towards the nimbus of her power, to be forever enslaved by her dark magic.

Finally, after many hours of brutal carnage, the screams of the city's inhabitants died down. The sounds of the fires that had consumed much of the city were all that could be heard. Her army had grown immeasurably during this latest conquest, and no more than a handful of frightened citizens of this once powerful city had escaped her grasp. Queen Karmina would be pleased with her progress.

Nadarru had finally come to the port area of the city. A huge network of harbours, piers and warehouses, where the lifeblood of Xhaan flowed in and out. At her express command the port had been spared the worst of the fighting and the buildings here had not been put to the torch. She needed the ships that were bobbing up and down in the gentle waters, protected behind the ancient breakwater. There were many vessels here, which would do the job of transporting her invasion force admirably. Her army was now sufficiently powerful and she longed to unleash it against the true target.

'Bring the Aellindi woman here,' she demanded.

Her warrior priests hauled the still unconscious form of Saven from the wagon and dragged her across the harbour, dropping her on the ground before their Ligarian mistress. Nadarru sent out a swift jolt of energy from her outstretched fingertips towards her captive, who shuddered at the impact of the aetheric assault. Saven awoke and looked up at her captors, her eyes narrowing as she recognised Nadarru as the leader of the invading army.

'Who are you?' she asked, her voice still weak.

'I'm in command here,' replied Nadarru, sending another powerful wave of pain into Saven's already injured body, causing her to double over in agony. 'Why are you here, Aellindi?'

'We came to investigate the reports of an army that had been spotted approaching from the east,' replied Saven, somehow unable to resist answering the Ligarian's question. She continued to look up at the lithe form of the fur-covered woman, whose tail swished behind her as if she were agitated.

'How many more of you are there in the city?'

'There are no more Aellindi here. I'm the last.'

'And what of your home island?'

Saven tried to resist the commanding voice of her captor, the fear of betraying her people helping her to overcome the sudden compulsion to answer the Ligarian. She spat towards Nadarru's skeletal mount and looked away, feeling triumphant at the apparent return of her inner strength.

G'Valk uttered several short, clipped words, and three of the other warrior priests grabbed her roughly, hauling her up onto her feet. He then took two swift steps forward and struck her in the face, rupturing her upper lip and sending one of her sharp pointed teeth skittering across the cobbled floor. Saven grunted in pain, spitting blood onto the ground. G'Valk continued his assault, violently attacking the prisoner while his fellow priests held her in place.

'Enough!' shouted Nadarru, immediately halting the brutal assault. 'I ask you again, fool, how many of your pitiful race live on your home island?'

Saven looked up at Nadarru, one eye heavily swollen and already closing shut. 'Our numbers are vast, and we're ready,' she hissed.

'We'll see how ready you are,' chuckled Nadarru, 'very soon indeed. Now, tell me of the stones of power. Where are they kept?'

'I don't know,' replied Saven truthfully. 'They've been moved and I was not informed of their new location. But they'll be heavily guarded, and you'll not find them easy to obtain.'

'No matter,' replied Nadarru, staring down intently at the injured Aellindi warrior. 'I'll determine their location after we've destroyed your homes. All of your towns and villages will be razed to the ground and your people enslaved.'

The Ligarian woman signalled to her priests and Saven was once again hauled to her feet. She was dragged towards the largest of the vessels that floated in the harbour of Xhaan, where she was gagged and then roughly tied to its main mast. From there she watched, through her one open eye, as the enemy army swarmed aboard every vessel in the port. The ship's decks were soon filled with the creaking skeletal warriors. She spotted her fallen Aellindi comrades amongst the mass of reanimated bones, standing taller than the other hapless servants of the evil Ligarian. She desperately hoped that they could no longer feel pain, and that their original consciousness had died along with their flesh.

Givas, my friend, she thought, *I hope you've managed to get a message back to the council, for this army is about to leave Thalmira on a heading for Nesteris, and it will require a powerful force to halt it.* She tried to reach out through the aether to make contact with her fellow councillor, who had returned to the scrying outpost. But alas, her connection to the aether was not strong enough to reach him. *Good luck*, she thought, as the large ship moved out of the harbour. It was guided by some unseen force, some magical wind, no doubt created by the Ligarian and her Visnaer followers, and headed out into the waters of the grey expanse towards the peaceful island of Nesteris.

*   *   *

Mizarius walked back into the council chamber, nodding to Endina as he approached the central wooden table. He had just returned from the scrying chamber and wanted to inform her of the dire news that he had recently received, and the message he had subsequently sent to the Kingdom of the Isles. The room was constantly guarded by a full troop of elite warriors, and the remaining councillors maintained a presence here at all times. Endina looked tired, and Mizarius fully intended to relieve her, to allow her to go and rest, just as soon as he had reported back to her. He would gladly stay here for the next watch.

'The look on your face, Mizarius,' hissed Endina, as he approached the table, 'tells me that something important has just occurred.'

'Very perceptive, my old friend,' he replied, trying to maintain an air of calm. 'I've just returned from the scrying chamber. We've received a message from Givas.'

'What did he say?' asked Endina, her fatigue suddenly replaced by a feeling of nervous tension.

'Saven's been captured by the enemy. Also, the undead creatures have set sail, bound for Nesteris.'

'What about our other forces at the outpost?'

'Givas cannot be certain, for he's alone there, but he fears that only Saven survived. They had been inside the city of Xhaan when it had been breached. Saven had led her warriors in a valiant attempt to allow Givas to escape. He managed to reach a small village, some distance from the city, where he took passage to the outpost. But as yet there's been no word from Saven, and none of the warriors have returned to the outpost.'

Endina was quiet for a moment while she absorbed the news. 'How long until the enemy fleet reaches us?'

'We don't know for certain, but Givas has detected a powerful aurora off the coast of Thalmira, and suspects that the enemy is utilising magic to propel their ships. If this is indeed the case, we might not have long!'

'We must mobilise the rest of the navy straight away,' hissed Endina urgently.

'I've already issued the command. The remaining ships will be leaving the harbour as we speak to join up with Admiral Mochus.'

'Have you sent word to King Elridan? Updating him on the latest news?'

'Yes, just before I came here to see you. He's already replied.'

'What did he say?'

'His navy is preparing to set sail for Nesteris. Tordin had already contacted him, warning him of the danger. The King has pushed his troops hard in order to prepare them, and his finest general will soon be in the capital. He's bringing with him many of the Kingdom's newest troops, with their advanced weaponry. They'll accompany the fleet and deploy onto Nesteris to aid us in the defence of our people!'

'And the stones!' added Endina.

'Yes,' replied Mizarius, 'especially the stones.'

'So these . . . Visnaer,' hissed Endina, 'I've found a few references to them in the ancient texts. But they don't give us much to go on!'

'What have you learned?'

'As Givas suspected, they were, or are, an offshoot of the Visnach. Their heritage is purported to go even further back, to a time before the Visnach, Vilnarri and the Visnaer became separate races. They were once a peaceful people, much like their distant cousins, preferring to live high up in the mountains in harmony with nature.'

'So what happened to them?'

'Some unknown disaster befell them. I couldn't find reference to what happened exactly, but it would seem that they unwittingly unleashed some terrible power amongst their settlements and their numbers dwindled rapidly after that. Those that remained turned to the worship of Evixius, the ancient god of the dead!'

'Evixius!' repeated Mizarius, a shudder overcoming him, filling him with a cold dread. 'I haven't heard that name in a while.'

'No, he's no longer worshipped here. Although the Visnach do occasionally leave offerings for their departed loved ones in the hope of keeping the dark god's mood jovial, to protect their souls.'

'So what happened to them after they turned to the dark god? How come we've not seen them on our world since the cataclysm?'

'It's believed that they had all perished, that Evixius had finally claimed them. But, it would seem, that wherever this Visnaer queen is located, we'll find the remains of their long lost civilisation.'

'Do you think she's here on our world?'

'No, I don't. Fireen is certain that she's located on another fragment, which would mean that in order for some of them to be here on our world, accompanying the Ligarian female, they must have the means to travel between fragments.'

'But that's not possible,' hissed Mizarius, 'surely there's no way to cross between fragments!'

'Ordinarily I would agree with you, my young friend, but the evidence would suggest otherwise!'

'Did the ancient scrolls hint at anything else?'

'Nothing regarding the Visnaer, but I have several scholars scouring them for mention of necromancy, or the worship of Evixius. We need to know how to reverse that abominable magic that has been used to reanimate the dead!'

'Let's hope that they find something soon, before that army gets here!'

*   *   *

Tordin paced across the confined bridge of the *Hammer*. He had just received word from young Mizarius that the enemy was on its way, and he was nervous. There had been no word yet from Fireen, and he was concerned about how their rescue attempt was progressing. He had hoped to travel to the *Beacon of Olon* to see what was happening, but that was no longer an option.

The *Drake* was keeping pace with him, ably commanded by Marcus's students and accompanied by Leandra. He was not really sure what use the *Drake* would be in a fight, as she was armed only with whatever magic her young crew could muster. But at least she was solidly constructed and could ram the enemy ships if they got too close to Nesteris.

The Aellindi fleet was also on high alert, and the last few ships were moving out into the seas around their beloved home, pushed through the water by teams of Aellindi magi. Although their ships were few in number, they were swift and crammed with elite warriors, who would board the enemy vessels and wreak havoc on their decks. In addition to the Aellindi marines, the council had posted scores of magi to the navy vessels, where they would unleash the fury of the aether in the hope of destroying the enemy ships before they got within striking distance of their homeland.

His only fear was that the numbers would be against him. His own vessel was certainly the most powerful afloat, but she was only one ship. The others, although powerful individually and defended by valiant warriors, might soon be reduced to piles of floating debris if the enemy arrived in the vast numbers that he anticipated. The Aellindi fleet was small, and would be no match for a sustained assault by a much larger foe.

His hope now rested on the arrival of his own navy from the Kingdom of the Isles. They must set sail soon, for even with magically enhanced wind spurring them onward, they were going to be cutting it fine if they hoped to arrive before it was all over. *Hurry*, he thought, *you must hurry!*

*   *   *

Arthen was nearing the capital city of Brind, his small regiment of soldiers having pushed their tharen beyond the point of no return. He just hoped that their strength would hold out long enough to reach the station. He had received another message from the King, while he was still about half way between Rothford and Brind, informing him that an invasion of the Aellindi homeland was imminent. He had stopped at the next military outpost for just long enough to switch their tired tharen for fresh animals, and then he had pressed on. They had ridden continually ever since and were all fatigued by the rapid deployment. His outward demeanour was that of a confident general, leading his troops to the front line, but inside he feared that they would be in no condition to fight should the need arise any time soon.

'Here we are,' said Major Tassik, 'the outskirts of Brind!'

'Good, we're nearly there,' replied Arthen, inwardly relieved.

'Of course . . . we have to ride on that new contraption first. Hopefully it won't blow us all to bits!'

'I think the engineers have made a lot of progress since that little . . . accident,' said Arthen, smiling at his officer's apparent discomfort.

'I sure hope so!'

The small force arrived on the outskirts of Brind, where a huge military outpost had recently been constructed around the new railway station. At present, this was as far as the network extended out of the capital city, although work had been started on laying further track northward.

Arthen could see a long train, with its locomotive sat at the platform, ready for them to climb aboard. While several of Marcus's technological wonders had been used to improve their military prowess, there were other individuals who had been interested in the myriad ways in which it might improve their way of life. The steam locomotive had proved to be a great success, and even after a few accidents, some of which had been fatal, the engineers had continued with their endeavours and had finally created a working prototype.

The initial locomotives had been powered by coal, just as they had on Marcus's own world. But at the professor's insistence, they had turned to the magically charged crystals that had proven themselves admirably in Tordin's navy. Marcus had been extremely pleased with how the project had developed, commenting that it was amazing to see such clean looking steam trains.

Arthen paced up and down the platform as his men and equipment were hastily loaded onto the train. He walked down towards the locomotive, which Marcus had named, for some strange reason, *Flying Scotsman*, and preceded to talk with the driver. He was a wiry little magus from the college, who could keep the crystals fully charged, but who also seemed to have an affinity for the technology from Marcus's world.

'Are you nearly ready?' asked the driver.

'Yes,' replied Arthen, 'just a few more wagons to unload and we'll be ready to depart.'

'Good. Can I ask you something, General?'

'Sure,' replied Arthen warily.

'You know Marcus quite well . . . right?' continued the driver, to which Arthen simply nodded his head in affirmation. 'Well . . . what the heck is a Flying Scotsman?'

'I have no idea,' replied Arthen, 'but I'll be sure to ask him when I see him.'

The train pulled into the central station in Brind after a short trip from the outskirts. It had been much quicker than if he had continued by wagon, reassuring him that the insistence on building these steam engines was justified. With the network extended up to Rothford, his journey time back to the capital would be greatly reduced. Their lives had truly been turned upside down since the arrival of the stranger from another world.

'Arthen, over here!' shouted a familiar voice, interrupting his musing.

Kat was there, standing on the platform, and she looked beautiful. He had missed her terribly. He clambered down from the carriage, with wisps of steam from the engine blowing around him, and smiled at the King's daughter as she ran to greet him. She jumped into his arms and kissed him fiercely, as though she had not seen him in years.

'Easy, Kat,' he said, chuckling to himself, 'that's no way for the heir to the throne to behave. What will people think?' He hugged her back, flashing his most dashing smile. 'I've missed you too!'

'We must hurry,' replied Kat, suddenly serious. 'Father wants to see you straight away. Something terrible is happening on Nesteris!'

Twelve

Fireen stood at the edge of a dark, seemingly impenetrable forest. Its trees were short and stunted and covered in slimy black bark, as if they had been afflicted with a foul poison designed to rot them from the inside out. Her rescue party had walked only a short distance from the portal before they had come across the huge wall of trees. They could only see a little way inside the forest, through the dense foliage that clung to the twisted branches like swarms of parasitic leeches.

There was an ominous feel to this place which was amplified by the foetid dampness of the very air around them, and Fireen did not relish the idea of scrabbling through the unwelcoming woodland, not unless they had no other choice. Upon leaving the safety of the *Beacon of Olon* she had instinctively known in which direction they should travel. She had decided that they would follow the edge of the forest until they either found a way through, or had skirted it completely. They could not turn back at the very first hurdle.

Panx had visited the dark world once before, when he and his companions had travelled through the portal to rescue Marcus. He had already warned the Aellindi what to expect when they arrived here, but the reality of this foul place was far worse than any of them had been prepared for.

The sky was the colour of blood. There were clouds drifting through the heavens above, but these did not promise to deliver a cooling rain to wash away the oppressive feeling that weighed heavily upon them all. No, the clouds here seemed to hang in the sky above them with ominous intent. They looked pregnant with danger and charged with powerful energies, seeking to unleash destruction upon those below them. In the distance they could see a storm raging, hurling great tentacles of brilliant white fire down towards the ground with titanic fury. They all silently prayed that it would not detect their presence somehow, to seek them out and reduce them to charred corpses. Even the air here was foul and difficult to breathe. It was laden with the stink of death and heavy with bitter humidity, which left them feeling lightheaded and giddy. Panx had tried not to inhale too deeply, to avoid the constant gagging sensation that accompanied every breath, but he finally gave in to the rank air before he passed out.

The Aellindi were on edge too, including Fireen, who was usually the epitome of self-control. The guards had fanned out, stalking away from the portal to ensure that the area was secure, and once Fireen had determined their direction of travel they had moved off with a nervous tension that Panx had not witnessed before. Even Rikoth, who was by far the most fearsome warrior that he had ever met, seemed apprehensive, even jumpy. The great warrior walked quietly beside Fireen with his ancient two-handed warhammer resting over his broad shoulder, yet Panx could sense that he was ready for action, like a coiled serpent waiting to strike.

As it had been before, when Panx had first entered Valken's domain, the aether seemed unusually weak. Its presence seemed shrouded in some way, as if it had been all but consumed, leeched away by some powerful ritual so that only a residual trace was detectable. Fireen had immediately commented on the lack of connection to the magical forces, seemingly frustrated by her inability to control the aether. Panx had assured her that the power was there, although they would have to find a way to tap into its energy. They had each tested out their powers in an attempt to re-establish the connection, to restore the comfort that they felt as the aether coursed through them.

They continued to follow the edge of the dark forest and were now high up in the hills. Stretching out far below them they could see vast plains, covered in thick yellow grass, which seemed to go on forever. In the far distance they could make out a huge fortress, sitting ominously atop a huge rocky outcrop. Panx wondered if it was the same one that he had visited before, although he could not be certain. Beyond the forest, in the direction that they were ultimately headed, were vast mountains, with jagged snow covered peaks. They had so far managed to avoid detection by the demons that they all knew to inhabit this world, and so far there had been very little sign of life. Even small animals, such as tree climbing rodents or songbirds, were few and far between.

As the group marched along beside the gnarled tree trunks, searching for a way through to speed their journey to the hills beyond, they came across a road which snaked its way down towards the plains below. Where the road intersected with the edge of the forest it passed through an enormous stone archway that appeared to have been incorporated into the forest itself, with the trees seemingly grafted onto it. So far, the arch had been the only true opening into the oppressive darkness and the road headed straight off into the trees, rapidly disappearing from view. The edge of the forest continued as it had done since they had started to follow it, running along the contours of the hill. Fireen called a brief halt while she and Rikoth explored the strange archway. They disappeared inside the forest, followed by several of their elite guards, rapidly fading into the impenetrable gloom.

Panx busied himself studying the intricate etchings on the archway, which were somehow familiar to him, although he could not remember why. He quickly sketched a few of the symbols, silently wishing that Marcus were here with his mobile camera. How easy it would be to record the images on the archway with one of those devices. He had just finished copying the symbols when Fireen and Rikoth appeared from within the archway, their nictitating membranes closing briefly to help reduce the sudden brightness to which they were now exposed.

'There is a wide road inside the forest,' said Fireen. 'It appears to wind its way through the trees, and represents our best chance of reaching the hills beyond.'

'Much better than skirting the entire forest,' hissed Rikoth. 'Who knows just how large it is, or how long the journey would take.'

'Agreed,' added Panx. 'Is it very dark in there?'

'Yes,' answered Fireen, 'but for some reason the aether has a strong presence within its borders. I was able to conjure up some light, so you should have no trouble accessing your powers.'

'It's very strange,' said Rikoth, 'but it feels less malevolent inside, almost as if the outer ring of trees were deliberately seeking to dissuade intruders from entering.'

The companions passed through the stone archway and headed into the darkness, leaving the red sky and the dull light that it provided far behind. They trudged onwards, following a road that was made from a hardwearing white coloured stone. It reflected what little light was able to penetrate the dense canopy, affording the group an easy to follow pathway.

Panx and Fireen, as the two most powerful magi in the group, set up a series of light globes that hovered above them as they marched along. Panx looked out into the darkness around him, where shadows skittered around the thick tree trunks as the light globes glided quietly by. He spotted a large animal, just inside the tangle of trees, which reminded him of the forest dwelling medrin that lived in the hills outside of Brind. The creature, which sported huge pointed antlers, darted away, heading deeper into the blackness of the trees.

Rikoth spotted a smaller pathway, leading away from the large road on which they were travelling, and took off with some of his elite warriors to investigate. He returned soon after, reporting that the small path led directly to a settlement, ancient and long abandoned. They had found some signs of recent occupation, although whoever had sheltered there had not been present for some time. His scouts had reported that the little pathway was the only way into or out of the ancient settlement, and that it was totally surrounded by thick forest in all other directions. Fireen had been contemplating finding a suitable place to make camp, as they had been marching now for nearly an entire sun-cycle, but she felt uneasy using the abandoned settlement as a base. So the group decided to press onwards. Whatever secrets had been left behind in these ancient ruins would have to remain hidden.

As the group continued their march through the gloomy forest, the scant red light that had been filtering down through the trees suddenly disappeared and they guessed that night had fallen. Panx felt a cold chill running down his spine at the thought of what foul creatures might come out at night here, and he tried to fight down the rising sense of panic which had washed over him. Fortunately, their connection to the aether seemed to be quite stable here inside the forest, and so they continued to march along the road, their way illuminated by the light globes which hovered silently above them.

They stopped briefly for some nourishment and soon after found themselves emerging from the forest, through another huge stone archway. This one had been badly damaged and its intricate surface details appeared to have been brutally smashed off, making it difficult for Panx to determine if the markings were different to those on the archway that they had discovered earlier. Even at night, the sky on this world had a blood red hue, and was lit up eerily by two small moons that appeared like a pair of eyes watching them from the heavens above.

Fireen decided that, as they had now made it through the forest, they should make camp here and get a little rest. She was uncertain how long the nights lasted on this world or what creatures might be prowling through the wilderness, so she instructed three of the warriors to watch over them while the others tried to get some sleep. The guards would be rotated throughout the night so that they might all get some rest. Rikoth joined two other warriors to stand first watch over the group, and the three Aellindi stalked off to find a good place to conceal themselves.

Panx fell asleep quickly, although his dreams were haunted by dreadful visions of his last visit to this world, where Navesh had been mortally wounded and had chosen to stay behind to face the oncoming demon horde.

The next morning, as the sun rose into the red-coloured sky, the group continued their journey towards the mountains that rose up before them. They left the forest behind and pushed on up into the foothills that would lead them all the way to the base of the huge peaks.

'I hope we don't have to go all the way up there!' said Panx, pointing up at the snowy mountains. 'It looks like a really tough trek.'

'I do not think that we will need to venture far into the mountains,' replied Fireen. 'I am certain that we are close to our goal now, and I think that we will find our friends somewhere in those foothills ahead of us.'

Rikoth appeared on the path in front of them, stalking back to commune with Fireen. He had scouted on ahead and had clearly returned with some important news.

'There's an abandoned camp ahead of us,' he said, stepping in beside Panx and Fireen.

'Another one?' replied Fireen. 'Like the one you discovered in the forest?'

'This one's different. It's very ramshackle in nature and doesn't look to have been created by the occupiers of this world. It looks distinctly out of place.'

'Navesh?' Panx asked hopefully.

'I didn't see any movement from within the camp, but it's certainly possible that our people are there, or were there recently.'

'Lead the way,' said Fireen, indicating for Rikoth to take them to the camp site.

They stood in the centre of the camp. It was abandoned, of that they were now certain. It had however definitely been occupied by their own people, although not as recently as they had hoped. There were crudely constructed huts covered with roughly thatched roofs, although many had caved in since they were last inhabited. Not much had been left behind to indicate who had been here, but Fireen had chanced across something of great importance.

'Look at this!' she hissed with an excited sibilant outcry, holding up a torn piece of cloth.

'What is it?' exclaimed Panx, as he hurried over to see what she had discovered.

'It is a message from Navesh,' she said, handing him the piece of dirty fabric. 'That is his family crest!'

Panx stretched the cloth out to reveal two crudely drawn images, hastily scribbled using a piece of charcoal. The edges of the images were faded and blurred by time and water damage, but Navesh's family crest was still clearly visible, as was the *Beacon of Rhasad*. There could be no mistaking the origin of the artist. Their people had been here.

'This has been here for some time,' said Rikoth, peering over Panx's shoulder at the clumsily drawn pictures. 'How can we be certain where he is now, or if he still lives?'

'We cannot!' replied Fireen. 'But we must take heart. We are on the right path and must keep going. We are close now, Rikoth.'

It was then that the demons found them.

A scream from the other side of the encampment alerted them to the danger and Rikoth swiftly raced to the aid of his wounded warrior, brutally dispatching the three skittering creatures that had managed to creep up on her. He helped her back to the centre of the camp where the others had congregated, leaving her in the care of Fireen and Panx, while he and the remaining warriors fanned out to receive the imminent assault.

The sound of the hunting horn sent a chill down their spines. It was a deep, bellowing noise, and Panx looked up at Fireen, fear showing on his young face.

'There is nothing more we can do here,' she whispered, indicating the injured guard, who had recovered sufficiently under their limited ministrations and was limping back over to rejoin Rikoth and her fellow warriors. 'We must prepare ourselves for battle.'

The warriors stood in silence, peering out into the curious yellow mist that had descended upon them, listening to the thunderous horn which seemed nearer and nearer with each blood curdling blast. They could hear the sounds of snarling animals coming from all around the camp, and they held their weapons at the ready.

The creatures attacked in a sudden, chaotic rush. They were huge, muscly beasts that bounded towards them on all four legs, each of which ended in a huge paw with multiple razor-sharp claws sprouting through the thick fur. Their eyes were blood red and glowed with an inner light. Thick gobbets of saliva dribbled from their gaping jaws, which were crammed with vicious looking teeth.

One of the beasts leapt at the nearest Aellindi warrior, who deftly stepped to one side and smashed his sword pommel into the creatures flank as it thundered past him. Rikoth dispatched the beast with one swift blow of his warhammer and then moved forward, intent on driving the rest of the hunting pack out of the camp. He smashed several more of the howling demon spawn into the ground, maiming or killing the animals with every stroke of his ancient weapon. He moved forward with each swing, laughing hysterically as he pummelled the beasts into the ground. His warriors followed his lead, expeditiously killing the creatures as they tried to engage them with tooth and claw.

One of the Aellindi warriors was caught momentarily off-guard, with four of the creatures leaping at him from out of the mist, pinning him to the ground and tearing into his flesh with savage hunger. Panx whirled his arms in the air as he completed the incantation that he hoped would unleash the power of the aether, allowing him to help his embattled friends. So far, since leaving the strange forest, the power of the aether had once again diminished and he hoped that he would be able to draw sufficiently upon it to be of some use here. As he had hoped, the flames shot forth from his outstretched fingertips, lancing with deadly precision into the snarling beasts that were tearing at the stricken warrior. To his surprise, the aether flowed easily, as if he had somehow connected with the untapped power that he suspected to be hidden on this world. The magical fire continued to erupt from within him, dislodging the snarling, nightmarish creatures from the warrior, who rolled aside and retrieved his weapon from the ground. He did not seem too badly injured and moved away from the burning animals, looking for another foe to engage. Panx continued to focus the power of the aether and soon the creatures had been reduced to a fine black ash, which gently settled onto the damp ground.

Fireen had also successfully tapped into the magical force, although she was directing her power towards her warriors, healing their wounds and enchanting their weapons, imbuing them with lightning speed or colossal strength. Rikoth had disappeared into the gloomy mist, following a group of the animals as they tried to circle around the camp. They could hear his triumphant cries as he caught up with the pack and slaughtered them all.

Suddenly the fight was over and an eerie quiet fell over the camp. The horrific sound of the hunting horn had ceased, as had the howling of the demonic hounds. Fireen stood beside Panx, looking out into the mist and surrounded by her warriors. They were all breathing heavily after the ferocious battle and waited nervously for the assault to begin anew. Their muscles ached terribly as they held their weapons at the ready.

Panx spotted something in the mist, his young eyes suddenly aware of movement just beyond the perimeter of the camp. He warned the others and they turned to face the threat, whilst quietly muttering the words to another spell, preparing to unleash its power on whatever appeared from the gloom. Their tension abated when Rikoth stalked out of the mist, his warhammer held firmly in his clawed fist, a look of pleasure on his face.

'That was fun!' he said as he approached his companions.

'You sound like you enjoyed yourself,' replied Fireen, shaking her head in disbelief.

'Yes I did,' hissed the Aellindi champion. 'It's been a while since I had such a challenge. Saven is good, but there's no jeopardy in training with a friend.'

'Look out!' cried one of the Aellindi warriors, pointing her sword into the mist behind Rikoth where a huge dark shape had suddenly appeared.

The creature that emerged from the yellow haze was unlike anything they had ever seen before. A huge monster with pale skin and thick blue veins, which looked as if its flesh were infested with grotesque burrowing worms, sat astride a powerful and heavily armoured beast. The demon warrior, no doubt the master of the hunt, thundered towards Rikoth swinging a huge spiked flail about its head. The charging animal had six powerful legs that drove it forward at tremendous speed. It was armoured from head to hoof with thick metal plates and two serrated horns protruded from the tip of its snout. The beast lowered its horns as it charged, attempting to spear the mighty Aellindi warrior from behind. Its master lashed out with the spiked ball as they closed in for the kill.

Rikoth turned to face the new threat, but was a fraction too slow. He narrowly avoided a gruesome death on the end of the animal's horns, but could not escape the vicious flail. The heavy ball hit him directly in the chest, denting his ancient armour but fortunately not piercing the enchanted plates. He was sent flying through the air, landing in a heap on the hard ground.

The charging beast continued its assault, this time aiming its vicious horns at Fireen who stood in the very centre of the encampment. The Aellindi warriors moved closer, forming a protective shield around their beloved leader. The beast did not slow as it approached and the demon huntmaster was once again swinging its crude weapon high above its head.

Something snapped then inside Panx's mind. He had been holding a spell on the end of his fingertips, waiting for the perfect moment to unleash it, but it had suddenly died, the words of the incantation sticking in the back of his dry throat. He watched the titanic creature as if it were moving in slow motion, hurtling towards Fireen, who looked defenceless and vulnerable. Suddenly his powers returned. It was as if he had unlocked the wellspring of the aetherium and released its energy in one colossal strike. The power erupted from within him like some thunderous storm, brutal and deadly. It was neither fire nor lightning nor winds which he unleashed, but a violent combination of them all, twisted into one devastating assault.

The demonic steed was hit with the full force of his attack and was knocked backwards, dislodging the rider from the saddle. The young magus continued to focus the power of the aether, afraid of the raw energy that was now surging through him, but unwilling to let go of the magic, fearful that it might fail him once again. He directed his fury at the demons, causing the spell to intensify further, and within moments the creature and its mount had been obliterated, torn to shreds in the magical conflagration. As the power died down, there was not a trace left of the demons. It was as if they had never existed at all. Even the yellow mist, which had appeared just before the beasts had first attacked them, was rapidly dissipating, allowing the blood red sky to shine down on them once more.

'That was different!' said Rikoth, limping over to where Panx and Fireen were standing. 'I've never seen that kind of magic before. What school is that, Panx?'

'I . . . I'm not sure what happened,' replied the young man, his voice failing him. 'Somehow I tapped into the aether and it all came flooding out of me.'

'Such raw power,' whispered Fireen. 'It must be something to do with the strange barriers that hold back the aether on this world. It is as if you either cannot form a connection at all, or it is so strong that it is almost uncontrollable. You must be careful!'

'I agree,' he replied. 'It felt as though the power was about to overwhelm me.'

'Indeed,' hissed Rikoth. 'I'm not a powerful magus, as you all know, but I think you're lucky to have survived that particular incantation. However, I'm glad that you managed to destroy that thing. It was some beast!' He placed his clawed hand on Panx's shoulder and squeezed gently in an unusual show of affection.

'Let us tend to the wounded,' said Fireen, 'before we become the target for another hunting party. We must leave this place as soon as possible and continue the search for Navesh. We have already dallied longer than I had intended.'

The group continued up into the foothills of the mountains, following Fireen's intuition as to the direction in which they would find their friends. After travelling for some time, they passed the site of an ancient temple which appeared to have been destroyed in a terrific battle between foes wielding tremendous power. There were shattered stone pillars strewn about the site, and the huge stone alter had been smashed into several large pieces. The broken remains of the temple lay on the ground and had been all but covered by a strange fibrous moss, which appeared to be dissolving the once smooth stone.

Fireen was certain that she had seen this place in one of her visions. She recalled seeing her people as they travelled up into the hills at the foot of the mountains, and this strengthened the resolve of her little rescue party. They were on the right track.

As they gained altitude the air began to feel a little colder than it had when they had initially entered the dark realm. Rikoth had been quiet since leaving the encampment, and he walked along in silence with his warhammer resting over his shoulder, looking around intently as the group made their way through the wilderness. He had admitted to Fireen that he had let the battle fury get the better of him when he had left the camp, stalking off alone into the mist to take the fight to the enemy. But he had been taken by surprise when the hunter had charged into their midst, and he vowed that he would not make that mistake again. And so he remained silent, ever alert as the group marched onward.

'There's movement up ahead,' whispered Rikoth as he readied his warhammer.

'I don't see anything,' replied Panx.

'It's straight ahead of us, behind those boulders.'

Panx slowed down, whispering the words of a defensive spell, trying to call upon the power of the aether once again. Fireen was also chanting and the Aellindi warriors had spread out around them.

A shrill whistle cut through the air, echoing off the hills around them and the group stopped walking, looking around for the enemies who were undoubtedly waiting to ambush them. The whistle was answered by two more high pitched calls that reminded Panx of the shrieking mountain garits back on his own world. No sooner had the answering whistles ceased echoing off the mountains, than a group of individuals stood up from behind their hiding places and advanced towards Fireen and her party. They were armed with crude looking weapons and were clearly ready to fight.

'Stay back,' shouted one individual, with a distinct Kingdom accent.

'I think we've found our people,' Panx whispered to Fireen.

'Yes, I believe we have.'

'What's Rikoth doing?' asked the young magus.

The Aellindi champion was stalking forward, his huge warhammer held high above his head and a war chant hissing from between his razor-sharp teeth. With tremendous speed he closed the distance between himself and the newcomers. They scattered as he approached, desperately trying to avoid combat with the fearsome warrior.

'Rikoth, those are our people!' shouted Fireen, trying to rein him in. 'Come back.'

She scurried forwards with Panx and her guards at her side, trying to look as unthreatening as possible, continuing to call out to Rikoth, who was desperately trying to engage their would-be ambushers.

Suddenly, a towering figure rose up from behind a large boulder directly in front of the berserking Rikoth, his arms raised in the air in a placating manner. Although he was leaner than when she had seen him last, Fireen immediately recognised the imposing figure and called out joyfully to him. But Praevir had not heard her, so focused was he on Rikoth, who was now circling him and swinging his warhammer towards his head. Praevir deftly stepped aside and moved in closer, wrapping his strong arms around his old friend, trying to calm him down before he could break free and slaughter them all.

Fireen came to stand before the pair of Aellindi councillors, who were still struggling with one another. She called out to Rikoth, desperately trying to convince him that he had made a mistake. The others, who had been concealed alongside Praevir behind the boulders, stepped out from their places of concealment. They held their crude weapons at the ready, although not daring to come between the pair of struggling Aellindi warriors. They looked emaciated and scrawny and were clothed in the dirty, torn remains of their once-fine military uniforms.

Finally, at Fireen's command, the other Aellindi guards moved in to restrain their frenzied champion, pulling him roughly from the struggling Praevir and gently restraining him. They removed his warhammer from his vice-like grip as Fireen approached the battered Praevir, who was still lying on the ground where he and Rikoth had been brawling.

'It is good to see you again, my dear friend,' she said, holding out her hand to him, helping him to stand.

'You too, Fireen,' replied Praevir, 'but what's wrong with Rikoth? Why did he attack us?'

'I do not know, Praevir, but he has not been himself since our arrival in the dark realm. His warrior spirit appears to be agitated and very easily stirred from its slumber.'

Praevir walked over to where the guards were holding Rikoth in check. The Aellindi champion appeared to have calmed down and watched as his old friend approached.

'You can let him go now,' Praevir commanded authoritatively.

The guards immediately complied, recognising him as a member of the Nesteris council. Rikoth took a step forward and Praevir stiffened slightly as the two warriors came face to face.

'I'm truly sorry, old friend,' whispered Rikoth, bowing his head before Praevir in a show of deep regret. 'I don't know what possessed me to attack you. All I could see through the blood rage was a band of vile demons that were intent on capturing us. Can you ever forgive me?'

'Of course, Rikoth,' replied Praevir, resting his hand gently on Rikoth's shoulder. 'This place does strange things to one's mind and some of us are still struggling to adapt to life here, even after all this time.'

'Two years is a long time to spend in this awful place,' said Panx, stepping forward and introducing himself to the tall Aellindi warrior.

'Two years?' replied Praevir, a look of confusion appearing on his gaunt face. 'By our reckoning, it's been over six full revolutions since we were trapped here!'

'Six years!' exclaimed Panx, unable to believe what Praevir had just told them. 'But how is that possible?'

'I don't know,' replied Praevir, 'perhaps the sands of time blow more quickly here, but we have judged it to be six cycles since we were brought here against our will.'

'How have you survived for so long?' asked Fireen.

'We managed to escape the dark citadel and fled into the hills beyond. For a long time the demons pursued us, hunting us down, but we finally found a place of refuge where the demons don't come. We've managed to survive here, if you can call it survival. Tell me,

Fireen, what happened at Rothford? I assume we won the war, but at what cost?'

'Yes, my friend, we won the war. But the cost was great. I promise that we will tell you every last detail, but first, where is Navesh? We must leave this place as soon as possible.'

'He's up there,' replied Praevir, pointing further up into the hills. 'Our settlement lies just over that ridge. He'll be overcome with joy to see you. I can't believe that you're truly here. It's like a dream, and I'm afraid to wake up to discover that we're still alone here.'

'If we had known that you had survived, Praevir,' whispered Fireen, 'we would have come to find you sooner. You must believe me.'

Praevir nodded and indicated that they should follow him. The two groups headed up towards the settlement. Some of those who had been trapped on the dark world asked questions about their homeland and the battle of Rothford, hoping for some news of their friends and family. Others, who were clearly traumatised by their capture and subsequent exile on this world, walked along in silence, glancing up furtively at their apparent saviours.

Praevir led them to the mouth of a small cave and beckoned for them to follow him inside. Fireen watched Rikoth very carefully for any indication that his battle fury was about to take control of him again, but he seemed to be quite calm and trudged along in silence. Panx scurried alongside Praevir, asking him questions about how they had managed to survive here for so long. The Aellindi warrior's answers were brief, and he seemed unwilling to elaborate further. He kept saying that, for some reason, the demons did not come to this place, and that Navesh would be able to explain it to them.

Finally they emerged from the cave and returned to the red-coloured daylight.

'There are children here, too!' exclaimed Panx, pointing to a group of youngsters who were chasing each other around the settlement.

All around them they could see people, the survivors of those who had been seized by Valken during the demon war. And there, in the centre of the small settlement, stood Navesh.

Thirteen

Marcus peered through the glass dome at the pier leading back to the veil at the edge of the world, his breath fogging the cold surface with each exhalation. The shock had not yet worn off and he was having trouble comprehending what he was looking at. Instead of the waters of the ocean, which he was expecting to see, and which always looked as though they were about to spill into outer space, there was nothing but icy tundra. The ancient energy veil sat over a frozen wasteland. There were large patches of snow with stunted yellow grass peeking through in places and small rocks scattered across its surface. The veil itself looked different too, and the light seemed to flicker with an alarming regularity. It appeared to be fading in and out of existence, allowing Marcus to catch brief glimpses of the world inside, which was normally obscured by the energy barrier.

Something in the back of his mind was yelling that this was not the same *Beacon of Olon* that he had left just minutes earlier. He was reeling from the events that had occurred since leaving Indrani, Idris and Tethine to watch over the portal into the dark world. The more he thought about what had befallen him, the more he was convinced that there was another *Beacon of Olon* that he did not know about. Or that something terrible had happened to his beloved Indrani since he had recklessly left to explore the new beacon in the desert. Could it be that somehow the journey back from that beacon had sent him hurtling forwards in time, to a point after some terrible disaster had taken place? What if the demons had returned, forcing their way into the world while he had been selfishly exploring the new beacon? For all he knew, the world of the Aellindi may have already fallen to the creatures from the dark world.

What the heck am I going to do? He thought. *I'm trapped here, wherever here is, and I have no idea how to get back. Marcus, you're a bloody idiot!*

It was freezing cold here and the shock of his predicament was beginning to weigh heavily upon him. He feared that if he were unable to get the beacon operating again, he would succumb to the icy temperature and freeze to death at the edge of outer space. It was as if the beacon were somehow exposed to the depths of the cosmos in which it appeared to be floating. Whenever he had been here before, the atmosphere inside the chamber had always been warm and pleasant. Something was very wrong, and he had no choice but to try and correct the problem before it was too late.

He picked up the tools that he had brought with him and busied himself removing the covers of the beacon's control panels. Before long he had revealed the dense tangle of wires, switches and relays that he had grown accustomed to whilst working within these ancient constructs.

However, after spending some time trying to revive the beacon, connecting systems together and bypassing others completely, he finally admitted defeat. No matter what he did, he could not squeeze any power from the reactor core, located deep underneath the beacon. He had not brought a portable power unit with him, and cursed himself for the oversight. He had felt so useless, waiting at the portal for Panx and Fireen to return, and had given in to his reckless desire to check out the new beacon. That same recklessness had ultimately been responsible for his arrival on the world of the Aellindi, when he had sent his plastic yellow duck on a journey through time.

Finally, he threw one of the tools across the chamber in an unusual display of frustration, and then stood up, uncertain of what to do next. As far as he could determine, he had two realistic options. He could head downstairs and try to gain access to the underground chamber that housed the power core, or he could head back along the pier and see if there was a way to get through the veil and go in search of help. He doubted very much that the first option would be successful, as the only way he had found to access the underground chamber was via the central lift, which was currently inoperable. The second option did not appeal to him either, but he considered it to be his best chance for survival.

He retrieved his discarded tools and swung his backpack over his shoulders, adjusting the straps so that it was as comfortable as possible. Casting one final glance around the chamber he desperately sought something that he might have overlooked, some way to reactivate the beacon that he had not yet considered. But, unusually for him, he was stumped. The apparent damage to the beacon's systems was beyond his ability to repair, at least with the limited tools that he had brought with him.

He headed towards the stairs, intent on going down to the pier, when he heard a noise. The sound was coming from the stairwell. It was a quiet shuffling sound, as if someone were slowly hauling themselves up the long winding staircase, puffing slightly as they went. He also heard muffled whispers and realised that whoever was approaching, they were not alone. He looked around for a weapon, realising that he had taken his sword belt off whilst working on the beacon's damaged systems and had failed to retrieve it. *Still not thinking like a warrior,* he thought, *Saven would never let me hear the last of this!* He retrieved his trusty blade and, gently drawing it from its scabbard, stalked over to the top of the stairwell, ready to defend himself from whomever, or whatever approached.

Of all the things that his imagination had conjured up, from snarling demons to muscly bandits, he was not prepared for the two individuals who emerged from the stairs. They were both Aellindi, of that he was certain, but they were of a type that he had not yet encountered. They were old, too. Older than any of Fireen's people that he had seen so far, although they still had an air of vigour about them and did not appear overly frail. One was male and the other female. Both were tall and slender in form, with purple scales that seemed thin and almost translucent. They were clad in thick animal hides, which were better suited to the deathly cold atmosphere within the beacon than Marcus's thin clothing.

The two aged Aellindi stopped when they saw Marcus standing there, holding his sword in a defensive posture. They looked at one another and Marcus could almost sense the psychic messages passing between them.

'Hello there,' said Marcus, as pleasantly as possible, sliding his sword back into its scabbard and letting it hang once more from his belt.

'So, you are finally here!' said the Aellindi male.

'We've been waiting for you to arrive for many years,' added the female.

'Do not be alarmed,' continued the male, looking down towards Marcus's sword, 'we mean you no harm.'

'Who are you?' asked Marcus, perplexed at their apparent anticipation of his arrival.

'We're the Aellindi,' replied the woman, as if that should have been obvious.

'Yes, I can see that, but who are you and where are you from? Where is Fireen?'

'I am sorry, my young friend,' replied the Aellindi man. 'My name is Endellion, and this is Tuuvar, my mate. We do not know this . . . Fireen. We are from the settlement of Varfell, which is inside the veil. It is our turn to keep vigil at the beacon and we were watching from the end of the pier when we noticed strange flashes of light emanating from the observation chamber.'

'We knew it would be you,' hissed Tuuvar excitedly, 'so we hurried here to greet you. Welcome, friend!'

'Please, call me Marcus,' replied the astounded professor, unable to think of anything better to say. 'You say that you were expecting me to arrive and that it was your turn to keep watch. How is that possible? How could you know that I was going to be here?'

'It's written in the prophecy,' replied Tuuvar.

'Oh,' replied Marcus, a sudden feeling of dread settling into the pit of his stomach, 'another prophecy. I ought to have guessed!'

'Yes,' hissed Endellion, 'we are members of an order known as *The Watchers*, a small enclave of Aellindi who have dedicated our lives to *The Prophecy of The One*, and we have been waiting for generations for you to arrive.'

'And what does this prophecy say?'

'It is said that a stranger will come from another world and, in our moment of greatest need, will lead the people of this world to a place of safety.'

'I'm afraid,' replied Marcus, frustrated with his apparent ability to get himself into trouble, 'that I can't lead you anywhere at the moment. The beacon is dead, I have no idea how to reactivate it, and I don't know where the heck I am!'

'You should come with us?' hissed Tuuvar. 'Our leader will explain the prophecy to you. Then we can determine the next step.'

'Okay,' replied Marcus warily, unable to think of an excuse not to go with them. 'Where is your leader?'

'He resides in Varfell,' said Endellion, 'within the boundary of the veil. It will take some time for us to get there, so we should hasten.'

They descended the stairs and headed out onto the long pier, which led back towards the edge of the world. Marcus had forgotten the quietness that pervaded the strange place that existed beyond the veil, having only been on the pier once before. It was eerie, like he was walking within some vacuum chamber where no sound was able to reach his ears. He carefully looked over the side of the pier, and a sense of vertigo washed over him as he stared down into the depthless black void. Endellion grabbed his arm protectively, steering him closer to the middle of the walkway. Clearly he did not want to lose their saviour over the edge, not after they had waited for generations for him to arrive on their cold world.

As they neared the end of the pier, where it was rooted to the edge of the world and protruded out into space, Marcus could see a group of large tents huddled together on the frozen tundra, just outside of the flickering veil. There were animals there too, amongst the tents, which looked like huge wolves. He assumed that the Aellindi had brought them, to drag some sort of sled across the frozen ground, much like huskies did back on his own world.

'Where are the rest of your people?' he asked, breaking the silence. 'You said that *The Watchers* were in Varfell, but what about the others? Are they still on Nesteris?'

'We've never heard of Nesteris,' replied Tuuvar. 'We originally come from Braefell, a city near the centre of the world fragment. Most of our people are there.'

So, thought Marcus, *if this is still the world of the Aellindi, what has happened to them since I left the beacon in the desert, and what has happened to their beloved Nesteris?*

'Okay ... so what about the Visnach, on K'vith, and does King Elridan still rule over the Kingdom of the Isles?' he asked, trying to build up a clearer picture of the current state of affairs on the world.

'The Visnach?' hissed Endellion, sibilantly. 'They are scattered across the world, living in small nomadic tribes and forever hunted by their dark cousins, the Visnaer. I have never heard of K'vith, or King Elridan, and there is no such kingdom here that I am aware of. I am not sure where you have come from, Marcus, but clearly you are far from home. Rest assured that the leader of *The Watchers*, Arkadin, will be able to tell you more.'

This was too much to take in. Who were the Visnaer, and why were they hunting the Visnach? Marcus suddenly remembered the huge map that Panx had discovered, and the truth dawned on him. He had not been sent hurtling into the future, but had instead been transported across the vacuum of space. Somehow, he had ended up on another fragment of the Ancestors' ancient homeworld. The thought was sobering and he followed the two Aellindi in silence as they neared their encampment.

The pack animals were yapping loudly by the time their masters had returned from the beacon, as if they were communicating with the two aged Aellindi. Endellion disappeared inside one of the tents and returned moments later with a large bundle of clothing which he handed to the shivering Marcus.

'Here,' he whispered, 'put these on. It is very cold here, this close to the edge of the world.'

'Yeah, I noticed that,' replied Marcus, his teeth chattering as he fumbled with the sinewy strands that held the bundle together.

He finally managed to pull a large animal skin around him, trapping a layer of air inside the thick fur which soon began to warm up. The cloak was a little long for him, being made for these tall and slender Aellindi, but it offered protection against the invasive cold. He pulled on a hat and a pair of mittens and, slapping his palms together, proceeded to coax his freezing hands back to life.

While Marcus was donning his new clothing, Tuuvar went to prepare the sled, attaching it to the harness that held the excited pack of animals together. The beasts were given chunks of bloody red meat, which they devoured ravenously, leaving bright red stains on the snowy tundra. As Marcus stood watching the gruesome spectacle, Endellion informed him that the animals were known as bavnok, a rare breed of tundra hound that the Aellindi had domesticated and trained to haul their sleds across the frozen landscape.

The bavnok were huge, easily the size of the wild wolves that still roamed the remote wilderness of Alaska, back on his own world. They had four powerful legs and were covered in thick, brilliant white fur and had long, tooth-filled snouts which were currently stained red with blood. Marcus was wary of getting too close to the creatures, lest they mistake him for a threat to their masters. However, the two Aellindi assured him that they had already told the pack who he was and that he need not fear the animals in any way.

After spending a little time at the encampment, which Marcus used to warm himself by the fire and to eat a little food, the Aellindi indicated that they were ready to depart. With Tuuvar's assistance, Marcus climbed aboard the sled and hunkered down next to their packs. The Aellindi stood at the front of the sled, calling out instructions to the bavnok, which yelped and barked in reply. At first the noise was deafening, but soon the yapping animals quietened and Marcus felt the sled begin to move, easing gracefully over the frozen ground. To begin with the animals struggled to haul the large sled, but after a while they were almost flying across the icy terrain and the bavnok howled, as if in joy, as they headed into the veil.

Tuuvar clambered to the back of the sled and settled down beside Marcus, indicating that Endellion would control the pack for now. She would swap when he needed to rest. They were passing through the veil now and Marcus looked up at the flickering energy barrier, which appeared to be changing colours rapidly. It was totally unlike the one he was used to seeing on the other world fragment. There was also a faint buzzing sound as the power of the veil discharged out into the vacuum beyond, its once protective energy leeching away with every passing moment. The veil was obviously failing and Marcus wondered just what kind of life had managed to survive on this fragment, which was essentially open to the cold depths of space.

'What's happening to the veil here?' he asked.

'It's been failing for several generations now, but has rapidly worsened of late. It started a long time ago, with a bright yellow flash illuminating the sky and tremendous winds that assailed us for almost an entire revolution of our world fragment. The winds have died down but the intense coldness of the void continually seeps into our world, creeping inexorably towards the inner lands. We believe that a critical point has been reached and that we have only a short time remaining before the veil gives out altogether and we lose what little protection it still affords us.'

Marcus was truly saddened to hear that news and his mind began to consider the possibilities, to think about what he might to do to help these people avoid an icy death. Perhaps there are other beacons on this fragment, as there were on his own. Perhaps he could find some way to reactivate them and use the portals to cross over to Nesteris. If he arrived here via a beacon portal, then it stood to reason that just such a portal might offer them a means of escape.

As he considered the twist that his life had taken, they emerged from beneath the veil and the world inside was fully revealed for the first time. Ahead of him, far in the distance, lay a range of huge, snow-capped mountains. Beneath the giant peaks, the tundra stretched onwards for almost as far as his eyes could see. In the distance, at the base of the mountains, the tundra rose up slowly, giving way to foothills that led up towards the snowy peaks. There were no animals here, other than those that bore the sled across the desolate wilderness, and Marcus assumed that the climate must be too intolerable, even for the hardiest of creatures.

'How far is your settlement?' he asked.

'Still a long way to go yet, Marcus. We'll not arrive there much before the sun sets behind the mountains,' replied Tuuvar, pointing to the towering peaks ahead. 'We'll need to stop frequently to rest and feed the pack, for even they tire quickly in this unforgiving place.'

The sled moved swiftly on, passing further into the world on which Marcus now found himself marooned. The veil had faded into the distance and a snow storm had descended from the heavens above, settling thickly around them. They covered themselves in extra layers of waterproof skins in an attempt to ward off the worst of the freezing weather.

After many hours of travelling they slowed down, as the bavnok started to haul the sled up into the foothills at the base of the mountain range, along a well-used track. It was early evening now and the snow storm had finally abated, although the sun was rapidly dropping, taking with it the faint warmth that it had provided. The air temperature was dropping and Marcus's breath began to freeze as he exhaled, leaving ever growing ice crystals on his fur-lined hood.

The terrain levelled off once more and as they rounded a huge pile of boulders, which had tumbled down during some long forgotten avalanche, Marcus spotted the Aellindi settlement of Varfell. He was expecting something small and temporary, like the encampment where his two Aellindi guides had resided, but what he saw far exceeded his expectations.

Varfell was clearly very old. The dwellings reminded him of those that were common throughout the island of Nesteris. Most were made from the same white stone as their counterparts on Nesteris, which here, on this freezing world, blended in to the snowy landscape. Even the rich blue-coloured stone insets, made from highly polished pieces of lapis lazuli, were present here. It was as if the same architects had overseen the design and construction of both settlements. At the centre of Varfell, rising up above the smaller stone buildings, was a large temple complex that bore a magnificent statue of some Aellindi hero on its roof. The warrior held a spear aloft, as if crying out in triumph, having just vanquished some ancient foe. Marcus was reminded of Navesh, who had carried a similar weapon during their quest to defeat Valken's army of darkness.

There were many Aellindi hurrying about the settlement, many of which looked similar in form to Endellion and Tuuvar, as well as some types that he had not yet encountered. They stopped to watch the sled pass by, obviously recognising the two Aellindi who were most likely returning from the veil before their assigned time. Marcus could feel their eyes boring into him as they headed deeper into the settlement. He could sense their hope radiating out and he feared that he might let these people down, feared that he would die here without ever seeing Indrani and their child again.

'We'll head straight to the temple,' said Tuuvar.

'Arkadin will be overjoyed to see you and will wish to speak with you immediately,' added Endellion, pointing to the temple which was growing nearer with every passing moment.

The bavnok navigated the streets with practised ease and came to a stop outside the huge temple complex. A large crowd had gathered around them, quietly watching as Tuuvar and Endellion hopped down and gathered up a few items from the back of the sled. The two aged Aellindi beckoned Marcus to follow them and then headed through the huge wooden doors and into the temple.

Marcus took one final glance around, smiling as casually as he could at the Aellindi that had gathered there. He knew that they recognised him as a stranger from another world and that they all thought him to be their saviour, but he simply did not know what to say to them. So he took a deep breath, coughing slightly as the cold air was drawn into his lungs, pushed open the doors and went inside.

Fourteen

Navesh stood there with tears trickling over his golden scales, leaving four wet trails across his gaunt cheeks. He was like a statue, rigid and immobile. Several small children pulled at the hem of his ragged, dirty cloak, pointing towards the newcomers and asking him who they were. But he did not answer, his voice having caught in the back of his throat. Panx could see that his friend's body was trembling slightly as he struggled to contain the emotions that threatened to overwhelm him. In the end it was Fireen who broke through the quiet, awkward silence that had descended upon the centre of the ramshackle settlement.

'It is good to see you, my dear friend,' she hissed, walking over to Navesh and embracing him in an unusual display of affection.

Navesh stood motionless for a moment longer whilst Fireen hugged him closely, and then he finally put his arms around the Aellindi leader. Panx and Rikoth exchanged glances and then moved forward, emboldened by Navesh's response to their arrival. Praevir gently ushered the inquisitive children away, promising that everything would be explained soon and that they were, at long last, going to go home. Navesh finally disengaged from his emotional embrace and looked around at the others who had made the dangerous journey to find him.

'I never believed, not truly believed, that I'd ever see you again,' he whispered, his voice quiet and raw with emotion. 'I've been calling out to you for years now, through the aether, but after a while I resigned myself to the fact that the messages hadn't reached you. I was going to cease calling, but Praevir persuaded me not to give up. I'm so glad now that I heeded his advice.'

'We have only recently begun to receive your calls, my friend,' replied Fireen. 'I have been having visions in which you were trapped here, calling out to me. And Idris has been having dreams about you too.'

'Idris,' hissed Navesh softly. 'Yes, I've called out to him on many occasions, and to Tethine. Idris, my dear Idris!'

'It is thanks to him that we are here now,' continued Fireen. 'Had he not come forward to tell the council of his dreams, I might have concluded that my own visions were nothing more than past memories settling into place, or my own mind finally coming to terms with your loss.'

'We should go inside,' said Navesh, awkwardly steering the conversation away from the topic of his mate and children, lest his emotions overwhelm him once more. 'There's much to tell you all.'

Navesh and Praevir led the newcomers into a small tent, which had been constructed with thick branches and covered in the skins of some large animal. Fireen followed closely behind, with Panx and Rikoth entering last. The Aellindi guards remained outside, ever alert for a demon incursion, and the inquisitive children crept up towards the tent, spying on the strangers. Navesh poured them all a drink of fresh, cool water, which he explained was from a small spring that had been discovered in the area, around which their small settlement had been built.

They all had many questions and, in an attempt to avoid a disjointed, garbled conversation, Fireen indicated that Navesh should begin with his own tale. The gaunt and malnourished Aellindi remained quiet for a moment as he marshalled his thoughts, and then, after taking several deep calming breaths, he told them everything.

He told them of how he had fought the demons in the dark citadel, gravely wounded and aided by the Aellindi warrior that had chosen to stay and fight by his side. However, neither had perished that day. For just as the fight looked to be at and end, when they both thought that they could hold out no longer, several Aellindi warriors had appeared from within the keep, led by Praevir and Maevar, with others from the Kingdom and K'vith trailing behind. They had all been captured during the battle of Rothford and brought back to the dark world where they had been subjected to brutal torture.

With the aid of the welcome reinforcements, they had swiftly dispatched the remaining demons and escaped the citadel. They were pursued by several inquisitors but managed to evade them for long enough to render aid to Navesh and his guard, enough to prevent them from dying, but not sufficient so as to fully restore them. Fireen noted that her friend walked with a slight limp and looked as though he might still be in pain, even after all this time.

'We ran from the inquisitors, who hounded us without pause,' hissed Navesh. 'They gradually whittled down our numbers, but we finally came to a large forest with dark, almost impenetrable trees along its borders.'

'Yes, we came that way too!' whispered Rikoth.

'The archways that led into the forest seemed to offer some protection from the pursuing demons,' continued Navesh, 'and they refused to follow us into the trees. We stayed there for a short time, exploring as much as we dared, even discovering a small settlement. That's where I began to reach out to you, as the aether seems particularly strong within the borders of the forest.

'But we didn't linger in those trees for too long, as we soon discovered that the forest was home to other dangers. We were attacked by creatures that we couldn't see or hear, and so we followed the road out of the forest and continued our desperate flight.

'Finally, we came to this place, and soon determined that the demons wouldn't follow us here. For the first time in a long while we felt safe, and we've remained here ever since.'

'How did you free yourself, Praevir?' asked Panx.

'We think that when Valken was killed, his hold over us was disrupted and we were able to escape the confines of his citadel.'

Finally, when Navesh and Praevir finished recounting their extraordinary tale of survival, they indicated that they would very much like to hear the news from their own world. They were desperate to find out what had happened since the war. Fireen informed them that the battle for Rothford had been won, although the cost had been great. Had it not been for the heroic efforts of those who had sealed the tear in the void, casting Valken back to his own world, he would have been unstoppable and all those who fought against the demons would have perished. They had been within moments of defeat when the army of darkness had simply vanished. Navesh looked close to tears as Fireen told him how his little band of adventurers had ultimately saved their world.

She recounted how the demons had broken free of the aetheric prison in which the Aellindi had held them, and how they had then rampaged across Nesteris. His golden colour faded from his scales when she informed him how many Aellindi had been slaughtered in the brutal incursion, and that during the chaos, one of the three stones of power had been lost. Navesh was distraught, and kept saying that if only he had managed to mend the tear in the rift sooner, perhaps some of the loss of life might have been prevented and the stone would still be in the hands of the Aellindi.

'Do not blame yourself, Navesh,' said Fireen, trying to comfort him. 'You did everything that you could. Nobody could have asked more of you.'

She went on to inform him that her visions, which were usually centred around him calling out to her, also showed tantalising glimpses of the lost stone of power. She had become convinced that the stone was now in the possession of a blue-skinned female, likely the queen of an as yet unknown people, and a powerful necromancer.

Navesh pondered all that Fireen had just divulged. But he could not explain why his reaching out to her would have induced a connection with these blue-skinned people.

'I've not seen these blue-skinned warriors that you speak of,' he said, confirming what Fireen already believed, that these creatures were not part of Valken's evil army. 'That's not to say that it's not possible,' he added, still considering what he had just been told, 'but I've not seen them. Perhaps it was the power of the stone itself that connected with my call for help, from whatever world this blue-skinned queen inhabits?'

'Perhaps,' replied Fireen.

Fireen finished her tale by informing them that the remaining council members and Admiral Mochus from the Kingdom were monitoring the approaching army of the undead, waiting to see what it would do. She wanted to head back to Nesteris as soon as possible to find out what had occurred in her absence. She had not heard back from Saven or Givas before travelling to the *Beacon of Olon*, and feared that something terrible had befallen them.

'Where's Maevar?' asked Rikoth.

'She was killed, several years ago,' Praevir replied sadly, 'when we were ambushed by a group of those inquisitor things.'

'I am so sorry to hear that,' said Fireen. 'She was a good friend.'

'Yes, she was,' replied Praevir, 'and will be forever missed.'

'Do you know why the demons haven't followed you here?' asked Panx, after a brief silence, in honour of Maevar.

'Yes, Ambassador, I believe so,' replied Navesh. 'Although I must confess that I don't fully understand it.'

Fireen, Panx and Rikoth looked quizzically at one another, not quite understanding Navesh's cryptic remark.

'Perhaps it would be easier if I just showed you what I meant,' added Navesh, seeing that his friends did not understand his meaning. 'Follow me and I'll show you what I've discovered.'

They followed Navesh and Praevir deeper into the foothills, climbing higher into the mountain range that surrounded the little settlement. They had left the guards behind to watch over the camp, although Navesh had assured them that it was not necessary. The little group walked for most of the day before reaching the outskirts of what appeared to be an ancient settlement. The buildings immediately looked familiar to Panx, who commented on their similarity to those that he had uncovered around the *Beacon of Andin*.

At Navesh's inquisitive glance, he quickly apprised him of the excavations that had been performed on the small island and what they had found there. He told Navesh of how Marcus had managed to reactivate many of the functions of the ancient beacons and that they were now used in order to travel rapidly between them.

'You've been very busy, Ambassador,' hissed Navesh, clearly excited by the news. 'When I get back home I'll want to come and see these excavations for myself!'

'Of course. I'd be delighted to show you.'

As the group continued into the abandoned settlement they saw a significant number of ruined buildings. It was as if the entire city had been subjected to a brutal, destructive invasion. Many had been reduced to no more than fragments of splintered rock, although the odd one or two had been spared and survived mostly intact. Panx drank in the sights hungrily, darting in and out of the buildings, noting the wondrous artefacts that still remained inside some of them.

'This is amazing,' he said, his voice full of childlike delight. 'Some of these buildings are just empty, ruined shells, but others still contain a few astonishing items. It's a real shame that we have to leave all this behind.'

'Don't worry,' replied Navesh, 'I've collected a few items which we'll take back to Nesteris for further investigation. It may also be possible in the future to open up a portal directly to this site, allowing us to return here and explore further, without the fear of a demon attack. But, my friends, this is not the sole reason that I've brought you all here,' he added, waving his arm theatrically across the ruined city. 'Follow me!'

He led them further into the city ruins, weaving his way through the rubble-strewn streets. They passed many strange buildings and constructs, including several odd looking carriages that appeared to have been built without wheels. As the sun dipped down between the huge mountain peaks that surrounded the city, Navesh finally stopped and pointed across a large open area.

'There,' he said triumphantly, 'look at that!'

The others looked in the direction that he was pointing and were greeted with a most wondrous site. Across from where they were standing was one of the Ancestors' beacons. It had been badly damaged, almost destroyed in some ancient battle, and had toppled over. But it was still perfectly recognisable for what it was. The fact that it had toppled over onto the surrounding buildings explained why they had not spotted it before now. Perhaps it had fallen at the same time as the city, or perhaps its destruction had heralded the final days of the people that had once lived here. They simply did not know.

As they moved closer to the ruined beacon, they noticed that the glass dome had been shattered, either by some titanic release of energy or simply during its collapse from its once lofty height. Interestingly, the metallic framework that supported the glass dome, which was usually transparent, was now fully visible and looked like the skeletal remains of some long dead creature.

'The demons don't come here,' whispered Praevir, as if the original occupants of the city might overhear his words. 'Perhaps this place was once home to beings which, even to this day, the demons are wary of.'

'There is still power here, somewhere,' hissed Navesh, 'although we've not been able to locate its source. It's a pity that Marcus was not able to come with you. I'm certain that he'd have been able to revive this ancient structure.'

'He'll be sorry that he missed this, that's for sure,' replied Panx, his eyes darting around the site of the toppled beacon, looking for clues as to its origin. 'He'll definitely want to come back with us later!'

'But this would indicate that our Ancestors were here, a long time ago,' said Rikoth.

'Yes,' replied Navesh, 'I don't believe that Valken and his minions are the first to have inhabited this world.'

'So did the demons invade them and steal their world? Or were they already gone by the time Valken arrived?' asked Panx.

'I don't know, my friend,' replied Navesh, 'and we may never find out the answer to that question.'

The group spent a little more time looking around the toppled beacon, before Navesh indicated that they should set up camp for the night. As the evening drew on and the two moons shone down on them from the eerie red-coloured night sky, they took in turns to recount their tales. Navesh was overcome to find out that Marcus and Indrani had named their child after him, and he vowed to renew his friendship with the stranger from another world as soon as they returned to the *Beacon of Olon*.

The companions made it back to Navesh's settlement shortly before noon the next day and immediately set about preparing the citizens for the journey back to the portal. Fortunately, as Fireen had homed in on the forest where Navesh had initially called out, the refugees would not have to travel as far as they had when escaping from the dark citadel. They only needed to make it back to the portal, located a short distance beyond the far edge of the forest. They would spend another night in the safety of their little settlement, setting out at first light the following day, hopefully entering the safety of the forest before sundown. Navesh had assured them that although the forest appeared to be haunted, the group would not be lingering long enough to attract the attention of its spectral inhabitants. They should be able to pass through safely, although one night inside the forest would be preferable to camping in the open land beyond, where the hunters roamed.

As the sun dipped toward the horizon, Fireen considered how long they had already been here. She had consulted Navesh on the passing of time in the dark realm and he had assured her that he and his charges had been here for a little over six revolutions. This fact was confirmed by the age of some of the children, who had not been born until after the group had escaped the demon pursuit. So, Fireen deduced that although many days had passed since she had travelled through the portal, only one in every three of those days would have passed by on her own world. She desperately hoped that things had not deteriorated too badly on Nesteris.

The screams shocked her from her musings, alerting her to some nearby danger. She rose from her meditation within the tent and emerged into the failing light outside. Rikoth was already there, his huge two-handed warhammer in his hands, as was Navesh, Praevir and many others. Looking around the settlement, she did not at first spot the assailant until Rikoth smashed his ancient weapon down on one of the human refugees, splitting his skull with brutal force and knocking his ruined body to the ground. It was then that it finally dawned on her. Rikoth had lost his inner struggle against his agitated warrior spirit, and there was now a real danger that he might kill everybody in the camp.

Navesh and Praevir were approaching him with arms outstretched, trying to calm him with soothing words and friendly gestures. But Rikoth was clearly beyond their help. His eyes had lost all focus, the pupils dilating wildly, masking all trace of his irises, and they now appeared as nothing more than dark globes filled with glistening black oil.

He swung his warhammer again, narrowly missing Praevir, who had been attempting to restrain him as he had done before. Navesh had drawn his golden spear from within his tattered travel cloak, its glowing shaft erupting from the ornate handle and coalescing into solid form. But he appeared hesitant to use it on his friend and waited while the others attempted to subdue the frenzied warrior.

Rikoth suddenly broke free from the circle of Aellindi guards that were trying to corral him towards a quiet area of the settlement. He swung his warhammer around his head in mindless rage, causing the others to take several steps backwards. The moment he was free of his would be captors, he set about attacking anyone within his reach. He crushed skulls and smashed bodies to the ground, where they lay still, bleeding profusely into the dirt.

Chaos ensued as the inhabitants of the settlement tried desperately to flee the carnage. The children were screaming and Rikoth made a sudden move towards them, intent on destroying the vermin that had infested his land. Fireen called out to him, drawing upon what little power she could muster from the unpredictable aether. But it was not enough. Rikoth ignored her and continued to rampage across the settlement, followed by Navesh, Praevir and the other Aellindi, who were still trying desperately to subdue him.

It was then that Panx arrived. He had been talking to one of the Visnach survivors on the other side of the settlement, when he had heard the commotion and had come to investigate. As he rounded one of the large tents, Rikoth's warhammer swished past his face and he took several steps backwards, thankful for his quick reflexes. As the rampaging warrior surged past him he noticed the bloody carnage that had been left in his wake, leaving him feeling nauseous and angry.

'Rikoth – Stop!' he shouted in a commanding voice.

The Aellindi hero faltered, shaking his head, trying to dispel the authoritative command that Panx was trying to enforce upon him. He took another step forward, resisting the young magus, slowly casting off the invisible chains in which Panx was trying to bind him.

'RIKOTH – STOP!' repeated Panx, much louder this time and suddenly the aether flowed from him, unrestricted and powerful.

An intense white light enveloped the enraged Aellindi hero, holding him still. Rikoth was unable to move and simply stood there, looking menacingly at the young magus, his pointed teeth bared in a vicious snarl and his black eyes promising extreme violence. Panx stood his ground, holding his arms out, keeping the inert Rikoth within his magical grasp.

Fireen approached, looking with undisguised awe at the tremendous power that Panx had just unleashed.

'How long can you hold him?' she asked.

'I'm not sure. I'm not under any strain at the moment though. What should we do now?'

'We should tie him up,' replied Praevir. 'He's already done this once before, and I fear that we can no longer trust him.'

'Perhaps when we get home he'll come to his senses. Once the influences of this vile world have worn off,' added Navesh.

'That is it!' replied Fireen, as if suddenly enlightened. 'It is not his warrior spirit that is agitated, but his very life force.'

She recounted how Rikoth had fought Valken during the battle of Rothford and that, had the demons not been dragged back to their own world, would have surely been killed. She proceeded to tell them of how she and Panx had restored Rikoth to full vigour, using the stolen life essences from within the dark lord's wicked blade.

'So you think that some of Valken's own life force may have been transferred into Rikoth,' hissed Navesh, anticipating what Fireen was about to say, 'and now that we're here on the dark world, the demon is somehow reasserting control?'

'Yes, that is exactly what I think,' she replied. 'We must expunge this foul spirit before we lose our friend forever!'

'But how do we do that?' asked Panx, still holding the raging Rikoth within his aetheric grip.

'The guards will restrain him and then we must work together to forcefully remove the spirit of Valken from within him,' replied Fireen, motioning the guards to disarm and subdue the huge warrior.

'That sounds very risky,' replied Panx, looking rather worried at the prospect of removing Rikoth's life force from within him. 'What if we cannot precisely control what we are removing? We could kill him.'

'Yes, my young friend, it is extremely dangerous. But we have little choice. The ritual might cause serious harm to Rikoth, depending on the degree of corruption. But to do nothing would risk further outbursts of rage that we might eventually be unable to contain, forcing us to kill him.'

'We've got no choice,' added Navesh, 'we must perform the ritual, right now, while we still have a chance.'

'Please, Fireen, get this thing out of me,' whispered Rikoth, in a moment of calm lucidity. 'I don't care if it kills me. Release me from this endless torment. I don't want to watch from behind my own eyes as I kill more innocent people. DO IT NOW. PLEASE!'

'Guards, hold him steady,' commanded Fireen, as Panx finally released the spell that had contained the berserking warrior, who had started muttering in some unknown, garbled tongue. 'You must provide the magical energy, Panx, as you seem to have regained a strong connection to the aether. Channel the power into Navesh and I, and we will redirect it into Rikoth, seeking out the corruptive forces and casting them out of his body.'

Panx nodded and then reached inside of himself, connecting with the power of the aether that he alone had somehow managed to unlock. He gathered his strength and then let the power flow with such force that those around him were aware of a shimmering haze extending from his outstretched hands and pouring into Fireen and Navesh. The two Aellindi magi stiffened slightly as the full force of the power reached them, struggling to contain the raw energy that Panx was discharging.

'Easy, Ambassador,' hissed Navesh in warning, 'we cannot control this much power.'

'That is much better,' whispered Fireen, as Panx modulated the flow of aether and the shimmering haze became no more than slight disturbance of the air around him.

Rikoth continued to struggle as Fireen and Navesh approached him with their arms outstretched, as if they intended to make physical contact. But they halted a short distance from his body and began to chant in perfect unison. Rikoth stiffened, as if in pain, closing his eyes and screwing up his scaled face, desperately trying to resist the ritual that was being forced upon him.

'DO IT!' he muttered, gritting his sharp teeth in barely controlled rage, the two conflicting aspects of his inner mind fighting for control of his faculties.

Fireen and Navesh continued the ritual, increasing the tempo of their chanting, extending the magical aurora to encompass their friend's entire body.

'I can feel it,' whispered Fireen, her eyes closed tightly in concentration, 'such anger and cruelty. We must focus on that, Navesh. Draw it out and cast it back whence it came.'

Rikoth screamed as the magic perfused his tense, rigid body, seeking out the corruption that had slowly manifested itself since their arrival on this world. Panx was also feeling the strain and his body trembled visibly as the power flowed through him. But it was working. He could see a faint black aurora around the struggling Rikoth that was darkening with every passing moment, as they drew the demon from within him. Rikoth struggled intensely, almost breaking free from the guards that were restraining him. He thrashed and spasmed wildly and then, suddenly, slumped back into the arms of his people, who gently supported his limp body.

Finally, when Panx felt the aether begin to fail, the ritual fizzled and died. Rikoth was still being held by the guards, although his visage was peaceful, less agitated, and his face was calm once more. The black aurora that had formed around the possessed warrior, like a dark storm, was dissipating into the air around them, growing fainter with every passing moment as the evil essence fled back to a place of safety. For a brief moment, Panx thought that he had heard the sound of malevolent laughter coming from all around him, but he could not be certain and soon all was quiet in the little settlement.

'Lay him down over here,' whispered Navesh, indicating that the guards should help Rikoth down onto the soft yellow grass where he could get some rest.

'Restrain his hands,' added Fireen, 'just until we are certain that all traces of the corruption have been removed.'

'Do you think that part of Valken has now been restored to life?' asked Panx, disturbed by the evil laughter that he had heard.

'Yes,' hissed Fireen, 'I believe so. But do not fear, my friend, I do not think that Rikoth contained the dark lord's entire life essence, only a small fraction of its power. It is unfortunate that we have returned Valken to some level of self-awareness, but rest assured, he will not pose a threat for many years, if ever.'

'That's a relief!'

Leaving the sleeping Rikoth on the grass, restrained and guarded by the Aellindi warriors, they resumed their hurried preparations to leave the dark world behind them.

Fifteen

Indrani paced up and down the control room, her face fixed in an angry frown and deep worry lines creasing her usually smooth skin. It had been almost an entire day now since Marcus had recklessly gone through the portal, never to return. She was furious with him, with his impetuous behaviour, and she was frantic with worry, desperate to find out if he was safe.

Except for when it was her turn to keep watch, she had spent all of her time trying to re-establish the link to the new beacon. But she had not been successful. In fact, the new beacon seemed to have disappeared altogether, as if it had never existed at all. Idris and Tethine had managed to sketch the glyph that had briefly appeared, so that when they finally returned to Nesteris they might be able to determine to which beacon Marcus had travelled.

'It's like the system did it on purpose,' she fumed, hitting the shiny control screen with her balled fist. 'It's like it came to life, just for Marcus, and then lured him away knowing that he'd be unable to resist.'

'I'm not certain that's true,' replied Tethine, who was standing watch over the portal. 'I think it's more likely that the system malfunctioned when Marcus stepped through and he's unable to return. That's probably why the glyph has disappeared. He seems like a resourceful man and I'm sure he'll find his way back to us.'

'When we get back home, we can find out which beacon is represented by that glyph,' added Idris, trying to offer what little comfort he could to the distraught Visnach magus. 'I'm sure that my father will know which Ancestor it belongs to, and then we can find out where the beacon is located and go and rescue Marcus.'

'You're right, both of you,' replied Indrani, letting out an exasperated breath. 'I'm just so worried about him. What if he's in trouble?'

A bright light appeared suddenly in the centre of the chamber, right beside the active portal into the dark realm, and within moments a second oval shaped window began to coalesce. Indrani stood up excitedly, desperately hoping that her beloved Marcus was about to step back through. She crossed her fingers, a silly habit that she had picked up from him, not really believing that it would have any bearing over the outcome of the next few moments. But she did it anyway, just in case. Finally, when the new portal was fully formed, her hopes were dashed as Endina stepped through from Nesteris.

'Greetings,' hissed the Aellindi woman, smiling at the three who were keeping vigil at the portal, unaware of the pent up tension that was about to explode from the usually calm Indrani. 'I came through to see how things were going and to apprise you of the situation back home . . . Where's Marcus?'

Indrani told Endina everything that had happened since the group had arrived at the *Beacon of Olon*. She described how Fireen had led her group through the portal, venturing off into the dark world in search of Navesh, leaving the four of them behind to keep watch. She then described the appearance of the glyph on the beacon's portal screen, and how Marcus had recklessly travelled through. She then berated herself for letting him go.

Endina listened patiently, whispering a few calming words in an attempt to sooth the agitated magus. She promised to take the sketch of the glyph back with her and to begin the search for answers as to its origin. When Indrani was finally pacified, she told them that the forces of the Aellindi were now on high alert, keeping a nervous vigil around the island, waiting for the enemy fleet to arrive. She believed it would be a few days at most, if Nesteris was actually the target. Finally, before heading back through the portal, she promised to send a few more people through to help alleviate the tiring task of standing guard at the portal.

'I didn't think it would take this long for Fireen to find them,' she said, before walking towards the portal that led back to Nesteris. 'I hope they return soon, for I fear we're about to face a wicked and cruel enemy.'

Endina disappeared back through the portal, which closed rapidly behind her, its edges fizzing wildly as the shimmering window shrank down to a fist-sized ball of pure energy before vanishing altogether. Indrani went back to the control panels and continued her fruitless attempts to re-establish contact with the new beacon, desperately hoping that Marcus was safe and unharmed.

'I'm going to kill him!' she muttered under her breath.

*   *   *

Marcus stood in the temple of Varfell. He was surrounded by *The Watchers*, a group dedicated to waiting for the arrival of *The One*, the prophesied saviour of their doomed world. Endellion and Tuuvar stood beside him, and their leader, Arkadin, stood before him, his face set in a look of undisguised awe.

Arkadin was tall and slender, much like Endellion and Tuuvar, and also shared their purple scale colouration. His head rested upon a long slender neck, much like that of Fireen, and swayed gently from side to side in that odd way that Marcus had grown used to.

The inside of the temple was gloomy, unlike most of the Aellindi buildings that Marcus had visited on Nesteris. It was a large structure with a domed roof that was held up by slender stone pillars. The cavernous interior was poorly illuminated, with numerous candles set into ornate holders, their flickering yellow light struggling to chase away the shadows. It was warm inside, and Marcus assumed that some magical aurora repelled the icy chill that would ordinarily have crept in from the frost-covered land outside.

'Welcome, Marcus,' Arkadin said pleasantly. 'We've been waiting for you to arrive for a very long time and I'm glad that you're finally here. It's a most desperate time for our world and its people, and we were beginning to despair, wondering if you'd ever come.'

'Thank you, Arkadin,' replied Marcus, unsure of what else to say. 'I'm pleased to meet you.'

Arkadin looked at Endellion and then at Tuuvar, with a confused look upon his face. Clearly he was expecting some grand speech from the newly arrived professor, and was a little underwhelmed at Marcus's awkward, hesitant greeting.

Endellion explained that he and Tuuvar had been waiting in the camp, beneath the failing light of the veil, in quiet meditation. They had become aware of flashing lights at the top of the *Beacon of Olon* and had immediately gone to investigate. They had discovered Marcus in the top chamber and, recognising his importance, had persuaded him to accompany them to Varfell.

'If I may ask, Marcus,' said Arkadin, 'how did you come to our world?'

'Well . . . ' said Marcus, pausing slightly to gather his thoughts, 'I'm not entirely certain. As I told Endellion and Tuuvar, I was working in the chamber at the top of the *Beacon of Olon*, on the world fragment where I'm from, when a new beacon glyph appeared. I travelled there, hoping to discover another of your Ancestors' wondrous constructs, but unfortunately it turned out to be malfunctioning. When I tried to return, something went wrong and I was transported here instead, to your master beacon. I was rather hoping that you might be able to help me find a way to return to my friends.'

Arkadin looked at him for a while longer, clearly unsure of what to make of the new arrival. *The Watchers* had waited for generations for the appearance of the one who would deliver their people from the doom that hurtled towards them. Nobody had ever appeared in the *Beacon of Olon*, until now. But could this nervous, bumbling stranger really be the saviour that they had been waiting for? There could be no other explanation for his sudden arrival, and Endellion and Tuuvar certainly believed in him. But something about Marcus and his arrival here left Arkadin feeling anxious. He was sure that there was more to his appearance than they had bargained for.

'Come with me, Marcus,' hissed Arkadin, 'I have something to show you.'

Marcus followed after Arkadin, with Endellion and Tuuvar in tow, leaving the other members of *The Watchers* to wait in the cavernous temple hall. The tall leader strode purposefully out into the cold streets of Varfell. Marcus pulled his warm fur cloak tightly around his shoulders and hurried after Arkadin as he rapidly walked across to a smaller building and went inside.

Endellion closed the door, once the four of them had entered the building, shutting out the cold of the night. Arkadin muttered the words to a familiar enchantment, sending a small glowing ball of light up into the rafters, illuminating their immediate surroundings. Marcus could see that it was a library, a storage facility for the histories of these people. There were books and ancient scrolls on every table and Tuuvar began fervently searching for a specific item.

'Here it is,' she hissed, carefully unrolling a yellowed scroll on one of the small tables.

Marcus looked down at the scroll and the ornate text written upon it and, to his surprise, was able to read the passage for himself. He hoped that it might explain what had happened to him, or reveal a way home. But rather than answers, he found only the cryptic words of another prophecy.

The Prophecy of The One

When Olon's touch fails

A man will come

When the light of the veil falters and the cold of the void threatens all life

Look to the stranger for salvation

In the cavern of the dead

A way will open

Follow the saviour to a place of safety

Marcus looked back up at Arkadin, who was staring intently at him, his alien eyes boring into his skull as if he were trying to pry his secrets from within the depths of his brain.

'Does this mean anything to you?' he asked. 'Anything at all?'

'No, I'm afraid it doesn't,' replied Marcus, unable to shake the feeling of dread that had settled in the pit of his stomach. How could this be happening to him again? What had he done to deserve such ill fortune?

'This is useless,' muttered Arkadin. 'How are we to know what to do, or even if Marcus is the saviour that we've been waiting for?'

'I believe he is *The One*,' replied Tuuvar, trying to restore a little calm to the room. 'The prophecy doesn't say that the stranger will immediately know what to do, only that we should follow him.'

'Yes,' added Endellion, 'perhaps things will evolve as they are supposed to. Perhaps we are all expecting too much from Marcus. After all, he has just arrived from his own world fragment, torn away unexpectedly and deposited here on our dying world.'

'You're correct, of course,' whispered Arkadin, closing his eyes and taking a long deep breath. 'I'm sorry. I appear to have let my frustrations get the better of me, and for that I ask your forgiveness, Marcus. I guess I was hoping for an instant solution to our plight, but as I should have known, life is never that obliging! Tell us a little more about where you come from, and then we, in turn, will share our story with you. Perhaps we'll gain a little more insight into exactly what we're supposed to do next.'

Marcus explained how he had been working at the top of the *Beacon of Olon*, although this time he elaborated, filling in the details of his initially sketchy story. He told them about Fireen and the mission to rescue Navesh, who they believed to be trapped on the world of the demon lord. He described how they had defeated Valken, sending him back to his own domain, but in so doing, had lost one of the stones of power that suffused their world with magical energy.

Endellion told Marcus that they too had three stones of power, here on their own world fragment, which performed the same function as those on Nesteris. According to the ancient texts, each of the world fragments possessed three stones of power; ancient artefacts of the Ancestors, left behind to protect the Aellindi and the younger races that shared their worlds. Endellion was very knowledgeable about these matters, and Marcus found himself listening attentively to the aged Aellindi as he lectured them about the ancient world of the Ancestors.

When Endellion had finished relating the story of the stones of power, Marcus continued his own narration. He informed them of Fireen's visions of Navesh and of the lost stone of power, which she believed to be in the possession of a blue-skinned queen and her army of the dead. At the mention of the blue-skinned queen, the three Aellindi watchers looked worriedly at one another, causing Marcus to pause his storytelling and ask what had unnerved them so.

'The blue-skinned queen that you speak of can only be Queen Karmina, the leader of the Visnaer necromantic cult,' replied Arkadin. 'She and her followers have returned to the dark arts in order to raise a vast army of undead warriors.'

'The Visnaer?' replied Marcus, looking at Endellion. 'Didn't you say that they're the dark cousins of the Visnach?'

'Yes, my friend,' replied the aged Aellindi. 'They are both ancient offshoots of an even older progenitor race. According to legend, both races lived in harmony for many ages. But for some reason the

Visnaer were corrupted by Evixius, the ancient and evil god of death. They began to practice the foul art of necromancy, in the hope that they might prolong their lives.'

Marcus remembered back to when he had first met Panx, and the young man had introduced him to the world of magic. He had asked Panx about necromancy, as that was the only type of fairy-tale magic that he had been able to think of at the time. He remembered the distraught look that had washed over Panx's face, and how the young magus had asked him never to speak of such things again. Only now did he fully understand his friend's dread and fear.

'Since the ancient cataclysm and the fragmentation of the old world,' continued Endellion, 'the Visnaer had all but disappeared, and those who remained were freed from their servitude to Evixius. But, for some unknown reason, Queen Karmina has renewed the ties to the old ways and her cult has once more begun to worship their dark god.'

'Is she here on this world fragment?' asked Marcus.

'Yes,' replied Arkadin. 'Her realm lies far across the continent, beyond the frozen sea and high up in the mountains.'

'So . . . ' replied Marcus, thinking things through. 'That would mean that the lost stone of power from my world fragment is here too!'

'Which also means that there is a connection between you and us, Marcus,' hissed Tuuvar joyously, pleased to have finally determined that they shared some common link and that Marcus's arrival might actually have been for a reason after all.

'Why did Queen Karmina return to the worship of Evixius?' asked Marcus.

'Some say that she simply craves power,' replied Arkadin. 'That she desires to rule over this fragment.'

'But this world is slowly dying!' replied Marcus. 'That doesn't make sense.'

'No it doesn't,' replied Arkadin, 'not to us anyway. Perhaps Evixius has promised her dominion over the dead on this world, which very soon will represent a vast kingdom. Who knows what bargain she has struck?'

Arkadin explained how their world fragment was once lush and verdant, and that after the ancient cataclysm the Ancestors populated each fragment with their wise Aellindi children, to lead, teach and protect the younger races. He recounted the story about the failing of the protective veil. Although no one knew for certain what had happened, the world had been in a slow decline ever since the veil first started to show signs of collapse. But gradually the cold of the void had begun to turn their world into a frozen, inhospitable wasteland. At the centre of the fragment, where the cold touch of the void had yet to reach, it was still warm and pleasant, blessed by the aetheric sunshine which the Ancestors gifted to their children before they departed.

'So what's the Queen's problem?' asked Marcus.

'She blames the Ancestors for the decline of our world,' replied Arkadin. 'She's spreading terrible lies, telling everyone that they left us here to die. She claims that only Evixius has the power to prevent that from happening.'

'Yes, by turning all of his servants into walking piles of bones!' hissed Tuuvar, almost spitting the words in anger.

'Well, whatever her reasons,' replied Marcus, 'it's clear to me that we must escape this fragment before it freezes solid. And we must take back the lost stone of power from Queen Karmina, without getting turned into zombies!'

'What do you suggest?' asked Arkadin, enthused by the professor's heroic outburst. 'Our warriors are skilled, although *The Watchers* are few in number, but we're open to your ideas, Marcus.'

The four of them continued to talk throughout the night, huddled around Arkadin's light globe. They studied ancient texts and scrolls and located the beacons of this world on the detailed maps that *The Watchers* had brought with them to Varfell. Marcus indicated that he had some kind of affinity with the Ancestors' beacons and that it might be a good idea for them to begin their quest at one of these ancient towers. The nearest was the *Beacon of Rhasad*, located in the Aellindi city of Braefell, many days journey from here towards the inner lands. Marcus was surprised to discover that the beacons here shared the names of those on his world fragment. It was testament to the fact that the same Ancestors were responsible for the many fragments into which their homeworld had been split. Braefell had only just begun to feel the touch of the void, and was still inhabited by the Aellindi, who would no doubt be honoured to aid them in their quest.

Marcus had elicited a gasp of astonishment from the three watchers when he had activated his pocket camera, and they had peered inquisitively over his shoulder as he manipulated the image of the ancient map that Panx had discovered. They had watched, transfixed, as he zoomed in and scrolled around the detailed map. He had searched for landmarks that could be used to determine their current location, comparing their hand-drawn maps with the one on the device.

All three Aellindi had been startled, jumping slightly and looking at one another in puzzlement when Marcus had shouted "Eureka!" He was pointing excitedly towards a small area on his huge map, indicating that he had found their fragment. Only when he carefully showed them what he meant had they finally understood his excitement. They could now see for themselves where their own little world fitted together with the other fragments, to make up the whole of their ancestral home.

Suddenly, the events of the previous day caught up with him and Marcus, yawning deeply, indicated that he desperately needed to get some sleep. Tuuvar said that she would take him back to the temple where he could get some rest and, bidding them goodnight, they headed out into the cold, leaving Arkadin and Endellion deep in conversation.

The next morning, barely a few hours since he had left the library, Arkadin came to wake Marcus from his sleep. The professor had dark black rings around his eyes, which were bloodshot and watery. He informed the leader of *The Watchers* that he had barely slept. He had been haunted by dreams of the Visnaer queen, who had relentlessly hunted him and his wife across the vast white tundra, desperate to add them to her burgeoning army of the dead. Arkadin indicated that they were ready to depart and that he and Endellion had toiled throughout the night to prepare *The Watchers* for their final journey, to escort their prophetic saviour back to the ancient city of Braefell.

He had dispatched two messengers already, who would hurry on in advance of the main group to inform the council of Braefell of their arrival and of their chance discovery of *The One*.

Endellion appeared and, seeing that Marcus had slept poorly, began to invoke the aether, suffusing him with its restorative power.

'*The Watchers* are not martially powerful,' indicated Arkadin, 'but we draw power from the stones in order to live in harmony with our world.'

'But you do know how to fight?' asked Marcus. 'There's a good chance that we might need to defend ourselves.'

'Do not fear, Marcus,' replied Endellion, 'we are fully capable of defending ourselves and our allies should the need arise. In fact, there are a few amongst our number who train specifically for just such a purpose.'

Marcus looked out across the snowy tundra as *The Watchers* were carried over its icy surface by huge packs of yelping bavnok. They had travelled for most of the day, stopping frequently to rest and feed the hungry animals. As the sun began to dip down towards the horizon, Marcus looked back and was surprised to see just how far they had travelled.

Varfell was no longer visible, and the mountains in which the settlement was located were receding into the distance. There was still no sign that the cold touch of the void was beginning to lessen its grip here, but his companions assured him that they had made good progress. They planned to travel through the night, navigating by the light of the moons and constellations, and Marcus hoped that he would be able to sleep through the bumpy motion as the sled was dragged over the frozen ground. Endellion assured him that he would get used to it, although he promised to invoke the aether as he had done before, if sleep would not come naturally.

As he watched the icy terrain speed by, Marcus considered how dreadfully familiar all of this seemed to be. He was beset by the same feeling of despair that he had felt when he had been displaced from his own world and drawn into the desperate struggle against Valken. Why did this keep happening to him? He finally drifted off to sleep, still thinking about the events of the past two years as the sled bumped gently over the frozen grassland.

'Wake up, Marcus,' whispered Tuuvar, gently nudging him out of the deep sleep into which he had fallen.

He had slept well, without help from Endellion, and was feeling refreshed and ready to face the challenges that were no doubt coming his way.

'What is it?' he replied, noting the urgent sibilance in her voice.

'We've spotted a group of people up ahead. Arkadin thinks that they're prisoners of the Visnaer Queen.'

'What?' he muttered, standing up and moving over to where Arkadin and Endellion were standing in hushed communion, pointing towards some distant object.

'Ah, good morning, Marcus,' said Endellion. 'I think we have chanced across one of Queen Karmina's slaver groups. No doubt they are being herded back to her palace to be indoctrinated into her cult.'

'You mean . . . '

'Yes, Marcus. Killed and reanimated by the powers of Evixius.'

Endellion told Marcus that their scouts had returned after spotting three Visnaer warriors up ahead, leading a large procession of magically subdued prisoners toward some unknown location. He surmised that they must be utilising some sort of portal transport system, as the Queen's domain was far away. There were also many undead warriors marching along behind the Visnaer, apparently shepherding the captives towards whatever fate awaited them.

'What can we do?' asked Marcus. 'Surely there must be a way to help these people?'

'Maybe, if we can prevent the Visnaer from using the portal,' replied Arkadin. 'Out here on the tundra, the Visnaer and their walking dead warriors are outnumbered, and with the numerical advantage we might prevail.'

The Watchers gathered together, huddling around Arkadin, checking their weapons and readying their connection to the aether. Marcus loosened his own sword, thinking back to the training that he had received, hoping that he would not be a disappointment to Saven. Finally, Arkadin indicated that they should get going and the bavnok once again pulled their charges rapidly along the icy landscape. Marcus noticed that the animals now moved in total silence, as if they understood the need for stealth.

Arkadin informed him that he planned to take the sleds to the other side of a group of hillock, in the direction that he anticipated the Visnaer to be travelling. His hope was that his people would be able to take them by surprise and rescue the prisoners before their captors could react or call for reinforcements.

They came to a halt behind the small hills, and *The Watchers* set about unharnessing the bavnok from the sleds, clearly intent on utilising the animals in the upcoming rescue attempt. There they waited. Marcus's heart raced and he checked and double-checked his sword, loosening his muscles and gently practising his swing as Saven had instructed him to do.

The Aellindi scout returned, appearing as if from nowhere to stand beside Arkadin, indicating in rapid sign language that the Visnaer and their prisoners were close and would be in sight within moments. The group waited tensely and finally Marcus got his first sight of the Visnaer. From this distance they looked superficially like the Visnach, although their skin was a pale blue colour and their hair was as dark as pitch.

Arkadin and Endellion stepped out from behind the rocks that had been concealing them, raising their hands towards the approaching Visnaer.

'Release the prisoners!' shouted Arkadin, 'or face the consequences.'

The lead Visnaer, a powerfully built female warrior, sneered back at the two Aellindi, whispering something to her two companions. She unsheathed her weapon and stepped forward, followed by her two henchmen, while the skeletal army skittered forward to form a defensive shield around their masters.

The rest of the Aellindi had now moved out to join their own leaders, drawing weapons and readying whatever magic they favoured. The two groups of adversaries faced off, neither prepared to stand down or retreat. Behind the Visnaer warriors and their skeletal host, Marcus could clearly see the subdued prisoners, standing as if drugged behind their captors. In amongst the human captives he spied several Aellindi and a lone, red-haired Visnach woman who instantly reminded him of his beloved Indrani.

'Oh what the heck,' he muttered as he drew his own blade and walked over to stand beside Endellion.

Sixteen

'I once saw one of the merfolk,' said Tordin, a faraway look settling across his face.

'What did they look like?' asked Klestin, with undisguised awe.

'Oh, she was beautiful, that's for sure. Sitting on the rocks and playing with her long hair. She waved at me as my ship sailed by, beckoning me to come and join her.'

'Long hair?' asked Brune, a puzzled look on his face.

'Yeah, lovely golden hair it was. She was combing it through with a brush made from white fish bones. She was something else, let me tell you! Sitting on that rock, with her tail swishing in the calm blue sea. I fell in love that day, and I've often wondered what would have happened if I'd followed my heart and leapt overboard to be by her side.'

Leandra raised her eyebrows at Lethis and Samir, shaking her head in mock frustration as the Admiral told yet another of his grand tales. Samir giggled slightly, looking over at Klestin and Brune, who were completely under Tordin's spell.

'Why didn't you go?' asked Klestin. 'Were you afraid that she'd turn you into one of her kind?'

'No,' replied Tordin. 'I can't swim!'

The Admiral laughed raucously and clapped the little Vilnarri man on the back, sending him stumbling forward.

Suddenly the *Drake's* powerful radar started beeping loudly, disturbing the Admiral's jovial mood, bringing him back to reality.

'What is it, Lydia?' he asked.

'I have detected a large number of ships heading this way,' replied the Drake's A.I. control system.

'In which direction and how far away?'

'They are coming in from the east and are currently forty miles out.'

'Thanks, Lydia,' replied Tordin, grabbing his sea jacket and heading out of the bridge. 'I'll head back over to the *Hammer* and then we'll get the fleet moving out to meet our guests! I'll be in contact with you, so keep the channel open at all times.'

Leandra and the students acknowledged the order and Tordin hurried down to where his small boat was waiting to transport him back to his flagship.

'So, finally we get to see what we're up against,' Klestin muttered nervously.

The *Hammer* gave a thunderous bellow and started to move eastward, followed closely by the *Drake*. The fleet of small Aellindi vessels swiftly followed, travelling as fast as their magi could propel them. Several ships stayed behind to guard the entrance to the harbour, in case the enemy made it through Tordin's blockade. They too readied themselves for action, loading weapons and reaching out towards the magical power of the aether.

*   *   *

Nadarru looked out across the sea towards the island nation of Nesteris. Her ship was the largest in the fleet and travelled through the choppy waters of the grey expanse, surrounded on all sides by the smaller vessels of her flotilla. She was impatient to get to her destination, to unleash chaos amongst the Aellindi and take their home from them. Two of her Visnaer warriors had taken command of ships at the very edge of her fleet. She reached out to them, urging them to increase their speed, just as she channelled more power from the aether into the straining sails, pushing her ever closer towards her goal.

Saven stood, bound to the main mast and gagged to prevent her from calling upon her magic. She had been beaten several times during the long voyage across the ocean, and was weak and cold from having to endure the bitter sea air that had battered at her endlessly. The muscles in her legs were fatigued and in a constant state of burning cramp, as she had been unable to sit or move around at all during the crossing. She stretched as best she could, in an attempt to keep the blood flowing through her abused limbs. Her face was swollen; a result of the harsh beatings that the Visnaer priests had inflicted upon her. She squinted into the blinding sun, trying to catch a glimpse of her homeland, which she deduced to be their destination.

She continued to work at the bonds that held her captive, gently stretching the thick, wet rope and scratching at it with her clawed fingers. Although her captors had enjoyed torturing her, they had not checked her bindings since leaving the ruins of Xhaan, and she had finally worn them away sufficiently to release one of her hands. She looked around at her captors, hoping for a chance to free her other hand. The Ligarian female was in deep conversation with one of the Visnaer, who seemed to be the leader of the warrior-priests. The three other Visnaer were standing at the prow of the ship, looking out to sea, and most of the skeletal warriors were below deck. Now was her chance.

After a brief struggle with the rope that still held her other hand to the thick mast, her arms were suddenly free and she reached up to remove the gag from between her teeth. Her mouth was dry, as the only water that she had obtained during the voyage was from a brief rain shower that had thoroughly soaked the gag. With a furtive glance to make sure that her enemies were still looking in the other direction, she gingerly bent down and placed her hands on the ropes that held her legs to the mast. This would be the most dangerous part of her plan, but she had no choice. Calling upon the powers of the aether, she whispered the words to one of the few spells that she was proficient at. She was primarily a warrior and not a powerful magus, but like all of her kind, the power of the aether was in her blood. The flames flared to life, burning through the ropes before her captors were aware that she was free.

She grabbed a nearby skeletal warrior, snatching its short sword from its bony fingers, and leapt towards the side of the warship, grabbing at the rigging as she clambered up onto the gunwale. A deadly curved blade bit into the wooden railing beside her, and Saven looked down at the lithe Visnaer priest who had noted her escape. Fortunately, the blade was now deeply lodged in the gunwale and the priest wasted precious moments in trying to free it. Saven clambered higher into the rigging, out of the reach of the blade and leapt into the air, unfurling her stiff wings as she momentarily plummeted towards the choppy water. She moved away from the ship, slowly at first, but with ever increasing speed as her wings gained strength and her momentum overcame her lethargic take-off.

As she gained height and the ship grew ever smaller beneath her, several bolts of searing blue energy cut through the air around her.

She clumsily dodged the bolts but was not quick enough, receiving a glancing blow to her thigh, causing her to scream out in pain as the bolt burnt her flesh. She called upon the power of the aether to numb the pain and, finally out of reach of the Visnaer weaponry, continued to gain height and headed off towards her homeland.

'Let her go,' said Nadarru. 'We can take another prisoner when we reach their island. For now, let's concentrate on carrying out Queen Karmina's plan.'

G'Valk nodded his head, accepting her authority and moving off to speak with the other members of his order.

'There's a fleet of ships approaching,' said one of the Visnaer priests, coming to stand beside Nadarru and G'Valk.

The three of them moved up to the prow of the ship, coming to stand beside the other two Visnaer as they looked towards the approaching vessels. Nadarru could see the enemy fleet ploughing through the choppy waters, clearly intent on engaging with her as soon as possible. There were two ships steaming ahead of the fleet, looking decidedly out of place. They certainly did not belong amongst the sleek warships of the Aellindi.

'What manner of ships are those?' asked one of the Visnaer, pointing towards the unusual looking vessels.

'I don't know,' Nadarru replied angrily, 'I'm not a naval expert! But they'll sink like any other ship. Go and ready the troops.'

A squadron of sleek Aellindi warships peeled away from the main fleet and attempted to hit the enemy from the side. In response to this manoeuvre, Nadarru motioned for some of her own fleet to move out and engage them. The two small groups of ships moved towards one another, propelled through the water by aetheric winds.

As the distance narrowed, the Aellindi crews started to fire their huge ballistae at the incoming ships of the dead, scoring several hits and snapping off the main mast of one unlucky vessel. With no such long-range weapons at their disposal, Nadarru ordered her ships to close in as swiftly as possible with the Aellindi fleet. She was determined to negate the advantage of range that her enemy was currently enjoying, and to unleash the power of her dark god upon them.

She did not have to wait long and soon the vessels of both flotillas were weaving amongst one another in a chaotic naval melee. Arrows flew from all sides as they coursed past one another. Many Aellindi were cut down in the deadly crossfire, as were scores of Nadarru's skeletal sailors. However, her warriors proved difficult to kill, and they simply stood back up, pierced by the long shafts of the Aellindi arrows but showing no ill effects from what should have been a deadly volley.

'We're too close to use the ballistae to maximum effect,' said one of the Aellindi captains, 'and their ships are clearly intent on engaging us at close range. Our arrows are all but useless against those undead creatures.'

'What should we do, sir?' replied one of the junior officers.

'Well, if we cannot withdraw to an optimal distance to fire the ballistae, then we've no other alternative,' replied the captain. 'We must play them at their own game, fighting hand-to-hand. Perhaps the skill of our warriors will have more effect on those unnatural monsters.'

One of the Aellindi vessels turned hard and hurtled towards the enemy, crashing into the side of one of the small wooden craft. A violent shockwave shuddered through the conjoined hulls and deadly splinters of wood flew through the air. Sailors on both ships were cut down in the mighty collision, as jagged pieces of wood sliced through flesh and bone. Many were sent sprawling across the decks by the violence of the collision and some were thrown overboard into the sea, where hungry razorfish waited for them to enter their watery domain.

Aellindi warriors poured over the sides of their vessel and onto the damaged enemy ship, swords raised high above their heads in challenge to those who would dare invade their beloved homeland. The undead warriors met their charge head on and a desperate struggle ensued. The Aellindi were better warriors, but the weight of numbers coupled with the tenacity of their skeletal foes, who simply rose up to begin fighting once more, soon began to take its toll. In the end the Aellindi captain called for a swift retreat and ordered his magi to set fire to the enemy ship, hoping to use magical flame to turn the enemy to dust.

'Well that didn't go quite as we'd planned!' cursed one of the Aellindi officers, clutching a wounded shoulder. 'There are too many of them, and they just won't stay down!'

The Aellindi ship eased away from the stricken enemy vessel, as the magi hurled bolts of superheated fire into the ranks of the undead. Several skeletons had crossed over onto the retreating Aellindi ship, but were swiftly overwhelmed and hurled into the water, where the thrashing sea creatures tore into them. Unfortunately, before it could fully disengage from the enemy, the Aellindi vessel started to burn. The crew frantically threw buckets of sea water across the wooden deck in a desperate attempt to extinguish the flames.

Several huge ballistae bolts tore into the enemy ship, cutting through the dense smoke to strike the small craft, smashing a huge hole in the side of its hull and toppling the mast into the water. Another swift vessel appeared from out of the smoke and came alongside the burning Aellindi ship, its crew urging the occupants of the doomed vessel to clamber aboard before the fire claimed them. However, the captain of the stricken ship frantically waved them away, having no desire to see more of his fellow Aellindi destroyed in the fiery conflagration. His sailors were still trying to douse the flames, but the magically induced inferno would not yield, and soon the sailors were jumping over the sides in a desperate attempt to save their own lives.

Suddenly a new ship appeared, larger than the Aellindi warships and with a hull that could better withstand the intense heat from the flames. The *Drake* pulled alongside the burning hulk, just as the flames were about to climb up the sails. Brune hurled the climbing nets over the side, enabling the Aellindi sailors to scrabble aboard.

'Hurry,' he shouted, as the Aellindi fled from their dying ship. 'You must hurry!'

Although the *Drake's* hull was constructed from thick sheets of metal, her rust-streaked red and white livery began to bubble in the intense heat, and Leandra feared that the flames might actually transfer across from the burning Aellindi wreck. She ordered Lethis and Samir, who were both proficient at wielding the mystical aether, to go down and help to repel the flames while the rescue operation continued.

Finally, with his sailors lying on the deck of Marcus's ship, the Aellindi captain clambered aboard and Leandra moved the *Drake* away from the flames, which had been sufficiently subdued by Lethis and Samir's combined use of magical water and wind. Lydia manoeuvred the ship away from the smoke and out into cleaner air. Leandra looked out of the window in horror as the full scale of the battle became clear. All around them ships from both sides were locked in a desperate struggle for supremacy. Burning hulks littered the sea and great rafts of debris floated on the surface.

The two fleets were fully engaged now. Tordin's ships had initially attacked at long range, having witnessed just how easily the magical fire could spread between them. Nadarru's fleet, which lacked the ballistae ammunition and trained operators, were simply unable to return that kind of firepower. She continued to command her ships to close the distance between them and their quarry and to engage at close quarters.

The Aellindi sent powerful bolts of lightning and huge fireballs streaking through the air, smashing into the enemy ships, which greatly outnumbered their own. The ordered battle that Tordin had desired had turned into chaos. His ships were everywhere, besieged on all sides by floating barges crammed with the dead, who leapt aboard the Aellindi vessels at every chance, killing many valiant warriors before they could be repelled.

The *Hammer* pushed through the debris-choked water, his men and magi firing arrows and hurling destructive energy into the enemy ships. The water was filled with skeletal warriors that scrabbled at her hull as she steamed past. Everywhere the Admiral looked he could see burning ships, or sailors fighting for their lives as the undead warriors tried to overwhelm them. He shouted an order down to the engine room and the *Hammer* picked up speed and altered course.

'Let's see how you like this!' he whispered, as his mighty warship headed straight towards one of the enemy vessels.

They collided with a gigantic crash as the larger ship smashed straight through the side of the wooden craft. Tordin smiled with undisguised pleasure as the *Hammer* pressed on, barely noticing the collision that had completely pulverised the enemy. However, the undead warriors were notoriously difficult to kill, and many of them had clambered aboard the *Hammer* during the collision and were now attempting to engage his crew with their rusty swords and axes, their mouths gaping as if in silent laughter. He set the *Hammer* on a collision course with another enemy ship and, loosening his naval sword from its scabbard, waited for the brutal fighting to reach the bridge.

Nadarru watched the battle with glee. She had deliberately kept her own vessel out of the frantic melee as she had another, more vital role to play. Although the Aellindi were inflicting heavy losses upon her undead warriors, her fleet was holding its own. Many of her ships were burning and the troops turned to ash, but she still had superior numbers at her disposal. There was no way that she could fail now.

'It's time,' she said, gesturing to G'Valk and the other three Visnaer priests. 'Let's begin the incantation.'

Nadarru and her lieutenants gathered around the main mast and began to chant, calling upon the power of Queen Karmina, begging her to imbue them with her might. A bright light shot up from Nadarru's outstretched arms, disappearing into the blue sky above. Four other pillars of bright white energy lanced up from the Visnaer priests, joining with Nadarru's own magical column. The light radiated outwards and formed a huge dome around her flagship.

She broke away from the battle and headed towards the island of Nesteris, which was little more than a smudge on the horizon. Numerous other ships had formed up with her, beneath the protection offered by the illusion magic that had just been invoked. And so, unseen by the Aellindi defence force, they slipped quietly from the battle.

Tordin parried the long, notched blade that the undead warrior swung towards his head, the metallic clang ringing in his ears and sparks flying from between their sharp edges. The undead warriors had swarmed onto the *Hammer* after he had rammed the second enemy ship, and had proceeded to engage the crew in ferocious close quarters combat. The skeletal warriors were mechanical in their attacks and were predictable and easy to knock down. But getting them to stay down was another thing entirely. Soon, many members of his crew had been wounded and the ship was in danger of being overrun. Reports had come in of a deadly battle raging in the engine room and, fearing for his ship, he had led his bridge crew down to join the melee before it was too late.

Fire had broken out as the magi tried to repel the undead creatures, and much of the wooden interior was now ablaze. Those who could be spared from the fighting worked furiously at the pumps, spraying cold sea water into the cramped corridors of the most powerful ship ever to sail the seas. But it felt like a losing battle as more and more Kingdom soldiers fell before the relentless tide of the undead. Tordin led a desperate counter-attack, charging through the vessel surrounded by his loyal sailors and magi. Slowly the enemy were pushed out onto the open decks and away from the burning interior.

Suddenly the ship lurched, sending Tordin sprawling to his knees. He did not see the wicked looking sword that lanced towards him, slicing through his left side and cutting deeply into his ribs. He screamed out in pain, falling backwards and rolling to one side in an attempt to avoid the follow up stroke.

'What just happened?' he screamed, as two of his men darted forwards to pull him to safety.

'The *Hammer* collided with more enemy ships, sir,' replied the sailor, as he toppled the skeletal warrior into the sea.

'Damn,' cursed Tordin, 'there's no one up on the bridge!'

He tried to rise, to drag himself to his feet, but the pain was too great and he almost blacked out.

'Find one of the bridge crew and get up there,' he shouted to the sailor. 'Get us moving again and get us away from those blasted enemy ships before we're all killed!'

'Yes, sir,' replied the sailor, darting away from the injured Tordin.

Tordin looked around, as if in a daze, watching his men fighting valiantly for their lives. Time seemed to slow down and the sounds of the battle distorted as he fought to remain conscious. He watched as more and more skeletal figures clambered over the side of the *Hammer* and began to attack his men. He looked around for his sword but could not find it. His counter-attack had failed and now his ship was doomed to be overrun by these ungodly creatures. His vision was fading and the sounds of battle grew fainter with each passing second. In a moment of lucidity he realised that he was dying and that, very soon, the loss of blood would reach the point of no return. He looked down at his wounded body and then looked around for something to staunch the flow of blood, but he was unable to focus his vision.

A shadow moved across the deck and he looked up, trying to figure out what was happening. The *Drake* was there, coursing through the water beside his own ship.

That can't be right, he thought. *Marcus is at the Beacon of Olon. He can't be here.*

As he continued to watch the battle raging around him, trying to keep his eyes open, Aellindi warriors poured over the side of the ship, jumping across from the *Drake* to lend their strength to a renewed attack. Hands grabbed him from behind and gently hauled him to his feet. A familiar voice was speaking to him, although he could not quite understand the gurgling accent. He felt himself being lifted from the deck and carried inside, held by a pair of strong arms, but by then the world around him was dark and quiet.

Leandra had manoeuvred the *Drake* in beside the *Hammer*, which looked like it was in serious danger of becoming swamped by the undead warriors. The Aellindi that they had rescued earlier had jumped at the chance to even the score and had taken the fight to the enemy. Within moments the battle had been turned and the skeletal warriors had been cut down, burnt to ashes or simply thrown overboard. Several of the undead creatures had clambered aboard the *Drake*, but had been no match for Leandra, Lethis and Samir, who had smashed them to pieces with a combined aetheric assault.

The fires had been extinguished and the *Hammer* had regained control of her engine room. Jebban and Chang, the Kingdom magi responsible for charging the powerful steam engine, had been injured in the brutal fighting. They were being tended by the Aellindi and would hopefully be strong enough to return to their posts before the heat crystals needed attention.

Tordin was their immediate concern. He was badly injured and unconscious, having lost a lot of blood. The Aellindi magi were unsure if he would survive, but were infusing him with as much healing magic as they could. All they could do was hope that he was strong enough to pull through.

The battle still raged around them and Leandra could see that their armada was in serious trouble. The enemy were just too numerous and she was momentarily panicked. It was Brune who snapped her out of her confused state; his strong, calming personality finally reaching through to her disorientated mind.

'We must retreat,' he said. 'Fall back and regroup at the entrance to the harbour. There're other ships there and we could use their strength.'

'You're right, Brune,' she replied, giving the order for Lydia to move the *Drake* back towards Nesteris. 'But I don't think they'll all manage to get away from these creatures as easily as we can,' she added, indicating the remaining Aellindi warships, currently locked in deadly combat.

'We'll send word to them,' said Lethis, indicating that she and Samir would reach out to the magi on those ships, informing them of the plan to regroup at the harbour. 'It's been a very costly day for my people and we need to preserve as many lives as we can.'

'There are more ships closing in on our position,' said Klestin, moving over to the window and pointing towards the huge warships that had suddenly appeared.

'We're in for it now,' muttered Leandra, berating herself for not keeping an eye on the radar display as Tordin had instructed.

'No, they're ours!' said Brune, coming to stand beside Klestin. 'You can see the Kingdom flag flying from their masts.'

Leandra felt her fear subside as the newcomers set about attacking the remaining enemy ships, bombarding them with huge ballista bolts, smashing the smaller vessels to pieces within moments of their arrival. The Kingdom magi, standing up on the prows of the approaching warships, hurled powerful blasts of energy at Nadarru's fleet, setting the wooden vessels on fire and turning the undead creatures to dust.

'Get us out of here, Lydia,' commanded Leandra, 'as fast as you can.'

The *Drake* turned rapidly and began to move out of the combat area, followed by the *Hammer* and those Aellindi warships that were still capable of moving. The Kingdom fleet continued to close in on their position, circling the area where, moments before, the fierce naval battle had taken place. Several Aellindi warships had been unable to fall back and so Arthen had ordered his smaller craft move in and assist their allies, transferring the stricken crew to the Kingdom vessels.

'Fire at will, Major,' shouted Arthen, as a bolt of blue energy hit the gunwale directly in front of him. 'And take out those two blue-skinned devils, if you please!'

A bugler called out the order and the Kingdom musketeers and riflemen, who were high up in the rigging, opened fire.

Many of the musketeers were still out of range of the enemy and their shots fell short of their intended targets, splashing wastefully into the sea. Some enjoyed better success, especially those on ships in forward positions, or those equipped with the latest rifle weaponry. They peppered the skeletal infantry with musket balls and rifle rounds, inflicting a heavy toll on them, knocking the creatures to the ground. However, the Kingdom infantry soon understood why this particular enemy was to be feared, as many of the skeletons simply stood back up. Some had been maimed in the furious assault, but most just picked up their damaged limbs and clicked the bones back into place.

Some of Arthen's ships had strayed too close to the enemy vessels and had been boarded. The sailors fought back tenaciously, but killing these creatures was proving to be difficult, and soon the smaller ships had been overrun. Skeletal warriors clambered up into the rigging and, through thunderous hails of musket shot, began to engage the Kingdom's elite soldiers in close combat.

Major Tassik, known throughout the regiment as the "finest shot in the army", fired round after round into the enemy below. His powerful shots tore into the undead warriors; splintering bones and smashing open the bleached white skulls of the unnatural creatures. As Arthen had asked him, he sought out the blue-skinned warriors that appeared to be coordinating the undead army. They had been firing their energy spears relentlessly into the approaching Kingdom fleet and several of the huge warships were now racked with flames. His personal weapon had been fitted with one of the experimental magnifying sights, developed from designs that Marcus had brought with him in the databanks of his computers. Whilst not as advanced as those from the professor's own world, they were revolutionary here and Arthen hoped to equip his entire force with them as soon as the design was perfected.

The Major scanned the enemy ships, looking for targets. His sights fell upon one of the Visnaer priests, who was unaware that she was being watched. He lined up the sight on her body, leaning against the mast to steady himself, and then fired his rifle. The shot rang out and Tassik looked back through the enhanced sight to see if it had been on target. It had. The Visnaer priest was clutching at her stomach, leaning on the gunwale for support, pressing her hands against the wound. She had dropped her energy weapon and Major Tassik knew that he would never get a better opportunity to finish the job. After rapidly reloading his weapon he aimed down at the wounded Visnaer priest and fired a second shot. This time the priest was knocked backwards by the force of the bullet and toppled over the gunwale into the sea.

The effect of the Major's shot was profound. The undead warriors on the enemy ship instantly collapsed as the power used to reanimate them was interrupted. Even some of the skeletons that had boarded the Kingdom ships were affected, and great piles of bleached bones clattered to the ground, never to move again.

'Find the other priest!' shouted Tassik, rapidly scanning the enemy ships.

Arthen's troops did not have to look far, as the Visnaer priest gave himself away. Blue bolts of energy crackled from one of the enemy ships, and the General ordered his entire force to concentrate on taking him out. Magical fire rained down on the ship, as did numerous musket balls and rifle shots, and within moments the Visnaer priest was obliterated and his ship shattered beyond all recognition.

With the removal of the second priest, the remaining skeletal warriors were finally halted. Arthen ordered the retrieval of the strange energy weapons from the shattered enemy ships, and then moved his fleet towards Nesteris, to join up with Tordin and what remained of the Aellindi defence force.

Seventeen

Fireen and Navesh led their people towards the dark forest, having set out from their settlement at first light. They had made good progress, with watchful parents ushering their playful children along the trail, trying not to panic them with stories of the demons that inhabited this world. On several occasions they had heard the chilling sound of the hunting horns, far off in the distance, and had continued on their way, hopeful that they would avoid discovery.

Rikoth marched beside Panx, still bound at the wrists to prevent him from suddenly attacking the refugees. He was in good spirits, saying that he felt like a different person since they had drained the evil life essence from him. It had been his own request that they keep him tightly bound and under close surveillance, just in case. But he had displayed no sign that he might revert to that brutal creature that had previously turned on them, although he did not fully trust that the ritual had truly worked. He was adamant that they should only release him when they had returned safely to their own world.

'You've grown powerful, Panx,' he said, nodding respectfully at the young man.

'Yes, you certainly have, Ambassador,' added Navesh, who was walking a few paces in front and clearly listening to their conversation. 'I'd be most grateful if you would show me how you managed to invoke those powerful spells using only a few simple words.'

'I'd be happy to share my theories with you,' replied Panx, 'although I'm not quite certain myself how I managed it! So far, I've had limited success using words of power, but on this occasion the aether just erupted from within me. Perhaps something has finally awakened?'

'Yes, I think that you may be right,' added Navesh. 'This certainly warrants further study.'

'There's really no need to address me by rank,' added Panx, slightly amused at Navesh's insistence on using his title as Ambassador to Nesteris. 'I'd be delighted if you just used my name.'

'As you wish, Panx,' replied Navesh, acknowledging the young man's request.

The group reached the damaged archway that would lead them into the forest. Navesh stopped for a moment to look at the runes on its surface.

'Do you recognise these, Fireen?' he asked.

'No, I do not,' she replied. 'The study of ancient language was always your speciality. What do they mean?'

'They're the symbols of our Ancestors. Waymarkers left behind from long ago.'

'Do you mean they're signposts?' asked Panx enthusiastically, 'showing us the way.'

'Yes, if you like,' replied Navesh. 'I can't read them, but I've seen depictions of similar archways before, in the Aellindi archives.'

'I've seen them too,' said Panx, showing Navesh the sketch that he had made on the other side of the forest. 'There are a few tomes within the Mages College that mention the Ancestors and attempt to reveal some of their language.'

'I should very much like to see them,' said Navesh.

'Sure, when this is finally all over, I'll arrange for you to visit the college.'

'We should be going now,' said Fireen, noting that the sun was dropping towards the horizon and not wanting to be caught in the open when night fell.

Navesh led the way, followed by Fireen, Panx and the rest of their little group of refugees. They headed deep into the gloomy forest, walking along the ancient trail that wound its way through the trees. Navesh strode confidently out in front, having spent a little while living under the dense canopies.

He took them to the area where he had brought the refugees several years ago. Those who had lived here previously began to gather up bundles of dead wood and soon had a small fire going in the centre of the ancient, long abandoned settlement. The children were running around excitedly, exploring their new surroundings, although their parents warned them not to stray too far.

Panx and Fireen followed Navesh as he took them further into the forest. He wanted to show them some of the things that he had discovered here and led them to several ancient ruins, some of which looked similar to those that they had found in the mountains. Clearly the Ancestors had been spread far and wide across this area of the world.

Panx rambled through the remains of the buildings, removing the choking bind weed that was clinging to the cold, wet stones. There were more of the odd looking wagons, which were clearly designed for transporting people and their wares, but which lacked the wheels that were necessary in order to travel across the ground. They had been toppled onto their sides and left strewn about the area in a haphazard fashion. *Could these carts have been capable of flying through the air?* He wondered, peering through a large crack in the smooth external carapace of one of the strange objects, although he was unable to make sense of what he saw inside. Navesh believed that the forest was not always so vast and that it had grown up around the ruins of an ancient city. He had admitted that he could not understand why the path, linked by the two archways, and the few buildings of the small settlement, appeared to be all that remained of the city. Nor could he explain why the forest had not swept in to claim them too.

'Perhaps there's still an ancient power at work here,' suggested Panx.

'Yes, I believe you're correct,' replied Navesh. 'Although I don't understand it.'

Navesh led them further into the trees and they soon emerged into a small clearing.

'This is where I first called out to you, Fireen,' he said, pointing down at a charred circle in the ground. 'It's strange how the foliage has not recovered here. My callings have not affected the terrain in the same way at the other locations.'

'Curious,' hissed Fireen, crouching down to examine the unusual circular mark. 'It is as if the aether has burnt the very substance of the earth here!'

She reached forward, picking up a small handful of the dry, dusty earth and slowly let it run through her fingers. Suddenly she wobbled and fell backwards. Panx and Navesh lunged forward in an attempt to catch her, but they were too far away and she was already unconscious when they reached her side.

*   *   *

She flew high above the rolling waves of the grey expanse, the water stretching out endlessly before her as she soared, with the sunlight twinkling off the surface far below. It was somehow familiar to her and, with warm air blowing across the clear blue waters, she spiralled higher, climbing on the thermal currents that billowed up from the depthless ocean. In the distance she could make out an island, and she flew towards it, riding the power of the aether as if she were a god.

The island grew ever nearer and she smiled to herself as she recognised its familiar terrain. The steep cliffs and the brilliant white stone buildings, inset with beautiful blue precious stones. There, in the distance, was the Beacon of Rhasad and she swooped down towards it, feeling the air rushing past her as she picked up speed. She had never felt this liberated before and she cried out in joy as the beacon of the Ancestors hurtled towards her.

Suddenly, she was wracked with pain and overcome with a terrible feeling of nausea. The sky flashed around her, in a display of raw, untamed violence, threatening to tear her apart with powerful bolts of lightning. Thunder boomed all around and the once beautiful sea was now sombre and grey in colour. The pain in her head was too much to bear and she swooped down towards the beacon, intent on landing and seeking help from those within. She never made it.

Her vision swam once more, leaving her dizzy and disoriented before resolving into yet another familiar vista. She was on the ground now, still on her island, but far from the port and the beacon. She stood up, her legs trembling with pain as she watched a group of Visnaer emerge from a glowing oval portal. She recognised the last person to appear as the one who now held the lost stone of power. The Visnaer Queen. They had not yet spied her and she pursued them stealthily, willing them not to discover her before she could discern their evil intent.

Once more her vision shifted and she watched, unable to act, as the Visnaer Queen killed the Aellindi guards and took the two remaining stones of power for herself. Her blue-skinned lieutenants had disappeared, although she could not remember where they had gone, or if they still lived. But it was clear that the Queen cared little for her minions. She desired the stones, and would not hesitate to *throw away the lives of her own people in order to achieve her goal. And now she had them!*

Fireen screamed in rage, but the Queen ignored her, unaware that she was even there. The Aellindi leader stood there, helpless to prevent the escaping thief, watching as if rooted to the spot as the Visnaer Queen summoned yet another portal and stepped casually through, disappearing for good. The last thing Fireen felt was a desperate feeling of loss as her connection to the almighty aether was severed. The stones were gone. All hope was lost!

*   *   *

'What's wrong with her?' asked Panx, looking down upon the unconscious form of Fireen as she lay on the ground, her body twitching slightly as if she were enduring some terrible nightmare.

'I don't know,' replied Navesh. 'I've never seen this happen before. It's as if she's trapped within her own mind, unconscious and enduring a painful vision. I'll try and wake her.'

'Is that wise? Will it hurt her?'

'I'll be gentle and not force her from her involuntary slumber. If the vision is too deep, then we have little option but to allow her to find her own way back to us.'

Navesh tried several incantations, gently nudging Fireen's unconscious spirit, subtly reminding her of their presence here in the real world. But no matter what he tried, he could not break through the barrier around her inner mind. At one point he delved a little too deeply and was cast out by a blinding light that propelled him backwards onto his rump, leaving him clutching at his temples, clearly in pain.

'She is, for now at least, beyond our reach,' he hissed, still massaging the sides of his head. 'We'll carry her back to the portal and hope that, once back on our own world, she can escape from the depths of her own mind.'

'Shouldn't we head straight for the portal now?' asked Panx, clearly worried about his unconscious friend.

'No. We cannot leave the safety of the forest at night. But we'll strike out towards the portal as soon as the sun has risen. Can you remember the way?'

'Yes, I can.'

'Trust in me, Panx,' added Navesh, seeing the concerned look on the young magus's face. 'I've lived here for many years now. We'd be nothing more than prey out there at night, hunted by the evil creatures that stalk these lands after dusk. We must stick to the plan, as Fireen would surely have us do.'

They made their way back to camp, bearing the unconscious Fireen with them and settled down for the rest of the night. Panx stayed with Fireen, unable to sleep, gently wiping the sweat from her troubled brow as she tossed and turned. At one point he thought that she might wake up, and she started muttering in some garbled language that he could not understand. He could make out the occasional reference to people and places that he knew, and he guessed that something was tormenting her terribly. She kept repeating the words "Nesteris" and "Stones".

Navesh returned to sit beside them and they both looked down upon Fireen's agitated face as she suddenly called out to Endina and Mizarius, who had been left behind to watch over their beloved homeland.

'Will she be alright?' Panx asked hopefully, resting his hand on Fireen's shoulder in an attempt to imbue her inert form with some of his own calm strength.

'Yes, I believe so. As soon as we get away from here, the vision will release her. She'll not forget the images, but the intense, raw pain will lessen and she'll be able to focus once more on the task at hand.'

'Good. I think we're going to need her before this is over!'

The next morning, as the sunlight filtered down through the dense tangle of trees, they emerged from the ancient archway that had first led them to Navesh's mountain refuge. Panx looked back at the receding trees, an intense feeling of relief washing over him as they put some distance between themselves and their oppressive arboreal hiding place. Although nothing else had occurred during their single night beneath the trees, they had all felt unseen eyes upon them, watching their every movement, and had slept fitfully. Navesh had warned them that if they lingered for too long within the forest, it would have appeared that the trees had awakened to drive them out.

They walked for several hours with the fatigued children struggling to keep up. This land was unfamiliar to those who had been born on this world, having spent most of their short lives in the mountains. The very air here was thicker and more oppressive than what they had been accustomed to, and the children felt it keenly.

Fireen was calmer now and less agitated. Panx estimated that they had been here, in Valken's domain, for the equivalent of two or three days on their own world. He was eager to return to Nesteris where, hopefully, the Aellindi leader would begin to heal. He was distracted from his thoughts when Praevir suddenly landed beside Navesh, having been scouting ahead of the slow moving group, checking that the way was clear.

'There are demons ahead of us,' he said, 'directly in our path.'

'How many?' asked Navesh.

'A considerable force. Mainly smaller beasts, but there are numerous large demons and a few of those hunters.'

'Can we go around them?' Panx asked.

'No, I don't think so,' replied the Aellindi scout. 'I think they'd discover us sooner or later.'

'We have no choice then,' added Rikoth, who had been listening to Praevir's report. 'We must attack them, before they realise that we're here, while we still have the element of surprise!'

'I agree, my friend,' replied Navesh, without hesitation. 'Praevir, gather the Aellindi and prepare for a surprise assault.'

'Release me, Navesh,' pleaded Rikoth. 'I can help.'

'I don't think that's wise, Rikoth. Remember what happened the last time you were armed? I'm afraid you might turn on us once again, especially with so many demons in close proximity. Who knows what corrupting influences they might bring to bear upon you.'

Rikoth closed his eyes for a moment, lowering his head, clearly distressed by the mistrust that his actions had engendered in his friends. He finally looked back up at Navesh through uncharacteristically tear-filled eyes.

'I feel so guilty about what I've done whilst we've been here. Even though I was not in full control of my body, I feel so ashamed.'

'Don't apologise, Rikoth,' said Navesh respectfully, 'it wasn't your doing.'

'Tell that to these people,' he replied, pointing at the refugees who were standing all around him, about to engage in a desperate fight for their lives. 'They will always blame me for the loss of their loved ones.'

'In a way, Rikoth, I'm ultimately to blame for your actions,' said Panx, causing the Aellindi leaders to look up at him in surprise. 'If I hadn't brought that evil blade back from Valken's citadel, then we would never have infused you with the corrupted life essence. I should have sensed that something was not quite right, before Fireen and I engaged in that ritual. It's unfair to hold yourself responsible for harbouring Valken's life essence, given that we allowed it to conceal itself within you, where it could lay dormant until it had a chance at revival.'

'Nonsense,' hissed Rikoth. 'You saved my life on that day. I was no more than a dried up husk, the shadow of my former self, and without your aid I would certainly have joined the Ancestors before very long. Please release me, Navesh. I want to atone for my actions. Please, before the demons detect our presence and launch an attack of their own.'

As if to further highlight the severity of their situation, one of the children started to cry and was swiftly hushed by his parents, who looked around, fearful that they may have been discovered.

'Very well,' replied Navesh, after a brief moment of consideration. 'I've known you for many years, Rikoth, and I trust your word on this.'

Rikoth's bindings were removed and his great two-handed warhammer returned to him. The Aellindi hero smiled as he once again felt the familiar weight of his weapon, and he bowed down before his friends before moving off to join the ranks of the Aellindi that had formed up beside Praevir.

Panx stayed behind with a few of the Aellindi guards and the human warriors, to help look after the children. Praevir and those Aellindi who could take to the skies leapt upwards, unfolding their wings and spiralling into the red-coloured sky. Navesh activated his golden spear and then he and Rikoth, followed by the remainder of the Aellindi warriors, moved off in the direction of the demon horde. Panx watched them go, silently wishing them good fortune as he readied his magic, hoping that he would be able to draw upon the unpredictable power of the aether.

'There they are,' whispered Navesh, pointing down through the trees at the large group of demons that had gathered there.

'There are too many of them!' replied one of the guards. 'How are we to take them all on?'

'The element of surprise will aid us,' replied Rikoth, holding his warhammer at the ready. 'Shall we?' he added, looking at Navesh and nodding slightly towards the demons.

'Just a moment longer,' replied Navesh. 'Let's give Praevir chance to drop in on our friends!'

'Oh, how I've missed you,' chuckled Rikoth, smiling back at his friend, placing one clawed hand upon his shoulder.

'And I you, Rikoth,' replied the usually taciturn Aellindi.

The battle started suddenly, with Praevir and the airborne Aellindi giving no warning of their approach. They swooped in low across the trees and dived down upon the oblivious creatures, hacking at them with their curved blades as they hurtled past.

'There's the signal,' muttered Navesh. 'Let's go, before Praevir takes all the glory. For Nesteris!' he shouted, breaking into a charge towards the startled demons.

'For the Ancestors!' replied the other Aellindi warriors.

Navesh was first into the fray, beating even Rikoth to the melee. He whirled his mighty spear around his head in a stunning display of skill and dexterity, slicing through the tough demon hide as if it were gossamer-thin. Rikoth was not far behind, crashing through the smaller demons with impunity, making his way towards the larger beasts, intent on removing the greatest threats before they could fight back. Praevir swooped down once more, decapitating one of the large hunter demons that had been about to blow its mighty horn, sending its blue-veined head hurtling through the air. He landed gracefully and, as his wings tucked in neatly behind his back, began to lay into the demons with desperate ferocity.

The enemy still possessed the edge, in terms of numbers, but the sudden attack and the superior skill of the Aellindi warriors soon began to show. Navesh pressed the attack, cutting down foe after foe with his razor-sharp spear, and dispatching the fleeing demons with bright lances of superheated flame conjured from its tip.

Rikoth was hidden from sight, deep within the ferocious scrum of violence. His fellow Aellindi would occasionally catch sight of him, surrounded by glistening black bodies as he swung his mighty warhammer in huge, powerful arcs, smashing the demons to the ground, breaking their bones and crushing their bodies to a wet, greasy pulp.

However, the noble Aellindi did not have the battle entirely their own way and several of Praevir's airborne cadre had been savagely dragged from the sky as they swooped down. They had been concentrating on a huge demon that had appeared from the rear of the enemy formation, but as they closed in on it, multiple tentacles had lashed out towards them, catching them off guard. Before they could evade the writhing mass of long black arms, three of them were plucked from the sky and held firmly in its grip as the creature began to crush the life from their bodies.

Rikoth and Navesh finally managed to engage the beast, just as it dropped the lifeless Aellindi corpses onto the bloodstained ground and began moving forward, searching for more victims. Navesh moved in swiftly, slicing into the creature with precise strokes, and Rikoth, hurtling at the demon from behind, smashed into the beast with thunderous sweeps of his mighty warhammer. The creature bellowed in pain, its tentacles flailing madly as it tried to engage its assailants. Rikoth was caught with a solid strike to his chest, although his ancient armour absorbed the blow, deflecting the tentacle and allowing the Aellindi champion to regain his footing. Smaller demons were sent flying, caught unawares by the injured monster as it sought to defend itself. The two heroes worked together, one darting in to attack the beast head-on, while the other moved into a new position, always trying to keep it off balance. Finally, after a brutal struggle, the fight was over. Rikoth clambered up onto the creature's back and hammered down furiously into its chitinous exterior, smashing through its thick armour and crushing its skull with powerful blows. He leapt clear as the creature toppled over, its titanic mass crushing more of the helpless demons as it fell.

'That was fun!' hissed Navesh, panting with the exertion.

'Sure was,' replied Rikoth, grinning wildly.

By now the remaining demons had been routed and were fleeing the battle, desperate to escape from the Aellindi warriors. The two remaining hunters had turned their giant mounts around and were retreating alongside their smaller brethren, apparently not wishing to engage the Aellindi alone.

'Let them go,' said Navesh, catching hold of Rikoth's arm, preventing him from pursuing the fleeing beasts. 'We must make haste to the portal, before the demons can regroup.'

'But we cannot let those things escape!' countered Rikoth. 'What if they alert more of their kind? They could come back and we'd be the ones on the receiving end of a surprise assault.'

'That's a risk we have to take. But for now we need to get out of here. I'll send Praevir ahead to keep watch, but we must leave now!'

'As you wish, Navesh,' replied Rikoth, grudgingly accepting his authority. 'But I hope that you're right,' he added, stalking back off towards where Panx was waiting with the rest of their group.

'So do I, my friend,' whispered Navesh, as he watched Rikoth walk away. 'So do I.'

'There's the portal,' said Panx, pointing towards to glowing oval window that led to the *Beacon of Olon* and the safety of their own world.

'Let's go then,' replied Navesh, indicating for Panx and Rikoth to lead the way.

The refugees left their concealment among the low growing trees and headed out across the thick yellow grass that covered the open ground between themselves and the portal. Some of them broke into a frantic run, desperate to finally escape from the dark world that had been their home for so long.

Navesh tried to rein them in, fearful that they would make easy targets should the demons return. But it was no use. Panic had taken hold of many of the refugees, and they scurried across the open ground, heedless of his warnings.

*   *   *

'I can see them!' exclaimed Idris, who was watching at the entrance to the portal. 'They're coming this way. And there's father!'

Tethine hurried over to stand beside her son, and was soon joined by Matixis and Rustara, who Endina had sent through to help bear the burden of watching the portal. Indrani was close behind, having been further away, still attempting to reactivate the portal through which Marcus had disappeared.

'What's that over there?' hissed Tethine in alarm, pointing towards a dense group of stunted trees.

Several large creatures had appeared from within the tangle of thick foliage and were dashing across the grass towards the fleeing refugees.

'Look out, Father!' cried Idris.

*　　　*　　　*

'Idris?' muttered Navesh, looking up, hearing his son's voice from the other side of the portal.

His thoughts were interrupted as he caught sight of the demons that had been tracking them. They had thought that they had shaken off their pursuers, before they had climbed the last group of hills and headed towards the portal. But it would seem that even after inflicting terrible losses upon the foul creatures, they had not been able to lose them.

'Panx,' he shouted, 'get the children through the portal. Everyone else, line up and be ready to defend it. We must not let them past us!'

Several huge minotaurs burst forth from the trees and began to trample through the long grass in a frantic attempt to reach the escaping humans. The Aellindi fought back, trading blows with the mighty creatures. But while they were distracted with the large demons, a group of smaller beasts skittered around and headed directly towards the human soldiers that were stoically defending their families. They were evil looking beasts, with sharp chitinous bodies and sticky black secretions dripping from their weapons. The humans prepared themselves for the assault, ushering the remaining children behind them.

Rikoth was suddenly there, appearing as if from nowhere, smashing his warhammer into the oncoming tide of demons and using his own body as a shield for the escaping humans. He smashed their vile bodies into the dirt, not waiting to see if they got back up again before moving on to attack another foe.

The human warriors, fearful at first of the Aellindi hero, worried that he was about to resume his butchering ways, slowly began to trust in their saviour as he drove a wedge through the oncoming demon horde. They hefted their own weapons and followed the enraged Rikoth, finishing off the injured demons that he left in his wake. Soon they were fighting beside the mighty hero against a seemingly endless tide of demons. Many fell to the vicious beasts, brutally cut down by jagged, rusty blades, or impaled on poison-tipped spikes.

But soon the tide had turned and the refugees became emboldened, suddenly believing that they might live through the day and actually get home. Panx continued to usher the non-combatants through the portal and soon most were safely through, including the unconscious Fireen.

The sounds of hunting horns filled the air, coming from all around them. The attacking demons fell silent and scurried away from the fight, leaving the refugees standing alone on the grassy plain, panting heavily, waiting to see what would happen next and not truly believing that the demons had given up.

From behind the retreating mob of demons came the largest beast that any of them had ever seen. It had pale skin, covered with red blisters and open sores. Its four muscly arms each held a gigantic sword, which the creature spun deftly in its oversized hands.

The refugees looked at one another, not quite believing what they were seeing. Many of the humans, who were tiny in comparison with this newest foe, stepped back slightly. Rikoth showed no such fear and stepped toward the advancing beast, muttering that this was his fight and for the others to stay out of it. This was, apparently, to be his atonement for the ghastly deeds that he had been forced to carry out while under Valken's influence.

Navesh and the other Aellindi stayed back, not wishing to interfere with the dual and upset their champion in so doing. The creature bellowed its challenge, huge teeth emerging from its mouth, spraying foul smelling saliva over the nearest of the Aellindi guards.

'Panx, get the rest of the refugees back through the portal,' shouted Navesh. 'We'll be along shortly, once Rikoth has finished with this foul beast.'

However, before Rikoth could engage the creature, more demons appeared from the trees around them, led by the terrifying hunters who sat astride their huge demonic mounts. Without warning, the hunters sent their smaller demons towards the waiting Aellindi warriors who had stopped to watch their champion as he took on the huge creature. Hundreds of demons hurtled forwards, accompanied by packs of hounds, with foul, bloody drool escaping from their gaping maws as they thundered towards their quarry.

'It's a trap,' hissed Praevir, landing beside Navesh. 'We're totally surrounded and vastly outnumbered. We need to get out of here now, or we'll be slaughtered within sight of our home!'

'You're correct, Praevir,' replied Navesh. 'We must escape now, before it's too late. Rikoth, it's a trap,' he shouted, 'we must go now. Head for the portal, before they cut you off!'

'Hurry, you hulking brute,' added Praevir, frantically trying to catch Rikoth's attention.

Rikoth, pausing to look around at the evolving situation, acknowledged his friend's command and hurried back towards the portal, angry at missing out on the chance to put down the demonic behemoth. Navesh was there, standing in front of the portal, beckoning him onwards. Panx was there too, standing beside Praevir and several Aellindi guards. He could see that the humans and their children had already gone through the open energy gate, and had taken the immobile form of Fireen with them. He was thankful for that. If he were to die here today, at least she would survive. Their people needed her leadership now more than ever.

'Rikoth, get down,' shouted Panx, as he unleashed a thunderous blast of energy towards him.

He rolled forward and remained tightly curled into a ball as aetheric heat passed a fraction above his head and smashed into the oncoming horde of demons. He resumed his hurried retreat, glancing over his shoulder at the destruction that the young magus had just wrought, and was shocked to see the huge scorched area littered with dead and dying demons. The huge monster, which had previously been used to bait him, was little more than a pile of grey ash blowing away in the wind. *Powerful indeed,* he thought, as he continued his retreat.

Navesh waited for him at the portal, clearly wishing to be the last one to leave the dark world. Panx, Praevir and rest of the Aellindi had already gone through, leaving just the two of them behind.

'Hurry!' shouted Navesh. 'We're the last and Panx is ready to close the portal.

Rikoth hurtled through the fizzing energy window, almost diving through. He turned around to see Navesh standing there, still on the other side, with a fresh tide of demonic abominations charging towards him.

*　　*　　*

'Father!' Idris shouted frantically. 'You're the last, father. You've saved them. Come home now, please?'

*　　*　　*

Navesh turned at the sound of his son's voice and walked, almost casually into the glowing blue energy portal. Panx removed the *Shard of T'nath* and the portal rapidly faded from existence, shrinking in diameter as the energy dissipated. They could all hear the terrifying sound of the hunter's horns and the demons still hurtling towards them, desperate to reach their hated foes before the portal closed. But soon there was only silence. Navesh and Praevir stood looking at one another, thankful that their terrible exile was finally over.

'Father!' cried Idris, running towards Navesh and hugging him fiercely. 'I knew you'd come back to us.'

Eighteen

Nadarru had approached Nesteris harbour from further along the coast, safely concealed within the aetheric shroud that she and her priests had weaved around her small breakaway fleet. With the aid of her lieutenants, amplifying her scrying powers, she could sense the presence of the two remaining stones of power. They were indeed here, on this island, held by the arrogant Aellindi in what they considered to be a safe location. Not desiring to engage the main Aellindi army, as the bulk of her skeletal army had been left behind to combat the enemy fleet, she had searched for a more secluded place in which to make landfall. One that would provide easy access to the city above, but which would allow her to disembark the remainder of her troops to act as a shield while she carried out the Queen's bidding.

'There,' she said, pointing towards a small harbour. 'That will do nicely!'

'It's defended,' warned G'Valk. 'We'd be wise to determine their strength before we commit ourselves.'

'I see barely a handful of pathetic Aellindi militia,' she replied acidly, 'but you're correct, we must be certain of success before we make our move.'

Her shrouded ships moved closer to the small quayside, their masts and rigging creaking gently in the wind. The island's defenders remained blissfully unaware of their presence, deceived by her wall of aetheric illusion.

'This is perfect,' she said, finally convinced that the Aellindi were few in number here and that she could make it safely to shore. 'Bring the ships in beside the quays and unleash the troops. Then we can begin.'

The little fleet glided gently towards the empty piers and the skeletal figures of their small attack force skittered across the decks and jumped down onto solid ground. This was their most vulnerable moment, for if they should be discovered before they were ready, the local garrison could easily raise the alarm.

G'Valk marshalled the troops at the quayside for as long as he could, keeping them within the concealment magic. But soon there were too many and, knowing that time was running out, he unleashed them upon the unsuspecting defenders.

Nadarru followed behind her army as they descended upon the Aellindi, who had been waiting just outside of the small harbour area, and who had moved swiftly to defend their nation. Although the defenders were highly skilled warriors, they were but few in number here and soon Nadarru's little band of undead warriors had eliminated the initial resistance and secured the local area. She wasted no time in adding the fallen Aellindi warriors to her own army, stripping them of their scaled flesh and reanimating their mighty bones. They would make excellent foot soldiers and, when coupled with the others of their kind that she had subsumed into her ever-growing force, the sight of their skeletal brethren moving against them would strike fear into the hearts of her enemies.

*   *   *

A wounded Aellindi scout landed heavily beside the officer in charge of the Nesteris defence force, who was angrily conversing with Mizarius.

'Sir,' he said, clutching at a deep gash on his side.

'Yes, what is it?'

'Sir, the undead army has landed along the coast. They've wiped out the local militia and are spreading out to secure the area.'

'How many are there?' asked the officer.

'Hundreds. Their leader is there too, with four of those blue-skinned Visnaer warriors. They're unstoppable!'

Mizarius looked at the officer in charge and some unspoken communication passed between them.

'I think we ought to redeploy the army, don't you?' he said, raising one of his eyebrows.

'Yes, councillor, I think you may be right.'

'Come with me lad,' said Mizarius, leaving the officer to mobilise his troops, 'let's see what we can do about that little scratch that you've got there.'

*   *   *

'The stones are near,' whispered Nadarru. 'I can feel them.'

'Shall we begin the ritual?' asked G'Valk.

'Yes,' she replied, with an unusual display of urgency. 'Let's waste no time, the Queen grows impatient!'

The four priests moved in closer, standing at equidistant points around her, forming a protective ring around Queen Karmina's instrument. They raised their arms into the air and began to chant, the timbre of the invocation raising and falling in a hypnotic fashion, their bodies swaying gently as they sang. Light burst forth from their outstretched fingers, shooting up into the sky before arcing back downward, lancing into the waiting form of Nadarru, who had fallen into a trance-like state. She shuddered slightly, as if in pain, as the aetheric light penetrated her body. But, after a few moments of extreme discomfort, she controlled the power, bending it to her will and redirecting it outwards, towards her chosen spot in an open area just outside of the harbour. The light coalesced into a solid sphere of dazzling bright white light that rapidly blossomed into an oval window of energy, a portal to another place. Finally the priests terminated their incantation and the last vestiges of power and light were swiftly absorbed by the newly formed gateway.

The vanguard of the Aellindi defence force arrived just as the ritual was coming to a close, their outstretched wings bringing them gracefully back to the ground, having flown as swiftly as they could to reach the incursion site. Waiting to greet them and creaking slightly as their bones rubbed together, were hundreds of reanimated skeletal figures wielding rusty swords and spears. Standing out in front of the frightful sight were the undead remains of their own people, the Aellindi who had already fallen in combat. This caught the vanguard momentarily off-guard and sent a wave of commotion through their ranks. Should they attack their own people, even though they were already dead? In the end, it was the officer in charge who led the attack, storming into the melee even though his warriors were outnumbered more than ten-to-one.

The battle was joined and the skilled Aellindi warriors hacked into the walking corpses that stumbled forward to attack them. Individually the skeletal figures were no match for the skill of the Aellindi, but all too soon the children of the Ancestors found themselves battling creatures that had already been slain many times over. Some had multiple missing limbs and there were even skeletons that had been decapitated but which kept on fighting, animated by some unseen force. One of the Aellindi had even been grabbed from behind by a severed arm that tried desperately to choke the life from him.

'It's no use,' shouted one of the junior officers. 'As soon as we knock them down, they get up again and come back for more!'

'Keep it up!' replied the officer in charge. 'We only need to hold them off for a while longer, just until the main force arrives. They're bringing the magi with them, and then we'll see how these monsters like a taste of pyromancy. Surely ashes and dust cannot fight back!'

The fight raged on around her as Nadarru slowly withdrew her power from the creation of the portal. It was an arduous magic to invoke, the opening of a gateway between world fragments. But the Stone Queen had chanced across an ancient scripture that detailed the required incantations, and had hungrily devoured its secrets. And now she was coming here, to join them in their conquest of the Aellindi homeland.

Her Visnaer lieutenants stood beside her, drinking in the sights of the mighty battle. They were impressed with the combative skill of their enemies, even though they knew it would all be for nothing. In the end, the defenders would be overwhelmed, worn down by an enemy that was already dead.

'She's here,' muttered G'Valk, looking into the fizzing energy gateway.

With that, the portal flared briefly and Queen Karmina stepped through. Her radiant blue skin shone in the warm sunny sky and her long black hair flowed down her back, over the regal bavnokskin cloak in which she had adorned herself.

'Ah, my children,' she purred, 'it's most pleasing to see you again.'

The others bowed down before her, kissing the back of her hand to show their obedience.

'I've located the stones, my Queen,' said Nadarru, standing up once more and pointing towards a narrow trail that led into the forest.

'Yes,' replied the Queen, 'I can sense them too, there is much power here. Let's go, while our enemies remain distracted.'

As the Queen and her followers headed away from the battle, the portal flared once more and a stream of fresh skeletal warriors emerged. They moved out to engage the already outnumbered Aellindi vanguard, pushing them back towards the main city from where they had just come.

*   *   *

Navesh held his son in one arm and his beloved Tethine in the other, hugging them close, not wanting to let go.

'I knew you were still alive, father,' said Idris, looking up at Navesh through red, tear filled eyes. 'I wasn't frightened by you, in the nightmares I mean. I knew you were calling out to me, asking for help.'

'I'm sorry that I alarmed you, my son, it wasn't my intention. Calling out through the aether is a difficult thing to achieve, and I fear that the vision I sent to you had somehow become warped and twisted on its voyage through the great expanse that separated us. I'm sorry, Idris.'

'It's okay, father, you're back now and that's all that matters.'

'Where is Keziah?' asked Navesh, turning to his mate to enquire about their young daughter.

'She's with my father,' replied Tethine. 'I didn't want her to be frightened by the events of the last few days.'

'I've missed you, Tethine,' he said quietly, smiling and kissing her on the forehead, holding her close. 'The thought of getting back to you and our children was all that kept me going through those long years that I was trapped on that foul world.'

He had briefly explained the difference in the passage of time on the dark world, and that for him it had been over six years since he had stayed behind in Valken's citadel, wounded and ready to give up his life in order to save his world. Fortunately, the Aellindi were a long-lived people, and these years had not noticeably changed him. The mental scars that he had acquired during his long confinement would heal fully, now that he was home.

'Where's Marcus?' asked Panx, turning to Indrani.

'I'm not certain,' she replied, eliciting a quizzical look from those around her. 'We were here, watching the portal, when a new beacon suddenly appeared on the system. He went through, rather recklessly

I may add, and never returned. I was hoping that once you'd all returned, you might help me find him?'

'I'm sorry to hear this,' hissed Navesh. 'I was looking forward to seeing him again, to find out more about what hallowed artefacts of the Ancestors he's been meddling with in my absence,' he added, with a look of mock irritation on his face.

Panx had given Navesh a full account of Marcus's achievements since the end of the demon war, including the miraculous reactivation of the beacons and discovering how to travel between them. Navesh had been fascinated and was clearly desperate to witness this wondrous ability for himself.

'However,' continued Navesh, 'things have spiralled out of control, as they so often do. We now find ourselves in a situation where Fireen has been stricken with some unknown ailment and we must return her to the familiar surroundings of Nesteris. I hope that this will aid her recovery and I promise, Indrani, that once the immediate emergency has been averted, I'll do everything in my power to help you locate and retrieve our wayward professor.'

'Thank you, Navesh,' replied Indrani, accepting, for now, his unemotional and logical argument. 'Here's the sketch of the glyph that appeared on the beacon's system. Idris and Tethine think that it might help us determine which beacon Marcus travelled to and to establish his location.'

'This is a good starting point,' replied Navesh, smiling down on his young son, proud of his rational thinking. 'I've seen this glyph before,' he added, inducing a look of relief from Indrani, 'but I must first consult the texts before I can confirm to which of the Ancestors it belonged, and the location of their beacon.'

'What should we do about Fireen?' asked Praevir. 'She's still unconscious, and I fear that her breathing is getting weaker.'

'We must waste no further time here,' replied Navesh, taking control of the situation. 'Let's get her back to Nesteris where she'll be in familiar surroundings. Once there, her soul will no doubt be able to draw strength from such sanctuary.'

He spoke briefly with the refugees that had lived under his protection for many years, promising them safe passage back to Nesteris and a place to live if they desired. He also promised that once the current crisis was over, he could arrange for their transport back to their homelands.

'But for now,' he said, 'I must leave you. You'll be cared for in Nesteris, and I'll see you all again soon.'

With that he indicated to Panx and Indrani that they should open the portal back to the city. As he watched, fascinated by the appearance of the doorway back to Nesteris, Indrani turned and asked him if he would like the honour of being the first to return.

'I'd like that very much!' he replied, and stepped through the portal.

*   *   *

Marcus parried a vicious attack, his blade growing heavier with every swing. Even though his training with Saven had taught him much and he now considered himself fairly proficient with the weapon, he was uncertain for how much longer he could continue. To fight a real and prolonged battle was far different than participating in a training bout. His arms were still not quite up to the task and he feared that at any moment he would make a mistake, or worse still, lose his grip on the blade, after which it would be over far quicker than he would like.

Suddenly, as if recognising his distress, Endellion was beside him, releasing powerful blasts of flame into his assailant, knocking them backwards and smashing their skeletal structure to smithereens.

'Even they cannot recover from that!' shouted his saviour.

'Thank you, Endellion,' replied Marcus, panting heavily. 'I'm not sure how much longer I could have held out.'

'You handled yourself well,' replied the aged Aellindi, 'but let me give your constitution a boost.'

Endellion placed his hand on Marcus's shoulder, sending the healing magic flooding through his fatigued body, instilling him with fresh vigour.

'Thanks, I really needed that. I wish I could tap into the aether, but I've never developed the knack for it.'

'You have your own part to play here, Marcus, so just be care—'

'Look out!' cried Marcus, pushing Endellion aside as a huge spear was thrust in his direction, sending him sprawling onto the ground.

Marcus smashed his sword down onto the wooden spear shaft, cutting through it with one savage blow. He followed up with a series of well-practised attacking strokes, knocking their skeletal assailant backwards, hacking off an arm in the process. Endellion clambered awkwardly to his feet and unleashed a further blast of fiery destruction as he re-joined the embattled professor. Side-by-side the two men fought, with Marcus driving the seemingly unstoppable creatures back and Endellion hurling powerful blasts of superheated energy at them, which was just about the only way to truly halt these abominations.

Although it seemed to Marcus that the battle had been raging for days, it had in fact only just begun. *The Watchers* had engaged the Visnaer shepherds and their skeletal entourage, closing in to fight with sword, spear and aetheric energy. The Visnaer had retaliated brutally, cutting down watcher after watcher with deadly precision. The lead priest of Evixius, a powerful woman, hung back and attacked from afar with her strange spear-like weapon, hurling bolts of deadly blue energy into the oncoming band of Aellindi.

Arkadin had soon determined that she was the deadliest threat and he personally led a desperate attempt to reach her.

'We're lucky,' he said, as he led them towards the blue-skinned female. 'She appears to be the only one armed with their mighty lance weapon, and the only one capable of summoning the powers of Evixius. Come on, we must reach her swiftly, before we're all pressed into the servitude of the Stone Queen and her evil master.'

Marcus followed Arkadin as he made his way towards the Visnaer warriors. Endellion and Tuuvar hurried along beside him, drawing continuously upon the power of the aether in order to help keep them safe. The bavnok were there too, tearing into the skeletal warriors as if stricken with insatiable hunger. He almost laughed hysterically at one point, when for some strange reason he remembered one of the television adverts that had been popular back on his own world. The brief sketch had shown a loving dog owner rewarding his pet with a huge bone, which it began to gnaw upon hungrily. It was, apparently, good for the health of the animal and he sniggered to himself as he recreated the scene in his mind. This time, though, with an enraged bavnok chewing on the leg of an enchanted skeleton as it desperately tried to escape.

He was brought back to reality when a blue bolt of energy struck one of Arkadin's watchers, right beside him, who began to scream out in agony as his body was torn apart. Marcus could do nothing but watch in horror as the bones clattered to the ground in a heap.

'There's nothing you can do,' shouted Tuuvar frantically. 'You must keep up, Marcus. We need to stop the Visnaer, before it's too late.'

Taking one final look at the pile of bones that lay at his feet, Marcus hurried after Arkadin, who had not stopped to wait for him.

The bavnok had raced on ahead and had launched themselves at one of the Visnaer shepherds, tearing the man to shreds with their powerful jaws and sharp teeth. Arkadin and *The Watchers* encircled the two remaining priests, who eyed them warily. The lead priest levelled her spear at them, as if warning them to stay back. The bavnok, having finished with their prey, now returned to Arkadin's side and waited patiently for his next command.

'Give up, while you still can,' he said, giving the Visnaer the chance to save themselves.

The Visnaer leader spat onto the snowy ground and then casually fired her spear at another of the Aellindi. The man was consumed in moments, but Arkadin did not stay still long enough to watch the gruesome spectacle. He charged forwards, with his followers and his pack of bavnok beside him.

'I gave you a chance,' he shouted angrily, 'and you repay me by killing another one of my friends in cold blood.'

Endellion grabbed Marcus by the shoulder as he tried to follow Arkadin into battle, shaking his head in a discouraging fashion.

'There's no need, Marcus,' he hissed. 'It will be over soon, so watch from here. You must not risk yourself needlessly.'

Marcus watched as the scrum evolved, the blue energy weapon flashing again and again, but it was soon clear that the two Visnaer priests were overwhelmed. Those watchers who had not joined the charge with Arkadin had been busy preventing the skeletal warriors from rescuing their doomed masters. The fight was quickly resolved and Arkadin walked slowly back towards them, clutching a wounded arm that bled profusely. He carried the strange power spear that he had taken from the Visnaer priest and, handing it to Marcus for safekeeping, headed over to Tuuvar, asking her to tend his wounds.

The skeletal army, reanimated by the power of Evixius, had dropped to the ground as soon as the head priest had been slain. Their subdued captives had also been freed and were now shaking off the mental shackles that had held them in thrall to the Visnaer. They looked around in dismay, wondering how they had ended up here, far away from their homes.

Marcus and Endellion walked over towards them, assuring them that they were now free, that they were once again in the company of friends.

*   *   *

On Nesteris the Aellindi were fighting back hard, the main army having finally relieved their embattled vanguard, desperate to drive the enemy from their beloved city. The energy portal remained open, although thankfully it had ceased disgorging further skeletal reinforcements. Mizarius had marched up with the main battle force and was fighting desperately at the centre of the Aellindi line. He sent jets of fire into the skeletons, which he found to be an effective way of destroying these sinister creatures, or expertly swung his curved blade in deadly arcs, cutting through their brittle bones whenever the creatures threatened to overrun their position.

'Where is the Ligarian?' he asked.

'I'm not certain,' replied the officer in charge. 'She was here with her priests, but they seem to have disappeared.'

'I don't like it. Why would they create a portal and then just vanish? It makes no sense, and it makes me nervous. Send some troops to determine where they've gone.'

As the officer was responding to his commander's orders, dispatching a small squad of winged scouts to go in search of the missing Ligarian and her lieutenants, the portal started to expand in size. It began to fizz and pop, crackling wildly with untamed energy, its blue glow lighting up the area in an eerie fashion and casting ghoulish shadows across the entire battlefield.

'What's happening?' whispered the scout leader.

'Never mind that!' replied the officer in charge, 'just go and locate our missing Ligarian, but don't engage unless you have to. Get back here and inform me what, in the name of the Ancestors, she's up to.'

Just as the scouts vanished into the trees the portal flared once more, expanding to epic proportions, its blue-coloured energy changing to a dark grey hue, as if something huge had momentarily eclipsed it. Mizarius watched in horror as a huge white dragon emerged from the gateway and hurtled up into the sky above the two armies.

'We're in for it now,' he muttered, as he watched the massive beast soar up into the heavens above, before turning around and swooping down towards them with terrifying speed. 'Ready yourselves!' he shouted, sucking in as much aetheric energy as he could muster, in the vain hope that he could resist such a powerful foe.

It made only a single pass on the Aellindi warriors, spitting its frosty breath across the bone-strewn battleground, killing both Aellindi and skeletal warrior without distinction, before climbing back up into the blue sky and winging its way speedily towards the harbour.

'Well that complicates things!' cursed the officer in charge. 'We cannot abandon the battle here, nor do we have the firepower to combat such a creature.'

'We've got no choice, we must remain here,' replied Mizarius. 'We have to gain control of this portal to ensure that the enemy cannot escape. We must have faith that our comrades back at the harbour will be sufficient to combat the dragon.'

The officer nodded at him and both men turned back to the combat, which had once again closed in around them. They raised their weapons and plunged into the tumultuous struggle.

*   *   *

The portal in the *Beacon of Rhasad* flared to life and Navesh stepped through, closely followed by his refugees and their rescue party. He had seen much in his life, but was unprepared for what he now observed as he looked down upon the harbour below the city of Nesteris. Many ships were waiting to dock and many more had already disgorged their warriors onto the quayside. Navesh recognised the livery of the Kingdom warriors and he assumed that King Elridan had sent his troops to aid the Aellindi, just as Navesh's own people had done during the demon war. What terrified him the most however, was the huge white dragon that swooped down upon the ships below, tearing them apart with its huge claws, or blasting them into tiny fragments with its powerful breath.

Nineteen

Queen Karmina led her party along the forest trail, towards the tower that held the stones of power. She could hear the sounds of battle behind her and by now her undead army would have received some of the reinforcements that she had amassed back on her own world. G'Valk had just emerged from the dense forest, having scouted forwards to locate the entrance to the tower.

'It's heavily defended,' he said quietly, 'although a swift strike would be sufficient to take most of them out.'

The Queen shook her head, indicating that such an action was unnecessary and beckoned her disciples to follow her into the trees.

'Stealth will be our ally here,' she whispered, weaving a subtle illusion around them to conceal their approach.

She unslung her own energy spear, in case they should be detected by some unknown power. The weapon made a brief high-pitched whining sound as it awakened from its slumber, as if sensing that its power was required, and the group resumed their furtive march through the forest.

The tower appeared through the trees and the Queen stood for a moment, looking up at its majestic splendour, the top levels bursting forth from the forest canopy above. She had seen Aellindi architecture before, in the city of Braefell, and was struck by how similar this ancient edifice was to those on her own, totally separate world fragment. The structures of the Ancestors truly were designed to last forever.

'My Queen,' G'Valk whispered awkwardly.

'Speak!' snapped Queen Karmina, irritated by his interruption of her quiet contemplation.

'I mean no disrespect, my Queen, but is it wise to enter the tower with so many guardians outside? If we were to be discovered, we'd be open to a counterattack and possible entrapment within.'

'Do not fear,' cooed the Queen, tenderly touching his cheek and caressing the smooth blue skin. 'The power of Evixius will guide us.'

G'Valk nodded and stepped back, forming up with the others, waiting for the Queen to lead the way.

As the Visnaer priest had indicated, the entrance to the tower was heavily guarded by the Aellindi. The Queen waited patiently, observing the scene and evaluating the strength of the garrison that held vigil here, guarding their most prized possessions. Although she believed in her god's ability to keep them safe while they conducted their stealthy raid, she had also listened to G'Valk's words and wanted to be certain that she was making the right choice.

'Let's begin,' she whispered, finally satisfied that stealth was the correct course of action.

She led her followers out of the trees and walked casually towards the tower entrance. As expected, the defenders had not detected their approach and they walked straight past the guards and into the tower. The structure was huge and without the aurora from the stones of power to guide her, they might have spent days searching the myriad of floors and rooms which filled its interior.

Carefully reaching out to the aether, following its lines of power back to their source, Queen Karmina allowed her mind to wander the hallways and stairwells of the tower. Moving like an ethercal spirit through stone and timber, she determined exactly where the stones of power had been secreted. She returned to her own body and opened her eyes once more, motioning for G'Valk to lead the way down a passageway that would take them to the catacombs beneath the tower.

The thieves descended a long spiral staircase, lit by strange glowing spheres and which grew cooler the further they descended. Moisture coated the surface of the stone walls and small patches of iridescent algae grew around each of the light globes. They emerged into a wide hallway that disappeared off into the gloomy distance and which was also guarded by the noble Aellindi. They moved unseen, disappearing around a corner and descending another set of stairs, which were narrower than before and this time barely illuminated by the guttering torches that were held in rusty sconces along the wall.

After weaving their way through the seemingly endless catacombs, they emerged into a small round chamber with a large ornate pedestal standing in the centre, on which lay the two remaining stones of power. Queen Karmina gasped at the sight of them, their power radiating out from their smooth green surface. The chamber was guarded by a handful of Aellindi warriors who stood to attention beside their two tiny charges, oblivious to the presence of the intruders.

Certain that these would be the finest warriors that the Aellindi could muster, ready to spring into action without hesitation, G'Valk and his priests burst from their concealment to strike swiftly at their enemies. The Aellindi were taken completely unawares and were dispatched with barely a struggle, the sound contained by the Queen's magic, momentarily extended to encompass the skirmish.

'I can feel the power radiating out from this chamber, infusing the world beyond with aetheric energy,' said the Queen. 'It's almost too much to bear.'

She slowly approached the stones, stepping carefully towards the pedestal, aware that traps may have been laid here that would alert the Aellindi to their intrusion. She unconsciously held her breath, desperate to obtain the stones, and soon she was standing before them. The ancient artefacts were finally within her reach.

All was quiet in the depths of the Aellindi tower and, as far as she could tell, her presence had not been detected. She reached out and picked up the first stone, followed swiftly by the second. Just like the one that she already possessed, which she had discovered in the snowy wasteland outside her palace, they were warm to the touch and glowed softly with an inner light. She reached within them, gently caressing the power that coursed through their crystalline structure and drawing a little to strengthen her concealing shroud.

'Are you sure they're safe?' asked Nadarru, concerned that the Queen might unleash the power of the aether upon them. 'Aren't they supposed to contain the entire magical power of the world?'

'It's quite safe, my child. They don't actually hold the power within, for that would be impossible. They act as a conduit between the wellspring of the aether and the world fragment on which they're located. The Aellindi foolishly allow the inhabitants of this world to draw upon the well of the Ancestors, but that's about to change. I can tap directly into the power, preventing others from sharing it. I'll become all powerful and none will be able to stand against me.'

Queen Karmina held the stones in her hand, gazing down upon their beauty, before depositing them into a small pouch that was secured to her belt. With their mission here complete, she indicated that G'Valk should lead the way back to the surface. After ensuring that the shroud was firmly in place she followed her priests through the corridors of the catacombs. They hurried past the Aellindi guards, who did not stir as the band of thieves scurried by, fearful that the stones would be missed at any moment.

They emerged into the bright sunlight, their way barred by a detachment of warriors, headed up by an aged Aellindi woman who was leaning heavily on her ornately carved staff. Her scales glistened in the sunlight that filtered down through the forest canopy, and her head was adorned with bony plates that stood erect, giving her a fearsome visage.

'You cannot escape,' said Endina, staring directly at the Queen, dispelling the concealment shroud with a wave of her staff and directing her troops to surround the fleeing thieves. 'You must know this?'

Queen Karmina remained quiet for a moment, aware that somehow they had been discovered and that her aetheric disguise had been dispelled by this decrepit Aellindi witch. They would now have to battle their way back to the portal if she were to retain possession of the stones. The priests shifted slightly beside her, thumbing their energy spears to life as more Aellindi guards emerged from the tower.

'*Are you ready, my child?*' asked Queen Karmina, the question forming directly in Nadarru's mind. '*You must enlighten these savages with the love of Evixius . . . do you understand this task that has been given to you?*'

'*I understand, my Queen. I'm prepared.*'

'It's too late, Aellindi,' said Queen Karmina, with cold hatred. 'I have the stones and will not be stopped by the likes of you, old hag!'

Endina directed a powerful bolt of lightning at the intruders, hurling one of the priests across the trail, where he lay, injured from the blast, with smoke rising lazily from his body.

'Take them, now!' said the Queen. 'I'll have no further delays.'

The Visnaer fired their weapons, cutting down several Aellindi guards as Endina readied another blast of aetheric energy. The noble warriors moved in to engage their enemies and a desperate struggle ensued.

*   *   *

The main Aellindi army was beset on all sides, vastly outnumbered as waves of skeletal warriors poured through the portal. Mizarius fought beside the officer in charge, although the enemy were incredibly difficult to subdue. He ordered his magi to employ destructive pyromancy wherever possible, as this appeared to be the most successful way to destroy the skeletal constructs. But, as with any prolonged use of the aether, they were beginning to tire and relied more and more on the skill of their warrior brethren to keep the enemy at bay. They had been pushed back, away from the portal, slowly giving ground before the oncoming tide of reanimated bones. It was clear that their position was precarious at best, and that they were close to being overrun. They must turn the tide of the battle soon, before all was lost.

'Have the scouts returned yet?' he asked.

'No,' replied the officer in charge. 'Something must have happened to them.'

'Let me take a squad of warriors and I'll go and look for them. We must know what they found out and if they managed to locate the Ligarian.'

The officer in charge detached a small group of warriors and Mizarius headed away from the battle, running as swiftly as he could in the direction of the tower.

*   *   *

'We're in deep trouble,' said Navesh, looking down upon the chaos that had engulfed the harbour before scanning the wider city, where he caught glimpses of the battle in the distance. 'We must go to the aid of our people. I need to find out what has happened here. Rikoth, Praevir, come with me!'

The three heroes, joined by the other Aellindi and any Kingdom soldiers who were able to fight, headed swiftly down to the harbour. Those who were gifted with wings soared on ahead and rapidly disappeared from sight.

'What should we do?' asked Panx, looking over at Indrani.

'I've got an idea,' she replied. 'Follow me. I hope you're not afraid of heights!'

Panx hurried by, casting a quizzical look at Tethine and Idris, who had been tasked with the guardianship of Fireen and the remaining refugees.

They hurried out of the beacon, heading over the connecting stone bride that linked it with the island. The dragon roared overhead, spitting its icy breath at any targets that it chanced across. Many of the Kingdom ships lay in ruins, having just returned from the desperate sea battle. They had been shattered into large splinters by the beast as they floated in the harbour, completely at its mercy. A few ballistae shots had managed to find their mark and Panx was heartened to see red streaks running down the dragon's flank where the huge bolts had embedded themselves.

'Are we going up in that?' he asked, indicating Indrani's little airship.

'Got any better ideas?' she replied, as they hopped into the small gondola that hung down beneath the buoyant envelope.

'No,' he muttered, holding onto the little rope handles, feeling terribly exposed.

Indrani untied the mooring ropes and began to infuse the power crystals with aetheric energy, and very soon they felt the gondola lurch as the gas-filled airship began to rise.

'I hope you know what you're doing!' said Panx, watching in horror as the ground receded beneath them.

'Don't worry, Panx, I've done this several times now! Let's gain some height before we make our move on that dragon.'

'I knew you were going to say that,' replied the young magus, hurriedly tapping into the power of the aether, which was again proving a little temperamental.

He was uncertain why his magic was being so erratic, but perhaps he was still adjusting to the transition between the two worlds. Hopefully his control would return soon.

'You'd better have a few powerful spells up your sleeve,' said Indrani, as she brought the little airship to halt at the summit of the beacon. 'Shall we?'

'Okay, let's go,' replied Panx, not wanting to admit that he was terrified of failing his friends.

Indrani reached out with her aeromancy, tapping into the aether and into the energy crystal that was an integral part of her airship design. The craft responded instantly, deftly leaving the cover offered by the beacon and heading out over the harbour towards the dragon as it swooped down upon the Kingdom ships. She could see sailors jumping over the sides, fleeing in terror as the monstrous beast hurtled towards them. But it was too late for many of them as the sea around the ships turned to ice, trapping them within or cutting them to shreds as they fought to escape the razor-sharp shards of frozen water.

The airship picked up speed and, with the gondola swaying gently in the wind, streaked through the sky towards the monstrous beast that was laying waste to the dwindling forces that guarded the harbour.

*   *   *

Mizarius raced along the forest trail, desperate to reach the tower that housed the stones of power. He was worried that, even though he had increased the strength of the garrison and had moved the stones from their usual residing place, they were still vulnerable and he hoped that he was not too late. Endina was already there, commanding the warriors. She possessed a deep connection to the aether, although only passable skill with a blade.

'Over here, sir,' shouted one of his men, pointing to a group of Aellindi that had been brutally slain and lay in pools of their own blood.

'One of them is still alive,' replied Mizarius, hurrying over to kneel beside the wounded scout, lifting him up and resting him against his knee.

The scout, who Mizarius recognised as the squad leader, slowly opened his eyes.

'Councillor,' he croaked in greeting. 'I'm sorry, but we failed you.'

'Not at all,' Mizarius replied gently. 'Tell me what happened here.'

'We were following the Ligarian and her Visnaer protectors. However, it seems that we were the ones who were being stalked.' He coughed slightly, spitting blood on Mizarius's tunic, before continuing his report. 'They were waiting for us, appearing like phantoms from the trees, cutting down my men with such ferocity and skill. I've never seen such a display of brutality before.'

He lapsed back into unconsciousness and Mizarius gently shook him, desperate to hear anything else that he might have to say. After a short while the scout reopened his eyes and focused once more on his commander.

'Where did they go?'

'That way,' whispered the scout, nodding in the direction of the tower. 'She's not alone,' he added, causing Mizarius to look down quizzically at him.

'What do you mean?'

'There's another Visnaer woman, their queen I think, and she now commands them. Even the Ligarian defers to her authority. She's very powerful, councillor, you must be wary.'

Mizarius waited a moment longer, desperate for more information, but it was clear that the scout had once again lapsed into unconsciousness. After gently laying him on the ground, Mizarius infused him with healing magic and left him where they had found him, hopeful that he would survive long enough for them to retrieve him on their way back.

'Follow me,' he said, heading along the trail at a swift trot.

He was so desperate to reach the tower that he failed to notice the Visnaer standing directly in his path and only the frantic yelling of his men saved him. They dived to safety as the blue energy of the Visnaer weapons lanced towards them. Several of his warriors were cut down, their flesh turning rapidly to dust and their bones clattering to floor. The Visnaer were not alone either, and Mizarius's blood turned to ice as he realised that the undead creatures that accompanied them had once been Aellindi.

'You'll never get away from here,' he muttered, moving slowly towards the Queen, hoping to engage her in close combat.

'Pathetic creature,' rebuked the Queen, reaching out and hurling him backwards with a blast of aetheric energy, leaving him badly wounded.

He watched as the remainder of his warriors were brutally cut down and then swiftly reanimated by the Ligarian, using the dark arts of necromancy.

As the Queen and her entourage hurried away, back towards the main battle and the portal that had allowed her to penetrate his beloved island, Mizarius struggled to his knees. He was battered, bruised and his skin was badly burnt by the Queen's powerful blast.

He grimaced with pain as he tried to get to his feet, uncertain what he could do but determined that he would not let the invaders escape.

'Where do you think you're going?' said a quiet voice, from somewhere behind him.

He turned to see a Visnaer priest standing on the trail, spear held above his head, ready to strike. Mizarius closed his eyes and whispered a short prayer to the Ancestors, accepting that he no longer had a part to play in this desperate struggle.

*   *   *

Rikoth lashed out with his warhammer, smashing the skeletal warriors to the ground, irritated by their ability to get back up from all but the most powerful of blows. He and the other warriors that had raced up from the beacon had finally joined the ranks of the Aellindi fighting on the outskirts of the city, and had helped to regain the initiative. The undead army had not received any reinforcements for some time now and the Aellindi were slowly pushing them back towards the glowing blue portal, intent on driving them through.

'There they are,' shouted Navesh, pointing towards the Visnaer who had just emerged from the forest trail. 'We must stop them before they get away. She has the stones, I can sense their presence. We must hurry!'

Rikoth wasted no time and sprinted towards the escaping enemy commanders, followed closely by Navesh and many other Aellindi warriors. The Queen, having spotted their approach, ordered her reanimated Aellindi forces to move forward and engage them, before she herself hurried on towards the portal. The heroes were briefly swamped by the powerful skeletal warriors who charged towards them, but soon managed to break free of the skirmish, leaving their subordinates to deal with their reanimated foes while they valiantly tried to intercept the Visnaer.

The four priests turned around, hefting their spears and spinning them round with majestic grace, standing between the charging Aellindi and Queen Karmina. Rikoth hurtled into the fray, swinging his own weapon in a similar display of martial skill, catching one of the Visnaer spears on its tip as the priest attempted to cut him down. A second priest, recognising the Aellindi warrior for what he was, a true killer and weapon master of unsurpassed skill, joined her fellow and the two of them circled him warily.

Navesh had activated his own spear and the mighty golden shaft, tipped with a razor-sharp blade, rapidly coalesced into being as he resorted to one of his favoured tactics, disappearing from view altogether. He reappeared moments later, standing directly behind G'Valk who whirled around quickly and only just managed to deflect the powerful strike that was aimed at him.

The fourth priest found himself in a battle against Praevir, who had dropped from the sky and swiftly engaged him with powerful strokes of his mighty curved blade. He had already been injured during the encounter with Endina, and soon found himself struggling to parry the furious blows that Praevir was raining down upon him.

Although the Visnaer had fought the Aellindi on many occasions, they were not prepared for the prowess of these three warriors. Never had they faced such individual skill and determination and they were soon pushed back, towards their retreating queen and the portal that would take them home.

'Oh no, I don't think so,' hissed Rikoth, 'you're not getting away this time.'

He dived forward, rolling in under the reach of the two Visnaer, too close for their spears to be effective, and then struck out savagely with a clawed hand, slicing through one of their throats. The priest, a powerfully built woman, clutched at her neck as her lifeblood surged out, gushing down across her body. Rikoth, covered in Visnaer blood, took a single step backwards to afford himself a little room and then smashed the other priest in the chest with his warhammer. The blow crushed the Visnaer's ribcage, sending him sprawling onto the bloody ground and Rikoth followed up with a powerful stomp of his armoured boot, crushing his skull with an ear-splitting crunch.

Praevir circled the wounded priest, who was now bleeding from several fresh cuts. The winged Aellindi warrior was a master swordsman and easily deflected the Visnaer's attacks, deftly knocking them aside and landing his own strikes on the priest who seemed unable to defend himself.

Realising that he was outclassed, the priest whirled his spear around and tried to catch Praevir with a blast of energy, hoping to use the power of the weapon rather than rely on his own dwindling strength. It almost worked. But Praevir spotted the manoeuvre just in time, stepping in closer and thrusting his sword up into the priest's chest. The Visnaer drew in a sharp breath as the blade was forced deeper into his body and then fell backwards as Praevir withdrew it, kicking him to the ground and leaving him to his fate.

G'Valk was a skilled warrior, by far the equal of the other priests, which was why he had swiftly gained his Queen's favour and the position as her anointed protector. But he had never before fought someone as skilled as the warrior who now faced him. Navesh, hardened by years of combat experience in Valken's dark world, parried every blow that the Visnaer champion swung at him. As he frantically dodged Navesh's spear he watched in horror as his priests were cut down by these new arrivals. *Who were they?* he wondered, having never witnessed such dexterity before.

Navesh fought savagely, desperate to end the fight quickly and continue his pursuit of the retreating queen. His opponent was good and he narrowly avoided the razor-sharp spear as it sliced through the air beside him. But he was fighting for more than just his own survival. He fought for the survival of his people and the entire world and this fuelled his rage, giving him the strength to battle on.

'You'll never stop her!' taunted G'Valk, smiling at Navesh as they circled one another. 'I'll be the last thing that you'll see as she disappears with your precious stones.'

'Oh I don't think so, vile creature,' replied Navesh. 'It is I that will be the last thing that you see!'

Navesh stepped adroitly aside and vanished from sight. G'Valk turned around, frantically searching for his opponent. His eyes widened in shock as Navesh's spear burst from his chest, having been mercilessly thrust into his exposed back. The Aellindi hero did not stop to retrieve his ancient weapon, and snatched up G'Valk's own spear before sprinting off to intercept the escaping queen.

*   *   *

Indrani's airship soared through the sky, chasing the dragon as it swooped down towards the troops below. It opened its maw as it dived, spitting great spears of ice at the tiny warriors on the quayside and sending them diving for cover. The beast was injured from several ballistae bolts that had managed to catch it unawares. But despite these lucky hits, the dragon still reigned supreme here and the ships had finally ceased firing, their ammunition all but depleted.

Panx lashed out at the creature with a ball of superheated flame, having already discovered that it was susceptible to heat. But the spell missed its target, as the airship made a sudden turn, Indrani desperate to avoid the dragon's icy breath. His flames plummeted into the sea below, creating a dense, steaming fog.

'I think the dragon has damaged the airship,' shouted Indrani, struggling to keep the little craft under control. 'That last pass was a little too close for comfort. If you're going to do something amazing, now would be a good time!'

Panx searched the sky for the dragon. It seemed to be toying with them and had momentarily disappeared from view. He reached deep within himself, searching for the snaking tendrils of power that connected his mind to the aether. They were there, but for some inexplicable reason stayed just beyond his grasp, allowing him to draw upon just a tiny fraction of the magical energy.

'Come on, Panx!' he muttered as the dragon reappeared, causing Indrani to suddenly swoop down under the beast as it hurtled by.

He focused his mind, remembering how it had been on the dark world, when for some reason he had unleashed an almost unlimited torrent of power against the demons that threatened their escape. The dragon dived again, knocking the airship aside with a flick of its tail and Indrani desperately fought to regain control before they crashed into the harbour. At that moment Panx unleashed a terrific blast of energy at the departing dragon, which slammed into the creature's back as it began to circle around for another pass.

That's it! He thought. *I'm trying too hard. Just let it flow, Panx, just let it flow.*

He closed his eyes and relaxed, which was quite difficult as the airship seemed to be spinning around violently. When he opened them again the power was there, and so was the dragon, speeding straight at them, intent on dispatching them once and for all.

Panx unleashed a stream of fire directly at the incoming beast, which swerved violently as it tried to avoid the flames. But it was Panx who was in control now and he slowly tracked the aetheric fire across the sky. The huge white dragon was hit full on, the flames searing its flesh and causing it to scream out in agony. It was a terrifying noise that thundered across the harbour. But Panx did not relent in his assault, lest his power fail him once more. He kept the energy directed towards their foe, slowly forcing it down into the depths of the sea just outside of the harbour walls.

'It's over, Panx,' shouted Indrani, bringing the young magus out of his trance-like state. 'You did it. The Dragon's gone.' She was staring at him in wonder, as she gently cajoled the damaged airship back towards the *Beacon of Rhasad*.

*   *   *

Queen Karmina approached the glowing portal with hungry anticipation. She was almost home and just a few more steps would see her back in her palace, with the three stones of power from this world completely under her control. They would afford her an unlimited wellspring of aether to draw upon, one that only she would have access to and would make her the most powerful magus on her world. She would be like a god.

'Look out!' cried G'Valk, limping after her, blood seeping from his wounded chest and soaking into his tunic.

He was pointing towards the portal and she turned around, just as Navesh reappeared, blocking her way.

'Hand over the stones,' he hissed, pointing the energy spear at her. 'They don't belong to you.'

'Pathetic fool,' she cursed, reaching out with her mind and snatching the spear from Navesh's outstretched hands, sending it skittering to the floor.

As Navesh moved forward to engage the Queen, Nadarru leapt upon his back, taking him off-guard and causing him to topple to the floor where he struggled to detach himself from her sharp claws.

'Thank you, my child,' said the Queen, calmly walking towards the portal. 'I'll always remember you fondly,' she added, laughing cruelly as she stepped through the event horizon and disappeared from sight.

Navesh, having finally released himself from Nadarru's desperate grasp, dived towards the portal. He intended to follow the Queen through, but the portal winked out of existence before he could get there and he stumbled onto the dusty ground where the gateway had been only moments before.

Rikoth had finished off the dying G'Valk and came to stand beside Navesh, looking down upon the Ligarian woman who knelt at his side, tears streaming down her face as she looked towards the place where the portal had once been.

'She's abandoned you,' he said, feeling deeply sorry for her. 'She ran away and left you here.'

Navesh sat there on the dusty ground and looked around in a state of total shock, unable to focus on what was occurring around him. Fortunately, with the Queen's departure and the death of her priests, and with Nadarru in no fit state to extend the influence of Evixius, the undead army stumbled to a halt, their bones clattering to the ground. The Aellindi had survived the invasion of their homeland, but with the loss of the stones of power, the cost seemed insurmountable.

*   *   *

Tethine paced around the chamber at the top of the *Beacon of Rhasad*, nervously awaiting Navesh's return.

'Mother, come quickly,' cried Idris. 'I think Fireen is waking up.'

'What's wrong with her eyes?' asked Tethine, coming to stand beside her son.

Suddenly Fireen let out an agonised scream and her body was wracked by violent convulsions.

Twenty

Marcus rode beside Endellion as the bavnok pulled the sled across the plains, while Tuuvar sat behind them, deep in conversation with some of the rescued prisoners. There were so many of them and all had been eternally grateful to their saviours, eagerly accepting Arkadin's offer of transport to Braefell. Marcus was delighted to have played a part in setting them free and was left feeling elated at having done something so heroic. He could not comprehend the evil power of the Stone Queen, or what she had intended for these people, and was overjoyed that, on this occasion at least, her wicked plans had been foiled.

His eyes kept wandering to the red-haired Visnach woman that they had rescued. She looked so much like Indrani that it left his insides feeling knotted and painful. How he longed to see her again.

'Are you all right, Marcus?' asked Endellion.

'Yes, I'm fine. It's just that the Visnach woman reminds me of Indrani, and I can't help worrying about her. Things were a little . . . precarious when I left, and I hope that they've not deteriorated.'

He knew that she would be frantic with worry, but he also suspected that she was likely to strangle him if and when he ever got home.

They had made excellent progress since the battle and the seemingly indefatigable bavnok had carried them far from the icy fringes of the world, closer to the still-warm interior. They were still many miles from Braefell, the ancient home of the Aellindi on this world. But already the air was more pleasant and the grass, where it managed to grow up through the receding ice and snow, was a rich green colour. *The Watchers* had cast off the thick animal skins, and now used them as cushions to make the bumpy journey a little more bearable.

Arkadin called a halt at the edge of an ancient forest. The icy ground was nearly thawed here and several of *The Watchers* set about modifying their sleds. Marcus watched with fascination as they connected sturdy looking wheels that would aid the bavnok in hauling them across ground no longer covered in smooth, almost frictionless ice.

Marcus explored the immediate area and was excited to find a strange stone archway that provided the only access into the densely packed trees. It was covered in ornately carved symbols that reminded him of the ancient hieroglyphs adorning the statues, temples and tombs of the ancient Egyptians. A wide road passed through the archway and disappeared into the darkness beyond.

'Are we going in there?' he asked, as he returned to the camp.

'Yes,' replied Arkadin. 'It's the quickest route to Braefell. It's only a short distance through the trees, but the journey would take far longer if we went all the way around.'

'What are those archways? I've not seen them before on my world fragment.'

'We're not entirely sure, but we think they were left behind by the Ancestors. Some sort of entrance structure, would be my guess.'

'And the symbols?'

'We don't know.'

With *The Watchers* fed and rested, and with wheels fitted to their sleds, Arkadin ushered his people through the archway and into the forest. Once he had become accustomed to the initial darkness, Marcus found that sufficient light filtered down through the canopy and he looked around with fascination as the sleds trundled along. He noticed the road was made from the same curious material as the one that led to the *Beacon of Andin*.

'Will we have to spend the night in here?' he asked, remembering the horrifying attack from the giant insects.

'No,' replied Tuuvar, 'it won't take us long to get through the forest. We'll reach the other side before sunset. If I'm reading him correctly, Arkadin is keen to press on well after dark. He's desperate to reach Braefell and introduce you to the council of elders.'

'Oh,' Marcus replied nervously.

As predicted, the journey through the forest had been swift. Their wheeled sleds had rolled smoothly along the road, emerging from the forest well before nightfall. Also as predicted, Arkadin had not stopped, but had pressed onwards, eager to cover as much ground as possible.

Finally, many hours after sunset, the leader of *The Watchers* had begrudgingly called a halt. Marcus assumed that it was more to allow the bavnok to rest than out of concern for the comfort of his people, who were a tough, resilient group, used to living at the icy fringe of their world.

The huge animals and their carers rested for several hours but as the sun once again peered over the horizon, casting an eerie red glow across their makeshift campsite, Arkadin called his people to action. They stowed their belongings and set off once more, continuing their ardent march towards their home city.

'What's that up ahead?' asked Marcus, pointing to a vast circle of stones that he had spotted off to one side.

'An ancient temple,' replied Endellion. 'One of the Visnach stone rings.'

'Dedicated to Nurarian,' added Tuuvar.

'Wow!' replied Marcus as the group moved closer to the stone circle. 'Look at that statue, it's huge.'

The ancient temple was composed of huge monolithic stones, painstakingly chiselled into near-perfect oblong blocks and then placed into large, symmetrical rings. Some of the blocks had toppled over but many stood where they had first been placed, hundreds, if not thousands of years ago. In some way the temple reminded him of *Stonehenge*, back on his own world. It even featured huge lintel blocks, lying horizontally across the tops of other stones, which held them aloft like huge gateways into the temple interior. What made the scene different however was the titanic statue at the centre of the innermost stone ring. It was an intricately carved likeness of a unicorn, depicted rearing up on its hind legs, although there were signs of damage, likely caused by the ravages of time. One of the forelegs, which would have been reaching up towards the heavens, had broken off and lay on the temple floor. It had smashed the small stone alter and toppled several of the standing stones during the collapse. But it was still an impressive sight to behold and he suddenly recalled the temple that Indrani had discovered on her visit to Reznar. What were the odds of him chancing across such a similar temple on this separate fragment of the ancient Aellindi homeworld? He was overcome with sudden excitement and knew that he had to investigate it further.

Arkadin trudged over to Marcus's sled, which had, at the professor's insistence, been brought to a halt.

'He doesn't look very happy,' whispered Marcus.

'No, he does not,' replied Endellion. 'Although I expect he is just wondering why we have stopped.'

Marcus explained that he wanted to explore the temple, insisting that he could almost feel it calling out to him and that he could not pass by without taking a look. After a heated discussion in which Arkadin tried his best to dissuade Marcus from delaying their journey, he finally relented, having exhausted all of his reasons why they must press on.

'Very well, Marcus, we'll rest here while you explore the temple,' Arkadin conceded. 'But please don't linger too long. We still have some distance to travel.'

'Thank you, Arkadin,' replied Marcus. 'I'm sorry to delay our trip, but there's something about that stone circle. I just can't ignore it.'

With that Marcus hopped back on the sled and, under Endellion's skilful control, the bavnok carried them in the direction of the Visnach temple.

They halted just outside of the huge outer ring of monoliths and Marcus jumped down, heading towards a pair of stones which seemed to mark the temple entrance. Endellion and Tuuvar followed behind. They had paused to feed the bavnok and now hurried to catch up with the excited professor, who was almost running towards the temple. However, before they could enter the huge stone circle, a bright white light erupted, as if from nowhere, shrouding the entire temple in its glare. As the two aged Aellindi squinted towards the bright light, their nictitating membranes closing to protect their delicate eyes, Marcus, who had already proceeded into the circle, simply vanished.

*   *   *

Calm had settled once more across the island of Nesteris. The Aellindi had suffered badly at the hands of the Stone Queen and they now busied themselves caring for their wounded and laying their fallen comrades to rest. To most, the sudden attack had come as a complete surprise and they did not understand the purpose of the invasion. The loss of the ancient stones of power was, at present, known only to a few individuals and the true meaning of the theft had only just begun to sink in.

Fireen sat at the head of the table in the council chamber. She had awoken suddenly at the top of the *Beacon of Rhasad*, and had instantly known what had occurred in the real world, while she had fought to escape her nightmarish visions. Although her eyes were open, her sight had not returned and she now sat with her fellow councillors, listening to their voices but unable to see their faces. Her Irises had once been a striking golden colour, with a beautiful iridescent quality, but she now gazed vacantly towards her friends through milky, opaque eyes. Fortunately, her mental faculties appeared not to have been harmed by her prolonged comatose state, and she patiently waited for the rest of the group to arrive, eager to begin the urgent quest to retrieve the stones of power.

'We must not fail!' she muttered quietly.

'What was that, Fireen?' asked Panx, who had just entered the room and taken a seat beside her.

'We must find the stones,' she replied, 'we must not fail in this! How is Tordin?'

'He's going to be fine, but he'll be in the infirmary for a little while yet.'

'I think he's got a crush on one of your apothecaries,' added Indrani.

'Only Tordin!' said Panx, trying to lighten the mood, although feeling guilty for doing so given the grave peril that they faced.

'The students are helping with the repairs to the *Hammer* and the *Drake*, as is Leandra,' said Indrani. 'They really seem to have an affinity for Marcus's technology and should have the ships ready soon.'

'Are Navesh and Praevir here yet?' asked Fireen.

'No, not yet,' replied Panx. 'Navesh is in the archive, looking for one of the ancient tomes. Praevir is visiting Saven in the infirmary. She was found lying on one of the beaches on the south side of the island. She'll be all right, although she's very weak at the moment.'

Fireen nodded, glad to hear that Saven had been located. *One small miracle amongst such loss and devastation*, she thought, a tear trickling down her cheek as she remembered Endina, Mizarius and the others who had perished in the invasion.

Navesh finally appeared, strolling purposefully into the council chamber, grim faced and clutching a large tome under his arm. He walked straight over to Fireen and touched her gently on the shoulder.

'I've found it,' he said. 'Shall we begin?'

'Yes, Navesh,' she replied, 'we can delay no longer.'

Navesh rapped loudly on the wooden table, demanding the attention of all in the room.

'My friends,' said Fireen, standing up to address them. 'There is no easy way to put this, but our world is in great peril and stands on the very brink of doom.'

Everyone was quiet, transfixed on the Aellindi leader, staring intently into her milky-white eyes as she looked around the room as though she were still able to see them.

'We must recover the stones of power before their absence strips our world of its connection to the aether and the protection that it affords us. Who knows what other side-effects their loss will have or what long-term damage might be caused.'

'What do you suggest?' asked Rikoth, who was seated beside Nadarru.

'We must know more about the Stone Queen,' replied Fireen, 'and we must determine where she has taken the stones. Then, and this will be the most perilous of tasks, we must find a way to follow her and take them back!'

'What about Marcus?' asked Indrani, feeling awkward asking about her missing husband, especially given all that the Aellindi had so recently lost.

'He's not our primary concern, Indrani,' replied Navesh, as calmly as he could manage. 'As I said before, I promise we'll look for him, but for now our most important task, the most important task that we've ever undertaken, is to retrieve the stones. For if we don't recover them soon, our world fragment will lose its connection to the aether and once that happens, we'll never be able to go in search of Marcus. I'm sorry, Indrani. I know you don't want to hear it, but the stones are more important than any one of us!'

As if to reinforce his statement, an earthquake suddenly shook the island, causing widespread damage across the city and leaving the council chamber with a large crack in its thick ceiling. The entire room was silent, fearful that further tremors were imminent. But when the ground stopped rumbling and the dust finally settled, Indrani looked back at Navesh and simply nodded her head.

'So what do we do?' asked Panx, breaking the silence that had fallen across the chamber. 'I don't know about the rest of you, but I can already feel the aether draining away. There's a void where its power used to be, and it's getting bigger.'

'I can still sense the stones, and can still access their power, albeit on a limited scale,' replied Fireen. 'But until we determine their location, we risk losing the connection completely.'

All eyes turned to Nadarru, who had been captured when her Queen had fled through the portal and who was now seated beside Rikoth. He had not left her side since the invasion had ended and clearly felt that she needed protection from those who might wish her harm.

'What can you tell us, Nadarru?' asked Navesh. 'Where can we find the Queen?'

Nadarru sat quietly for a moment, collecting her thoughts. She no longer felt the presence of the Stone Queen's power in her head and that tiny voice, which had been screaming at her from the back of her mind, had finally been set free. She felt a sense of utter dismay and deep remorse at the death and destruction that she had wrought in Queens Karmina's name. It filled her with a burning desire to make amends in any way that she could.

'My name is Nadarru,' she began, 'and I'm a Ligarian from the eastern coast of Thalmira, as you have no doubt discerned for yourselves.'

She told them her story, of how she had been orphaned at a young age and spent years living on the streets, stealing and begging for food. Hunger had made her careless and she had been caught by the city guards and sentenced to death. However, Denir had taken to her and had paid them off. From that point on she had become his servant, spending many years travelling with him as his caravan crossed from one side of the great desert to the other, selling exotic spices, expensive wines and occasionally people.

She recounted how they had been camped out in the middle of the desert, below the ancient tower, when the caravan had been attacked by the Visnaer priests. They had slaughtered everyone except for her

222

and had then taken her through some magical doorway to the Stone Queen's palace.

'She used us all,' she said, after a brief pause, a look of disbelief registering on her face. 'Even her loyal priests. It was all part of one huge diversion. The invasion by her skeletal warriors and the death and destruction on the west coast of Thalmira. Even the dragon, which was forced to do her bidding against its will. It was all done to distract you. She wanted those stones and threw everything else at you in order to confuse you and divert your attention away from protecting them. I'm so sorry for what I've done, truly I am.'

'But why you?' asked Panx. 'Why did she choose you? Why not just invade us with her undead warriors and her Visnaer priests?'

'She needed someone from this world to act as an anchor for her magic. It has something to do with focusing the portal on this world fragment and it allowed her to specifically target my location on Nesteris. But she never intended for us all to escape. We were expendable; tools for her to use and cast aside when she was finished with us. I'm sorry but I don't understand why she chose me that day at the tower, and why she didn't just ensnare the first person that she came across. For some reason, she slaughtered the others and gave me the power to reanimate them.'

'Tell us more about this tower in the desert, where your caravan was attacked,' said Navesh.

Nadarru described the tower and they all agreed that it sounded very much like one of the Ancestors' beacons, set at the centre of a long-dead city and surrounded by the vast rolling dunes of golden sand.

'Have you seen this symbol before?' Navesh hissed excitedly, opening the huge tome and placing it down upon the table in front of Nadarru.

'I'm not certain,' she replied, 'but I think it was etched on the entrance to the tower, and also in the large room at the top. At least I think so.'

'Is that what I think it is?' asked Indrani.

'Yes,' replied Navesh. 'It's the glyph that enticed our wayward professor to go . . . travelling!'

'I do not believe in coincidences,' said Fireen, speaking for the first time since Nadarru had related her story. 'There must be a connection with this tower in the desert, and the sudden appearance of its glyph, just when Marcus was watching.'

'Agreed,' replied Navesh. 'This is no chance occurrence. We must travel there at once! I believe that we'll find Marcus there, or at least a sign that he's been there recently. I also believe that this represents our strongest link to the missing stones of power. This beacon is significant, Fireen. We must see it for ourselves.'

'Whose beacon is it?' asked Panx.

'It belongs to Errithad, one of the Ancestors,' replied Navesh. 'According to the texts, it was Errithad that fell from grace, allowing the ruinous powers to bring about the cataclysm.'

'It seems very fitting that this particular tower has been used as a conduit into our world, in order to steal the stones of power from us,' replied Fireen. 'Errithad might have just unleashed a second cataclysm upon us.'

'How do we get there?' asked Panx, desperate to hear more about Errithad but recognising that Navesh was in no mood for history lessons. 'Should we try to travel directly from the *Beacon of Rhasad*?'

'Yes, Panx,' replied Navesh, 'we could try that first. But remember, the glyph disappeared from the *Beacon of Olon*, so I fear that the direct approach may not work.'

'We could take the *Drake*,' offered Indrani, clutching at any chance to go to the *Beacon of Errithad*, where she hoped she would be reunited with Marcus. 'But then we'd have to travel across the desert for many days.'

'It may be our only choice,' replied Fireen. 'If we wish to find the place that Queen Karmina first entered our world and follow her back to her own, we may have to make the arduous journey east!'

'Nadarru knows the way,' added Rikoth. 'She could guide us?'

Before anybody could reply to Rikoth's suggestion, Saven limped through the doorway and into the council chamber, followed closely by Praevir. She made her way over to where Nadarru was seated and, looking down upon the black-furred Ligarian, spat vehemently at her, causing Nadarru to turn away, fearful that Saven would follow her first assault with one far more violent.

'Saven! What's the meaning of this?' hissed Navesh.

'Am I not a member of this council?' retorted the injured Aellindi warrior. 'Am I not permitted to join this meeting?'

'You know what I meant, Saven,' replied Navesh, trying to calm his friend.

'There's no way that we should ever trust this woman,' hissed Saven, looking down at Nadarru with cold hatred. 'I watched as she and her lieutenants slaughtered the people of Xhaan. She will betray us at the first opportunity.'

'Saven, we all understand your anger, but it has no place here,' Rikoth said calmly.

'How can you say that, Rikoth?' she replied. 'How can you defend her, after all that has happened?'

'There are many amongst us,' continued Rikoth, 'myself included, who have fought a desperate battle with some . . . inner demon. I'm sure that Praevir has told you of our journey into the dark world, and the terrible things that I did there?' he added, looking over at Praevir, who nodded almost imperceptibly.

'Yes,' replied Saven, her shoulders sagging and the tension in her stance easing slightly. 'I've heard about what happened.'

'In a way,' muttered Rikoth, looking down on the frightened Ligarian, 'I feel a kinship with Nadarru. We've both been possessed by another and we both must now live with the consequences of our actions, even though we were not truly in control of them. If you cannot forgive her, then how is it that you can forgive me?'

'But she killed hundreds of innocents and facilitated the theft of our greatest artefacts,' Saven replied angrily, her temper rising once more. 'Surely your own crimes are not of the same magnitude?'

'The theft of our stones, or the brutal murder of innocents,' said Rikoth, looking around at those in the council chamber. 'You must decide, Saven, which is the greater crime. If that's even possible. But the truth is that Nadarru, as I was before her, was no more than a puppet with a malevolent master pulling the strings.'

Fireen indicated for Saven and Praevir to be seated.

'We will not forget what has happened here, Saven,' she said. 'But neither are we a vengeful people. As we did with Rikoth in the dark world, we shall watch Nadarru for any sign of treachery. But she will be given the chance to redeem herself.'

Satisfied that Saven had, for now at least, been pacified, Fireen and Navesh turned their attention to the mission. They must travel to the *Beacon of Errithad* and enter the Stone Queen's world to take back what had been stolen from them.

Twenty-one

By now, Endellion, Tuuvar and Arkadin were in a state of panic and had combined their powers to hurl great spears of aetheric energy at the dome of white light that had engulfed the ancient stone circle. But their attempts were futile and the energy was simply absorbed into the shroud of light, strengthening it further.

'It is no use!' hissed Endellion, ceasing his assault and lowering his hands in defeat. 'Just as we find the saviour of our people, he is taken from us, ensnared by some cruel trap.'

'Don't despair, Endellion,' replied Tuuvar, 'we just need more power if we're to crack open this energy barrier.'

Arkadin summoned the remaining watchers and they tried again to penetrate the Visnach temple.

*   *   *

Marcus stood beside the titanic statue of Nurarian, squinting into the bright light that had enveloped him. He could see nothing but white light and the unicorn god's stone likeness, although the statue was slowly fading away, becoming difficult to focus on. He tried to move, to walk back out of the stones, but they too had disappeared and he could not discern in which direction to go. He could feel the solid ground beneath him but could not see it, as if he walked on an invisible treadmill, inside a white room.

'Endellion? Tuuvar?' he shouted, trying to reach his friends outside the temple, but there was no reply.

A slight movement caught his eye. The white light shimmered as if something not quite as bright had moved across his field of vision.

'Hello?' he yelled. 'Is someone there?'

'Do not fear, Marcus,' replied a gentle voice that was simultaneously all around him and inside his head.

'Who's there? I can't see you.'

'How about now?'

As Marcus turned towards the sound, which was now coming from somewhere behind him, his vision finally focussed on a frail old man with a bald pate and a long white beard, which he tugged at as he approached. The man was short and hunched over with age. He leaned heavily on a wooden staff adorned with a small green gemstone that glowed faintly with some inner light. In stark contrast to the clean white surroundings, the man was dressed in a ragged brown cloak, which looked dirty and bug-ridden, and he shuffled slowly forward as though his legs no longer wished to support him.

Although Marcus had been surprised at the old man's sudden appearance, the creature that walked at his side left the professor utterly breathless. Beside the aged, dirty looking old man, stood the most majestic and beautiful white unicorn that Marcus had ever seen. It had a bright white coat and light grey mane and exuded a power beyond all comprehension, shaking its horned head from side to side as the odd looking duo approached.

Just a few years ago he would have scoffed at the thought of standing in a room with a unicorn, but since his transportation to the world of the Aellindi he had become very open minded. He had even ridden one of these magical beasts himself, whilst visiting Indrani's parents on K'vith. But this unicorn was different. It exuded a terrific magical aurora, which outshone even the bright light of his surroundings and which made the hair on his nape stand on end and left his skin tingling and sensitive to the touch. Surely this could only be Nurarian, the Visnach god of the heavens, known commonly as "The Traveller".

Marcus was not a devout man and had been a disciple of Science back on his own world. But in the presence of these two beings he had to fight the urge to kneel down and kiss the old man's crusty feet.

'Who are you?' he asked, 'and where am I?'

'You are within the stone circle, Marcus,' whispered a magical voice inside his head, which he assumed to be that of the unicorn god. 'We have simply removed you from time.'

'Temporarily you understand,' added the old man, smiling at the professor and waving his staff around theatrically. 'To remove someone from time altogether . . . now, that's a little more difficult, although not impossible.'

'Who are you?' Marcus asked again.

'Allow me to introduce myself,' said the old man. 'My name, as it's known to your friends, is Malan, the god of time. And this is–'

'Nurarian?' said Marcus, interrupting the old man and suddenly feeling guilty about it.

'Yes, exactly,' replied the old man, ignoring Marcus's lack of decorum.

The unicorn stepped forward and lowered its majestic head in greeting, pushing its powerful nose in his direction, as if asking him to rub its brow.

'I've often thought about trying to contact you, Nurarian,' said Marcus, feeling foolish, 'but never knew how to go about it.'

'Yes, yes . . . we know,' replied Malan. 'But that's not why we've come here today.'

'What do you want from me?' asked Marcus, wondering whether he truly wanted to know.

'Oh, we've just dropped in to make sure that you're fully aware of your role here.'

'That you fully comprehend the important tasks that lay before you,' added Nurarian, speaking in musical tones directly into Marcus's mind.

'Before you go home to your lovely wife and children that is,' completed Malan.

'Children?' exclaimed Marcus, somewhat confused. 'I only have one child, a son called Navesh.'

'Oh bother!' cursed Malan. 'I've done it again. Always getting the past and the future mixed up.'

'Can you get me back to Nesteris?'

'Perhaps,' replied Malan. 'But why would we, when you're quite capable of getting there yourself.'

Marcus looked at the two gods, his head beginning to thump as the constant riddle-talk made him feel dizzy.

'So what do you need me to do?'

'It is simple,' replied Nurarian. 'Fulfil your role as the prophesied saviour of these people.'

'But how in the heavens do I do that?'

'We can't just tell you what to do, Marcus! Where would be the fun in that,' said Malan.

'Perhaps if we showed him what would become of this world should he fail?' said Nurarian, to which the old man nodded his head, as if it were an excellent idea.

'Allow me.'

'Have it your own way,' chuckled Nurarian, its musical laughter reverberating through the chamber. 'Like you were going to give me the option anyway!'

Malan swished his staff through the air and Marcus felt as though he were falling, although the strange white light in which he had been captured did not move at all. After a brief moment, during which he thought he might be sick, the bright white colour of the room began to change, slowly darkening until he stood in complete blackness. He was still aware of the gods beside him, but other than their divine presence he could not see, or hear, anything.

Suddenly a light appeared in front of him and he was treated to a panoramic view of the dying world on which he was trapped. It was as if he were at the cinema, watching a blockbuster movie on the huge screen. The image started to drift across the landscape, viewed from a bird's perspective, swooping through the cloud towards the mountains which he recognised as the location of Varfell.

'We thought you'd appreciate this,' chuckled Malan, startling Marcus from his entranced reverie.

'Hmmm . . . yes, it's somehow familiar, I guess.'

As Marcus continued to watch the show, the image plummeted down towards ground level and he could see the snowy tundra below. It appeared devoid of life and a tempestuous blizzard was assaulting the frozen ground. The snow was building up into vast drifts that seemed to grow in size with every passing moment. He watched in fascination as the image flew ever onward, passing mile after mile of totally white terrain with no sign of vegetation whatsoever.

Soon he reached the small enclave of Varfell, which at first glance appeared deserted. But as the viewpoint moved closer, swooping in towards the main avenue that led to the temple, he saw bodies lying out on the frozen ground and he was certain that Endellion and Tuuvar had been amongst them.

As the view shifted once more, Marcus was presented with an image of a refugee camp with ragged tents that had collapsed under the weight of the snow. He saw many different races there, including humans, Visnach and a few others that he had not yet encountered. They were all dead, frozen to the ground below him as he soared by. He could feel a tear welling up at the corner of his eye and the back of his throat felt as if he were trying to swallow his tongue.

'Surely some must have survived?' he said, his voice hoarse and croaky.

'Watch!' whispered Malan.

The image shifted again and Marcus was shown the world from extreme height. He could make out the *Beacon of Olon* in the distance, on its lonely pier, reaching out into the cosmos. But he could see no trace of the veil. It had completely failed. He flew rapidly across the entire world fragment, but there was nothing to see but a vast, never ending ice field.

He spotted movement and he pointed towards it, hopeful that there might be some survivors clinging desperately to life. But as the gods showed him more closely just what it was that he had spotted, he felt his blood turn to ice. The movement was not that of desperate refugees, but a vast skeletal army marching across the icy plains. They were led by a beautiful blue-skinned woman astride an ornate sled pulled by skeletal hounds. She looked towards him as he flew by, lashing out with powerful beams of light as he approached. He screamed out in pain as he started to feel his insides burning and his flesh melting from his bones.

'Have you seen enough?' asked Malan.

'Yes,' he screamed, 'please, make it stop. I can't stand it anymore.'

No sooner had he thought he was about to die than the images on the screen disappeared, leaving him once again in the white light of the god's prison, with the feeling of pain rapidly fading.

'We're sorry to have forced you to endure that, Marcus, but we thought it would better serve your cause if you knew exactly what is at stake,' said Malan.

'So the Queen wins?' Marcus asked.

'Not necessarily,' replied Malan, 'but it's one possible outcome.'

'But one that we want to avoid,' added Nurarian.

'What can I do against the Stone Queen? You saw her power, how can I do anything about that?'

'You have allies, Marcus,' Malan reminded him. 'Don't be afraid to call upon them.'

'*The Watchers*?'

'Exactly!' said Malan, nodding his bald head energetically. 'They believe in you, and you should start to believe in yourself too.'

'But why can't you just deal with the Stone Queen and repair the damaged veil? Why do I have to get involved at all?'

'If only we could,' said Malan, 'we wouldn't hesitate.'

'But we have battles of our own to fight,' added Nurarian.

Marcus's mind was suddenly assaulted by visions of darkness, of pain, terror and intense suffering. He was overwhelmed as he tried to make sense of what he was being shown and was left feeling nauseous, with sharp pains shooting down his limbs. For a moment he thought he caught sight of a huge, dark figure. It was shrouded in a black veil and exuded an intense, violent energy, although when he tried to focus on the image it refused to keep still and he gave up.

'Is that Valken?'

'Oh no. This is something far more terrible,' replied Malan. 'Something way beyond the comprehension of most people's minds.'

'Evixius?' he asked, finally understanding just what the gods were telling him.

'Perceptive, Marcus,' said the majestic Nurarian. 'Like we said, we have battles of our own to fight.'

'So you're battling Evixius and I'm to help save these people?'

'I told you he was sharp!' exclaimed Malan, clapping the unicorn on the rump. 'Didn't I tell you!'

Nurarian did not reply but instead trotted closer to Marcus, circling him, before coming to stand before him.

'There is one more thing, Marcus,' said the majestic, musical voice.

'What's that?'

'You will need to steal an ancient artefact from the Aellindi here, in the city of Braefell.'

'Steal? What artefact?'

'You will know it when you see it.'

'What's it for?'

'For another time, Marcus, and another place.'

'Thanks,' replied the professor. 'I'm no good at stealing. Won't they just give it to me if I say it's important?'

'You will understand, in time, Marcus.'

'Perhaps we should send him back now?' interrupted Malan. 'I think his friends are getting a little anxious.'

The strange screen appeared again and Marcus was treated to a view of the stone circle in which he was purportedly still standing.

He could see that the temple was surrounded by *The Watchers*, along with many of the rescued prisoners. They were throwing the power of the aether at the temple, hurling as much energy as they could muster, in an attempt to disrupt the concealing shroud that Malan and Nurarian had placed over the site.

'Yes, I think you are correct,' replied Nurarian. 'Before they empty the entire wellspring of the aether or before they attract the attention of our brother.'

'Remember, Marcus,' said Malan, 'only you can save these people, and only you will have the necessary knowledge to do it. Fulfil the prophecy and all will be well.'

'Will I see you again?' asked Marcus.

'Yes,' replied the two gods in unison.

'When?'

'At some point in the future. Or is it the past?' said Malan, chuckling to himself.

'Riddles!' muttered Marcus, exasperated with the entire situation.

'Goodbye, Marcus, my dear friend,' added the old man. 'I've waited a long time to see you again.'

Before Marcus could reply to Malan's odd parting words, the two divine figures disappeared and the light began to fade, leaving him staring out of the temple towards his friends. *The Watchers* had ceased their assault on the dome and simply stood there, looking towards their prophesied saviour with a look of profound relief.

'Are you well, Marcus?' shouted Endellion, cautiously entering the stone circle.

'Yes,' replied Marcus. 'Shaken, but not stirred.'

'What?'

'Never mind. I'm fine.'

Marcus tried his best to explain his meeting with the gods, and that they had shown him just how desperate the situation was here, although he did not mention the ancient artefact that he was meant to steal from them. Arkadin and *The Watchers* found it difficult to take in at first, but as Marcus relayed the things he had seen and the words of the gods, they began to look upon him with a sense of reverence.

'I knew you were *The One*,' said Endellion, causing Marcus to wince a little at the title.

'I'm just me,' he replied. 'But I do seem to have a knack for getting myself into trouble!'

'Well . . . ' said Arkadin, rubbing his clawed hands together, 'given the grim future that you've been shown, Marcus, perhaps we ought to make haste? We're still some distance from Braefell and I don't want to waste any more time here.'

'Sure thing, Arkadin. I'll check out the temple again later,' replied Marcus, which elicited a look of dismay from the leader of *The Watchers*, and a hearty chuckle from Endellion and Tuuvar.

*　　*　　*

Indrani's airship floated above the baking sands. As was usually the case, the sun beat down with ferocious intensity upon the great desert, through the clear blue skies that blanketed the continent of Thalmira. Panx stood at the front of the gondola as it swayed gently in the thermals rising up from the hot surface below, his youthful eyes straining to spot the beacon which lay at the centre of the desert.

The airship had been hurriedly repaired following the clash with the dragon, and the tear in the envelope had been sealed with a fresh piece of ixoden silk. Indrani had been shocked to find her lost wagons, filled with the expensive fabric, waiting for her outside the *Beacon of Rhasad*. They had not been there when she and Panx had taken to the skies to combat the beast and she had no idea how, or when, they had actually appeared. The controls of the small vessel were, for now at least, responding well. Although she was beginning to find it difficult to keep the crystals charged, due to the failing connection to the aether and she hoped that it would not fail out here in the barren desert.

Leandra and the students had stayed behind, attempting to restore the connection to the desert beacon. If they could re-establish the portal it would offer them a far quicker way of returning home, assuming they managed to retrieve the stones of power.

'I can see it!' Panx shouted excitedly, 'way off in the distance.'

Indrani moved over to stand beside her friend and the two of them peered through the thick heat-haze.

'You do have good eyes, Panx,' she replied, 'but yes, I can just about see it too.'

'Shall we tell the others?'

'Yes,' replied Indrani, moving back towards the controls of the airship. 'I'll turn us around and we can give them the good news.'

The rest of the group were far behind the ranging airship, waiting for the afternoon heat to subside before setting off once more through the ever shifting dunes, following the map that Nadarru had taken from Denir. As she had done when they had mounted the rescue expedition into Valken's dark world, Fireen had insisted on taking as few people as possible. She still believed that stealth would be their greatest ally, and pointed out that a smaller group would require fewer supplies. It had been different for Nadarru, as her army of skeletal warriors had needed only the sustaining power of Evixius in order to survive, and had tirelessly stalked across the burning desert sands to reach their destination.

They had tried to travel directly to the *Beacon of Errithad*, but nothing they did was successful in creating a portal to the recently discovered tower. They had even returned to the *Beacon of Olon*, just in case a connection could be made from there, but fortune was clearly not on their side. There had been no option but to sail across the grey expanse, towards the ruined city of Xhaan. From there they had headed out into the desert, looking for Queen Karmina's initial point of entry, hopeful that an aetheric tether still remained that they could use to pursue her.

The group had taken the *Drake* and the *Hammer* to Xhaan, under the command of Tordin, who was well enough to take to the high seas although his movement was still a little stiff. Their sudden disconnection from the powers of the aether had prevented them from completely healing him and he had opted to stay with the ships, where he still felt useful, leaving the others to strike out without him.

Arthen and his elite riflemen had also joined the expedition and he hoped that they would prove their worth. He rode alongside the group on one of the powerful desert beasts that they chanced across in the harbour district of Xhaan and looked down on the Aellindi as they strode purposefully along. They seemed tireless and did not require the use of mounts in order to advance across the desert sand, clearly at home in these inhospitable conditions.

Fireen walked at the head of the group, pointing with her staff, as if she were still capable of seeing the great sand dunes that stretched out before them and talking quietly with Rikoth, Navesh and Praevir. Their elite warriors guarded the flanks, ever alert for the presence of bandits or wild animals, armed with the energy spears of the fallen Visnaer priests.

Nadarru rode silently beside them, keeping as close to Rikoth as she could. The Aellindi warrior had been tasked with watching over her, which was something he relished. They had engaged in many conversations about her life as a slave, and he seemed best suited to coax her into relating what details she could recall about Queen Karmina and what they might find in her realm, if they ever found a way to enter it.

Saven had stayed behind. She was still weak from her ordeal at the hands of Nadarru and the Visnaer, and Fireen had insisted that she regain her strength, although Saven had guessed that it was her hatred of the Ligarian woman that had excluded her from the expedition. She had accepted Fireen's decision and stayed in Nesteris to oversee the monumental task of rebuilding their once beautiful city. The island had been wracked by terrifying tremors and Saven feared that she would be left presiding over a rubble-strewn city, populated by a panicked, fearful people. There had even been reports of small tremors from as far away as K'vith, and Fireen had secretly confided in her that if they failed to retrieve the stones, the tremors would spread and increase in magnitude and that their world may not survive beyond the next sun-cycle.

'They're returning,' said Praevir, pointing up into the sky. 'Hope they've got good news.'

Panx and Navesh stood at the top of the *Beacon of Errithad*, peering out through the clear dome, their eyes drinking in the glory of the ancient and long abandoned city.

'These dwellings look similar to those on the island of Andin,' said Panx.

'And those in the ruined city on the dark world,' added Navesh. 'This place definitely belonged to the Ancestors.'

They had arrived at the tower the morning after Panx had spotted it, having walked through the night, relying on the twinkling stars to keep their course in the darkness. After inspecting the remains of Denir's caravan they had ascended the tower, eager to explore.

There had been no sign of Marcus in the ruined city or at the top of the tower, although they had found some of his tools, left behind after he had tried to repair the beacon. This did at least prove that he had been here, but left them a little disappointed, as they had hoped that he might have been trapped here since his reckless journey through the portal.

There was great devastation at the top of the beacon, including signs of a desperate struggle and several large bloodstains on the floor. Indrani was fearful that Marcus had been injured, although Nadarru insisted that the damage had been caused when the Visnaer had first appeared, and that the blood belonged to Denir's guards.

They had been surprised to find that the beacon was active, at least partially, and their spirits had been lifted when Indrani realised that she might be able to open a portal. Their hopes were further raised when she claimed to be able to reopen the most recent portal, which should take them to the same place as Marcus.

Fireen was quiet for a moment as she pondered their next move. She did not want to leap blindly through the first portal that they created. They might not be able to return, should their destination not be all they wished for, and they might find themselves lost, with no way back.

'We must find a way to reach the Stone Queen's world,' she hissed, after deliberating for some time. 'If that is also Marcus's location, then we are indeed fortunate. But we must not lose sight of our purpose.'

'The only portal that we know of that has facilitated travel to a different world was the one that we created within the *Beacon of Olon*,' said Navesh. 'Perhaps we might try something similar here?'

'But we didn't bring the *Shard of T'nath*,' said Panx.

'No, we did not!' replied Navesh. 'But we have little option. And besides, I think that the *Shard of T'nath* is an integral part of the *Beacon of Olon* and would not aid us here, even if we had it.'

The group tried to open an inter-world portal using the incantations that allowed them to access Valken's world. But it was no use. The energy of the aether sparked, fizzed and finally gave out altogether, leaving the magi feeling weak and dejected.

They discussed why the portal might have failed to open, in an attempt to conceive a way to succeed. Navesh suggested that perhaps only the Ancestors had the ability to travel between worlds. That without their help, as they had previously been granted when crossing over to the dark world, the power to create this kind of portal was beyond them. Fireen also believed that the loss of the stones had in some way damaged their ability to wield such powerful energies.

'So our only hope is to follow Marcus through the beacon's last known portal destination?' asked Praevir.

'Yes, I believe so,' replied Fireen. 'Perhaps he will be able to invoke the power of the Ancestors and provide us with a way to follow the Stone Queen.'

'Forgive me,' said Arthen, looking a little bemused, 'but I thought you couldn't open a portal? Didn't you just try that?'

'They're two different types of portal,' explained Panx, looking over at Indrani for confirmation.

'Yes,' she replied. 'The portal which Marcus appears to have travelled through was one generated by the beacon itself. As with all of the beacons, when they're restored to power they can be used to travel to other beacons.'

'It involves no magic,' added Panx, 'but relies instead on the Ancestors' technology.'

'But the portal that we just tried to open,' continued Fireen, trying to explain the wonders of the Ancestors to Arthen, 'was one designed to allow us to leave this world fragment completely. We need to enter the Stone Queen's domain, which we hope retains some link to this place, it being her first known point of entry into our world.'

'These inter-world portals rely heavily on the power of the aether,' said Navesh, 'which is waning rapidly, and only appear to use the beacons as a focal point for their creation. Just like the one that we used to travel to Valken's world.'

'Oh,' said Arthen, 'now I understand.'

'I'm glad you do,' muttered Major Tassik.

So with their choice made, Indrani approached the beacon's control panel and activated what she believed to be the last destination, where they hoped to find Marcus. The portal flared into life, although it flashed wildly, fluctuating with random colours and hissing noises. The companions looked at one another as if seeking reassurance, and then stepped through the event horizon.

Twenty-two

Marcus had finally reached Braefell and was standing out on a wide balcony, overlooking the myriad of villas, temples and monuments. It was still warm here, although he detected the faint traces of a cool wind blowing across the city. He wondered how long they had before the devastating effects from the failure of the veil reached the inner parts of the world.

Unlike Nesteris, on its paradise island and covered in ancient forests, Braefell was built upon a vast grassy plain with uninterrupted views in all directions. However, the individual dwellings were reminiscent of those on Nesteris, constructed from bright white marble and inset with ornately carved blocks of beautiful blue lapis lazuli. Marcus was captivated by the similarity between the two distant cities, separated for countless years across the vast empty space between the two world fragments.

The balcony, situated on the third floor of the council building, looked towards the towering *Beacon of Rhasad* that rose up at the centre of the magnificent city. Marcus found it peculiar that the beacon here shared its name with the one that he now called home, back on Nesteris. Since meeting with the two gods, he had come to view these coincidences as signs that he was nothing more than a pawn in a much bigger game.

The one major difference he noticed about Braefell was the abundance of unusual symbols carved into nearly every statue and monument. They bore a striking resemblance to the Celtic knots that appeared throughout the ancient history of his own world. He had not noticed these symbols in Nesteris before, and was confused as to their meaning here. Many of the Aellindi in Braefell also favoured the wearing of long cloaks, featuring voluminous hoods that were often raised over their heads, giving them the appearance of ancient Celtic druids.

Back on his own world, before he had been transported to the world of the Aellindi, he had been interested in ancient history, particularly that of the Roman Empire. He had visited many ancient sites within the United Kingdom, remnants of the Roman invasion of what they called Britannia. He was struck by the similarities between the druidic clothing and the Celtic symbology referenced in books that he had read, and what he now saw here, in Braefell. *Surely this is more than mere coincidence!* he thought, as he watched the city's populace wander by, below his lookout on the balcony above.

'They will see you now, Marcus,' said Endellion, coming up behind him and interrupting his musing.

'Lead on, Macduff,' replied Marcus, chuckling to himself and earning a strange look from his Aellindi companion.

Marcus followed Endellion down an ornate staircase and onto the grand concourse within the council building. Tuuvar and Arkadin were already waiting for them at the foot of the stairs, and smiled in greeting as they descended. The elegant plaza made him think of the grand senate buildings that were used to govern the vast Roman Empire. There were ornate statues, realistic busts and beautiful tapestries lining the walls. He was acutely aware that the inside of the council chambers back on Nesteris were rather austere compared to here in Braefell, and he wondered what had made the two sets of Aellindi so different in their tastes. He was now more resolved than ever to get home, to see his beloved Indrani and their child, and, more importantly, to save the people of this doomed world.

'They're waiting for us,' said Arkadin, pointing towards a long corridor that led away from the plaza, indicating that they should leave at once.

The council of Braefell were waiting within the main chamber for their arrival. There were nine of them, as there were originally in Nesteris before the demon invasion devastated their island and its population. The leader, an aged female called Chylordin, stood up as Marcus and his three companions approached. She was totally different than Fireen, short and stocky in appearance and covered in bony ridges. She looked more like an older version of Rikoth, and Marcus wondered if, in her youth, she had been as fearsome a warrior as him. Like many of the Aellindi on this world, Chylordin had purple-coloured scales that seemed to shimmer slightly in the dappled light coming through the windows in the domed ceiling.

This room also held many wondrous objects that shared the Celtic designs of his own world. He looked around the chamber, his eyes glancing across the display stands that were set around its periphery and laden with ornate weapons, armour and beautiful jewellery. Chylordin herself was adorned with an exquisite looking torc made from shiny bronze. It wrapped itself around her muscly neck, glinting in the sunlight and giving her a most regal appearance.

'Greetings, Arkadin,' said Chylordin. 'It's been far too long, my friend.'

'Hello, Chylordin,' replied Arkadin, bowing slightly before the council. 'Please accept my apologies for my prolonged absence. My duties at the edge of the veil have kept me away from Braefell for too long.'

'No apology is necessary. It appears that your efforts have been . . . fruitful?'

'Yes, I believe they have. Allow me to introduce Marcus Klein, who I believe to be the one we've been waiting for. The one who will save our people from the doom that has inflicted our world.'

Marcus stepped forward, no longer intimidated by the strange appearance of the Aellindi people, bowing in greeting to Chylordin and the other councillors.

'So you are *The One*, Marcus?' said Chylordin, beckoning him to step a little closer.

'I make no claim to be anyone other than myself, Chylordin. I just happened to appear within the *Beacon of Olon*, having travelled from another world fragment. I was greeted by Endellion and Tuuvar, who believe that I might have a role to play here.'

'You come from a world fragment not afflicted with that which has doomed us?' asked another of the council members, a slender-necked male with green scales that made him stand out amongst his purple-coloured brethren.

'No, our veil has not been damaged, and the people who inhabit the world are not facing the disaster that threatens your people.'

'So how exactly do you propose to save us?' asked another councillor.

'Well . . . ' said Marcus, thinking carefully about his reply. 'I was hoping that by combining our knowledge and our efforts we might find a way of crossing over to my world. I'm not sensitive to the aether, but I do have an affinity for the technology of the Ancestors and I believe that the beacons hold the key to our survival.'

'We've not heard of this . . . technology, of which you speak,' replied Chylordin, 'but if there's a chance that we might yet survive, then we're willing to listen.'

'Could you simply help to repair the veil?' asked the slender-necked councillor. 'That way we would not have to abandon our home.'

This comment elicited a flurry of nods and a cacophony of rapid chatter as the Aellindi discussed their doomed world again, going over theories and plans that they had already conceived, but which had seemingly failed to help.

'Please,' interrupted Endellion, 'let Marcus speak.'

'But this is our home!' replied one of the councillors. 'We are right to fear leaving it. We've lived here for thousands of years, in perfect harmony with the land, ever since the Ancestors left us to guide and teach the younger races.'

'But that time has passed now,' said Arkadin, desperate to regain some semblance of order to the rapidly deteriorating meeting. 'Our world is dying and it's only a matter of time before it will no longer be capable of bearing its children.'

Arkadin then told of the vision that Marcus had been shown by Malan and Nurarian, which depicted the frozen bodies of the people of the world, reiterating that they only had a little time left before the vision became reality.

Endellion stepped forward, closely followed by Tuuvar and they informed the council that their observations at the edge of the veil indicated that the deterioration in the protective barrier had recently begun to speed up. Their initial estimation of how long they had before it failed altogether was now grossly inaccurate.

'And only Marcus, *The One*, has the ability to save us,' continued Arkadin. 'We must listen to him and act swiftly. Before it's too late.'

Chylordin called the council meeting back to order and the quiet, peaceful atmosphere was re-established.

'I promise that I'll do everything in my power to save your people,' continued Marcus. 'I freely admit that I'm neither a powerful magus, nor a ferocious warrior. But I'll not let your people fade into nothingness. However, if we're to survive, we must work together.'

'Where will we go?' asked one of the councillors. 'To your world?'

'Yes. I believe that's our best option, so long as we can find a way to get there.'

'What of the people already there? How will they receive us?' asked Chylordin.

'Fireen, the leader of the Aellindi on my world, will welcome you with open arms,' said Marcus, truly believing that she would do just that. 'In fact,' he added, 'your people would greatly enhance their nation, as they're slowly dwindling in number following the recent demon invasion. She'll be overjoyed to see so many new faces.'

'So what should we do?' asked Chylordin, after a moment's consultation with her fellow councillors.

'I think that the first thing we should do is to visit the *Beacon of Rhasad* and see if we can revive it,' said Marcus. 'After that, I think we need to take another look at that prophecy and figure out a course of action.'

*　　　*　　　*

'But this is the *Beacon of Olon*!' muttered Indrani. 'This cannot be right. Marcus didn't travel back here after he disappeared, so why did the portal bring us here now? Something must be wrong.'

The group had emerged from the portal, expecting to arrive at some unknown destination, ready to fight for their lives if the need arose. But the only thing waiting for them on the other side was the darkness of the cosmos, speckled with twinkling stars, and Klestin, Marcus's Vilnarri student who had come to try his luck reacquiring the glyph that had lured his teacher away.

'Nevertheless, this is where the portal has brought us and this is where we must now devise a new strategy,' Fireen replied calmly.

'So what do we do?' asked Rikoth, feeling somewhat out of his depth with the constant bumbling through portals and overall failure to engage with something tangible.

'I do have an idea,' replied Navesh. 'But it'll be risky.'

'What do you have in mind?' asked Fireen.

'I've been giving some thought to how the Stone Queen initially acquired the first stone of power, and how she subsequently determined the location of the other two. It stands to reason that the stone was taken from Nesteris during the demon assault, after they broke free from the aetheric prison. I think that it was in the process

242

of being transported back to Valken's citadel when the dark lord was ejected from our world. It's my belief that the stone was cast adrift into the void, somehow coming to rest on the Stone Queen's world where she chanced across it.'

'That's a good hypothesis,' said Panx.

'I think . . . ' continued Navesh, looking intently at Fireen, 'that when I first called out from the dark world, my calling not only reached you and Idris, but also latched onto the stone. This allowed the Stone Queen to spy on us, utilising a scrying power that was somehow tethered to my call for aid. She then followed the skeins of power from the stone and determined the location of its two siblings. And from there, by means unknown to us at present, she opened a portal to the *Beacon of Errithad*.'

'So, assuming this is correct,' said Rikoth, 'how does this aid us?'

'Well, I cannot reverse the damage that has already been done,' replied Navesh, 'but we can utilise the call for aid in a similar way to her. However, we'll need to return to the dark world in order to perform the ritual.'

'I was afraid you were going to say that,' hissed Fireen. 'But I think your idea has merit and can see no alternative. We must act at once, before the link between your calling, the lost stone and the dark world fades beyond our ability to manipulate it.'

'We'll need to return to the forest where I made the first call for help. Then we'll follow the thread of aether, which should lead us to her. We can then attempt to use this connection to open a portal directly to where the lost stone appeared on her world.'

The *Shard of T'nath* lay upon the control panel within the *Beacon of Olon*, its cool crystalline structure sparkling slightly in the reflected light from the stars outside. Panx picked up the ancient artefact reverently and gently offered it up to the orifice that was designed to accommodate it. As if receiving a signal to increase the power levels, the beacon came to life and its other control screens rapidly filled with scrolling text. The shard was taken inside the control panel, which morphed to conceal the entry point.

'There, we should be able to create the portal now,' said Panx.

'Gather around me,' said Fireen, beckoning all of the magi to step forward. 'I will need every last drop of aether if we are to succeed.'

Out of habit rather than need, Fireen closed her milky-white eyes and began to chant softly. The other magi, recognising the role that they must play, began to add their voices to the ritual, which was beginning to rise in pitch as its tempo began to quicken. Panx, Navesh and Indrani, as the most powerful magi amongst the group, drew heavily on the wellspring of the aether, struggling to direct the usually abundant energy into the ritual. The weaker magi added what energy they could. Even Rikoth, who was first and foremost a warrior, managed to augment the incantation with a little extra power.

At first it appeared that nothing would happen, but after a while Fireen began to exude a glowing aurora that grew in intensity with every passing moment. She continued to chant, invoking the power of the Ancestors, incorporating the energies of her companions into the creation of the portal. Soon a tiny ball of flickering blue light appeared, floating just above the floor, although it was rapidly growing in size.

Arthen and his soldiers, who were devoid of a connection to the aether, watched in fascination as Fireen directed the ritual, like some musical conductor drawing in power from one of her companions, adding it to that of another and seamlessly weaving the strands into her own energy stream.

Even though the magic of the aether was fading fast, there was just enough for Fireen to complete the ritual and after a prolonged incantation, the portal was complete. It stood before them, a glowing doorway into another world, its edges crackling slightly as the unstable energy arced out into the room.

As the group peered through the portal, Navesh noted that Fireen had managed to open it inside the forest, near the settlement where he had first called out to her.

'That's good,' said Panx. 'I was dreading the journey to the forest. Those demon hunters are probably still patrolling the area.'

'Fireen . . . are you well?' asked Praevir, coming to the aid of the Aellindi leader as she started to topple over, her knees buckling.

'I will be fine,' she replied, leaning on the tall warrior for support. 'I think that the energy of the aether has become tainted in some way and that drawing heavily upon it has left me a little weak. I shall recover . . . in time.'

Navesh took the lead, leaving Panx and Indrani to support their weakened leader, stalking through the portal, closely followed by Rikoth, Praevir and the Aellindi guards. Arthen and his men went next, rifles at the ready.

'This will be dangerous, child,' said Fireen, looking over at Nadarru. 'Are you certain that you wish to join us? There is no guarantee that we will return.'

'I wish to come,' replied Nadarru. 'If I can help in any way, then I will. I've much damage to repair, although I doubt that I'll ever be able to atone for what I've done.'

'We all make mistakes,' said Indrani. 'You were coerced into your actions. Give it time, Nadarru. If we make it back, I'm sure you'll find a way to make amends.'

'Thank you,' replied the Ligarian, 'I certainly hope so.'

'Klestin, you must keep watch, through the portal,' said Fireen. 'If we are successful in creating a doorway into the Stone Queen's world, I want you to remove the *Shard of T'nath* as soon as we go through. Do you understand?'

'But that will leave you stranded!' replied Klestin, his voice sounding more gurgled than usual. 'You won't be able to return to the Beacon.'

'That is a risk we will have to take, my young friend. We cannot allow the demons, or anyone else to find their way here. You must close the portal.'

Klestin nodded, indicating that he understood her instructions and wished them all good luck. Fireen gently placed her clawed hand upon the young Vilnarri man's shoulder and then, assisted by Panx and Indrani, hobbled over to the portal and stepped through into the dark world.

They appeared in the forest, with Nadarru following close behind. Navesh was standing beside the scorched patch of ground where he had first called out for help and where Fireen had been badly injured, losing her sight.

Panx noted how the aether here, which on previous visits had felt weak and inaccessible, now felt like a mighty torrent, straining to be unleashed. Navesh concluded that it was simply due to their altered perception. The loss of contact with the aether on their own world was bestowing them with the false impression that the dark world was rich in magical energy, although in reality the strength of the aether here was unchanged.

Fireen wasted no time, beginning the ritual to seek out the tendril of aether that had snagged on the lost stone as it careened through the void, in the hope that it would lead them to Queen Karmina. As before, the magi stood in a small circle around their revered leader. They syphoned what power they could from the world around them and redirected it to Fireen, who gradually wove it into the complex spell that she was attempting to cast.

As had been the case when he had last visited this world, Panx found that he was able to draw upon significant aetheric energy. It was as if he had finally overcome the mental obstructions that were preventing his access to the power, and soon Fireen's incantation had reached an energetic crescendo. She was now completely enveloped in a bright shaft of blue light, which extended up through the forest canopy and disappeared into the blood red sky.

However, just as the portal was beginning to form, its glowing blue edges starting to expand outwards, Fireen collapsed under the constant flow of energy. The magi instantly withdrew their power, concerned for her wellbeing.

'No!' she shouted, through the intense buzzing noise that had suddenly filled the clearing. 'You must keep going, and increase the power if you can. We must succeed here. Do it now!'

They resumed the incantation, sending the power towards Fireen as she had requested. Only Panx had been able to increase the flow of energy, and she now appeared to be in a great deal of pain, dropping to her knees as she desperately tried to maintain control of the ritual.

'Almost there,' she hissed, gritting her pointed teeth in agony. 'I just need a little more power.'

Panx let his mind reach out and touch the aether, searching for another reservoir that he might tap into. He probed at the streaming torrent for what seemed like an eternity, and any reserve he found he redirected to Fireen, bolstering what magical force she had to work with, hoping that it would be enough.

It was. The portal finally opened and the angry buzzing ceased. The light had grown so bright that they had been forced to close their eyes. But when they finally opened them, the familiar oval shaped portal was there, with blue-coloured energy crackling around its periphery, holding the doorway open.

'Fireen!' shouted Panx, rushing over towards the Aellindi leader, who had collapsed completely and was lying on her back.

She was still breathing, for which they were all eternally thankful. But she had been dreadfully burnt during the invocation as a result of the unrestricted barrage of aetheric energy. Her skin was bright red and covered in weeping sores and fluid-filled blisters. Her eyes were open, although they had turned from milky-white to a dark grey colour, oozing blood from within the deep sunken pits of charred flesh. Even though they continued to move from side to side in their sockets, her friends could clearly see that the damage was beyond repair and that her vision would never return.

'You've done it, Fireen,' said the young Magus, kneeling down beside her.

'That is good, Panx,' she replied, holding an arm out towards him. 'Help me up. We must leave immediately, for I fear that the portal is weak and unstable. We will not get a second chance.'

*   *   *

'Good luck,' muttered Klestin, as he watched the last Aellindi warrior step through Fireen's portal, disappearing from the forest clearing. He gently tapped the control panel and removed the *Shard of T'nath,* shutting down the portal into the dark world.

*   *   *

Marcus stood at the top of the *Beacon of Rhasad,* in Braefell, looking out over the ancient and beautiful city. He had come here, accompanied by Endellion and Tuuvar, to determine if he could activate any of its systems. In particular he wanted to try the gateway portal, which he hoped would allow them to escape the doom that was hurtling towards them. The only tools available to him were those that he had thrown into his backpack before he had recklessly left Indrani. But clearly the gods were watching over him, for everything that he required, he had brought.

Soon he was rewarded with active control panels, covered in lines of fast flowing text and icons that would allow him to remotely activate other parts of the beacon. The first thing on his list had been the lift, as he still dreaded the climb up and down the seemingly endless spiral staircase. Secondly, he visited the power reactor which, like its counterpart in Nesteris, sat directly underneath the beacon in a subterranean chamber, accessible only by the lift car. He was pleased with his progress and beamed at Endellion and Tuuvar, who watched him intently, in awe of the technology that had lain dormant for countless years.

'Clearly we have lost much of our ancient knowledge,' said Endellion.

'Yes, we're certainly not as enlightened as we thought we were,' replied Tuuvar.

'Don't take it to heart,' said Marcus, attempting to raise their spirits. 'It's the same as your . . . cousins, on my world fragment. They didn't realise the potential of the beacons either. I guess the Ancestors left so very long ago that you've all forgotten what the beacons were for, and clearly they neglected to leave the instruction manual behind when they left!'

They headed back to the control room and were excited to see another beacon showing up on the system. Marcus was more than a little shocked by the familiar glyph that now flashed on the screen in front of him. Unless he was mistaken, this was the same glyph that had lured him here in the first place. An icy chill crept up his back at the strange coincidence.

Endellion peered over his shoulder as he worked, taking an interest in what he was doing and asking a great many questions. The aged Aellindi informed him that the flashing glyph belonged to one of the Ancestors, an individual known as Errithad, who had fallen from grace long ago. He had been partially responsible for the great cataclysm that had shattered their world into many fragments.

'Be warned though, Marcus,' said Tuuvar, 'that it's Errithad's beacon that has been claimed by the Stone Queen. Her fortress palace sits just beyond it.'

'That's got to be more than a simple twist of fate,' replied Marcus, a little worried by the turn of events. 'It's the very beacon that we'll need to visit. Strange that it should show up now.'

'Need to visit?' asked Endellion.

'Didn't the prophecy say something about the cavern of the dead?' replied Marcus, stopping what he was doing and turning to face his friends.

'Yes,' replied Tuuvar.

'Well, it stands to reason, to me anyway, that we may well find this . . . cavern, within the Stone Queen's palace. After all, she is surrounded by the dead.'

'I think we should return to the council chamber,' hissed Endellion. 'Arkadin and Chylordin will no doubt wish to hear of this.'

'It sounds like a suicide mission to me,' added Tuuvar as they headed for the lift.

Twenty-three

Saven peered over the edge of the fissure, looking down into the black, depthless chasm that had opened up on the southern side of Nesteris. A violent, long-lasting earthquake had wracked the entire island, causing a vast amount of destruction across the great Aellindi city and devastating some of the smaller settlements that were dotted across it. This was but one of many large fractures that had appeared during the earthquake. It was as if the gods themselves had reached out with weapons of great power, slicing deep gouges across the landscape.

As temporary leader of the Aellindi council, it was her duty to ensure that her people were safe. She had spent the day travelling across the island, checking on the citizens of the affected areas and dispatching aid to where it was most needed. She now waited patiently for the climbers to return, to find out just how far down the fissure extended.

One small settlement had been utterly destroyed; swept into the roiling sea as the powerful tremors pulverised the cliffs into tiny fragments of splintered rock, carrying the Aellindi and their dwellings into the deep waters below. Saven and her brother, Dram, had grown up in this very village and she had wept openly to discover that many of her family and friends had been lost.

However, although her personal loss had been great, Saven silently thanked the Ancestors that the overall death count had been low. But she knew that it was only a matter of time before the world spirit's unrelenting fury returned to lay waste to the rest of their precious nation and she feared that the damage and death toll would soon reach catastrophic levels. Their very survival now lay with the small group of heroes, led by Fireen and Navesh, as they attempted to retrieve the lost stones of power and restore the aetheric balance of their dying world.

*   *   *

To the west of the island of Nesteris, on the continent of K'vith, the Visnach people were in great turmoil. Duchess Sybille, supreme commander of their armed forces, had just attended a meeting with the ruling council, where she detailed the futile attempts to rescue the citizens of the coastal city of Yemmath. Her account of the catastrophe had been utterly heart-rending, and she now stood outside of the ancient council building with tears streaming down her face.

The Visnach nation was built, literally, upon an ancient and dormant volcano. The vast circular crater had, at some time in the distant past, suffered a substantial collapse in part of its steep rock wall. This had allowed the waters around the volcano to flood into the crater, creating what had since become known as the shallow sea. But something even more profound had happened recently and the ancient volcano was now, apparently, no longer dormant.

Powerful eruptions had roused the Visnach from their slumber, and in the early hours of the morning they had emerged from their dwellings to find the island shrouded in a suffocating fog of noxious gas. Many had already succumbed to the poisonous fumes, and the ruling government had pronounced a state of high alert, mobilising their armed forces to help evacuate those most affected.

It had been during these hurried evacuations that the real eruptions had begun. Far above Yemmath, high up on the mountainous slopes, great explosions suddenly wracked the volcano wall, hurling great chunks of rock high into the air as titanic forces threatened to tear their nation apart. As the terrified inhabitants of this large and vibrant city looked on, several glowing streams of molten lava began to flow down from the hills above.

The army had done all that it could to rescue the city's panicked population as they started to flee for their lives. Given the impossibly short time that it had been afforded to prepare the evacuation, it was a wonder that any had survived at all. But time was something that they did not have in abundance, and many Visnach died as they hurriedly gathered their possessions; burnt alive by the searing heat of the pyroclastic flow. Others were overtaken by the rapidly approaching molten rock as it flowed inexorably towards them, destroying everything in its path.

*   *   *

Far to the south, beyond the jungle nation of Reznar and near to the southern edge of the great protective veil, a large sailing ship floundered in the choppy waters. A mighty storm had swept across the sea, appearing as if from nowhere and catching the crew of the ship completely off guard.

So swiftly had the storm appeared that the sailors had been unable to trim the sails before three of the great canvas sheets had been violently torn from the mast and swept into the sea, leaving the ship faltering in the massive swell. The captain had ordered the remaining main sails to be taken down, hoping to limp on with a few smaller sheets, enough to retain minimal control of the ship.

But good fortune was not with them today. The ship began to take on water through a large hole that had been smashed in her side. She was now listing dangerously, completely out of control.

However, as precarious as the condition of his ship was, the captain realised that he now had another, far more pressing concern to deal with. One of his men had spotted the veil, glistening in the squall, just off their port bow. They were too close and the storm was dragging them directly towards the energy barrier that surrounded their world.

Throwing caution to the wind, the captain ordered his crew to hoist the sails once more. He was desperate to regain control of the vessel and the need to avoid further damage to the canvas sheets or huge timber masts was suddenly a minor concern. But the storm was too powerful. Within moments of it being spotted, the ship was dragged inside the fringes of the veil, never to be seen again.

*   *   *

With Braefell's beacon reactivated, Marcus and the Aellindi had turned their attention to the prophecy of *The One*. They meticulously picked apart every line of the ancient prediction, looking for any clue as to how they might escape the fate that awaited them.

'I still think the key to our escaping this world lies somewhere within the Stone Queen's palace,' said Marcus, somewhat exasperated at the Aellindi's reticence to embrace his plan.

'But we cannot simply assault her stronghold!' Arkadin replied vehemently. 'If we follow that course of action, we would likely be subverted by Evixius as soon as we approached her icy walls. There must be another way?'

As ever, Endellion and Tuuvar were firmly on Marcus's side, their belief in him overriding their loyalty to their own kind. And so, for the rest of the afternoon the three of them verbally duelled with Arkadin and the Braefell council, desperately trying to get the point across that, if they did not at least try to reach the caverns of the dead, then they were likely doomed anyway.

'We've nothing to lose,' hissed Tuuvar. 'We'll certainly die here if we do nothing and at least Marcus's plan gives us a glimmer of hope. Why can't you see the logic in this?'

'Enough!' said Chylordin, after a moment of quiet thought. 'I can see that we've reached an impasse here, and that one side must ultimately yield. I'll agree to your plan, Marcus, but I'm still not convinced of the wisdom of a full scale assault. I'd like to obtain some proof that somewhere within her palace we'll find the means of escaping this doomed world. Until then, we must be cautious in our advances.'

'That's an excellent start at least,' replied Marcus, relieved to have finally made a breakthrough with the stubborn councillors.

'You claim to be able to gain access to the *Beacon of Errithad*,' continued Chylordin, raising an eyebrow questioningly.

'Yes,' replied Marcus, as confidently as possible. 'I can open a portal directly from the *Beacon of Rhasad*, which will take us to the Stone Queen's domain. It should come as a surprise to anyone who is waiting on the other side.'

'So if we're quick, we can capture the beacon and use it as a place to marshal our forces and reconnoitre the area outside?' asked Chylordin.

'Indeed. It'll be like a swift commando raid and, with any luck, we'll suffer only minor casualties.'

Chylordin was impressed with Marcus's answer and his apparent concern over the losses that her people might endure. She turned to one of her advisors, a stocky female who clearly belonged to the same class of warrior as Rikoth, and whose outward appearance was exactly how Marcus envisaged the younger Chylordin, before advanced age diminished her fighting prowess. They spoke quietly for several moments before the warrior nodded and left the room.

'It's done,' said Chylordin, looking him straight in the eye. 'I've authorised your . . . commando raid, and mobilised our army. I have the distinct feeling that we're going to need them very soon. Go now and refresh yourselves,' she added, to Marcus, Endellion and Tuuvar. 'We'll send for you later.'

The meeting was adjourned and Marcus departed, accompanied by his two Aellindi friends, leaving Arkadin and Chylordin deep in conversation.

The portal in the Stone Queen's tower flared to life. The Visnaer guarding the ancient structure were instantly alert, scrambling to their feet and patrolling the usually quiet chamber.

'This hasn't happened before,' said one of the priests, looking at the garrison commander, troubled by the sudden appearance of the portal. 'We've no hunting parties out. Are we expecting company?'

'No, we're not!' replied the commander, powering up his energy spear, suspicious of the unexpected activity.

His spear dropped from his hand as a ghostly blade appeared, as if from nowhere, swiftly removing the arm that wielded it. The Visnaer commander fell to the floor, clutching at his severed arm, trying to staunch the flow of blood as it pumped energetically onto the ground.

'What's that?' said another priest as something brushed past her. She spun on her heels, looking for the cause of the contact, but saw nothing.

It was at that point that the chamber at the top of the *Beacon of Errithad* descended into total chaos. Endellion, using the power of the aether to conceal the raiders, had bravely gone through with them. He unleashed a mighty incantation that plunged the chamber into near pitch darkness, and then swiftly retreated from the frantic melee. As he looked back he saw, with aetherically enhanced vision, the glowing forms of the Aellindi warriors as they descended on the surprised and somewhat outnumbered Visnaer garrison.

Marcus once again stood in the council chamber, talking with Chylordin and Arkadin. The raid had begun and they awaited the outcome of what they expected to be a fierce battle for the *Beacon of Errithad*. Endellion and Tuuvar, who were waiting at the *Beacon of Rhasad*, had explained to Marcus just how the raid was to be enacted. A small force of elite warriors was to go through first, concealed behind powerful magical wards. They would be all but invisible to those on the other side as they set about capturing the beacon. Once the goal was achieved, they would send a message through and the first wave of regular Aellindi forces would begin to travel through the portal. From there they would move out onto the icy wasteland beyond the beacon and establish a forward base while further reinforcements continued to cross through the portal. Endellion believed that, so long as the battle for the beacon was successful and that there was not a vast army of the dead waiting for them on the other side, the Aellindi should be able to move a significant number of troops through.

'The beacon has been taken,' said a messenger, entering the council chamber.

'Excellent,' replied Chylordin. 'Did we lose many warriors?'

'Just a single warrior,' replied the messenger. 'We struck swiftly and the resistance, although heavy at first, was soon overwhelmed.'

'Enemy survivors?' asked Arkadin.

'One Visnaer priest was captured alive and another is believed to have escaped the initial assault.'

'So we have announced our presence to the Stone Queen,' hissed Chylordin.

'But perhaps we can find out from the prisoner if there is another portal within the Stone Queen's palace,' replied Marcus. 'I'm convinced that the answer lies there, in the cavern of the dead.'

'Okay, Marcus, we'll interrogate the prisoner. Perhaps we'll learn something significant. But we must hurry and get the next part of the plan into motion, before she has time to react.'

The messenger left the room, closely followed by Chylordin and Arkadin. They would relocate to the *Beacon of Rhasad* and oversee the deployment of the army and send for Marcus in due course. So for now he was left alone in the council chamber. He moved around the periphery of the ancient room, studying the Celtic-style objects which the Aellindi used to decorate it.

As he moved between the display tables, looking upon ancient rings, swords, armour and even belt buckles, his eyes were drawn to a beautiful circlet, fashioned from polished bronze and inset with sparkling jewels. The knotwork was extraordinary, and the large green emerald that sat at the very centre of the headpiece gave it significant weight. He found that he simply could not contain himself. It was as if his mind had surrendered control to a more powerful entity, and he found himself reaching out to pick up the circlet.

A brief flash assaulted his senses and he stepped backwards, away from the display table, dropping the circlet onto the wooden floor. He took a moment to consider what had just happened and then reached down to retrieve the magnificent headpiece. Carefully picking it back up, he was ready when the flashes once more assaulted his mind. He managed to keep hold of the circlet, allowing the flashes to embed themselves within his consciousness, aligning with his own brainwaves until they became colourful visions that finally resolved into crystal clear memories. It was almost as if he were reliving something that had happened to him many years ago and he struggled to make sense of what he was being shown.

He stood within the mighty stone circles at Avebury, back on his own world. However, what he was seeing were not the stone circles as he knew them to be in his own time period, with stones missing or leaning heavily to one side and with a thick carpet of grass covering the entire site. This was not the familiar Avebury, with a road running through the small village that occupied a portion of the ancient monument. No, the image that he was being shown was clearly from a much earlier time period. There was no road or village. The stones themselves, mighty pillars and avenues of monolithic blocks, appeared to have been recently placed, with no cracks or patches of lichen to indicate that they had been sitting there for countless millennia.

As he looked around he became aware of other groups of people. There were druids everywhere. They waved in greeting, beckoning him to come and join them. Clearly an important ritual or event was in progress here and Marcus cautiously made his way over to where a large group of druids had congregated. They were dressed in ragged brown robes and wore their hoods over their heads, concealing their faces within the dark recesses of their accoutrement.

Marcus continued to watch as the ritual progressed and, as the activity reached a fever pitch, was surprised to see one of the druids begin to lower their hood. He observed the individual closely as the voluminous cowl was gently placed upon their shoulders, and was deeply shocked by the face that appeared from within its gloomy interior. The druid was one of the Aellindi. In fact, he was the spitting image of Arkadin, with purple scales glistening in the moonlight.

As Marcus was slowly coming to terms with the images that he had been shown, the vision began to fade and he found himself alone once more in the council chamber, in the city of Braefell.

What did I just see? He wondered.

His thoughts were answered almost immediately by the ghostly voices of Malan and Nurarian, reminding him of the need to steal an ancient Aellindi artefact. *'Marcus, this must be done before you return to your own world fragment. You must not falter now!'*

He was suddenly aware of the familiar voices of Chylordin and Arkadin. They had returned as promised, and he knew that time was running out for him. If he were going to carry out the gods' strange request, then he would have to act swiftly.

He stuffed the circlet into his tunic and moved away from the plundered table, which fortunately held several other objects, giving Marcus some hope that its disappearance would go unnoticed. He began to whistle softly and then jumped a little as Arkadin entered the room and called out to him.

'The beacon is secure, Marcus. We've put the next phase of the operation into action.'

'Would you care to join us now?' asked Chylordin. 'We're moving to the *Beacon of Errithad* to see for ourselves just what Queen Karmina has in store for us.'

'Yes, I think I'd like that.' replied Marcus, a little awkwardly.

'Are you alright?' asked Arkadin.

'Yes, I'm fine,' replied Marcus, desperate to recover his wits. 'Shall we go there now? There's no time to waste.'

*   *   *

Panx stood in the chill, frigid air. The fine hairs on his exposed arms were standing on end and he was shivering, trying to keep warm in the cold air of his new surroundings, which was a stark contrast to the heat of his own world. Fireen was lying on the snow covered ground beside him, as Navesh tried desperately to save her life.

She had been badly wounded during the creation of the inter-world portal and had suffered further injuries as she had made the transition through the void. Her burns and blisters had miraculously disappeared since leaving the dark world, but her entire body was now covered in thick leathery scars. Her hair was falling out in thick clumps and her hands had barely the strength to hold her staff. She had been standing when they had first appeared on the Stone Queen's world, but had soon collapsed; suffering what Panx thought was another seizure.

He watched with an increasing sense of helplessness as Navesh infused her with healing energies, and was relieved when her spasms began to subside as her second-in-command gently cleaned the milky discharge that had dribbled down the side of her mouth.

Fortunately for them the power of the aether was strong on this world, with a similar level of readily available energy to their own, before the stones had been stolen. Panx was able to restore his depleted energy reserves, infusing his body and mind with the intoxicating power of which he had recently found himself gravely deprived.

The group had arrived beside what they believed to be the very spot where the first stone of power had landed, after drifting through the void. They found a small circular patch of scorched earth which even now resisted all attempts by the ice and snow to reclaim the area. It was as if the aether was still focussed on that very spot, burning it with tremendous power.

The portal had collapsed almost as soon as the last of their party had emerged, sealing them off from the dark world and ruling out any chance of return. Not that they had any particular desire to return to that foul place. Fireen had only been able to bring them here due to the lingering effects of Navesh's call for help and there was no chance of her opening another inter-world portal, not without some focal point and an enormous source of power. All that remained of their entry point was a large circular patch of melted ice, which was rapidly disappearing as fresh snow began to settle on the ground.

'I can feel them,' said Fireen, coming to her senses once more, her voice rasping and raw. 'The stones are here.'

'But we still need to find them,' replied Panx. 'How do we determine their location?'

'They are close. I can feel their strength. In fact, I feel stronger again, knowing that we now have a chance to save our world.'

'There's a fortress up ahead,' said Praevir, landing gently in the soft snow beside Navesh, 'and a beacon!'

'That is where we will find the stones,' hissed Fireen. 'We must leave immediately.'

'But Fireen, you're in no condition to travel,' Navesh pleaded. 'Please, allow yourself some time to recover a little of your strength. We could build a shelter here.'

'There is no time, Navesh. We must head out immediately if we are to successfully retrieve our precious heirlooms. My health is of little consequence. Let us go.'

The group headed off into the stark white landscape, trudging through the deep snow drifts as the weather continued to deteriorate, rapidly changing from a gentle snow shower into an icy blizzard. With Navesh lending Fireen what support he could, they made their way down the gentle slope on which they had first appeared and into the valley below.

Twenty-four

Marcus stood in the glass-domed chamber at the apex of the *Beacon of Errithad*, looking across the vast icy wasteland that sprawled out around the ancient structure. The leaders of the Braefell Aellindi stood around the captured Visnaer priest. He was on his knees before them, watched over menacingly by six hulking warriors. They had been interrogating the prisoner since coming through the portal, attempting to ascertain what defences Queen Karmina had at her disposal. But so far the priest had refused to give them anything useful.

Arkadin was in a fitful rage at their inability to glean anything of value and Endellion was fussing over him, earnestly trying to calm him down. Marcus watched as Arkadin shrugged off Endellion's hand, which had been resting gently upon his shoulder, and then stalked forward. He kicked the Visnaer to the ground and then leapt onto his back like some wild beast. Tuuvar pleaded with him to stop, insisting that they were better than that, but Arkadin was beyond reason and grabbed the priest by his long black hair, yanking his head backwards. He whispered something into the Visnaer's ear, eliciting a look of fear and initiating a desperate, although futile struggle. But Arkadin's grip was powerful and he pulled the Visnaer priest closer, placing one of his clawed hands upon the man's head and speaking the words of some terrifying spell.

At first the priest resisted, closing his eyes and muttering a counterspell of his own, attempting to neutralise the power that Arkadin was using to infiltrate his mind. But the Aellindi magic was not easily overcome and soon the priest was sweating profusely as his own power was forced aside. Marcus felt a shiver run down the length of his spine as he watched Arkadin force his will upon the struggling priest and, although he realised that it was necessary and that time was against them, he felt a little uncomfortable as he observed the brutal violation.

But soon the struggle was over and the priest's defences had been torn asunder, allowing Arkadin to delve into his mind.

Arkadin spoke softly, as if reading the Visnaer's thoughts aloud. He described the interior of the Queen's fortress and gave an account of the strength of her forces, which would be valuable in the upcoming assault.

'She has a secret place,' he whispered, immediately grabbing Marcus's attention.

'Where?' he asked.

'She often spends time there ... alone,' continued Arkadin, speaking in an odd monotone voice, apparently having not heard Marcus's question.

It would seem that their prisoner was one of the Queen's high ranking priests and had been summoned on many occasions to deliver slaves for her dark uses. He had also observed her talking quietly to someone, although nobody else had been present. Marcus had become excitable when Arkadin discovered that the Queen's retreat was located in a cavern, and he started babbling on about the prophecy and the cavern of the dead.

He had to be hushed by Tuuvar as Arkadin began to speak once more, and the entire Aellindi command group had smiled enthusiastically when he spoke of a portal within the cavern. They looked at one another, as if finally agreeing that this entire mission had indeed been worth the effort.

'This is exactly what we're looking for,' said Marcus, still excited by the news. 'I'm convinced that this portal holds the key to our escape. It's unlikely to be a simple portal like the one we used to travel here from Braefell, as to the best of my knowledge these are generated only within the beacons themselves. This portal is something else entirely.'

'You're right, Marcus,' agreed Arkadin and Chylordin. 'We're sorry to have doubted you.'

'That's okay. You have the weight of your entire nation upon your shoulders,' he replied.

'Yes, we do. But apparently the weight of our entire world rests upon yours,' replied Chylordin, leaving Marcus wide-eyed and stunned, unable to reply.

While the Aellindi leaders had been interrogating the prisoner, their army had formed up outside of the beacon, on the icy ground beneath the Queen's palace. Hundreds had already come through the portal and hurried down the stairs, eager to bolster the strength of their attacking force and many more waited in Braefell, ready to join them.

However, their intrusion had not gone unnoticed and thunderous horns began to sound from within the Queen's palace. The Aellindi scouts returned, informing their commanders that the huge icy gates had begun to open, swinging outwards on great hinges. The vanguard of the Stone Queen's forces had been spotted emerging from within, led by her Visnaer priests. They were armed with their dreaded energy spears and followed by rank upon rank of shambling skeletal warriors.

'Will we have enough troops?' asked Marcus, looking out over the icy battlefield, aware that the Aellindi were vastly outnumbered by the tide of enemy warriors marching slowly towards them.

'Have faith, Marcus,' said Chylordin. 'Few in number we may be, but this army includes our greatest warriors and magi. Each is worth a hundred of Queen Karmina's abominable creations, and our numbers are growing with every passing moment. We're not defeated yet.'

As if to emphasize her words, an Aellindi warrior stepped through the portal, followed moments later by another. Both headed straight down to the battlefield, where their strength and courage would soon be tested as never before.

'Shall we join them, then?' Marcus asked, loosening his sturdy blade in its scabbard and heading towards the stairs. 'I don't think I can just stand here and watch.'

'They're nearly here!' said one of the Aellindi warriors.

'We must hold them off for a little longer,' replied another. 'Our own forces are still forming up.'

'Follow me,' replied the stocky female councillor, unsheathing her ancient curved blade, which glinted in the bright light reflected from the icy landscape. 'We'll strike hard against their Visnaer masters and hopefully slow them down a little. Come!'

The small group of elite warriors sprinted across the icy wasteland, followed by a group of Aellindi magi, rapidly closing the distance between themselves and the priests at the head of the enemy vanguard. The magi would focus their arts upon the skeletons, using destructive magic to shatter bones and reduce the freakish monsters to piles of ash, which was just about the only way to permanently defeat them.

The Visnaer fired their weapons towards the oncoming Aellindi strike force, engulfing several warriors in the searing blue energy. The withering hail vaporised flesh and spared only bones, which clattered to the ground around their comrades. The Aellindi magi swiftly destroyed the remains of their fallen brethren before they could be resurrected to fight for the Queen. They then turned their anger towards the enemy, hurling great bolts of lightning and streams of superheated flame into the ranks of skeletal infantry.

The Aellindi warriors engaged their hated enemies and began to tear into Queen Karmina's forces, cutting a great swathe through their number, heading directly for the priests. They were the greatest threat and had to be defeated at any cost.

'We're nearly there!' shouted the stocky councillor, swinging her mighty blade in a great sweeping arc, smashing several skeletal figures to the ground before pushing on towards their ultimate goal.

'Look out!' shouted one of her warriors, pushing her aside as a mighty axe cut through the air, narrowly missing her shoulder.

The two warriors turned and waded into the fresh band of skeletons that had appeared, having been reanimated by the powers of the Visnaer priests.

'We need more magi,' cursed another warrior, breathing heavily as he smashed foe after foe into the icy ground. 'They just won't stay down!'

'The magi are right behind us,' replied the stocky female councillor, 'we must trust in them and concentrate on our main target. Come on, follow me.'

The Aellindi sprinted into action once more, ignoring the skeletons wherever possible and only engaging when there was no other option. The magi continued to follow behind, destroying the Queen's minions as they went, intent on relieving the warriors as they struggled to reach the priests.

One of the warriors took a blast from a Visnaer spear, his body instantly beginning to burn and the flesh literally melting away within moments of the strike. Seeing her chance, the stocky councillor leapt past the final ranks of skeletons and hurtled towards the Visnaer. She dispatched the closest priest without mercy, her ancient blade piercing his heart in one mighty thrust, before performing a nimble pirouette and removing the head of another.

Her warriors, those that had survived the sprint through the ranks of skeletal soldiers, danced and leapt in a bewildering display of martial prowess. They were desperate to end the priest's unnatural control over the undead infantry, fighting with reckless abandon to bring down their hated enemy.

One of the Visnaer spears glanced off her ancient armour, leaving a dent in the breastplate and nearly severing one of the leather straps on the left pauldron. She turned aside, allowing the razor-sharp edge to slide away from her and then stepped closer to her enemy, head-butting the priestess with all her might. The Visnaer's nose was shattered, leaving her momentarily dazed, with a gory red smear spreading rapidly across her blue skin. Several teeth had also been dislodged and she spat them out onto the snow covered ground.

The stocky councillor did not wait for the priestess to regain her senses and drove her sword through her lightly armoured body, before picking up the Visnaer's fallen spear, leaving her own weapon deeply lodged in her enemy's chest.

The Aellindi magi had continued to unleash the power of the aether and great swathes of skeletons had been turned to ashes as they hurried to keep pace with their warrior brethren.

'They're beginning to flounder,' said the lead magi, hurling another powerful bolt of lightning into the ranks of skeletons, its crackling energy splitting into multiple tendrils, each blasting an undead soldier to bits.

Soon the Queen's vanguard was defeated and the remaining skeletal warriors dropped inert to the icy ground as the last priest was slain. The cost had been high and the stocky councillor returned with less than half of her original attack force. But she had successfully stalled the Queen's defences, and in the time taken to engage the enemy their own forces had been greatly bolstered.

'That wasn't so bad,' Marcus said naively, as the stocky councillor stalked back towards him. She carried one of the plundered Visnaer energy spears, her own sword resting once more in its scabbard.

'Don't be foolish, Marcus,' she hissed. 'That was but a fraction of the Stone Queen's power. She's toying with us.'

'We have more of their energy weapons now,' said Endellion, noting the mighty spear that the stocky warrior was carrying.

'Yes,' she replied. 'I've ordered them to be distributed amongst our forces; to take advantage of the enemy whenever possible.'

'We must always focus our attacks on the Visnaer,' added Arkadin. 'By destroying them, we interrupt the influence of Evixius and the undead army becomes no more than a pile of bones.'

'Agreed,' replied the Aellindi leaders.

With the Aellindi forces slowly increasing in number, the Stone Queen finally showed her hand. A bellowing horn announced that she had committed her army to the field. They watched as a seething mass of infantry began to emerge from within the palace, appearing as a black stain against the snowy background and moving inexorably towards them.

'We're for it now,' muttered Marcus, feeling tense and nervous about the impending battle.

'Do not fear, my friend,' replied Endellion. 'Whatever the outcome, it will be over soon.'

'That's reassuring,' replied Marcus.

Endellion had been correct and the Aellindi did not have long to wait, as the Stone Queen's forces swiftly closed on the beacon. The leading edge of her army engaged with the Aellindi warriors, who brutally hacked apart the skeletal warriors, while their magi tried to thin out their numbers with powerful blasts of fire and lightning.

'The Visnaer are staying back this time,' noted the stocky female councillor as she unsheathed her ancient blade and strode forward. 'I'll see if I can get a little closer.'

The mighty warrior hurtled off into the chaotic battle, followed by her elite guards, grinning wickedly as she ran to meet her enemies.

Marcus parried the skeleton's attack, stepping aside and striking back with his own blade. He and Endellion were working together, with the professor lashing out with his sword and the aged Aellindi following up with burning flames. Tuuvar was also using her magic to combat the enemy, although she focused on healing their injured, allowing them to return to the fray as soon as possible.

Arkadin had joined Chylordin and the remaining councillors and had moved forwards to stand with their warriors. Marcus was in awe of these individuals, who appeared fearless in the face of such overwhelming odds, and just hoped that his own actions were worthy of those that did not make it through the day.

'What in the heavens are those things?' he asked, pointing to a group of towering skeletons that were pushing their way towards Chylordin's command cadre.

'Those are, or were, Syldran,' replied Endellion. 'Evidently Queen Karmina has conscripted them into her army.'

'They're huge,' replied Marcus, trying to imagine the towering creature that once fitted around those mighty bones. 'They're like the lumbering giants from the fairy tales on my own world, easily twice the height of your biggest warriors. Have you ever fought them before?'

'No,' replied Endellion. 'They are a peaceful people and not easily roused into violent rage. But I suspect that we are about to see just how tough they are! Follow me. I think we may soon be needed.'

Arkadin ducked, rolling through the Syldran's legs and lashing out with the looted Visnaer spear as he stood up behind the titanic skeleton. Chylordin and the council members were fighting for their lives, and the magi were frantically hurling blasts of fire and chain lightning against these mighty creatures. But their bones seemed to resist all attempts to destroy them.

'We must concentrate on one at a time,' hissed Chylordin. 'They're just too strong.'

Arkadin fired the energy spear at the nearest Syldran. It seemed to be the only weapon powerful enough to take them down and soon the bones of the creature had been turned to dust. But there were so many of the creatures, and they had too few of the Visnaer weapons at their disposal. He activated the spear again, but this time it failed to engage, leaving him with no option but to swing the razor-sharp edge in a conventional attack.

'Perhaps they take time to recharge?' muttered Chylordin, who had moved closer to him, unleashing an aetheric barrage at a nearby Syldran.

The combined efforts of the Aellindi warriors and magi slowly started to take their toll on the rampaging giants. Only a few of the mighty creatures now remained. Three Aellindi councillors and numerous warriors had fallen to the beasts' assault, but the danger was finally ebbing away with each passing moment.

All around them the army of the Aellindi was engaged with the enemy, which had all but surrounded the noble forces, leaving them only a narrow corridor leading back to the beacon.

Arkadin continued to fight against the skeletal forces, swinging the Visnaer spear and firing its lethal energy whenever it had returned to full power. He stalked forwards, away from Chylordin and the remaining councillors, towards one of the Visnaer. If he could kill the priest it would weaken the Visnaers' control over the skeletal forces in the immediate area.

But he never made it. A chance strike from an enemy's rusty short sword pierced his armour and he staggered to the side, a green-coloured stain spreading across his tunic. Marcus watched in abject horror as his friend was swamped by skeletal warriors, their weapons thrusting wildly, hacking into him again and again.

Chylordin pushed forwards, her warriors forcing the enemy back. But they were too late and Arkadin's body lay still, his blood already beginning to freeze on the icy ground. *The Watchers* had lost their revered leader.

*   *   *

Fireen and her companions skirted the hill that they had been following. They had chanced across a narrow trail that wound along its contours and decided to follow it, hoping that it would lead them to the beacon. Sounds of battle could be heard nearby, the clash of metal on metal and the cries of desperate warriors as they charged towards their foes. Panx and the other magi could feel the energy of the aether as it was unleashed in powerful assaults, the air radiating with eldritch energies.

'Down there,' said Praevir, pointing towards the conflict that was raging below them on the ice fields between the beacon and the ominous fortress.

'Those are Aellindi warriors,' replied Rikoth, 'and they're engaged in a fight against those Visnaer devils and their undead abominations. We must go to their aid.'

'Yes, my friend, we must help,' replied Fireen, staring blankly at the other members of the expedition through her sightless eyes. 'Take the warriors and go. Be safe, all of you.'

The entire group paused for a moment, looking over at Fireen, detecting a hint of sadness in her voice.

'I will take the rest of our group into the Queen's lair and look for the stones,' she added, drawing deeply on the power of the aether, imbuing her with fresh vigour and offsetting her lack of vision by enhancing her other senses. 'They remain our ultimate priority. We must find them and perhaps, while the Queen is distracted with the battle, we might yet prevail. If we do not return, know that it has been a great honour to have served you for all these years.'

The Aellindi looked sad, not daring to reply, fearing that they might never see their beloved leader again.

'Is that Marcus down there?' Panx shouted excitedly, pointing down into the battle that was evolving below them, dispelling the sad moment that had enveloped their little party.

'Once again, Panx,' replied Indrani, coming over to stand beside the young magus, 'you have terrific eyesight! That's Marcus alright. He's here, on this world. I didn't expect that!'

They could see their lost professor down on the battlefield, standing beside a pair of aged Aellindi. He swung his blade with proficient skill as he defended himself and his companions as they blasted the skeletons with aetheric flame.

'I'm sorry, Fireen,' said Indrani, moving over to stand beside Rikoth as the warrior checked his armour and hefted his mighty warhammer, 'but I've got to go to Marcus. He might need me down there and I could never forgive myself if I lost him again, now that we're so close.'

'I understand,' replied Fireen, 'go and save our wayward hero!'

Rikoth leapt over the edge of the hill and raced down to join the battle, followed closely by his elite warriors, eager to relieve their embattled brethren. Praevir took to the sky, along with those Aellindi gifted with wings, and swooped towards the enemy, intent on unleashing a deadly aerial assault on the Visnaer. Indrani hurried down towards her beloved Marcus, who was valiantly fighting for his life. Only Arthen's troops remained on the hill, looking for a suitable position from which to fire upon the enemy with their rifles.

'Aim for the Visnaer,' shouted Arthen, as his men settled down behind a group of snow-covered boulders.

The General lifted his own rifle and looked through the enhanced viewfinder, centring it on one of the Visnaer priests. With the rifle resting gently on the rock, he pulled the trigger. He did not see whether the shot had found its mark as the weapon's recoil caused him to lose sight of the target. So after reloading as quickly as he could, he found another target and fired again, hoping that his shots had been truc.

'Fire at will,' shouted Major Tassik, as he squeezed off several shots into the dense melee, taking out the nearest Visnaer priest with casual ease. Great swathes of skeletal warriors fell to the ground as the reanimating energy abruptly ceased.

Rikoth had raced down the hillside and waded directly into the nearest knot of enemy warriors, smashing bones with impunity as he pushed ever deeper into the endless ranks of skeletons. He had spotted a small group of Aellindi warriors surrounded by the enemy and struck out in their direction, hoping to relieve them before it was too late.

He found himself fighting alongside a powerful female warrior. She was short and stocky, as he was, and protected behind an ancient suit of armour that was the twin of his own. If it were not for the difference in their skin colouration and their favoured weapons, the two weapon masters might have been siblings hatched from the same brood. She smiled as he leapt into the fray, knocking down a handful of undead warriors with one mighty swing of his warhammer and nodding to her as if in casual greeting.

'I don't recognise you, friend,' she hissed. 'But you're most welcome.'

'Rikoth, at your service,' replied the noble Aellindi hero.

'Gethed, at yours!' replied the purple-scaled warrior. 'Shall we?' she added, nodding her head in the direction of the writhing mass of skeletons.

'It would be a pleasure,' replied Rikoth, grinning with undisguised glee.

The two kindred spirits worked together, cutting a great line through the enemy forces. They left a trail of dismembered skeletons in their wake, which their magi vaporised with aetheric fire as they followed behind. Between them they slew many Visnaer priests, their constitution seemingly without limit. Rikoth laid waste to the enemy with his mighty warhammer, charging with all his might and fury into the brittle skeletons, while Gethed deftly separated bony limbs with her ancient curved blade. None dared go near them for fear of the violent rage that the pair exuded.

Praevir and his winged cohort swooped low over the battlefield. He had spotted a group of three Visnaer priests, engaged in a ritual to reanimate their fallen infantry.

'Let's put a stop to that, shall we?' he said, altering his course and gaining height.

His warriors followed him, and soon they were circling above their prey. Praevir was first to attack, banking sharply into a nosedive, his sword ready to slice into blue flesh.

One of the Visnaer spotted their approach and fired his spear up at them, catching an Aellindi warrior in the face. Praevir heard the scream as her flesh began to melt, leaving nothing but bones to crash into the ground.

Praevir took the priest's head in one single swing, sending it careening through the air. He raced past at breakneck speed, hoping that his warriors had successfully dispatched the other two priests, and then soared back up into the sky to search for further prey.

As he looked back, he could see that an entire section of enemy infantry had been decimated; the puppeteer's strings cleaved when the priests had fallen and their necromantic influence rendered inactive.

Spotting another group of skeletal warriors, one of the flyers dropped down to engage them and Praevir moved to follow. As he swooped in, keeping low, blue fire shot towards him. He jinked to one side, deftly dodging the blast while keeping his eyes focused on his intended target. He did not see the other priest, standing to one side. The spear arced through the air beside him, slicing through his wing and sending him tumbling from the sky. He smashed into the ground, rolling across the icy battlefield and landed in a twisted heap before the oncoming tide of skeletal warriors.

'Hold on, Praevir!' shouted Rikoth, who was nearby and had observed the entire incident.

Rikoth and Gethed, accompanied by their warriors, proceeded to smash through the writhing wall of bones, desperate to reach the fallen Praevir, who was injured and fighting valiantly for his life.

Indrani hurried down the hillside as fast as her legs would carry her. She was desperate to reach Marcus and hurled powerful gusts of wind towards the enemy, scattering them in all directions. Marcus was in the thick of the deadly combat, and his little group of Aellindi protectors were beginning to look a little overwhelmed. She was nearly there, just a little further.

Marcus suddenly went down, pulled to the ground by some hulking skeletal monstrosity, disappearing beneath the frantic scrum. She screamed out, hurling powerful energy at the skeletal army, scattering bones with tornado-strength winds and running even harder, desperate to reach him.

'Marcus, are you alright?' asked Endellion, hurling a powerful jet of flame into a large Syldran skeleton, burning it to cinders.

'Yes, I'm fine,' he replied, 'it's just a scratch.'

'You should go back to the beacon,' said Tuuvar, coming to stand beside the injured professor. 'You're just too important to lose.'

'I can't leave you now,' he replied. 'I won't sit meekly inside the beacon while your people fight this battle,' he added, hacking at a skeletal arm as its owner strayed a little too close. 'I'm fine, honestly.'

'But without you, Marcus, this entire fight . . . all this loss of life . . . will be for nothing,' pleaded Tuuvar. 'You must be kept safe.'

'I think we've just received some welcome reinforcements,' said Chylordin, coming over to stand beside Endellion. 'It appears that we have new allies,' she added, pointing up towards the surrounding hills.

Marcus heard the gunshots echoing across the icy battlefield and spotted King Elridan's flag fluttering wildly in the chilly wind. He cheered loudly, having never felt such joy in all his life, realising that he was no longer alone. His friends had come.

'They are friends indeed,' he said, suddenly remembering the words of the gods, reminding him that he had allies. 'Somehow they've crossed over from my world to aid us.'

'They're already fighting within the melee,' said Tuuvar, pointing towards Rikoth and his warriors as they fought valiantly beside Gethed and the native Aellindi.

'That's Rikoth!' shouted Marcus. 'This is fantastic news.'

*   *   *

Fireen led her small party stealthily towards the fortress gates, which had remained open after disgorging the Stone Queen's army, but which now seemed unguarded and quiet.

'Do you know where we're going?' asked Panx.

'Yes. I can feel the power of the stones. We are close now, my young friend. But we must remain vigilant, as the Queen is powerful and I fear that she is somehow drawing upon the combined energy of all three stones. Her strength will be beyond all imagining and we must combine our efforts if we are to succeed.'

The group skirted the fortress walls, hugging its outline closely, concealed behind an aetheric shroud. Panx considered Fireen's words as he crept along behind her. If the Stone Queen was able to draw upon the power of all three stones, what chance did the four of them stand against her? His heart was pounding and his mind raced wildly as they made their way inside the citadel, towards Karmina's seat of power and the final confrontation.

Twenty-five

The battle beneath the *Beacon of Errithad* continued to rage, with the two armies equally matched. While fewer in number, the Aellindi were ferocious warriors, trained from birth to defend their nation. However, the skeletal forces of Queen Karmina were seemingly without end. Targeting the Visnaer priests had been the Aellindi's most promising tactic, allowing them to interrupt the reanimating power of Evixius and decimate rank upon rank of skeletal warriors. But no matter how many they killed there were always more undead creatures ready to step forward and fill their position.

Gethed and Rikoth stalked boldly through the ranks of the enemy, always seeking out the Visnaer in the hope of destroying the skeletons once and for all. However, it was becoming obvious that the Visnaer were merely pawns in the great battle, redirecting the power of their god. There was something else in control here, some higher power over which the Aellindi had no control.

'Marcus!' shouted Indrani, trying desperately to be heard over the noise of the battle and finally closing in on his position at the rear of the Aellindi line. 'Marcus, I'm here!'

Marcus turned around, certain that he had heard his name being called and was shocked to see a red-haired Visnach woman running towards him at full pelt, waving her arms furiously in the air.

'Indrani, is that you?' he muttered, moving towards her.

'It could be a trap, Marcus,' cautioned Tuuvar, holding on to his arm as he struggled to go to his wife.

'It's Indrani,' replied Marcus, shrugging off Tuuvar's protective grip. 'I'd know her anywhere.'

Indrani finally reached his position and pushed her way through the Aellindi warriors that guarded the command cadre, wrapping her arms tightly around him and holding him close.

'I thought I'd never see you again,' she said, hugging him fiercely, not wanting to let go.

'Me too,' he replied. 'I thought I was going to remain trapped here forever. I thought I'd never get back to you and little Navesh.'

Indrani pulled back slightly, looking at Marcus through tear-blurred eyes, and then punched him straight in the face, knocking him backwards onto the ground.

'Don't you ever do that to me again, Marcus Klein,' she sobbed, 'or so help me, I'll . . . I'll . . . '

'It's all right,' said Marcus, motioning for Tuuvar to move back, indicating that it was not actually the trap that she had feared. 'I guess I deserved that,' he added, getting back to his feet and gently hugging the sobbing Indrani, pulling her close.

*   *   *

While the battle continued outside, Fireen stalked furtively through the hallways of Queen Karmina's palace, closely followed by Panx, Navesh and Nadarru, all concealed by an aetheric shroud. She could sense the power of the stones radiating out through the walls and, with Nadarru's aid, guided her little group towards it.

Panx looked around at the interior of the palace as they slowly made their way towards the Queen's lair and what was likely be an energetic and violent confrontation between powerful magi. He noticed that the palace shared many similarities with the internal structure of the Ancestors' beacons although, strangely, he noted that the floors were not level. The entire palace seemed to be tilted slightly, as if it had been sunken unevenly into the icy ground. He pointed these things out to Navesh, but the Aellindi hero was clearly not in the mood to discuss the architecture of the enemy's sanctuary, so instead he focused on what was about to happen. He began to prepare his most potent spells, in the hope that they would prove useful in the retrieval of the stones.

They had been descending for some time now, heading deep into the bowels of the Queen's palace, still following the energy trail that they believed would lead them to the stones. The air was icy and their breath condensed into a thick, warm fog with each exhalation. The floors were still tilted at an odd angle, and the occasional slippery patch of ice made accessing certain areas of the palace quite treacherous.

There were long-dead control panels spaced at regular intervals along the dimly illuminated corridors, many of which had been badly damaged at some time in the past, their screens smashed in or access hatches torn asunder. Panx could see thick, fibrous clusters of wires inside some of the control panels and was more certain than ever that this place had been built by the Ancestors.

'Where is everyone?' he whispered. 'We've not seen a single person since we entered the palace.'

'Perhaps they're all on the battlefield,' replied Navesh.

'Quiet!' Fireen cautioned them. 'We are close now. The concealment spell is still in place, but I do not want our presence to be detected before we are ready. Prepare yourselves.'

The group emerged from the icy corridor onto a wide balcony, which looked out across a vast cavern that disappeared off into the gloomy distance. There was a wide walkway that appeared to encircle the entire inside edge of the cavern, leading away from either end of the balcony. The edge of the walkway was guarded by a sturdy metal fence, to prevent the room's occupants from falling into the depthless cavern below. The walls were braced with huge ice-encrusted girders that were made from a similar material to that used in the construction of the beacons. It was as if they were standing inside the empty ribcage of some titanic creature, looking out across the space where its vital organs once rested.

Panx cautiously looked over the railing and was beset by a sudden feeling of vertigo. The floor of the cavern was barely visible, and he was certain that the entire *Beacon of Olon* would fit within the chamber.

'There she is,' whispered Fireen, her deep connection to the aether clearly compensating for her lack of vision.

She was pointing towards a Visnaer woman seated on a large throne some distance away, further inside the chamber. The walkway would lead them directly to her and so Fireen strode forwards, not waiting to see if her companions were following, eager to confront the Stone Queen.

As the group approached the Queen she looked up, somehow alerted to their intrusion. She had been gazing into an unusual looking device and had clearly been surprised at their sudden appearance. Panx felt Fireen's protective shroud being lifted, which left him feeling naked and vulnerable. He was acutely aware of the deep chasm that yawned beside the walkway on which they all stood, and he moved several paces towards the comforting presence of the solid wall.

'Give back the stones, Karmina,' hissed Fireen angrily, moving as swiftly as she could towards the throne in an attempt to capitalise on their surprise appearance.

Panx knew that Fireen was weak and that her scarred body was close to the limit of its endurance. She appeared frail and ancient as she hobbled towards the Queen. The young magus knew that she was relying entirely on her formidable connection to the aether, which fortunately had been restored now that they were on this world fragment.

As he began to call upon the mystical energy of the aether to aid Fireen in her confrontation, he spied Navesh out of the corner of his eye. The Aellindi hero had activated his golden spear and, as he started to move forward, disappeared from sight altogether.

Nadarru was unsure of what to do, now that she was once again in the Queen's presence. But finally she moved forward to assist Fireen, offering her arm so that the ailing Aellindi leader might lean upon her for support.

'You!' shouted Queen Karmina, pointing at Fireen. 'I've seen you before, spying upon me. You thought you were hidden, but I sensed your presence within the current of the aether. How did you get here?'

'I have come for the stones, Karmina. Give them back. Our world will die if you do not.'

'I don't care about your world, Aellindi witch! The stones are mine and nothing you do or say will alter that. And you, Nadarru, I see that you've joined forces with these wretches now. You could have had anything you desired. How far you've fallen, child.'

'Your power over me ended when you abandoned us, Karmina,' said Nadarru, filled with rage and contempt for the Queen. 'I see you now for what you really are; an evil sorceress who cares nothing for her followers, and whose only desire is for ever greater power. If only I'd been strong enough to resist you before.'

'Brave words, whelp!' screamed Queen Karmina. 'But you're nothing but a wretched Ligarian. Like all of your people, your mind is weak, and so easily corrupted. Why do you think I chose you to act as my pawn? Surely you didn't really believe that you were going to be my equal? Pathetic fool! We Visnaer have always hated your kind, and have hunted your people to extinction on this world. Imagine my joy at discovering you, hiding in the ruins of that long abandoned city. My joy at using you to act as my conduit, to enable me to enter your world and pilfer the stones from the Aellindi. You're weak, Nadarru, and you'll die now, alongside your new friends.'

As Panx observed the bitter verbal encounter between Karmina, Fireen and Nadarru, he spotted a slender dais beside the Queens' throne, and his sharp vision was able to make out the three stones of power sitting upon its shiny surface. Aetheric energy was radiating out of the stones although, surprisingly, it was not directly bathing the Queen with its powerful aurora. As he studied the colourful eddies emanating from the stones, he became aware of a portal in the background, further along the pathway that encircled the vast chamber. Beside it floated a dark cloud, its ever-changing shape seething with evil intent, like a roiling mass of thick oily smoke that threatened to choke them all with its foul stench.

He could not take his eyes off the cloud and slowly became aware of some level of sentience within the dense, oppressive darkness. It was as if some evil consciousness lurked at the edge of the cavernous chamber, filling it with hateful, violent thoughts and dark, angry energy. The power from the stones danced along a chaotic pathway, linking the dark cloud, the portal and Queen Karmina in one circular loop of pure aetheric energy.

'I will not ask again, Karmina,' said Fireen calmly, 'return the stones or face the consequences.'

'Consequences?' laughed Karmina. 'Don't threaten me, old hag! They're here,' she added, pointing to the three stones that rested on the slender dais, 'come and take them, if you dare.'

Fireen attacked without warning, her sightless eyes burning with their own inner light, sending a wave of flame hurtling towards Queen Karmina, who sat casually upon her throne. Panx watched as the Queen casually waved her hand in the air, causing the flames to bend away as if deflected, disappearing into the cavernous depths below. He too called upon the power of the aether, hurling his own flames towards the Stone Queen in an attempt to overwhelm her. But she easily blocked his magic too, as if drawing it deep into herself, drinking in the power like some withered plant after an unexpected downpour.

The Queen lashed out, sending the flames back towards Fireen, who was momentarily engulfed in the fiery conflagration. Nadarru screamed out and hurled herself at Queen Karmina, desperate to distract her, scratching her face with razor-sharp claws. Karmina repulsed the attack and struggled up out of her throne, grappling the Ligarian with titanic strength and hurling her across the walkway, towards the yawning depths of the great cavern.

Navesh made use of Nadarru's well-timed distraction to launch his own assault on the Stone Queen, reappearing suddenly beside her and thrusting in with his golden spear, its razor-sharp tip aimed directly for her heart.

'Fool!' she muttered, easily batting his weapon aside and grabbing the shaft as it glided past her face.

She picked him up as if he were nothing more than a rag doll and uttered several sharp words of magic, sending powerful bolts of electricity coursing up the spear and into his body. He screamed out, letting go of the spear and dropping back to the floor. Karmina casually reversed the weapon and thrust it back towards him, slicing deeply into his arm as he desperately rolled aside.

Fireen emerged from the fireball in which she had been engulfed, having conjured up a protective shield that saved her from a fiery death. Her skin, although badly scarred from the transition to this world, had suffered no further damage. If anything, she seemed even more enraged than when she had discovered the Queen sitting casually beside the stones of power. She uttered several words, sending a titanic blast of invisible force to batter the Stone Queen head on, forcing her to stagger backwards.

As Panx watched, he detected a change in the coursing power of the stones as they emitted their energy into the roiling black cloud, emerging once more to infuse the Stone Queen with ever greater strength. *If I could disrupt the flow of aether in some way*, he thought, beginning to form a plan in his mind.

While he considered the strange energy stream and the odd black cloud, which apparently only he had seen, he unleashed an attack of his own, sending out a powerful jet of water from one of his outstretched hands and a surge of lightning from the other.

Queen Karmina, bolstered by the latest burst of energy from the stones, erected a magical barrier and laughed evilly as their attempts to overpower her failed miserably.

Navesh attacked again, this time leaping onto her back and attempting to suffocate her with an arm around her throat. But she was too strong, even for the powerful warrior whose own strength was fuelled by savage desperation. She hurled him across the walkway, lashing out with violent jets of energy as he careened across the floor. Panx watched in horror as he slid over the edge of the walkway and into the chasm, his body steaming and his clothes charred and burning as he disappeared from view.

'You are nothing!' screamed the Stone Queen. 'Mere insects, come to annoy me with incessant buzzing and puny stings. I'll squat you like the repugnant bugs that you are.'

A lance of black energy hurtled from her slender outstretched fingers, smashing into Nadarru with terrific force and sending her to her knees. The Ligarian was writhing in agony, and Panx saw her topple over. When the magic flow ceased, Nadarru lay still on the walkway, her once beautiful form smashed and ruined.

'I've had enough of your distractions now,' said Queen Karmina, retrieving Navesh's spear and striding purposefully over to where Fireen was standing. The Aellindi woman hurled another blast of flame at the approaching Visnaer magus, but the Queen's energy shield flared to life once more and the aetheric assault was easily repulsed.

'Still you don't understand, even now, at the moment of your own doom.'

She unleashed a deadly barrage against Fireen, who tried valiantly to erect a defence of her own, to ward off some of the destructive energy that was streaming towards her. But the blast caught her in the chest and she was hurled to the floor.

'I alone can draw upon these three stones of power, plundered so easily from your pathetic world. I alone can control them and I alone will rule this world. Your time has ended, Aellindi.'

Queen Karmina raised the spear, intent on driving it into Fireen's prone body, which lay before her in a smoking, tangled heap.

'STOP!' shouted Panx, rushing to stand before Fireen.

'Young fool. Soon you'll all be dead and your bodies given over to me. By the power of my god, Evixius, I will rule here. You can do nothing to stop me. Your pitiful magic is no match for my mastery of the stones of power. I'll destroy you both with one stroke of this blade, and then reanimate your bones to fight at my side. Perhaps if you run now, boy, I'll allow you to escape. But there'll be no such pardon for your Aellindi friends.'

'There's something that you've overlooked, Your Majesty,' said Panx, showing no fear but feeling terrified inside. He took a few deliberate steps towards Queen Karmina, forcing her to look at him with suspicion.

'What are you talking about, fool. I've overlooked nothing.'

'I'm afraid that you've grossly overestimated your powers,' continued Panx.

'Silence!' shouted Queen Karmina, shooting more flames down upon the wounded Fireen, who struggled to resist the aetheric assault.

'You see, while you claim mastery of the three stones of power that you stole from our world,' continued Panx. 'There are now, in actual fact, six stones of power present on this world. And I can tap into them all!'

Queen Karmina looked up. Her expression clearly showing that she had failed to consider her world's own set of stones. She had never before been able to draw upon more than the diluted power that infused the world, and did not consider them to be a threat, especially when she now had three stones of her own.

Panx did not give the Queen time to fully take in what he had just said, but instead drew in the power of the aether, reaching out towards the native stones from this world and the three stolen stones that sat nearby on the slender dais. His efforts were instantly rewarded and he felt the energy flowing through him like never before. With a single word he hurled an intense bolt of lightning at the Queen. It was more powerful than anything he had ever unleashed before and threatened to overwhelm him completely.

Queen Karmina screamed as her defences were stripped away, her connection to the stones lost forever as her god abandoned her in her moment of greatest need. She screamed as the impudent young boy reached out with ever greater power, the lightning burning through every fibre in her body. She erupted into a seething ball of flame as the heat from the aetheric assault reached its zenith.

Panx did not let up, did not relent. He felt the power coursing through him and by now had begun to understand how to control it. He watched, as if from behind someone else's eyes, as the Queen burned. She fell to the ground, writhing in agony as he channelled the power from all six stones, fuelling his rage as he destroyed his enemy. Her smoking body rapidly turned into a charred wreck and began to disintegrate into a pile of black ash, which blew over the edge of the melted walkway, swirling around as his aetheric fury continued to erupt.

Nadarru came up behind him and gently put her hand on his shoulder.

'It's over,' she whispered. 'You've done it, Panx. She's gone.'

With the battle finally won, Panx lowered his hands and ceased channelling the aether through his body, interrupting the flow of magic and plunging the cavern into an eerie silence. He was aware that Fireen had dragged herself to her feet and was gingerly moving over towards him, her clothing torn asunder and her body damaged beyond belief.

'Where is Navesh?' she rasped, her voice husky and barely audible.

'He went over the side,' replied Nadarru, moving gingerly towards the railings and peering over into the chasm-like chamber, her own face a devastated mass of burnt flesh. 'There he is,' she added excitedly, pointing to a lower tier of the walkway onto which Navesh had fortunately fallen. 'I think he's alive, but we'll have to find some way of rescuing him.'

*   *   *

Outside the palace a thunderous noise assaulted the senses of those on both sides of the battle, forcing many to drop to their knees and raise their hands to their ears in a desperate attempt to block out the painful bellow.

'What's happening?' said Marcus, looking questioningly at Endellion.

'I do not know,' replied the aged Aellindi.

Without warning, a bright white light erupted from the palace and descended upon the army of the dead. So bright was it that the Aellindi were forced to shield their eyes, lest they become damaged by its fierce intensity. But when the light finally began to wane, they were treated to the most wondrous sight. The skeletal army had fallen. Every last one of Queen Karmina's abominable creations had dropped to the floor, creating a vast, unmoving pile of bones. The startled Visnaer priests were completely surrounded by their fallen warriors and simply stood there in disbelief. They were swiftly rounded up, their weapons confiscated and their hands securely bound behind their backs.

Indrani had informed Marcus that Fireen had taken Panx, Navesh and Nadarru into the palace in search of the Queen and the stolen stones of power. He deduced that something important had occurred and gathered up the Aellindi leaders and, followed closely by Indrani, led the way towards the palace.

*   *   *

'Are you injured, Panx?' asked Fireen, struggling to remain standing beside the young magus.

'No, I'm fine,' he replied, offering his arm to help his stricken friend and mentor. 'I was suddenly able to reach out to all six stones with my mind. And not only that, I was able to draw upon all of their power at once.'

'That is a rare gift, young man,' she said, suddenly collapsing to the floor, her body wracked with convulsions as it finally succumbed to the colossal damage that had been inflicted upon it during the past few days.

Nadarru moved over beside Panx, who was kneeling beside Fireen, attempting to infuse her with healing magic. Navesh had also reappeared, clambering gingerly up a small ladder that linked the lower walkway with the one on which the titanic battle had taken place.

'Hold on, Fireen,' said Navesh, adding his own magic to that of the young magus. 'Don't give up now, not after all we've been through to retrieve the stones.'

But their efforts were to no avail. Fireen was too badly injured, in mind as well as in body, and her life-force slowly began to fade away.

'The stones,' she hissed softly, 'bring me the stones.'

Nadarru shambled over to the slender dais, as fast as her own injured body would allow and retrieved the three stones of power before hurrying back to Fireen and placing them into her burnt hands.

Panx watched in amazement as the signs of pain and anguish faded from Fireen's face and, even though her body was cruelly disfigured, she looked somehow at peace. She clutched the stones to

282

her chest, repetitively muttering a string of quiet words to herself. She then offered them to Navesh who, at first, took a step backwards, shaking his head as if not wanting to touch the ancient relics.

'These are yours now, Navesh,' hissed Fireen, her voice little more than a faint whisper, 'as is the responsibility for our people. Take them home and restore them to their rightful place before our world is beyond all help.'

Panx felt warm tears running down his cheeks as Navesh gently took the stones from Fireen, and held her hands in his as the last of her life-force ebbed away. He watched in silence as Fireen took her last breath, her chest falling but failing to rise again. The stones had been glowing with an intense green light, but this gradually faded as Navesh gently placed Fireen's lifeless hands upon her chest, her spirit finally returned to the aether.

Marcus and Indrani arrived shortly after Fireen had perished. They were accompanied by Endellion, Tuuvar, Chylordin and a small contingent of Aellindi warriors, and approached Panx and Navesh with anguished looks. Marcus was overjoyed to see Navesh alive and well, and embraced him like a lost brother. But the situation did not permit the reunion that he had originally hoped for, and he knelt down beside Fireen, laying his hand upon her still form, tears streaming down his face. Indrani stood behind him with her hands resting on his shoulders, giving him support and allowing him to mourn. Fireen had taken him in when he had first arrived, after they had defeated Valken. But now he would no longer be able to enjoy her sage company.

'Marcus, we must find a way to return home,' hissed Navesh quietly. 'I promise you that we will all be allowed to grieve for our lost friends. But we must return the stones to their rightful place, before our world is beyond repair.'

Marcus looked up at Navesh and gently nodded his head, understanding the urgent need to escape from this place. If they did not act soon, both world fragments would perish.

'What do you make of this?' asked Panx, indicating the portal that had been active throughout the entire confrontation. 'It looks like an ordinary portal, like the ones used to travel between the beacons, but there's something else at work here too, some odd presence surrounding it.'

Marcus stood up, taking one last glance down upon Fireen, and made his way over to the portal that Panx was showing him. He could clearly see the roiling black cloud that Panx had described and was a little hesitant to approach it. He remembered the vision that Malan and Nurarian had shown him, with Evixius shrouded in an ill-defined black veil that exuded waves of intense, violent energy.

'You must leave now, Evixius!' he called out. 'It's over.'

The dark cloud started to move towards him, forcing him to take several steps back. He could feel the malevolence radiating out of the cloud, like a being of pure evil, intent on ending his life in a savage and bloody manner.

As he retreated before the slowly advancing cloud, he became aware of a bright white light, which contrasted with Evixius's dark form and slowly began to surround it, preventing it from moving and forcing it to shrink in volume. As he watched, he noticed that the others in his party had not seen the white light. They continued to look towards the portal, as if they were unaware of the mighty battle that was taking place between the three immortal siblings. He alone seemed to hear the soft whispering voice coming from the dark cloud as it slowly shrank in size. It was as if it were emanating from inside his own head, although he could not understand the language.

After a few brief moments, where the black cloud continued to shrink, it was all over and the darkness simply ceased to be. The bright light also began to fade away, revealing once more the glowing portal behind it, which started to splutter before dying altogether.

'What do we do now?' asked Panx, walking over to where the portal had been and looking around in despair, searching for a way to reactivate their only means of escaping this icy world.

'The portal was fuelled by the souls of those sacrificed in the name of Evixius,' replied Nadarru, her swollen lips and battered face making it difficult for her to speak. 'It has closed now that Queen Karmina is dead.'

'Her god has abandoned her,' replied Navesh. 'Gone to seek another champion to undertake his foul deeds.'

'So how do we get home?' replied Panx, asking the question that was on all of their minds. 'This portal is no longer of any use to us!'

'Don't be so certain, Panx,' replied Marcus, walking over to investigate the portal site for himself. 'This is no ordinary cavern, as you've all no doubt discerned for yourselves, and I don't believe that this portal was solely reliant on magical means for its creation.'

'Are you saying it's a technological portal?' asked Indrani. 'Like the ones within the beacons.'

'I think so,' said Marcus, pointing to a small cluster of instruments at the back of the walkway. 'I think this place is a remnant from the time of the Ancestors. Something akin to the beacons, but also something very different. It's clearly a nexus for their technological marvels and perhaps we can make use of it.'

'But the beacon portals are only capable of going from beacon to beacon,' replied Panx.

'Ordinarily yes,' agreed Marcus. 'But this place is more than just another beacon. And don't forget that the Stone Queen did, somehow, travel between her world and ours. This implies that somewhere there's a portal capable of taking us home. Perhaps this is it.'

'So what do we do?' asked Navesh.

'I'm certain that this room is important,' replied Marcus. 'All I need to do is find a way to reactivate this portal and then we can see if we can control it. Would someone be so kind as to return to Braefell and fetch my tools?'

Endellion dispatched one of the Aellindi warriors and the group settled in to await their return, watching with fascinated interest as Marcus and Panx removed the covers from the portal's control units.

Twenty-six

The portal behind the Stone Queen's throne flared to life. It filled the chamber with intense blue light, before its water-like surface settled into the familiar undulating appearance, with waves of energy gently rippling across the event horizon. Panx looked up from where he had been resting, seeking any sign that his friends were about to return. His nervous tension was relieved as Marcus emerged from the portal, closely followed by Indrani.

*   *   *

A short time earlier, the professor had managed to open the portal by linking it to a previously dormant power source. Clearly the Stone Queen had not known how to utilise the ancient technology, relying instead on the ruinous powers of Evixius. He had been uncertain exactly where the portal would take him, given that the display screen was damaged beyond repair, but he suspected that it would be the same destination that the Queen had first used to abduct Nadarru.

With no way of testing out his theory, Marcus had volunteered to go through first, assuring his friends that it would be safe and that he would return as soon as he had determined the portal's destination. Having only just been reunited with him, Indrani had not wanted to let her beloved travel through the portal alone, and so together they had made the journey into the unknown.

Fortunately his assumptions had been correct and the portal did link the doomed icy world fragment with that of his own, reaching out across the endless void that separated them. He had breathed a silent sigh of relief upon emerging inside the *Beacon of Errithad* in the centre of the ancient city in the great desert of Thalmira.

The beacon's control systems had somehow been restored to greater functionality than when he had last been there. Indrani had indicated that the beacon appeared to be active when she and the others had passed this way, and so Marcus assumed that some ancient repair mechanism had finally restored the damaged systems. His hopes were further raised when he spotted the glyph for the *Beacon of Rhasad* slowly blinking on the display screen, indicating that direct travel back to Nesteris was possible.

They decided that it was time to return to the Stone Queen's palace, and stepped back through with fingers crossed, hoping that the portal would permit two-way travel. All had worked out as he had desired and, after emerging from the portal, they hurried over to where the others were waiting, eager to make their report.

*   *   *

'Does it work?' asked Navesh, desperate to know if he could return home with the stones of power.

'Yes,' replied Marcus, 'the portal appears to be stable and links this place with the *Beacon of Errithad*, in the desert of Thalmira. From there the beacon will allow direct travel to Nesteris.'

'The desert beacon appears to be fully functional,' added Indrani, in response to the questioning look from Navesh.

'So, we're just two portal jumps away from Nesteris?' asked Rikoth, who had joined the group in the cavern, having finally rounded up the Visnaer prisoners above ground.

'Yes,' replied Marcus. 'I see no reason why you can't be back in Nesteris within minutes. I'll come through to the *Beacon of Errithad* with you and show you how to activate the portal to Nesteris.'

'Are you not coming back to Nesteris?' asked Navesh.

'Yes, I'll be coming back, but there are a few things that need to be sorted out here first.'

Marcus explained about the failing veil on this world fragment, which came as a bit of a surprise to the others. He told them that he had promised the Aellindi in Braefell, and any other people of this world, that they would be welcomed on his fragment.

'So you see,' he said, after relating the details of his adventures here, 'I cannot return until the preparations for the evacuation of this dying world have been finalised.'

'How long will that take?' asked Navesh.

'I'm not sure, but I expect they'll want to leave as soon as possible. We can't be certain how much longer the veil will last, and they cannot risk lingering too long. I believe that they've already begun to prepare, so I'll go and see what I can do to help.'

'Perhaps they could move into the ancient city in the desert?' suggested Nadarru. 'It'll require much effort to restore the structures, but there's water there in plentiful supply.'

'That's a good suggestion,' replied Marcus, looking over at Navesh, who was now the leader of the Aellindi on their world.

Navesh nodded in affirmation, his mind quickly decided, and moved over towards the portal.

'Come then, let's return to our own world and see what damage has been done,' he said. 'I just hope that we're not too late, or we too may be looking for a new home in the near future.'

Marcus and Indrani stepped through the portal, followed closely by those that had come through in search of the stones of power. Rikoth spoke quietly with Gethed for a brief moment, promising to help her people to settle into their new home, before he too passed through the portal. Navesh was the last to leave, having taken a moment to commune with Chylordin, promising to return as soon as he had restored the stones of power to their rightful place. He nodded respectfully towards the Braefell Aellindi and then lifted Fireen's broken body gently into his arms before stepping through the portal, disappearing from view.

The memorial for Arkadin had just finished, and as the masses that had attended the service began to thin out, Chylordin asked Marcus, Indrani, Endellion and Tuuvar to join her in the council chamber to begin planning the final stages of the evacuation.

Ambassadors had already been dispatched to the other races that shared their world, in the hope of persuading them to join the Aellindi migration to a new home. Chylordin hoped that replies would be quickly returned, especially given the grave peril that the world's inhabitants were in.

'I would like Endellion and Tuuvar to go through with you, Marcus,' said Chylordin, 'accompanied by Gethed and her elite warriors for protection.'

'Agreed,' said Endellion and Tuuvar in perfect unison.

'Marcus has secured Navesh's consent that we can repopulate one of our Ancestors' long forgotten settlements,' continued Chylordin. 'I'd like you to take a look at the site, to determine if it would be possible for us to live there.'

'Of course,' replied Endellion. 'When will the rest of you follow?'

'We'll continue to settle our affairs here, and gather up everything of value from Braefell. The outlying Aellindi communities will be arriving soon and then we'll start the crossing, bringing with us the sum of our possessions, wealth and knowledge. That which we can carry.'

'I believe that the portal is stable,' said Marcus, imagining the Aellindi trying to bring their entire city with them. 'You have time to gather your histories and bring them through, but don't delay. We have no way of telling how much longer the veil will hold out. You must prioritise what you bring with you and return later for the rest if you can.'

'I understand what you're saying, Marcus, but we cannot simply abandon our city without at least trying to preserve what we can of it. But I know that you're only thinking of our continued survival. Rest assured that we shall heed your wise words.'

'Thank you,' replied Marcus, relieved to have made his point. 'Perhaps we should leave immediately?' he continued, looking over at Endellion.

'Yes,' replied Chylordin, 'that would be sensible. Send word as soon as you're through and keep me apprised of the situation.'

Endellion and Tuuvar both nodded and headed out of the council chamber, closely followed by Marcus and Indrani. They made their way to Braefell's beacon, and from there travelled back to the Stone Queen's palace via the *Beacon of Errithad*, crossing the now-empty ice field outside, where signs of the recent battle were still plainly visible.

*   *   *

'The tremors have ceased,' said Praevir, looking out of the high window over the forest, 'and perhaps now that the stones have been returned, our world will begin to heal?'

'Yes, I believe so,' hissed Navesh, looking down upon the three stones of power. They were once again resting in the cradle that had held them for countless years, high up in the tower in the forest. 'I think that we may yet feel the earth shifting beneath our feet as the energy stabilises, but the worst appears to be over.'

The two Aellindi councillors had ascended the tower to check on the stones, which had been hurriedly transported here when they had first returned from the doomed ice world. Since then the terrible dying groans of their world had abated, and they had started to believe that they may have actually recovered the stones before it was too late.

*   *   *

Fireen had been given an elaborate funeral service, with most of the inhabitants of their island nation travelling to the city to pay homage to their beloved leader who had selflessly descended into the unknown to save them. Her body had been laid within the council chambers and a constant stream of mourners had visited. But now her frail and ruined form had been brought here, to the tower in the forest, to be interred within the catacombs where many of their greatest leaders now rested in peaceful, eternal slumber.

Navesh had been the last to leave the great tomb, wishing to stay a while and quietly pay his own respects. He never did truly get to thank her for leading the rescue party that had secured his return from Valken's dark world and he, and the other survivors of that terrible place, owed her a debt that could never be repaid.

'I truly hope that I can prove a worthy successor, Fireen,' he had whispered. 'I don't feel that I deserve such a position, but I'll make every effort to guide our people with the same devotion that you always displayed. I won't fail you, or those who have recently come to our world seeking our help and a place of refuge. They'll be treated with the respect that I know you would have shown them. Goodbye, my dearest friend, may the Ancestors protect you.'

*   *   *

Marcus was also struggling to come to terms with Fireen's death. When he had wished them well as they headed off to rescue Navesh, he never expected that to have been the last time that he would see her. His emotions were threatening to get the better of him and he sat at the top of a high cliff, beside one of his new generator buildings. He looked out over the limitless expanse of sparkling blue ocean, desperately wishing that things had worked out differently.

'Ah, there you are,' said Indrani, walking up the slope that led back to the city and seating herself beside him on the rocks.

'Hi,' he replied. 'Sorry, Indrani, but I'm pretty bad company today.'

'That's alright, Marcus, none of us are feeling much like talking at the moment. We each need to deal with the recent events in our own way. I'm just glad that I found you again,' she said, looping her arm through his and resting her head on his shoulder.

'Is it time?' he asked.

'Yes. Navesh wants us to accompany him to Thalmira.'

'I guess we shouldn't keep him waiting then,' replied Marcus, standing up and dusting himself off.

'I hear the Aellindi, I mean the other Aellindi, have named their new city in honour of the leader of *The Watchers*?'

'Yes,' he replied. 'Arkadia! A fine name for a city, wouldn't you agree?'

'Yes I would,' she said, as they slowly made their way back to the harbour.

* * *

Navesh emerged from the portal, stepping out into the *Beacon of Errithad* where Chylordin was waiting to greet him and his party. The two leaders spoke quietly to one another as the rest of the Nesteris delegation arrived. He introduced Saven and Givas, whom she had not met before, and then they all headed down to the city of Arkadia, towards the new council building that was being constructed.

'I see that you've made great progress,' said Marcus, as Endellion joined them in the dusty city streets.

'Yes. We have also made many fascinating discoveries and truly believe that this will make a great home for our people.'

'Don't try and tempt him away with the promise of fascinating discoveries, Endellion!' said Indrani, smiling mischievously at the Aellindi man.

'Of course,' he replied, laughing out loud and clapping Marcus on the back. 'He is all yours.'

'So how many refugees have come through?' asked Marcus, eager to steer the subject away from his earlier recklessness, which Indrani seemed determined to refer to at every possible moment.

'A constant stream! It is all Tuuvar and I can do to keep up with it.'

'So not just your own people?' asked Indrani.

'No. Most of the Aellindi are here now, helping to restore the city. But we have received many others who were desperate to escape our dying world; the mountain tribes, Visnach nomads and even some of the Visnaer people.'

'Really?' replied Indrani, raising an eyebrow. 'After what they did!'

'We cannot turn them away. They were merely pawns in the battle between Evixius and his godly brethren. But now that they are freed from his servitude, they are eager to begin a new life.'

'Where did they go?' asked Marcus. 'Surely they're not here, in Arkadia?'

'No. They realised that they would not fit in here, at least not yet, so they headed out into the desert to seek their own place in the world,' replied Endellion. 'Nadarru went with them,' he added, eliciting a surprised look from Marcus and Indrani. 'She said that she must also make amends for her actions and left with the Visnaer, hoping to help them to find their own peace, now that they were no longer slaves.'

'How is she?' asked Marcus. 'Have her wounds fully healed?'

'For the most part, yes. But she refused to allow us to heal her scars. She wants them to be a reminder of what has occurred, lest she forget the damage that the evil god has wrought.'

'I hope she finds what she's looking for,' added Marcus.

'And what of the others?' asked Indrani, keen to hear about the Visnach people that once inhabited his world. 'Where did they go?'

'The others were sent to the city of Xhaan, at the behest of Navesh. I understand that it was almost destroyed when Queen Karmina's forces rampaged across your world. The council of Nesteris believes that the refugees from my world would be welcomed there.'

'A good idea,' she replied. 'Perhaps we should visit there someday, Marcus?'

'Definitely,' he said, as the group turned the corner of the dusty street and entered the council building, which was still without a roof, but which would serve for now.

'You've made great progress,' hissed Navesh, addressing the council of Arkadia, 'and the Aellindi of Nesteris welcome you to our world.'

'Thank you,' replied Chylordin. 'On behalf of the people of Arkadia, and all those who have made the journey from our world to yours, we thank you for receiving us so readily. Perhaps, when we've further restored our new city, we can host a great banquet in honour of your gracious people?'

'We would welcome that,' replied the usually taciturn Navesh, holding out his scaled hand towards Chylordin, who firmly took it in her own. A cheer erupted up as the two leaders declared their intentions to work together in restoring this world to its former glory. The two groups of Aellindi, separated for countless years across the dark void of space, were finally reunited.

'So what should we do next?' asked Indrani, looking over to where Navesh and Chylordin were deep in conversation. 'I thought that we could go and pick up little Navesh from my parents and then head down to Reznar. I've still got to show you that temple down there. You remember the one I told you about, dedicated to Nurarian? I think it might be enlightening, for all of us.'

'I think I've already been enlightened enough thank you. Let's just go home and rest,' replied Marcus, squeezing her hand and smiling at her. 'I'm too tired for any more adventures right now.'

Epilogue

The fine sand blew across the baking desert, the gentle breeze slowly shifting the dunes in an endless rippling motion. The heat gave rise to a fuming haze, appearing as if a great expanse of water lay at the edge of the horizon, but always just out of reach. The skies were an intense blue colour and not a cloud could be seen as the sun gazed down upon the two figures that slowly meandered through the sand dunes, their footprints visible for miles behind them.

The old man plodded along, leaning wearily on his wooden staff, with his hood pulled over his bald head in an attempt to protect it from the fierce midday sun. Beside him was his constant companion, a magnificent white unicorn, which trotted along, lashing out with its tail at the tiny flying creatures that persistently tried to attach themselves to its skin.

The old man pointed to a group of objects that were coming into view, far off in the distance. A huge stone pyramid was being constructed in the shadow of the pair that already dominated the landscape. The two companions could just make out the tiny figures of the men and women that were fervently working on the huge structure.

'So what should we do now?' asked the old man, reaching his hand out to idly scratch the unicorn behind the ear.

The unicorn snorted loudly, causing the old man to laugh.

'Always in a hurry,' he said, shaking his head in dismay. 'Don't worry, we have plenty of time.'

The unicorn made another sound, almost as if the majestic beast were tutting at an obstinate child.

'What?' said the old man, coming to a halt in the baking sand. 'You *are* always in a hurry!'

The unicorn fixed him with an unyielding gaze and the old man chuckled and started walking again.

'I tell you what, let's just have a look at what these folk are building and then we'll get back to business. How about that?'

The unicorn shook its head and whinnied, before following the old man, catching up with him in several long strides.

'Just a quick look,' he promised, as the two figures continued their march across the baking desert.

*   *   *

'Marcus, you have to come and see this!' said Panx, excited beyond all measure.

The two friends were investigating a large cavern that had recently been discovered on a small island off the coast of Nesteris.

'Wow!' replied Marcus, whistling slightly as they descended into the mouth of the cavern. 'This rock fall looks relatively fresh, wouldn't you agree?'

'Definitely. I reckon it opened up during the tremors that followed the theft of the stones of power.'

'So about a year ago then,' Marcus replied rhetorically.

They continued to follow the winding path of the cavern, with Panx lighting their way with a large globe of aetheric energy that hovered silently above them. Finally they discovered a set of stairs, made from the same material that the Ancestors utilised in their ancient structures, which descended towards a vast doorway.

'It reminds me of the underground cavern on Andin's island,' said Panx. 'I wonder if the door's open?'

'There's only one way to find out,' replied Marcus, scurrying down the stairs.

'This is unbelievable!' said Marcus, looking around at the contents of the large cavern that they were now exploring.

The huge door had been damaged and had allowed them to access a small antechamber. After passing through a second doorway they had emerged within the cavernous space in which they now stood. All around them were huge cylindrical sarcophagi, standing up in long rows that extended all the way to the back of the cavern. Many had been badly damaged, with their glass covers cracked or smashed open by some ancient disaster and their skeletal occupants clearly visible, standing motionless in place as they had for countless years.

'Can you hear that?' asked Panx, tilting his head slightly and trying to ascertain where the gentle humming sound was coming from.

'I think it's coming from further back in the cavern.'

'There's a light back there,' muttered Panx excitedly, hurrying along beside the rows of damaged sarcophagi.

'These remind me of the cryogenic chambers that were often depicted in the science fiction films back home.'

'You've seen these before?'

'Well, not these particular ones. But similar devices featured heavily in our fantasy literature. In fact, they were such familiar objects that our scientists were actually attempting to create real-life versions for use during long space voyages.'

'Marcus . . . these ones are intact! The lights are coming from the panels on the side.'

'And the humming noise!' replied Marcus. 'Can you see inside?'

'I'm afraid not. The front covers are all misted up.'

'I think we should go and fetch Navesh. He'll want to see this for himself.'

'Agreed. Let's go.'

As the two friends hurried back to Nesteris to summon Navesh and the council, they failed to notice the fresh row of lights that had appeared on some of the sarcophagi. They had blinked into life as the two men were clambering back up the steps and began to pulse with increasing rapidity. Finally, the lights stopped their incessant pulsing and remained permanently illuminated. Several sarcophagi emitted a short hissing sound as their systems finished reactivating and the foggy glass covers began to clear, revealing the faces of those contained within.

Printed in Poland
by Amazon Fulfillment
Poland Sp. z o.o., Wrocław